Vampire Grail

THE SEVENTH AGE

Steve H Hakes

Vampire Grail

The Seventh Age

Steve H Hakes

Paperback ISBN: 978-1-8380946-5-2

Hardback ISBN: 979-8-4483881-6-3

E-book Copy ISBN: 978-1-8380946-4-5

V250813103858:   simbolinian@outlook.com

Thanks to...

- Sheridan Le Fanu's non-lesbian, *Carmilla* (1872)

- Christian songwriter/vampire writer, Sabine Baring-Gould's, *Margery of Quether* (1891)

- Bram Stoker's folk-Catholic, *Dracula* (1897)

THE HAUNTING

Come with us, ye whose hearts are set, on this, the present to forget. For know that once upon a time our planet hosted some rather remarkable creatures, proud creatures that had never tasted blood, whose fate would reverberate through many of the Ages of Arda. For a time they had seemed to be creatures of the Dark. But from the Dark, unbeknown to his own people, Wulfgar of the vampires had killed off the last of that flea-ridden race, at least of those which had settled on this woe-begotten world. But the Kingdom of Night, his kingdom, must never know, and he lived now in fear. As you might expect, a few of the Necros knew, but why should they dob him in?

Such was self-conscious life, replete with both rational and irrational bitterness, stabbings in the day and stabbings in the night. There was no cause to give way to Usen, your enemy, but even the enemies of your enemy could be your enemy. So don't let down your guard. Never! And never is a long time, a very long time. If all the world's a stage, and the Children are players, having their entrances and their exits, well, their fleeting ages, their petty parochial stages, were as nothing compared to the Ages of Arda. And Arda was old, very old, old even before the Ages of the Children had begun.

Five Ages had now come and gone. Necuratu's first fall had ended the first. The Necromancer's first fall had ended the second. His final fall had ended the third. Manwë's fall had ended the fourth. Toba's fall had ended the fifth. Wulfgar had seen it all, for he had begun as a free soaring spirit of will before Arda existed. Now he was keeping his head down. He was something of a loner, truth be told.

At times he felt a slight twinge of remorse, remorse for the needless genocide he had been forced into. At times he even felt despair. He had gotten away with worse than murder, yet he still suffered some pangs of shame, an inner lash, an inner prison from which there could be no escape—he was judge, jailer, and jailed. Still, inner condemnation was not a weakness to be open about, and the world was stirring again. Best look to the future, not to the past—let it die, and live on.

Some deadly game was now afoot, some game-changer as yet unknown. But a titanic storm was certainly coming. Clouds of doom hung oppressively over both the Night and the Necros, the kingdoms of the vampires and the diaboloi. You could almost feel it in the air, weighing you down, brooding, close. Usen was stirring. In times like these, the enemy of your enemy could be your friend. The Night and the Necros, both of the Dark, had recently made an uncommon alliance to combat the threat and to ward off the Light. Beyond a doubt, an invisible yet perceptible invasion force—portending a seventh Age—hovered over the horizon of space and time. Alarmingly the Beyond was Becoming, breaking in at some undiscovered beachhead, or at least lurking in the wings—some vast force of unimaginable power. These were troubling times for the oppressed of Usen. But Wulfgar would survive. He had to. Death would be the beginning of an end that he stubbornly refused to face. He feared that death wasn't as safe as some made it out to be.

The Kingdom of Night was a worldwide network of vampires who, under a monarch, were basically united by their hatred of the Great Enemy. In unity there was strength, safety for their people. As a matter of fact, their enemy didn't usually bother them too much, and it almost seemed as if he had dumped them as prisoners on some inescapable and mysterious island, then smartly sailed away, leaving a few of his underlings to keep some sort of order until he returned. It was better if he never returned, but now you could feel him in the air, a brooding presence, lurking, watching them as a cat might watch a mouse. The vampires were not natives to this island planet, but they had developed a taste for the natives. Still, the natives should not be blamed for their absent landlord, and relations between the vampire Pneumata, and the native Psuchai—the human species—were by and large that of tolerant co-existence, live and let a few die.

Yes, the vampires levied a blood tax, but there is a big difference between the purposeful use of blood, and the purposeless waste of blood. The rebel Powers, the Turannoi, the Necros, they were the ones who went in for purposeless waste. Death and destruction made their day. But now an unholy alliance had formed between the Dark Powers and the Dark Pneumata.

Of course all vampires were equal, but some were more equal than others. Not that they had a power structure based on inheritance—that was a silly human thing. No, for one thing, vampires could not be born, though they could die. Axiomatically, overall numbers could never go up, no, not in a billion years—they could only go down. Inheritance? No, they were basically given titles and authority—dominance—according to their strength and reliability.

Their titles, and their organization, had begun with the advent of the Children of Usen, and their titles have always kept rough approximations with the realms of the Children in which they have lived, though those who have written of their accounts have sometimes used approximates to their own cultures, so that their audiences might understand. So within Europa in her later years, they came to use such terms as queen, prince, duchess, count—at least for the more powerful and more trusted within their global hierarchy.

Such entitling helped them to blend in with humanity, which posed a lethal threat—hiding within was wiser than exposure without. But theirs was a judicial, not a military, command. That said, they could be summoned together to fight under various nobles or royals—Formings, like wolf-packs, were very much feared by their victims.

Before the dawn of man, Simbolinians—as they were known in far flung space before they became vampires, Earthbound bloodsuckers, had adopted physical frames for convenience, at first crystalline, later biological. Now weakness kept those frames of necessity. Indeed, a vital necessity, for to destroy the physical body, even by extreme severance, sped the vampires into the Land of the Dead.

Death was their last line of defence, a buffer zone, and yet few believed that it was totally secure, totally safe, for it bordered on Life Beyond. It was safest never to die. They had long maintained an assortment of shapes—for most the primary shapes were humanoid, wolf, and bat. One of their number—something of a troublemaker but out of harm's way—had created a dragon shape, a design long ago stolen and commandeered by Necuratu, head of the Necros.

When news of that theft had gotten out, many of those who had sought a permanent alliance with the Necros, had put aside their darker thoughts: why trust a thief? But Dark still called unto Dark—the fellowship of fallen spirits.

Wulfgar's main shape was humanoid, the obvious choice, really, but he often loved to lope through the woods and wilderlands as a lone wolf. For pleasure, some, like Lilith, preferred to fly above the woods and the wild, partaking of the bat form. Some simply preferred to stroll along in the shape of the Children, because for them, the swapping of shapes had become too strenuous. But at the end of the day, it basically boiled down to individual tastes. And invisibility, and unfamiliar shapes, always required even more concentration, more thelodynamic power. It could be too draining.

The Necroi, on the other hand, found it far easier to maintain their invisible form, and they hated the biosphere anyway. For covert operations, visibility could be useful, but since the Fifth Age, Usen had forbidden the Turannoi to directly shape-shift into the humanoid shape, whether of the firstborn or of the secondborn, or even of the adopted. That command cramped their style, but like him or loath him, best to obey him, for his power seemed limitless.

It was as well that he spoke but seldom, though Ruach constantly worked insidiously in the background, tweaking circumstances, feather-weighting events to tip certain ways, working Usen's will. The diaboloi were permitted to materialise, but only for short stints. For the Great Game, they were allowed to play with the human scum. Usually for that they simply played *Ghosts*, for apparitions weren't too taxing. Materialization was indirectly shape-shifting, using a substance they formed around human players in the Great Game, and so it didn't break the rules, only bent them a little. It wasn't easy but hell, what you put into the game, you get out of the game. Ectoplasm was normally good for a few hours of unclean fun.

Why, you may ask, did Usen limit their shape-shifting? Good question. Perhaps he thought that they were already too seductive to the evil heart of man. Perhaps he thought that they at least should no longer speak in human form with human tongues. As for the firstborn, those who had remained in Middle-earth were now almost deaf to the Turannoi, anyway, and secreted themselves in the hidden places of the world, well below the surface of history. As backwater history, Necuratu sought them not.

But well whyever, Usen had unilaterally imposed this limitation, and the Turannoi were content enough anyway to merely bear bestial shapes, such as the dragon, the snake, and the scorpion. Morquamar the Necromancer had used most terrifyingly the shapes of bat and of wolf. He had finally been expelled through the Doors of Night into the Timeless Void, never to darken this world with such terror again. Necuratu himself had long been chained in futility beyond the Orb of Arda. There were others of the Dark who had come forth from the Dynamic Bubble at the same point in space and time as had the Necromancer, but had lived south of his kingdom. Many names these others had had—in the south the secondborn spoke in hushed fear the name Apophis. Yes, they of the Light had nothing good to say of Apophis the Serpent. Had he grown out of some evil murk vomited forth from the nether darkness of the abyss, wishing to bury the very sun within the vile vapours of his vindictiveness?

Another who came later from the Timeless Bubble was Set, one of five Powers whom Lord Thoth and Lady Nut summoned forth to be their children. Yet they misjudged him, for his bent was to evil, into which he soon grew, showing himself a true son to Apophis, not of Thoth, though at one point he had been forced by Ra to fight against the evil Apophis. Yet soon he sought the throne of Khem, to reign over the secondborn of Usen, but was opposed by his brother Osiris and his sister Isis.

Set was very much a law unto himself. Short on loyalty, he dwelt alone as a typhonic beast, a one-of-a-kind spirit in the desert. And he was now seated within a stone alcove, upon a throne hewn out of cave wall. He appeared almost human, yet his head was bestial, a shape of intimidation and of malice. But before him now stood Wulfgar, unfazed and nonchalant. "Wulfgar of the vampire people, welcome to thee and to thy guests. What brings thee thus to my lonely abode, servant of the Night?"

Both knew the answer. The question was purely ceremonial, seeking servitude. Obligingly Wulfgar bowed low in token of obeisance. "Lord Set, my people are ever honoured to be welcomed to your dark domain, noble lord among the Necros. We need no other reason than the honour we feel deeply. However, I come now commissioned by my queen to join the hunt for Hamashiach, for his time is foretold and now is nigh, and we of the Darkness are one. You, O mighty one, we welcome as our marshal."

"Some Sheep," began Set, "live again in Alexandreia and its scattered surrounds. Fearing that birth, at first we caused them all to drop their unborn, but calmer now we watch as we can like wolves, allowing their brats to be born. For too much unnatural death stirs up the Light, and the Time of Edfu is not yet. Already the Falcon has doubled his watch and has avenged those mothers whose unborn we bore to the grave. For he and his aggeloi have crippled many of my finest diaboloi.

"A heavy price we have paid, and for what? For the fun of slaying their unborn lambs? Enjoyable, yet an indulgence we have paid for dearly, and can ill afford. Well, our hands burnt, we now limit our watch to the vile virtuous among them. Those they drop in birth we watch, yet so far such brats appear as normal—admixtures of vice and of virtue, as befits the human vermin. So we let them live, lest the Eye of the Falcon becomes the red eye of wrath. Especially, we look for lovers of wood and of their ancient lands—such shall be slain. Since Usen limits our numbers in this land, the many eyes of thy kind are sorely needed in the hunt."

"And to that end, vampires will gladly help, my lord", replied Wulfgar deferentially. "My queen has reached out to me, and to many more from other lands, for a Forming here. But we come not to savage the land, lest we be uncloaked and our kingdom revealed. Our search shall be by stealth. But what is this Time of Edfu?" asked Wulfgar innocently. "For long I have lived in a far island, and know not of this time."

"Then dost thou not know of my bitter defeat?" demanded Set angrily. "The Great Falcon, son of Isis and Osiris, sought ever to avenge his father whom I slew, and to sit in the seat of pharaoh where I sat. His father, straying back from the Land of the Dead into the Land of the Living, guided him, teaching his hands to fight. That son I would have dismembered as happily as I had the father, but falsely was I played by a false jade, and breathing time was given unto my foe.

"Yet in time I slew the Falcon, but unfairly didst he return from the Duat to slay me in turn. Alas, all too well had Osiris trained him. My human slaves he turned against each other, by a blindness that bordered on madness. An army of diaboloi I unleashed—they too perished, and I escaped by the skin of a snake. Yet at the isle of Edfu he came at me as a giant man might attack a giant hippopotamus, and he speared me to the howling of hideous applause. In clamorous celebration, a temple—now long gone—did the rabble of this land build. Though it perished, another like unto it now stands in its place—will mine foe never be forgot? Still he abides as a Guardian within the Kingdom of Ra. And it stands written that at Edfu shall end the Last Age yet to be, and usher in The Aphtharsian Beyond, the Eternal Khem for the true worshippers of Ra. So we must rip the Seventh Age from its womb; we must abort Hamashiach. Do I not live each day in fear, and hast thou not heard?"

"Of such matters I know little, my lord Set. Within the Night we have faint whispers, inklings, but perhaps few speak sooth. It is ours to survive if we can and as long as we can, to hide within the Darkness, to feed off the Light, and to punish those who stray into it. It is enough to us to destroy he who is to be born to our death, even Hamashiach, the New Moyshe—if that is what he would be. To this end I do unquestionably submit unto you. Assign me my humble place in the search, my lord." Wulfgar bowed low. Though information sharing was wise, ever Wulfgar sought to shield his heart and mind from the Necros. But then, that was what he was, a loner, a hidden card, a dark horse, a nightmare. Even his guests knew him but in part, and they had agreed not to speak of what they knew, for he was a safe house for them—who undermines their house?

Approaching the Necros was a thing which even vampires of the Night preferred to avoid, for it was deadly. Many vampires had come with Wulfgar, but they were content to hang around outside and to wait patiently. Enough for them that their captain had gone inside to receive his orders. And glad were they when at last he returned—without his host—and led them forth to their assigned tasks.

Little weight did they put on the prophets of the Necros, let alone on the prophets of the Sheep People. Their trust was in their own prophets, among whom Zalkeesh had foretold that a baby boy would be born in poverty in a troubled house under a shining light—perhaps of the full moon creeping through the windswept clouds. That he would be a woodworker, and would leave Khem to visit an oppressed people. A little unclear, to say the least, but is that not the way of prophets? And whatever Set might believe, it wasn't absolutely clear to them that Hamashiach would belong to the Sheep.

True, the Sheep themselves were rumoured to speak in their own fuzzy way, of the same or some similar prophecy. But then what dejected and rejected people didn't prophesy up a deliverer for themselves? That they were favoured by Usen above other peoples, had long been clear, but what if they were false favourites, chosen scapegoats to throw the Darkness onto the wrong scent? Curiously his favour to them seemed to be as an oyster is favoured by the irritation of grit. If an oyster brings forth a pearl of great price, it pays for pain without gain. If such is an honour, it is an honour many would prefer to pass over them, like an angel of death.

Be that as it may, for the task in hand, neither Necros nor Night could cover all the bases alone, and so both had come together in unholy alliance, and had still to focus on the most likely scenarios. Fear makes strange bedfellows. Overall it seemed probable that another Moyshe would be born in Khem—probably among the Sheep—and sooner or later leave for the land wherein that flock mainly dwelt: another exodus, so to speak. But whatever the people, the place was certain. All eyes were therefore on Khem, that languid world of legend. The trick was to identify Hamashiach at an early stage, and to eradicate him before things got out of hand. Actually, Wulfgar had deceived Set. He had known about Set's defeat—although he hadn't known about the Time of Edfu. "Yes," he said silently within himself, "if this Moyshe survives overly long, he might become as Horus the Falcon, too strong to take down."

Assigned the Eastern Delta district around the slowly dying city of Avaris, Wulfgar was pleased to have joined the hunt. Long had he travelled aloof from his kind, lonely but never alone. Long had he travelled with guests innumerable yet unseen, petty diaboloi whose power did not match his, but whose combined power supplemented his. For he was weak, weak beyond count of years, yet still strong among his kind. The weakening which had affected them all, had afflicted him more than most.

That perhaps was the hand of judgment at work, for maybe Usen—whom some called Elroi—saw all the deeds of Darkness, deeds done in the dark. The nights were the time for duty, searching to extinguish the Light. Now the day had dawned once more, and concealed from sight, he reflected alone. This land was still fertile and well watered, not that he and his people needed water. Once upon a time, a tiny enemy had floated helplessly upon those waters, floated by right under the noses of the damned dunamoi. Such an oversight must never happen again.

And now they were after bigger game. The new infant must be quickly identified and destroyed, well before he could identify and destroy them. But today was a scorcher, and nothing seemed to be happening among the secondborn. Why did Usen bother about such weak and weedy layabouts? But then for Wulfgar, the heat of the blazing sun was little different from the frozen seas of the far north, though the light did bother him. Like his special forces, he needed no sleep, and could sense hostiles afar off. He could easily bury himself for days in the baking sands. He had the strength of many men, and a speed they could not dream of matching. His big weakness was simply the sunshine, and so he often rested in the hours of the sun. Not that he slept—another weakness of these pathetic little bipeds: his body rested; his mind travelled. He might in fact wish for the weakness of dreamless sleep, for often his unoccupied mind travelled over time, reliving a recurrent past, a slaughter of an innocent.

Silently it had grazed in grace, the last lonely beast of its kind within Earth's orb, grazing in the grace of the Kingdom of Night. It had fallen out with the Necros; shown sympathies with the Light. Night itself had had its run-ins with the Necros. Hostile takeover bids it had opposed. It had survived as a free and independent kingdom. Navigating the wild waves of life, inevitably encountered some super-rogue waves now and again. Necuratu usually invited, sometimes demanded, total obedience, subservience. And he had fought skirmishes to bully, where he could not bind. Still, by and large, peaceful coexistence subsisted between the Dark Wings. Necuratu did not wish to tempt the Night into the Light as to a safe harbour, nor did the Night wish to be radicalised into the Necros. *Push us too far and we might push away.*

But the vampires had not been the only show from beyond this planet. Other Pneumata had become entrapped by the Eighth Law, as had the Simbolinians, and had also resented Usen. One such people had become known as the Unicorn People. They had initially snubbed Usen, but they—a less powerful and less numerous people— had at length shifted their position into the Grey Zone. Necuratu had understandably resented that. He could put up with aggeloi being aggeloi, but he could not tolerate diaboloi becoming aggeloi—not that any did! Fact is, you don't want *your* kind of people becoming the *other* kind of people, though the *other* kind of people becoming *your* kind of people is fine. Conversion Therapy should only be in your direction.

Disobedient to that diktat, the Unicorn People had slowly slidden from friendship with the Dark, into the forbidden unfriended zone. The Necros hadn't seemed to mind, but many suspected that it had expedited their demise. The Night's policy was not to protect other peoples, but it had had some sympathy towards a similar people, kindred spirits likewise snared within the orb of Arda, who like them had donned biological shapes. Their chosen shape had been the unicorn, nowadays naught but a mythical beast of legend.

And like the vampires, these thelosomatics, having joined with the biosphere for convenience, found that they had come to need it as an essential. Those who sit in chairs too long become dependent on chairs. But unlike the vampires, the unicorns had found flora sufficient for their needs and tastes, and become herbivores rather than sanguivores.

The Night had had no beef with this thelodynamic race, and had been pleased to welcome them as a big brother might welcome an unexpected addition to the family, a late arrival they assume will know its place. Similarly, a solitary prisoner of long-standing, on suddenly receiving a short-term inmate to share their cell, might enjoy a common invective against their warden—fellow sufferers together. But all too soon the little sibling hadn't needed big brother's help; the new prisoner didn't think the warden so bad after all.

Towards the end, vampire attitudes towards the unicorn people had become a little confused, a little grey. Still, it is true to say that more united than divided were these two races, and the Night, while not prepared to actively assist the unicorns, was prepared to passively assist in providing a safe haven to shield the last of their dying race. They had not been without offspring, but neither they nor the vampires could multiply according to their kind: spirits do not give birth to spirits. They had however mated with the Phusika, playfully playing around with embryonic DNA. Creatures weird, woeful, and wonderful, had come from these shapeshifters—such, it was said, as the mighty minotaur that had disturbed the island of Minos—even as the long-gone Nephilim had come from the Sleeping Count, he who had brought calamitous woe upon his own people, and whom they in turn had put to sleep for his crimes against humanity.

Wulfgar's hidden sin was not against the Children, and he had not been brought to book. Indeed it had been the Children who had hunted down the unicorns, even if had been as some suspected that the Necros had put them up to it, had been the unseen hand that guided the bow. At last they had been whittled down to one, which had sought protection. The Night had given it a safe haven, ensconced where the secondborn hunters ventured not. Then, driven by his guests, Wulfgar had done the dirty, though espied by none. His deed could not be undone; Humpty Dumpty lay irrevocably shattered at the base of the wall. The Unicorn People had all been of the water-type—their bodies had left no lasting trace, all gone. Their only trace lay as a ghost in Wulfgar's soul, their haunting revenge.

Within human history, myths abounded, but myths, once decoded, were useful sources of information. In enemy-occupied territory, they were a common way in which Usen spoke with his children. Therefore most had useful insights into him, though they usually came directly from the Philikoi kingdoms that he had set up to teach and to guard the secondborn—quite elementary lessons, really. The Children—as most students still today—did not always heed what their teachers taught. Some preferred to teach than to learn, and developed their own trajectories—if not the blind leading the blind, at least the myopic leading the blind and both teetering on the edge. Some even abused the knowledge of the Guardians for selfish ends. Sifting true words from Usen had become problematic, a mixed bag, fields of wheat and weeds.

But Wulfgar and his team weren't simply to patrol like mindless machines, seeking out signs of intrauterine life, awaiting developments. No, the set plan of Set was to be selective, not least because of their limited search capabilities. So they had to study the clues, and the clues might well be within the myths, that pool of ideas that had seeped into the human psyche, a pool muddied by human input, and also, it must be admitted, by Necuratu himself in seeking to upset Usen's teaching program.

Wulfgar's patrol sector was the land from where Moyshe had come. There had been nothing supernatural about his birth, though Ruach had played a part in protecting and perfecting that life. Then Usen had taken the people of Moyshe out from Khem, out from slavery. Well, out from human slavery, at least. That special relationship was the reason why Set had a particular problem with that peculiar people. Once more they were slaves, bound within an empire of iron, though perhaps believing themselves to be free. Their zealots fought for former freedom, but it was a long walk back. Surprisingly Usen's sheep had gained exemptions from the belief system of that empire, and Wulfgar's Delta Team reported that that people, the Sheep, sometimes managed to gain classmates from other peoples. In short, they punched above their weight, for the deadly Hand of Usen was upon them.

But no need to look to the east, for in The Prophecy of the Chosen One, Zalkeesh had been very clear at this point: Hamashiach would come *from* Khem. That made sense. Many of the Sheep had recently migrated west to Khem, and potentially they could as easily migrate back from Khem, so they still had to be carefully watched. Some Sheep had casually been questioned. However, it simply seemed they expected a deliverer, another Moyshe, to arise from within their Promised Land, not from Khem. That didn't meet expectations. Well, it was a waste of time to pin too much weight on their misguided myths: cover all bases; focus on Khem.

Amusingly the Sheep sported a rather novel notion of parthenogenesis, undoubtedly ignorant of basic biology. The vampires knew that nature could produce human girls by this method, for the gene code of girls was the same YY chromosome of their mothers. The only way to produce an XY chromosome was through normal human mating, and yet some of the Sheep seemed to believe that their deliverer would be a virgin-conceived *he*, not a Deborah! They obviously did not understand the human genome as well as vampires did, but then vampires had been masters of nature from the earliest stages of life—the secondborn still had much to learn.

The Khemites had toyed with this idea, too, but perhaps for political clout. They knew—they thought—that something like that had happened within the Kingdom of Ra, for Horus the Avenger, son of Isis, was said to have been conceived after his father's death. Well, there were many avian divinities assembled under the name of Horus, falcon-shaped lesser Guardians who looked for lordship to Horus the Elder, and later to Horus the Younger, son of Isis. And their doings were sometimes attributed to their lord, making it difficult to always tie down any particular story to any particular Guardian. But on this, all spoke clearly as to the what, though not as to the how.

Some Khemites assumed that having died, Osiris could no longer father, and so presumed that the child was only his mother's; some reckoned that his widow-wife drew code from his DNA, and so the child was theirs; some cynics reckoned that Isis had simply cheated on her deceased husband—any fool can be a cynic. All in fact were dead wrong. The Guardians didn't do parthenogenesis, for the simple reason that they didn't do birth. The secondborn tried to conceive of the Guardians in human terms, in biological terms. None understood that Horus the Avenger had been a spirit called forth from the Dynamic Bubble by those two Guardians, and so had become their son for a mission.

Crazy ideas by crazy people, thought Wulfgar. Why, it'd be an absolute miracle if the Sheep's parthenogenesis ever got off the ground. But he knew that some humans across the globe had piggybacked on such ideas, to simply get out of trouble or even to elevate their political status by claiming to be direct offspring of the Guardians—understandable, really, in the quest for power. Why, in this very land the scammer Amenhotep 3 had caused to be written that while his secular sire had been the good pharaoh Thutmose 4, yet his spirit father, at Thutmose's request, had been a shapeshifter, the Guardian Amun-Ra! This particular 'divinity conception' was allegedly through the Great Royal Wife, his mother Mutemwia. It was an inventive way to strengthen the awe of the pharaohs in general and of Amenhotep 3 in particular.

Not surprisingly the Sheep, having lived in Khem, copied that idea— or had they? After all, the Sheep had the unique idea that Usen was not some divinity messing around with the secondborn, not really someone likely to sire human children. No, Wulfgar could not understand that puzzling people that seemed to say both yes and no to the same question. But not all the Sheep followed the same voice, even if they all prayed for another Moyshe—and some didn't pray. A mixed bag, really.

Through a telepathic relay system, Wulfgar reported back to his queen. "Your majesty, I Wulfgar, your humble servant, have at your command joined with Necuratu's agent, Set, who governs the diabolical principality of Khem. You need not, I think, visit this land at this present moment in time, although more vampires would be welcome at large. My own patrol area, from where once the Sheep escaped from slavery, seems calm—but is it the calm before the storm? I have divided my team to gather intel. Some pose as humans professing to be midwives or matchmakers, thus collecting data from the secondborn, whether of Khem, of the Sheep, or of other foreigners. Others search window by window in stealth mode. There is a general belief in this land that bats keep the diaboloi away, yet also that their blood holds healing powers, so while there is some slight danger searching in this form, some occupants seem to speak the freer in our hearing.

"As I have indicated, so far there have been no positive sightings of any signs of Hamashiach's conception here. Nor have we either seen or heard any signs or gossip concerning betrothed brides who have strayed to false men and are with child. We know of none who boast in—or seek refuge in the claim of—visitations by the Philikoi. I do not confine our search to such. In human guise we mill and mix town to town, seeking for any son born who seems to be exceptionally usenic, has a penchant for wood, and has wider family outside of Khem, unto which he might go. We also look for the signs of illumination of his birthplace. My troops are under strict orders not to engage in bloodlust, and to feed in strict moderation, lest the human population should disperse. For who knows, in such dispersal Hamashiach could slip through our nets in a general stampede. Contained, he should be easier to pinpoint. I remain sanguine that we shall have him if he should be born within the search area assigned to me, Wulfgar."

It was a satisfactory report, so far as it went, but Queen Lilith, rummaging through all the Khemite reports, remained dissatisfied. If the sword dangling over your head is on a thin thread, does it ease your mind to know that it hasn't yet fallen? She yearned to know beyond reasonable doubt that such a threat had been positively identified and neutralised, his tiny body floated away down the sewers, flushed away, end of story. She had always been an active advocate of extinguishing the Light.

It is said that those who hate the Light do so because their deeds are Dark. That principle is certainly at work within the human domain. Apart from times of war—which are fairly frequent—the secondborn usually choose night times to break into homes to steal, to kill, and to destroy. It is a natural time for concealment. Sure, such activities also occur in daylight hours, and there are many daylight robberies, but again, the element of concealment is usually factored into these crimes, masking one's face in darkness. Even when crimes are committed against the weaker classes, concealment is usually factored in, so that while the villain does not bother to conceal their crime to their victims, they certainly conceal their crimes from their peers and from police—unless they receive a cut. The 'night' of anonymity is blest—if our deeds are evil.

Lilith was committed to the Dark, and she had committed a deed of Darkness that deeply disturbed her soul. For she had once fallen in love with Tauresgal, a sindeldi prince, and together they had had a daughter. He had recently been killed, a mere three millennia or so ago, but the memory of him would always live within her heart. But in her heart he lived as in grief, for not long after he died his daughter, Lona, their daughter, had died, killed at the hand of she who had been his wife. In her heart he knew this. Did he, she wondered, know this in his own heart, where he dwelt west of this world? Would Lona have pained him by, or protected him from, the knowledge of Lilith's anger, she wondered? He could not return to her, but could she, would she, return to him? And if so, could he, would he, forgive her for killing their only child? If only Lona had realised that having lost him, Lilith had needed, oh so much she had needed, Lona to remain only her own.

But how could Lona have known of her motherly need-love, since Lilith had had to conceal her motherly gift-love until death did them part? Lilith belonged to the Kingdom of Night, and affection-love was, like forgiveness itself, almost an unforgivable sin, and certainly queer, inexcusable in a queen. Her peers could perhaps overlook the fact that she had been a wife and a mother, so long as they presumed that it had been merely a dalliance, an amusement, a one-night, nay, a one-minute or so, stand. More like one minute, that is, in human terms. For to those who had lived billennia, one hundred thousand sun years seemed more or less equal to one human night, and one hundred years as but one human minute. To kill your spouse or child was considered good practice, whereas caring instead of killing was considered shameful practice. The vampires of the Dawn disagreed, but they had already long been expelled for heterodoxy.

Unsurprisingly, Lona had not felt a daughterly pull to remain with her seemingly uncaring mother. She had gone off, gone and gotten herself married, and become a loving mother. It had been in suffering under a bitter sense of betrayal, that Lilith had killed her as an ingrate. It had seemed highly satisfying at the time, but alas, how bitter now was the sense of having butchered your own child. The secret festered within, and that was where it must remain buried. All the more reason for Hamashiach to die, for it was said that he would unearth all buried secrets, exposing the darkness in which they hid. So far the reports seemed satisfactory, but, still unsatisfied, to Khem she swiftly flew, not knowing what would await her there. Pleasantly it was the sound of mourning that greeted her, as she descended upon the Delta town of Tjaru at the going down of the sun.

Sabaf had died, and his funeral procession headed west towards the setting sun. His shadow box journeyed with him. Sabaf had been a priest, an embalmer, high up the pecking order, and yet had died well before his time. An accident, some said. Jealousy, others said. The word 'poison' was softly whispered—the baleful work of viperous vindictiveness. It is indeed true that he had risen rapidly up the ranks, a true servant of the Powers promoted above his older and less conscientious peers. Now he had died. But does a sacred priest ever really die? His mummy, his former physical body, his *khat*, was prepared for burial with his heart intact. His khat remained the anchor for his immortal identity, his *akh*. The coffin was of wood, yet inlaid with gold as befitted one so worthy of high honour. Lilith glided down to silently watch, that which never ceased to transfix her. The coffin was led by an honour guard; the mourners held gifts for the life beyond life; priests chanted words of power, and sang hymns to the Powers. Sabaf was being escorted to the Duat.

But all these trimmings were symbolic, without real power, for the Powers could not be swayed by human sentiments. Of what weight are the judgments of mortal man? No, Sabaf's immediate fate would be decided within the judgment hall of Osiris. All this Lilith knew, for though a vampire, she had once spent time—along with her friend Ishtar—as a placement within the Kingdom of Anu, working as a paraprofessional to the Guardians. In the Kingdom of Ra, intermediate dwellings were naturally determined a little bit differently, for each guardian kingdom was permitted its variations in line with the mood of their province. The Kingdom of Anu shared the Mesopotamian monotony of hopeless despair; the Kingdom of Zeus shared the vitality of breath-taking beauty; the Kingdom of Odin shared the northern coldness and the bitterness of heroic fatalism. The Kingdom of Ra shared a stuffiness of heat and death, yet life flowed through its veins.

Yet she knew that in whichever province they crystallised, the Philikoi taught that their judgments were but temporary and rudimentary, and that one day a global judgment would span the entire history of the secondborn. Speculation, of course, pure speculation, the gullible teaching the gullible. What Usen really planned for the vermin no one could really know, could they? Personally, she couldn't see why Usen ever bothered with such creatures—some speculated that like wine he matured them to drain for his pleasure. Was he the supreme sanguivore? That would be ironic. But what was happening with Sabaf?

It was given to Lilith to see beyond the eyes of mortal Children. She saw through the first portal into the first region of the Duat, with its six fire-breathing serpents of Apophis, and between whom the Mesektet Boat of Ra, its glory dimmed, glided over the ghostly river of death—would the sinful souls on board seek those shores of horror and dismay, hoping thus to escape divine justice? Some would always jump from the fire into the frying pan. Within that boat lay as if lifeless, the body of Ra, as a felled actor in a drama who now would neither hinder nor help them on this their crucial night of destiny.

An hour long was that voyage, after which the Second Gates loomed large. There, keeping out the evil of the besiegers, were stationed lesser guardian spirits of Great Ra, exuding thelodynamic power as poisonous flames. But the gates were flung wide open in welcome as his boat approached. And the protective field of power was stilled, so that the Mesektet Boat and the souls who sailed within her might sail through unharmed. Within this region lay a strong temptation to souls to disembark and to dwell upon sweet shores, yet their hope would cheat them, they who sought to forge their own future.

The third gate opened up to the land of Amenti, the third region of the Duat, through which the judgment seat dwelt—were they willing by virtue to venture on? For the night had set in, and Osiris had taken his nightly seat as lord of the Duat, the lord of judgment. Each night the *kas*, the detachable souls of those buried that day, sailed in that ghostly boat to meet their judgment, each carrying their own *ib*—

their heart—in their hands. Funnily, it seemed as if the less righteous sailed with more confidence than the more just—such is man's arrogance.

Each night fresh entrants were first tested on their knowledge of the words of wisdom, words which allowed them to pass the doors into the judgment hall and so to have any chance of life. Such tests were designed to probe whether the deceased had been interested before death with after-death, and were pretty superficial, preliminary tests before the real exam. Each had left the group separately through a guarded door, individually being tested on who it was that they believed was its guard. In the Duat all doors were potential test fails, tests as to how well the kas had bothered in the khat to learn religious instruction, details which had been given to the people and which was varied from time to time—though less frequent was that change than the change of their pharaohs.

Once they had disembarked, the boat sailed on onto the other regions of the Duat night, leaving the kas to face Osiris alone. Each night Ra had to defeat his old enemy, Apophis, if the light of blessing was to rise again upon Khem in the light of day. Priests prayed in the long night hours for his victory—it kept them on their toes. So far, Sabaf had sailed through the tests, and now he stood in silence, as did they all, yet far aloof he stood.

Most rehearsed the stereotyped recital about evils they had not done, hoping thus to fob off the panel of judges. As they moved down the line they would greet each judge, and say such things as "I have not been sexually immoral. I have never betrayed Ra. I have not cheated on my spouse. I have never been a homosexual partner, neither dominant nor passive. I have not stolen from my peers. I have never been excessively greedy. I have not been a binge drinker. I have never abused my servants. I have not been a serial swindler." By exposing sins they had omitted, they could hide sins they had committed, and since even a minimum pass is a pass, why not drop a few peccadilloes? For they had learned that there were 42 judges, each with a special interest, and so memorizing personalised lists of 42 denials—negative confessions—had become the standard defence upon which they would be tested. Before death, each ka tried to list 42 ways in which it could truthfully defend itself after death, each item being to satisfy each judge on their specialist concern.

The reality was perhaps to train citizens in the avoidance of general vices, and also in the ways of virtue well before they died. Sabaf's friends had helped him write up his 42 point defence, but Sabaf now clenched his fists, pounding his chest again and again. He knew that he would not stand the test before glorious Osiris. Indeed he yearned to fail since he knew that his welcome would contaminate that saintly kingdom of the red and the white crown. Nevertheless, he hated to be cut off from Ra, though confessing that cold had been his warmest thoughts towards his king. He seemed stuck between a rock and a hard place.

No, he was unworthy to enter Ra's holy house, yet though Ra's children should first be fed, even his dogs were permitted the scraps that fell from their table—or were thrown through their windows. Yes, perhaps as a dog he might be allowed to live outside the divine windows, looking in unseen, a harmless ghost looking without touching, without defiling. He had had hammered home *The Book of Coming Forth by Day*, the funerary advice to protest one's innocence, but it now seemed so unreal, so pointless to claim that black was white, that he was good, for the eyes of the Powers would see right through him. "Ra, be merciful to me, a sinner", he cried.

His fellow kas, hearing his lament, were disturbed. They of course weren't crooks, evildoers, adulterers. But Sabaf? Well, well, well, so he had been a secret sinner all along, masquerading as a priest—the jolly old hypocrite! Now he would get his comeuppance. Well, there was no need for him to disturb them as they prepared for the penultimate exam, was there? They'd soon see him no more, and good riddance to bad rubbish. The kindlier souls however seemed to pity him, rather than to sentence him. And still Lilith watched, her telepathic vision extended almost to its limit. The fate of a soul in the balance is so fascinating.

None had seemed more surprised than Sabaf when he, having shamefully denied 42 sin-types before the 42 judges, passed on to the final exam. Momentarily hope flickered faintly in the gloom of expectation. But then all hope fled from the face of Sabaf as he beheld the face of Osiris, who was seated before him as one slain, yet as a warrior king in the full vigour of his manhood.

With his destiny dangling in the balance, Wolf-headed Anubis kindly assisted the shuffling Sabaf over to where stood the Scales of the Duat. Here those who remained would be tested for virtue, and stand before four witnesses, even the four shining sons of Horus: Hapi of the north; Imset of the south; Tuamutef of the east; and Qebehsenuef of the west—they who have been called the sons of Isis. After acquitting himself of what he had not done, what he really was like at heart would come out.

His fate was far from certain, for one who passes a theory test can yet fail a practical. Would he sail through? He seriously doubted it. And part of his heart wished to fail before the Guardian King of the Duat, as one unclean and unworthy, for he yearned for truth to come out, he who believed himself to be so false.

He believed in the Three Ways. Punishment was the lot of many. Perhaps eventually it would end if hearts could be cleaned—he knew not. Then above punishment there was the way of pleasure at the right hand of Ra, within the Field of Peace. Then below punishment there was the way of nonentity, when souls died even to death, and their *ren*—the sum of their experience—was remembered no more, for having been fully condemned, there was no more *them*. The latter fate he studiously shunned, since it meant that such souls had been meaningless. Please Ra, no. No, he would rather live under exceeding punishment than that, but then it was not his judgment to make.

At last, he stood before the Shining Ones, witnesses for or against the defendants. He would have to endure a telepathic probing into his very heart. Tentatively he stepped onto the lowered scale, and was hoisted to the midway point by Anubis. This was iconically depicted as a scale holding the human heart—which in turn represented the centre of the human mind and will—being balanced against a pure featherweight of truth. And what heart can be so free of sin that it weighs less than a feather, that it can't be laid low by a smidgen of truth? For he whose throne is set upon a stream running clear and deep, sought virtue, not simply un-vice. Why bless those who had selfishly sought to avoid evil, yet had no selfless love for virtue? Was not their selfishness itself evil?

Nay, Osiris sought those who had desired the good—they alone had his goodwill. It is they who have, without desire of gain, protected widows from the wolves, adopted orphans, housed the homeless, fed the famished, and clothed the threadbare. For Osiris himself has known great misery and understood it, having had his body sinfully slain by a brother, cast wretchedly adrift far from home in the Great Green Sea, and then cut into many pieces to deny him his future. But he had also had a sister selflessly risk her life to seek out his body, so as to put him back together again—for the body is the anchor to the soul within the Orb of Arda. Ultimately virtue would triumph over vice. It was the will of Usen.

So it was that Osiris looked upon the scales, where suspended in the balance by a feather-shaped rod, stood his servant Sabaf, with whom he was well pleased. For this night Sabaf alone had besought Ra for mercy, yet with a humility that veiled his own virtue even from his own eyes. To the unseeing eye, the secondborn of Usen seemed like cheap and common clay pots, easily broken and not much to look upon even unbroken. But Osiris saw within Sabaf a pot of gold, the treasure of a heart pure without dissimulation, an eternal flame from the flame imperishable. Anubis looked to Ma'at, and Ma'at smiled—she who stood for harmony, for justice, and for order. Sabaf was surely as pure as the great Bennu bird of Suten-henen. But judgment was not hers to give, and into the hand of Anubis had she bestowed her rod of office.

For a season it befell to Anubis to nightly weigh up each heart, to hear testimony from the four witnesses, and to exercise his own intuition. Then, with Ma'at's rod—like unto a white ostrich feather—he would either raise or lower his side of the scales of judgment. Woe betides any whose side was lowered, for Osiris would show little mercy to those whose hearts Anubis had judged to weigh heavier with evil than with goodness. But those that were exalted by truth were his delight.

Yet only with mixed emotions did Anubis ever upraise the Feather of Truth, and watch the fallen fall down to their doom. For though his nature delighted in mercy, it would be false mercy to mix together both malefactors and benefactors. For the evil, no longer being able to dominate, would be sore chafed by the virtuous, and the straight, no longer able to redeem the crooked, would be saddened that love was helpless. No, better for all concerned that the evil be despatched as black moths to the black fire pits of Apophis, he who lurked in the nether regions of thick gloom.

But as Sabaf was vindicated, what joy was in the heart of Anubis as he lowered his side of the scale, thus exalting the virtuous! Thoth himself joyously shouted aloud good news of great happiness, and to the Field of Reeds within the *sekhet-hetep*, was Sabaf escorted in high honour, to dwell in the house of Ra. Lilith could see no further, and so her eyes left Sabaf to his fate.

Neferu his son could see no further, and so his eyes left Sabaf to his fate. Sabaf's tomb was sealed. He had gone to meet his beloved pharaoh, Cleopatra, the new Isis. As to Neferu, his marriage to his beloved Kiya was all arranged. Having lost his mother and now his father, Kiya would comfort him as his companion in the life-way. Together they would be one until Ra summoned them to judgment. The Powers took, but they also gave, such was the circle of mortal life. He had first met his sweetheart while she was out walking with Hebony her dog, alongside one of the daughters of the Iteru. She had shown prudence, for it was safer for a young maiden to walk with a dog, for even the Iteru, the Lifeblood of Khem, could pose dangers, both in her mystic waters and around her shores.

All the more dangerous with the Romans and their riff-raff about. Why, Neferu had even heard that one wild incomer had wilfully killed a cat—he had gotten swift and fitting retribution! Neferu did not like foreigners, but their frontier town—once the abode of outcasts—was now within, and facing, the Roman Empire. There was some benefit in that, insofar as they now needed few defences, but the new lords, busy skimming off the cream, still used their soldiers to re-educate the locals in foreign customs. He knew what the foreigners could jolly well do with their claptrap customs. He was sure that one day his people would revolt and take back their own, but whether in his days or beyond, he knew not. But even his bitterness over bolshie incomers was offset by the charming sweetness of Kiya. It had been love at first sight. They were ready and eager to put away childish things and to enter the adult world hand in hand.

As the father had been, so the son was. As a priest, he walked each day in the blissful knowledge of the Powers. In his heart, he thanked the Philikoi for their boundless blessings. Moreover, he was mindful to daily repent of selfish actions and wrong attitudes of his heart, and to help as he would be helped—within certain limits of practical convenience, of course. And Kiya? She like him was loyal to the revelation of their ancestors, and took her faith seriously. That was her intermediate beauty. She stood before him, a smile of love on her beautiful face. "Kiya, my beloved, there is none like you. Evil alone do you lack. Alas that my late lamented mother knew you not, that she might see a son of her son, and a daughter to cherish. And now gone is my beloved father, too good for this world, by the world taken, maybe—for I know of the dark rumours of his downfall. Yet the marriage settlement has been signed and sealed. The dowry has been paid, and gifts to your parents given. Both sides have been warm to welcome us, as we welcome each other."

"Neferu," she replied, "I am ready and glad for your home to be our home. You I know will provide me with clothing and all that is needed for a happy life and a happy home. You shall give me children to our blessing; unto you I shall give the gift of life—if Ra be pleased with me. And a son shall carry your name when you go to greet your father, who this night has begun his new life, and shall see Isis of the Iteru. This night I shall enter your home, for I am your wife." So it was with joy, touched with sadness, that together they combined loss of life with the hope of new life. The silvery moon shone through the windows upon them, and the weeks fled by in bliss.

As soon as could be expected, Kiya felt the joy of new life stirring within her. Neferu had indeed proved to be a good husband unto her, handsomely fulfilling his obligations. On one thing alone they disagreed—she longed to leave Khem. It wasn't that she didn't love it. It was solely because she was concerned about a dark curse that had descended on it. In fact they both were, but Neferu was beholden as a priest to brave the curse.

The talk of the town was that this curse even struck down the newborn. Their people were recently suffering from a strange malady which caused a draining of blood, resulting in enfeeblement or death. Death was not to be feared, but neither was it to be befriended. The curse seemed to be limited to Khem—why were they being targeted? It wasn't the numbers who suffered from this malady which disconcerted the people, so much as the uncanniness about it. Had Isis sinned, thus allowing Iuppiter to defeat her, and now this? Had they sinned, in allowing the robbers of the north to seize their land and goods? Octavianus had swept to power; the defeated people had to bow the knee; Anubis was even mocked as a yapping dog; Octavianus was called by some pharaoh. Yet if that was why they were cursed, why had the curse been so delayed?

As a priest taught to know—and know about—the divinities, Neferu knew that different peoples had been given differing revelations through different sets of Guardians. In the Two Lands, that of Deshret and Hedjet, a pharaoh had once striven with the idea that there was One above the Guardian kingdoms who encircled the whole earth, to whom the Guardians were but emissaries. Akhenaten had been that pharaoh, and doubtless would have enjoyed the northerner's philosopher Platon, who had visited once and apparently had proclaimed the same message as Akhenaten to later generations.

Nevertheless, along with his people, Neferu believed that this One—to whom the Guardians bowed—had given the peoples of each nation their own Guardians to obey and to worship. Therefore, unless the One ordered otherwise, mankind was right to worship his local servants in spirit and sincerity. It was said that Akhenaten had caused the dickens of a problem by trying to force his deep insight into shallow times. He had happily bowed to the king, and then unhappily expelled the king's governors! Anyhow, Neferu had not heard that the Guardians were displeased with the worship they received, and if they were not ill-pleased, neither would he whom they in turn worshipped be displeased. He believed that within their framework, their judgments counted most.

But were the Guardians of Khem—under the One—now standing back, allowing Set to work his evil way? Was it a judgment upon the people of Khem? Once more, it was said, a spotted leopard had been seen prowling around the daughters of the Iteru, and bats were creeping into homes at nights around their mother. Had Seshat turned against them, even as Sekhmet had once devoured the enemies of Ra? Or had Hathor returned to her old bloodlust? They knew by now that a new Sekhmet had taken the place vacated by she who was now Hathor. But whether it was Seshat or Sekhmet who sought their blood, who would embalm those who fell and save their souls if the priests fled?

Kiya of course was right, that as a backup job he could earn their keep as a skilled carpenter elsewhere. A friend and foreigner named Yosef had helped hone his secular skills, and for a few years they had worked well together—not to make their fortunes, but to make honest quality goods to benefit their customers, whether rich or poor—what some quaintly called neighbourliness. Yosef was one from whom he had learned much about some rather unique customs and ideas, and he had been sorry when his mate and workmate had left, but life had moved on.

And after his father's death his duties had increased, so his sideline had taken a back seat. For Neferu had inherited his father's priestly office of *cheriheb*, a position of high honour, one vital to his community. Maybe the curse would soon be lifted, but whether it was or wasn't, to desert his people in this their hour of trouble, would be tantamount to dishonouring his father's name. Unknown to him, vampires picked up that this worker in wood, Neferu, had a wife who had become a mother of a child as yet unborn, and who wished to depart Khem. This was a backwater town, and vampire resources were thinly stretched, but the local agent would keep this family on her visitation list as she walked among the locals, trading, collecting gossip and rumours.

Though history is a pretty good teacher, students can be pretty bad learners, often needing lessons to be repeated. Plagues and chaos had befallen Khem before—as a matter of fact many a time—and the admonitions of Ipuwer the Sage, were but some of many memories that filtered down about curses upon her. In days of yore there had been the Sheep, and some reckoned that it was about them that Ipuwer had raged. The Sheep had been welcomed with open arms, had amply repaid their welcome, but had gotten too big for their own boots and been brought down a peg or two. Okay, maybe Khem had been guilty of overkill, cracking the nut with a sledgehammer, and some even wondered whether the pharaoh in those days had been misled by Set to attack Kurion, the Chief Shepherd who protected the Sheep. Well, whether Khem had been at fault or not would continue to be endlessly debated as long as folk had nothing better to do. She had certainly paid the price of a stinging rebuke upon her army, when with rearguard action Kurion had turned and sorely smitten her.

But whatever the rights and wrongs of the past, the Sheep seemed happy enough to live once more in Khem, for some had immigrated under the Ptolemies. Nowadays within the land, they were free to be themselves, and they wished to worship only Kurion, whom—dismissing all other divinities as 'not for them'—they likened to

Aton—whom some named Usen—much as Akhenaton had done. The Sheep believed that Kurion coordinated the whole show, invisible, untouchable, and yet they held the incompatible idea that he was one divinity among many. It was almost as if they had two levels of language, a poetic and a precise. A somewhat fickle people, the Sheep, but they could be friendly enough, as Yosef had shown. Neferu often remembered Yosef—a history buff—lovingly.

Unlike Neferu, the Darkness was disturbed by the presence of the Sheep, who had flocked again to the land of Khem. Were they were a sleeping volcano which might ignite the Light? Why were that people called the Sheep, you ask? Well, there were different reasons. But to them it was a term of contentment, for they believed that they alone were Kurion's flock, given special insight into his covenant name. And they were happy to be called the Shepherd People, believing that someday somehow they would shepherd other peoples.

But beyond their petty borders, many deemed them to be followers of a false Power, fools to blindly go where no fool had gone before. For some, they were a flock of weaklings, as prey to wolves to be devoured. Indeed the wolf was oft at their doors. They had had their heyday and had long since come down in the world. But still they kept going, though finding it difficult to quite find their way as a community: their shepherd spoke less to them than of old—the prophetic voice could only manage a whisper; its shout had long died.

The vampires continued to study the land, seeking for signs of invasion, seeking the Sign of Akaz. Unbeknown to them, and well off the radar, among the Sheep a couple far away came silently together, having found the will of Kurion. These two were Yosef and his wife, Miriam. But even in the will of Kurion, unexpected difficulties now knocked on their doors. And Yosef welcomed indoors a friend, a friend whose face looked sad and serious.

"Yosef," began old Zattu, avoiding his eyes, "understand that I am not blaming you, but well, my wife has an eye for these things, and your betrothed I fear has strayed beyond her bounds."

For a pregnant pause, Yosef pondered Zattu's meaning. "What do you mean, Zattu? Miriam's an upright a young woman as it's been my privilege to know, and I'm honoured to have her as my wife. She's bound to me, and as true a worshipper of the lord of heaven and earth as anyone could wish. If you mean what I guess you mean, I must say you're making a big mistake. Such things do go on, but neither she nor I have strayed."

"Yosef, my friend, for the life of me, I do not mean to imply that you have done the dirty. But well, we both know that there are certainly men around who would take advantage of a woman young in the ways of men. My wife has the eyes of a midwife, Yosef. I speak only as a friend. And well, if you want my advice, it is to kick up a fuss and cut her off from your life, period. For if you stay with her, you will either be branded an evildoer—thus never be permitted to divorce her—or you will be branded a fool for letting a soft head overcome a sound mind. By publicly repudiating her sin, my friend, you will not only take back your bride gift for a more fitting woman, but you will keep her dowry as some small recompense for her sin against us, and all will admit you to be a wronged man, shamed but shameless."

Yosef found this conversation to be distasteful, but it had to be faced. "But what of Miriam? Let's say you're right. Who knows, Zattu, maybe she was unwilling—though she's not protested her innocence, nor seems unhappy of any wrongdoing. That said, she seems a little queer—quiet and peaceful, like. I can't figure out what's going on in her head, and I candidly confess that I'd begun to harbour some suspicion. But Zattu, I don't wish to add to her shame—if she *has* cheated on me, which I don't wish to believe for one moment. Are you saying that it would be best for her if I simply divorced her without a fuss—if you're right, that is?"

"No, a hushed-up divorce won't do, Yosef. No, you must go public. Sound it from the rooftops, if only to deter others. As for her, well, she deserves stoning to death, and there are plenty of womenfolk who would be more than willing to remove such a blight that defiles the land. Look, even if you only go for public divorce—as her being stone dead to you—that at least will protect your own reputation as a decent man. It has got to be clear to everybody exactly why you divorced her. You will only keep alive any chance of marrying a good woman, if you come out loud and clear with your own innocence. Besides, your poor parents could not without shame allow you to sleep under their roof ever again, unless they see that you do not share her guilt, man. And well, as to her, she has proven unfit to marry, and a bad name will mark her down as unmarriageable—protect good men from her, that will. But you have got to move smartly. Take my advice: do not put off till tomorrow, what you should do today."

"No, Zattu, not today. This night I must sleep on top of prayer, seeking wisdom from the father of our people. Tomorrow is time to speak to my wife of my heart and mind. Shalom to you and your family, Zattu."

"Shalom, Yosef."

Zattu left, relieved that his irksome duty was over and done with. That Yosef was infatuated with Miriam was clear enough to the whole town. That he was a righteous man was equally clear. That Miriam was a moral lass—or rather had been—was equally clear. Zattu walked slowly, weighed down by his reflections on the evils of life, evils which some said all began with a woman. No, he thought, that was too simplistic an explanation for the fallen heart of man. Well, what would Yosef decide to do? Hopefully nothing too soft-hearted.

After all, he could only protect the innocent by prodigalising the guilty—that was justice, that was. Besides—and he could have kicked himself for not having made this point—Yosef was the legal claimant to the royal throne, not that any were likely to fill that seat while the people were under the Iron Heel. But good heavens, that would make Miriam *Queen* Miriam, at least in name—a rather horrid idea in the light of the foul deed she had done. And putting it that way, well, that made her sin the sin of high treason against the king, against his people, and against his bloodline. By rights of things, her paramour should be cut off from the people! But his name would probably never be known unless Miriam, facing death, betrayed him who had betrayed her and her whole community. Well, maybe Yosef could sleep on it, but it was probably going to be a sleepless night for Zattu as he mourned for his cuckold friend.

In point of fact, Yosef tossed and turned a fair bit that night, being more troubled than he had let on about Zattu's frank advice. He knew well enough that babies didn't just happen out of the blue. He couldn't be the father—indeed he couldn't understand how anyone could treat a girl like that—but some cad was lying doggo. Since Miriam had not claimed assault and indeed seemed almost beatific, the obvious conclusion was that of willing consent. Yet she was not the kind of woman to consent to such uncommon abuse against common integrity. Of course it was just barely conceivable that she had neither been willing nor knowing. Stories were told about how women among the Unclean Peoples could awake from binge drinking, violated unawares.

And not just women. Thinking about it, even among his own people there was a story of one guy, Bo'oz of Bet-lekem—his hometown to boot—who had had a nasty turn when awaking after a drop too much. After a party, he had been happily sleeping it off outdoors in the harvest fields—he should have been safe enough. But in the middle of the night, waking to find an unidentified woman lying at his feet, he had felt that his goose was well and truly cooked. Fortunately nothing untoward had gone on—although he had at first felt framed—and in the event all turned out well, very well indeed. Yes, the inebriation of Bo'oz, awoken with paralyzing terror, had swiftly fermented into the intoxication of joy. But one must take care around booze.

Strange, come to think of it, but that young woman of Bo'oz' dreams had come from the Unclean Peoples, had been adopted into the Flock, and without her Yosef would not have inherited his kingship. Truly the hand of Kurion had been at work behind the scenes in ancient times, but that hand seemed so withdrawn in his own miserable days, made the more miserable by Miriam's apparent condition. Anyway, the unawareness of wine could hardly have been her bad excuse, for she had never tripped into tipsy land, had she? Well, she had had a recent and rather extended visit to a respectable cousin, Eli-sheba, but she would have been her chaperone.

He tried not to think but to sleep, but at best it was a fitful sleep. It was during the third watch of the night, within that fuzzy in-between state of subreality and reality, when enlightenment came to him. Had some phantasm called his name, Yosef ben Heli? Opening his eyes, he found that he was trapped in the dreamworld, unable to awake, try as he might. No phantasm was this, but rather one of the aggeloi, they who act independently of the Powers when under the direct command of Usen himself. He was held fast bound in the land of dreams. With unmoving lips the aggelos spoke directly into his mind.

He knew—he said—of Yosef's fear that Miriam, by being his wife, defiled the royal line which his paternal grandfather had inherited through marriage. Fear not, Yosef. He spoke of Huion's plan to invade this world, which would become the beachhead for cosmic conquest.

That, he said, was what lay behind Miriam's pregnancy. She had not done wrong, but on the contrary that she had done right, was chosen, was enviable beyond all other women even until the world's end, the mother of the great synthesis between super-nature and nature, the transcendent and the immanent, the bridgehead into the biosphere.

Yet her doom would devastate her. So so far from divorcing her, Yosef should support her and her son—let the world believe what it would. The child, legally his own, would inherit the key to the throne, and that key, unimportant legally, would symbolise the true kingdom which was not of this world. Still, for a season the reality had to be concealed that the child—Yosef could not process all the data—was somehow the human vessel of Huion, who from beyond time and space had entered this world and become at one with its people, a seamless blend.

Throughout, his true identity had to remain hidden, for he had to be rejected by his world, even by the Sheep to whom he had come as a Lamb, so that Clean and Unclean Peoples would play their restless parts, until shalom ended their segregation. Meaning coded into the ancient prophecies was about to be decoded in terms of fulfilment, shadows giving way to substance. But beyond the need to know, absolute secrecy remained imperative until Hamashiach had set up his planetary command post. For this special mission, Ruach himself had been, and would continue to be, a key player. The first stage of the mission was nothing less than overthrowing the Necros and allowing the great escape from the Darkness into the Day. Though Miriam was key, Yosef too had been chosen. His part was to play a supportive role, supporting Miriam while he could, and so the wedding must go ahead as planned.

Having spoken, he of the aggeloi stood silent, allowing Yosef time to assimilate the information. His mind was in turmoil, going around and around and around. Coming to actually believe the prophetic belief of his people was proving more difficult than he would have believed possible. Told that a very good or very bad will happen, you can believe it loosely, yet still be gobsmacked when it happens, for the distance between head and heart is vast.

To Yosef, Hamashiach had been an unreal belief, an unfocused myth. If asked, "What if this present were the world's last night?" would we not say that it was possible but of course it won't be? Now the prophecy was unfolding before his very eyes, the myth had become fact—crystallization of the amorphic. This was the very best good imaginable. And to think that he and his wife were pivotal to it, indeed that they had been prophesied!

But could he bear being misunderstood to be a bad man, when all his life he had striven to be good? Would his own parents despise him? He now knew full well that he was not to let them into the secret, so sadly they would only think the worst—who wouldn't? And would they believe if he told them, anyway? Had Miriam told him, he defo would not have believed her! How would they treat her? How would they treat him? Long he remained transfixed, as slowly slumber strove to reclaim him, and the light of memory dimmed and died down.

As the light of dawn awakened the chorus of birds, Yosef slowly awoke with a thumping headache, but with no lovely lady at his feet. Perish the thought! Giving thanks to Kurion above, he had a quick breakfast, before going to visit his betrothed wife, soon to be his wedded wife. She likewise gave thanks to he who is above, that her betrothed husband had seen the light, had likewise been visited by the aggeloi. It was with some heartbroken disappointment in them both that Zattu, going along the road, saw from afar their obvious delight in each other. They obviously had eyes only for one another, and had he shouted, they might not have heard. "Well," thought Zattu shaking his aging head, "that explains things well enough. I wouldn't have expected it of either of them, let alone from both of them. Well, I say, don't let them dare ask me for my blessing, that's what." Quickly he passed by on the other side as they held hands in the doorway, oblivious to the outside world.

To Yosef who now had ears to hear, Miriam could now tell all that she had been told. Namely that her baby was a boy; that Yosef would welcome him as his son and heir; that their son would be a warrior-king who would save his people; and that he would always be their king. As to how these things could be, she had pondered long and hard for weeks. Somehow the oppressors would be defeated, but would the victor be deathless, or was the world soon to be wound up, if his reign was *never* to die. Or might it be that after death he would still reign over his people in a kingdom beyond death? Motherhood had not been forced in her. Her permission had been asked and given right willingly, obedient ever to the will of Kurion her lord.

She reminded Yosef that interstate her cousin Eli-sheba had also experienced a minor miracle: the hands beyond nature can kick-start nature; the king may work even in a hamlet. The thing with Eli-sheba was in itself a confirmation to the couple. Not that at that point in time they needed any confirmation that their personal revelations from deep heaven had been kosher.

And presumably the development of their son's character would be a confirmation in itself. Actually, one can suffer from too many confirmations, take comfort in them, or find them a mixed bag. As said, weeks earlier Miriam had, by divine directive, visited her cousin, Eli-sheba, who by Ruach's revelation had immediately proclaimed Miriam—still less than one week pregnant—to be with holy child. Even Eli-sheba's baby had gotten in on the act, excitedly registering with his feet his vote of welcome of the glorious unborn.

That was a story in its own right, for given her age, Eli-sheba's pregnancy was rather remarkable, and she hadn't even been the first to know. The first to know had been her husband, a pure priest of the old order, who by word from the aggeloi had told her that the season of her unfruitfulness had been ended by *fiat*. Beyond belief she was finally going to bear a child, and not just any old child, special though any old child is. No, their child would be the boy long prophesied to prepare the way for Hamashiach himself. An awesome and enviable task, exceeding even that of Moyshe the Mystic, and like him, he would not himself enter the new land of promise. So, well before Yosef had come into the loop, both mothers were getting excited by the good news of great joy for the whole world. That had been a welcome confirmation.

Confirmation was also welcome the night when Miriam gave birth. For local shepherds came with joy in the night. They had been visited by a happy band of aggeloi and directed to the house of Yosef's parents. For even before Kurenius became governor of the Surian, given the political uncertainties of the day it was demanded that Yosef's people would face a special tax, each man to pay in the town of his birth. That tax, tagged on to a rolling regional poll tax that that year had focused on Khem, had necessitated Yosef, and his wife Miriam, to return to his hometown, Bet-lekem.

And she, wearied though she was by the journey and the heavy load she bore, had not even been given a look in at journey's end. For his parents, being good folk at heart, snubbed them both as if tainted. Far from offering the guest room to their firstborn son or to his betrothed, they said that the pair of them would simply have to make do on the ground floor, and bunk down in the barn with the family goats. Another son, arriving the same hour, was treated warmly and billeted upstairs in signal preference, though seeing Miriam's condition he had protested his readiness to sleep below for the greater good. The attitude of Yosef's parents was patently hard and hostile. Clearly they blamed Miriam for their son's sin: ha! let the erring couple learn their lesson, until they beg our pardon.

Oh how Miriam sorely wished that her in-laws had had confirmation, instead of having to be kept in the dark. Knowing them well, Yosef had predicted that their initial frostiness would chill—eventually. Perhaps worse parents would have given them a warmer welcome, for standards would have been lower. For hedonism indeed makes a pleasant dream, though cannot but end as a nightmare. So perhaps thank goodness for moral in-laws, but then the better the people, the worse the hurt. And it hurt still more when in draughty surround her firstborn was born, crying loudly as if he had come to announce a message to the whole wide world. But his infant voice was neither heard nor heeded upstairs. Either Yosef's parents were hard of hearing, or hard of heart.

And then at last the blessed confirmation had come, with the shepherds arriving in the courtyard, gazing wide-eyed at the newborn that was sleeping on a bed of hay laid snugly in the feeding trough. They festively proclaimed that Kurion's shalom was upon all those who welcomed Hamashiach into the world. Their bluff and merry voices ascended to the rooms above, and then through the streets around. Some neighbours cursed the revellers, whose rowdyism woke up their young bairns, but only then did Yosef's parents come down and bow down, convinced through their testimony that indeed Hamashiach had at last been born to his people. Who better than shepherds could recognise the Chief Shepherd come to his flock?

Many years later a minstrel would sing this lay: *Silent night, holy night, in the dark—Usen's light, shining where that mother so mild, looked upon her holy child—he, the light of the world—yes, he was the light of the world. Silent night, holy night, shepherds quaked at the sight, glory came from deep heaven afar, aggeloi sang of zed-a-kah. Hamashiach was born—yes, Hamashiach was born. Silent night, holy night, gift of Light—oh how bright, Usen smiled through that pure infant's face. Hark! the dawn of redeeming grace, he was king at his birth—yes, he was king at his birth.*

The very next day, the guest room was hastily converted to cater for the latest addition to the family, and happiness all around was the order of the day. But Miriam and her son alone were ensconced above, since Yosef elected to billet downstairs with his brother, waiting for the blessed day of his wedding. Time flew by. Was it only a few short weeks later when, as her wedded husband, Yosef played host to special visitors from the east?

This confirmation was a rather puzzling and unwelcome one. Oh, the visitors were friendly enough, but they were royal astrologers—occult operations did not sit too well with Yosef. Nor was he exactly over the moon with the fact of them being *foreigners*—although he had always gotten on well with *righteous* foreigners, and firmly believed that all races were branches of the one world tree. Nor was he chuffed by the fact that in searching for the true covenant king, they had first visited the official king and blabbed about their mission. It had seemed logical to them at the time. Getting *him* into the mix only spelled trouble, as any fool could see, since the true line for kingship would not exactly rhapsodise the *de facto* king.

Still, the Easterlings had meant well and had simply been following such limited light as they had been given, travelling with their entourage off the beaten track to the little town of Bet-lekem, maybe just big enough to boast a village inn. But for all their goodwill they had doubtless stirred up a hornet's nest, and they had realised it by daybreak, for unearthly warnings had come in the night. In different ways had the aggeloi spoken—even to Yosef.

∞

On most nights there were dusky forms with sly little jeering faces, crouching in the corners of the king's room, bending over his bed, tempting him towards madness, spirits that tempted him to murderous thoughts. The hours of the sun were now little better, for waking life was becoming crowded by confusion, by visitations, by unwelcome visitors. Poor Herodes Magnus, unhappy usurper. King, as they called him, political appointee, heir of a new dynasty. He had just spent a few disturbing hours in conference with visiting magi, who stirred up his old fears. Some years earlier he had married a lady he feared might usurp his throne, for rich royalty flowed in her veins. Bit by bit, fed upon lies and innuendoes, he had become paranoid about his tenuous hold on her, and about her loyalty to him—his mind was more prone to poison than was his stomach. Finally he had become so wound up that he had her and her family executed, wiping out that threat, but still it seemed that she threatened his sanity.

The years had flown. He no longer remembered her form nor her face, but he vaguely remembered that she had been beautiful. In the bright moonlight nights within the quiet of his room, whenever he snapped out of sleep, he could see some fragmented image of her standing still and motionless, with long luxurious hair whipped up by no earthly wind, and sad lacklustre eyes staring fixedly upon him, chilling his very soul. For having truly loved her, his grief had been as great as his name, and he had wallowed in the grief of the blood he had spilled. Was he going mad, he wondered? In the name of sanity, should he kill himself?

He knew not that in the background, diaboloi had been at work, stirring up mischief for the pure devilment of it, softening his mind to suspicions suggested by his sinister sister, she who had combined her fear of her brother's overthrow, with her hated of his wife. He knew not that they played with his mind in the moonlight hours, donning the face she had worn, as was their wont. To them that was all part of the Great Game, and they played with humans as humans play now with chess. As a matter of fact, they had been a little disappointed that civil war had not broken out, for the effusion of blood was ever their prime joy.

Now here again was a prime chance for them, stirring again the king's fears. And he had become more cruel than ever was wolf to wounded beast, more prone to bipolar flare-ups of passion, having been given enough authority to cause significant mayhem. Foreign magi had visited the land as an embassage from their king, seeking the one born king, of whom the heavenly lights had spoken. And where else but in a palace would such a king have been born? Theirs was a genuine mistake, but the local diaboloi twisted that fact to seem like it had been an intentional snub by foreign potentates, whose delegates were too untouchable to be tortured for their gall.

And yet to the king's tortured mind the alternative seemed also to be true, that the delegation really did not know and were asking him for directions, blind rabbits before the cunning fox. Was his overthrow really foretold in the stars? Could he not outfox the stars? The mad, it is said, can be shrewd, and he had masked his mind before them, feigned joy, even assembled priests and consultants to review the ancient scrolls for these magi. And then, once the scribes had come up with a probable site, he had blessed the astrologers, bidding them to go in peace, begging only that once their mission was accomplished, that they return to him for their mutual joy, telling him where to go so as to pay his respects to the newborn king. He did nothing to raise their suspicions, neither sending an escort—they had their own—nor spies to track them—they might be spotted.

To the astrological mind, not even the greatest of mortals would dare to challenge the immortal stars. Moreover, as faithful servants to the stars, surely they would not have been misguided to their occlusion. In short, the palace, though not the birthplace, had surely been a stopover that they had been destined to make. Thus, with sincere souls and hopeful hearts, did they take their leave of the king. It was quite touching, really, that he had wished them the happiness of first contact, and in humility had been happy to take a back seat until they returned to their lords—one artist at a time.

In truth he had feared lest they, servants of the stars, should suspect him of sinister designs on the one born king. But he had done his best to allay any such fears, for he could not afford to defy the stars to their faces. Besides, those gullible men seemed best placed to pinpoint the child, and since not suspecting his duplicity would—on their way out of his kingdom—naively report back to him the exact location. Then he could pounce on the unsuspecting victim, and assassination would be sudden and sure without international protest. He who had murderously killed sons of his own, had no inner compunction against killing someone else's son. But he must exercise due caution, knowing that his emperor already had doubts about his mental state. A surgical strike was needed.

As it was, upon nearing Bet-lekem the magi needed no star to guide, since word had been spread a while ago by local shepherds. That news had largely gone unreported in the big city, which anyway wasn't likely to get overly excited over a risible rumour that a dull as ditch-water town had finally found its moment of fame. Nah, besides, many in the big city didn't believe that the time was ripe for Hamashiach, or at least they didn't wish to antagonise their overlords. Hamashiach? Surely not! Why, even the magi didn't know the true identity of the king whom they sought. Big deal! But as it stood, it was ironic that foreigners were at least more in tune with the ancient prophecies than were the people of the prophets.

And their search did not go unrewarded. At last they had discovered and paid their homage to the young king, delivering the token treasure chests which their king had sent with them to set up trade agreements between sovereign nations. It seemed like the table was not quite ready for trade discussions. As royal diplomats they had well concealed their surprise at the, well, shall we say somewhat unusual setting for one highly favoured by the stars?

But then they knew enough about history to see that sometimes regime changes sprang from the underdogs. Had not Mandane of Media's son, having been cast out from the king's court to the shepherd's cot, turned and overthrown the dirty rascal who had had another's son butchered and cooked for an unholy banquet? And thus the underdogs had become the masters, and the masters had become the underdogs; the mighty were toppled, the lowly exalted, and the rest was, as they said, history. Yes, maybe the new king needed a few more years before he took the reins.

So what about the king they had just left? Suspicions only slowly arose concerning Herodes Magnus, and they stroked their beards in contemplation. Before heading back home they took a little time out to talk with Miriam, a pleasant enough young woman and seemingly a tough cookie—and she might need to be. Then, talking late into the night with the lad's father, they came to understand the local politics, seeing from the people's point of view that Herodes Magnus was something of a bloody tyrant, fuelled by the paranoiac flames of perdition. And it was to him that they had dutifully promised to report back!

To these masters of wisdom, a promise was a promise, inviolate to selfish thoughts, but ultimately subservient to altruistic ones. Such were their thoughts as they left the house and bivouacked on the outskirts of the town. It was destined that theirs was not to be a deep and dreamless night. Being disturbed by bad dreams in the night, they soon awoke and all agreed that it was best to depart without further ado: better to obey the ancient stars than the old king. Thus they upped stakes and departed, adding speed and secrecy into another route out of the king's domain—the stars of these people, under which they now walked, would protect their true king.

Yosef and Miriam, and indeed the whole village, had been fair amazed at such a foreign embassage traipsing through. While a few rowdy shepherds would hardly make front-page news, royal visits to an outback town would certainly be splashed about the big city before many more days were past. Even before they had politely taken their leave, Yosef had decided in his heart to take his family and flee to familiar haunts in the east and lie low, but to depart on the morrow would leave too easy a trail for any pursuers from Bet-lekem to read. Perhaps in a few days, when curiosity had died down. With such thoughts he yielded his weary eyes unto sleep.

By the morning the locals were buzzing like bees around a beehive, what with super-animated shepherds and fashionable foreigners and all—what was it all about? Had hope at last come? But such hopes were soon to be dashed, for that day the new celebrities were nowhere to be found, having upped and disappeared as silently as snowflakes in the night. No forwarding address had been left! For behold, in a dream more real than the waking of day, an urgent warning had come that night to Yosef, warning him to there and then take his family to Khem. If sunning on your rooftop you see invaders racing towards you, you don't hang around to pack for holidays. Awoken with alarm he had acted with alacrity—the foreign gifts sure came in handy to bankroll a long journey to friends and relatives afar.

Funnily enough, there was a time before when Kurion had sent his son into that land as a paying guest, but Khem had sought to swallow that lad into slavery, and Moyshe had been raised up to force the land to cough him—Kurion's son—back up. Khem had proved untrustworthy. The son that had gone to help had been made a slave, but nevertheless to that land Kurion's special son was now being taken, he who would end tyrannical slavery, he who could escape all chains of bondage. But then he had come to be a slave, and to give his life to ransom many. Anyway, Yosef had scarpered off as swiftly as if he just escaped a longterm lockdown, leaving a cold trail.

For his part, after giving the magi a few days of slack, Herodes Magnus had gone ballistic, finally realising that he had been outfoxed—by foreigners to boot. Despite a possible charge of mismanagement—which could be presented by his enemies before Overlord Octavianus—he felt it imperative to order a blanket elimination of all possible challenges to his throne. If brought to book, he could always argue that he had merely acted in the spirit of the *Pax Romana*, Octavianus' baby, but of course if he could hush the whole thing up it would be safest and simplest, and that shouldn't be too difficult. Bet-lekem had royal antecedent, but it wasn't a big name nowadays, and he could always smooth things over by reducing taxes for the town. After rewarding their silence, they would surely refrain their voices from weeping, their eyes from tears, and be comforted. With such reasonings in his mind, he sent in his special forces to purge the town of wannabe kings—bash their brains out; dash them against the rocks! Unsure about whether the star sign had come at, after, or even before the birth, he set the killing parameters from zero to 2-year-old boys, just to be safe: overkill beats underkill every time.

For their part, the local diaboloi never really connected this event to the birth of Hamashiach, since so far as they were concerned, he would come from Khem, where the Dark Alliance was on full alert. They therefore should not be blamed for spectating, when they should have been reporting. Should they not enjoy the fruit of their labour? All work and no play, you know. They had been at the king's side when the astrologers had confabbed with him, and on the spur of the moment they had put the king up to a nice bit of mischief— Usen knows he was used to it. It had certainly been nice to witness the slaying of yet a few more innocents—an innocent enough pastime, they had chuckled.

But it had only seemed to them to be some local excitement, some local blood. From their point of view, the dozen or so boys killed were a mild and pleasant diversion from the dull drudgery of their miserable existence. With hindsight, they had wondered whether they should have calmed the king down. For maybe in a few years the pretender to the throne would have arisen, leading an open revolt against the king, and then things would have become much more interesting indeed—lots more blood and chaos. But as it stood, they had wanted some fun, had not wanted to wait, and the threat had surely been neutralised. And after the show—and they always loved to see women weeping—it had not seemed worthwhile reporting upline. So they didn't bother to report it, and Hamashiach slipped unseen through their fingers.

None too soon had the special family escaped to Khem. For the Powers of Darkness had descended on Bet-lekem, and great sorrow had ensued, but then, what was new about that? The state of their oppressed people was such that it really did seem that Rakel, the people's beloved matron, wept with unquenchable tears for her children—hope lingered on. Many a time her children also wept, knowing that by their rebellion against their shepherd—the father of their nation—they had invited foreign wolves in. And they had lost their spiritual compass, knowing neither their way back nor their way forward. They were not even agreed as to whether they should go back to Kurion—he who had led them out of Khem. Had he not sent them to dine with the swine? Should they not settle down and build new alliances, befriend the pigs, live like pigs?

And so there were some who worked hand in glove with the new lords, currying favour, and there were some who simply stuck their knives into the backs of any who collaborated with the invader. But for the most part they simply carried on with life, baring their backs to the whips of injustice, lumping, if not liking, what they had. Even their priests were divided and of dubious sanctity. The purists of the people sought either to sort the priests out—as did the prayer warriors, the Perushim—or to undermine them altogether by denying their legitimacy—as did the Zadokim. All but the priests agreed that the priesthood was faulty. It was a land of conflict and of tears. Bet-lekem was but one sad little town among big tears, hoping to lie quiet and so ride out the storm. It did not heed that it need not fear, but as long as Hamashiach lived, hope lived, and not just for the Children of Rakel.

A week or so later, tired, dusty, but safe at last at Tjaru, Yosef knocked on Neferu's door. He had to knock several times, as darkness like sleep had descended. Again knock, knock. Hebony barked as if in welcome. "Who's there?" barked a gruff voice from inside, as a light was unmasked.

"It is I, Yosef ben Heli", came the reply. Quickly the door was unbolted, and the lamp shone upon him and his young family.

"Yosef, welcome. Come in, come in. But what brings you here—with your wife?" Another voice was now heard within the house, that of a sleepy woman, asking who it was who was visiting so late at night.

"Kiya, it is my good friend" shouted Neferu, "Yosef ben Heli, a straying sheep, it would appear. He has come it seems on a long journey. Please, some refreshments, for he comes with a young mother and child." Kiya soon joined them and made them welcome, and introductions were made.

"Neferu, we need help, yet we could be dangerous guests, I fear. As I think you may know, I hold the title deeds among our people to the kingship, but the Iron People of Etruria have appointed a royal dynasty of their choice to reign over our land. And now my son is heir apparent to the throne, and the portents suggest that at last my people will regain their freedom from the yoke. Nevertheless, a great darkness is upon our people, and its power has been stirred up to the killing of our son, who is the hope of our people—for he is the one spoken of by our prophets. Therefore we have fled our land, warned and shielded by the holy aggeloi, and to this land we were sent. Now therefore help us I pray, for the sake of our friendship and that of our people. Indeed I believe that the fates of our peoples are tied together. Will not the saving of our people be for the saving of all peoples? Did Kurion not create all, even Ra whom you serve?"

Neferu looked at Yosef with approval. Yes, he too had come to see that all divinities were under deity, though he still believed that his particular divinity was deity. But ah, the myopia of parochialism can carry some fantasies a wee bit too far for comfort. No, as a well-educated man, Neferu could see that deity must be too holy to be directly in touch with humanity, too strong to be endured—his slightest touch would surely unmake Middle-earth. Anyway, were he to focus on one people, he would not fail them so badly as to allow them to be subjugated by any human power.

Well, he and Yosef would chew the rag during his friend's stay, and he'd take the opportunity to convince his friend through cogent reasoning, that the One was above Kurion and Ra and Iuppiter, and above every name that could be named, for that matter. But why had he come to Khem? Yosef was nobody's fool, and too down to earth to have been spooked into a long migration. If prophecy and politics had been at work, Neferu wasn't too keen to be a part of any clash between Kurion and Ra, and he could well do without Iuppiter. Ra had once before welcomed Yosef's people into the land, and both peoples had been blessed. That had started with a Yosef, too. Perhaps blessings new would start with this Yosef, and not finish on bad terms. Such thoughts aside, for the sake of friendship Neferu would happily house his friend and family.

"My help you shall have, friend Yosef, since it seems that I am fated to ever befriend you. You don't know, Kiya, that when Yosef lived among his people in our land, he was badly beaten up by robbers who were never caught. Were it not that I was passing by, he might not be here tonight. I attended to his wounds, then took him on my donkey to a nearby inn, paying upfront for his care while I attended to my priestly duties elsewhere. On my way home I stopped off at the inn where he had stayed, and we became fast friends. It turned out that he and I were carpenters, and he taught me a fair few tricks of the trade that have stood me in good stead, more than repaying his bill."

Yosef's face beamed with relief for the now, and gratitude for rescue in the past. "Yes Neferu, I don't know what I would've done had you not turned up. Some of my own people passed by but hurried on, I guess afraid lest I'd been left as bait by the muggers. But then they had sacred duties, perhaps, and didn't wish to defile their hands by my blood. Such things are important to us. I still don't doubt our ceremonies, but it did make me think about what the deeper lessons of life might be, and whether when called for, mercy might not be better than sacrifice. But what if that mercy comes from those we call unkosher? What if mercy is withheld by those we call kosher? What are the inner and outer distinctions? Might the vessel be unkosher on the outside yet clean within, perhaps contrariwise? Once I wouldn't have supped at the same table as you, but necessity drove us into fellowship, and what I once deemed contaminating I now deem an honour."

"And since necessity drove you to me once more," said Neferu, "I do not turn you away. Stay as long as you deem fit, Yosef, for we will shield you and your family. Yet it might be best not to tempt fate too much, my friend. Our house is spacious and ideal for those who would remain hidden. I guess that knowing your way to my late father's house, you enquired not along the way, and timed your arrival for concealment? Yes? That is good. It is better that you go not forth in the garb of your people. Our clothing you may wear if you wish to stretch your legs, keeping your distance from others of our town, and walking in our likeness. Thus you shall be concealed from the Iron Hand that covers our lands. Your child is even of the age of our child. So, by your presence we are blessed and multiplied, for the one has become two."

And so it was that though there now dwelt there two families, the outside world knew of but one. Naturally, the border town of Tjaru had its own complement of diaboloi, but they were fairly slack in their duties—diaboloi seldom put themselves out. Shadowmenacing, mischief-making, blinding, such things were their main business, everything nice and easy, the way they liked their bit of amusement. Even now they gladly left to their allies, the vampires, the main job of seeking out news of Hamashiach. And their allies had already noted the birth of the carpenter-priest's son.

And Wulfgar knew of that, but he also knew that the last check had shown that Neferu was determined not to take his son out of Khem. Vampire spies would keep tabs on town gossip, and would soon pick up any new signs of emigration among its populace. He knew that some families were already on the move, many moving south, senselessly keeping with the familiar, but a fair few were either fleeing east to escape the unnatural curse, or taking ship to the north. His people were perhaps taking a little more blood than they really needed, but their disobedience might actually help the cause rather than hinder it, flushing out the game, so to speak. Still, it was slow work, and although he was the Delta zone supervisor, he felt the eagle eyes of Lilith upon him. She was checking up on progress in his sector. From afar he sensed her nervousness.

Unknown to him, Lilith had recently established her base of operations around Avaris. Never had the Enemy seemed so close. The very air seemed tense. Had the Enemy landed? If so, how best to counter-attack the beachhead? If not, how best to secure possible beachheads? Not much was positively known about the Enemy's plans. Ever since their prophet Zalkeesh had raised the alert, they had debated the issue thoroughly. His data seemed insufficient to ensure success, but at least sufficient to give them a fighting chance. Usen was a fool to have allowed his plans to be leaked to the prophetic community. Yet he must have felt secure enough in himself being able to offset any attempts to derail his plan. As the hour of danger approached, her people had tried to do what they could, but they were always fighting a losing battle, for Usen had such unfair advantages. Even the beachheads were his, but at least they could occupy them, fortify them, watch and wait, they and their allies. And they could continually search to see if anything had gotten through. For every cat that watched a hole, two more searched the room lest the mouse was running loose.

She hated her ally, the Kingdom of Necros, but her fear of Usen far exceeded her hatred. It was as if having marooned them, he now returned—or was returning—to persecute the normality which they had so painstakingly created within their captivity. He was plumb spiteful, the cosmic sadist, and had to be cancelled, silenced for eternity. To different sectors of Khem she had sent nobles from among her people, and under them were many lesser vampires. Had she appointed the right generals to the right sectors? Had they sufficient backup?

Her own people did not always work well together, at least not with finesse. Formings were normally for fighting, and that they all did well, when pinch came to shove. Unsurprisingly none wished to be killed. Therefore they usually preferred to drive lesser soldiers to mop up enemy attacks, but in fighting mode some got so caught up in the fracas that they even forgot about their own mortality.

Yet now they had to systematically search, enquire, chat, sense. Lilith had left Prince Draven in charge of her kingdom, but Princess Ishtar had joined her in Khem. Ishtar had become her daughter and friend, one of only two who really knew her heart and—a secret that must never come out—cared for her. Caring for others was frowned upon by the vampires as being weakness, a betrayal of the stark nihilism of the Darkness, and only a hop, skip, and a jump, from unforgivable love—pah! Lilith and Ishtar sat together in human form, ruminating.

"Reports from my generals seem phlegmatic so far", said Lilith with a sigh. "Among the old men, none seem to match expectation. Few have such selfless dedication as we must expect, even among the priests. Nor have the young men and boys offered much likelihood of being him. The begotten and the newborn we must wait to see, but all who seek to leave we must doubly check and shadow if needs be. For thus spake Zalkeesh.

The mind of the Enemy is subtle, and only by subtlety shall we reveal it. I doubt not that he toys with us, taunting us, for some twisted sense of pleasure. In the extremity of such need, I wonder if it would be wise to awaken the Sleeping Count. What think you, daughter-friend?"

"There are indeed few of our people given to such a task as this, but against the Count I must speak, my queen. Firstly, his sleep is upon him both for his good and for ours. Think of how Usen, enraged by him, has punished us all. Have we not paid dearly the price for the Count's pride? Awakened too soon, will he not run amok, to our discomfort? Does he not need many millennia more to come to better wisdom, and mayhap become an asset rather than a liability? Secondly, if awakened, will he wear the yoke of servitude? And if forced to comply, will he prove trustworthy? Nay, a very unreliable servant would he prove, I fear, and I for one would not know if his yes was yes and his no was no. A danger is he, and like to be of little help, I deem."

"Perhaps, yet he has the skills for such a task, and perhaps the fear of death would keep him on the straight and narrow. The need is desperate, Ishtar, and we cannot afford to be too fussy in choosing our friends. There is danger in him, yes, but is there not also salvation within the Count? In awakening him, does not what we might gain, outweigh what we might lose?"

"My queen, the hasty strike often goes amiss. We certainly cannot be sure that he would play our game and not his—he is a wayward arrow. And I suspect that he has a vendetta against you in particular, and perhaps against our people in general—for who among us have supported him? His goal has long been to gain the ascendancy of our kingdom, and if given high trust might he not sway our generals to side with him? For will it not seem to them that he has escaped yet again his just deserts, and incline them to him? Take care, lest the arrow target your throne. My friend and mother, you must stand firm and let him sleep on, relying on your subjects who are loyal, not exalting the disloyal, no matter how high their skills be exalted."

There was a long pause before Lilith spoke once more. "Be at peace. I wished but to know your mind, my daughter-friend, though the decision is mine to make. Alas that such skills as we seek are entombed within one so unworthy, for they would have served the kingdom well at a time like this. Alas, he asks not how he can serve the kingdom, but merely how the kingdom can serve him, for his mind is twisted like the Necros.

I yearn for a day when we may release him as repentant, as one awakened into wisdom.

"But so far there is no sign given of such change. Even in his waking and wandering escapades—which unbeknown beyond these cave walls, I have wrought—he has shown no hints of hopefulness. Yes, I fear that should he be awakened in folly, yet attain to power, that he might then seek to bow the vampires unto the will of the Dark Lord, and that success for him would be disaster for us—should the full fury of Usen descend upon us. From of old, Drac the Dangerous has seemed to believe that he could escape the consequences of his folly, seemingly unconcerned as to whether or not others likewise escaped. He is a strong sword that cuts the hand of they who wield it, a swift sword unwise to unsheathe, alas. Therefore he must remain a sleeping dragon." Concerning Count Drac, Necuratu had been wise enough to make that request to the Queen of the Night, and wise enough to leave to her to treat her own as she should choose. He would be disappointed, but not too surprised, to discover her choice.

Meanwhile, life in the Delta went on as usual in that timeless land, where life seemed but conception, and death seemed but birth. Ever the humans there seemed to dwell between the grace and wrath of the Powers, as Light and Dark continued their ceaseless conflict, now stirring, now slumbering, in endless cycle. The two households in one, were getting on with life, adjusting how to live with each other in harmony. Providentially located on the outskirts of the town, it still seemed to the locals to be but one household. If Miriam walked in the garden in the cool of the evening, Kiya did not, and Miriam walked ever ready to quickly scuttle indoors if townsfolk were spotted approaching. By careful management of their egress and shopping, their duality remained unknown to both the town and to the wider community. Unknown to them, it was hidden even from the Necros, for aggeloi had raised a fuzzy telepathic block around the house. And rarely did the Sheep family come forth, though when they did they came forth arrayed in the garb of Khem, and avoided close contact with other folk.

Yosef completed his concealment by a total shave, even as like to the priests of Khem. Among his own people, priests made such symbolic shaving but once, and that was upon their commissioning. And in keeping with the dictates of symbolic separation, they never ever styled their beards, unlike the men of the Unclean Peoples—as they sometimes smugly, sometimes sadly, or sometimes spiritually, termed those not of their own race.

Among his own people, shaving was at times commanded for deep mourning, and verily Yosef mourned the enslavement of his people, enslavement which had caused him to flee from the land in which Kurion the Landlord had let them dwell. Yet not in mourning, but in concealment, did he now shave every day as did his host, so that none who sought the holy child might find them. His very brothers might have bowed down to him as to one of the High Khem, had they journeyed to that land. But had the veil of his secrecy been lifted, had they recognised him, they might have recognised one who had pondered in his heart whether one day the divide distinctions—the religious apartheid between his people and the Goyim—would be needed no more.

Ironically, had he unveiled his heart, his own brothers might have preferred not to recognise him, for their brother Yosef was a radical. One can't choose one's siblings, of course, yet perhaps it was for that very radicalism that Kurion had chosen him to be the adoptive father of Miriam's firstborn, for by definition radicals are they who rest not until they get to the root of things, and Yosef sought out the deep things of Kurion, even his unimaginable mind. Nay, perhaps chosen first, and then radicalised by Kurion, for would he have sought for Kurion unless Kurion had first sought for him? Yosef had certainly become an extremist—extreme towards the Light; discontented with the Dawn; dismissive of the Darkness. That quality now endangered his family, or say rather that by that quality he was eminently qualified to be the head of such a dangerous and endangered household, knowing when to flee, and when to face, danger most grave. And if it were not enough that the diaboloi and the vampires of the Dark were searching for his son, even the wife of Gaius Turranius was searching.

In the land of Khem, Gaius Turranius was a conscientious governor, and an honest worshipper of Iuppiter, and it is but unhappy coincidence that his name should seem like unto that of the Turannoi, the Powers of Darkness. It is true that the Khemites, whom he governed, did not seemingly worship the divinities whom Gaius worshipped, but the Iron Empire grew on the basis that foreign divinities were just as valid its own—tolerance on essentials. Personally he confessed that he did not know whether the same divinities simply went under different names among different peoples, or whether similar divinities existed among all peoples. What he did know was that many in the land of Khem had become deeply despondent because their land was part of the Empire, and had lost faith in their own divinities, as if they were to blame. Such irreligiosity wasn't going to help anyone. For a happy land, you needed happy divinities, and if worship dried up, the people would too. Khem lived on inundations, and if the divinities dried up, the inundations might dry up, and then Khem would be of little use to the Empire, a drain not a gain.

So, how could Gaius boost true worship in spirit and reality? He knew that many of the priests were little more than timeservers, in it for the job security and the prestige it afforded—besides other little perks—rather than as true believers fulfilling a true vocation. With that in mind he was carrying out an audit of the priesthood, looking to drastically prune numbers back to the spiritual core, lopping off the hangers-on, the parasites, the spongers. His wife was genuinely committed to him, ever seeking to help him in the background. He did not exactly know what she did, but suspected that her source of knowledge—often useful—came from high magic. For augmenting his analytical skills in auditing the priestly activity of priests, his wife helpfully provided insights drawn from the invisible realm, a realm which he feared to enter except through traditional devotions. But his wife? Well, generally men are stronger than women, but women are tougher than men. She seemed to survive the deeper things of the spirit world, things which might have unmade him.

In her inner room she now sat, in front of Manetho, old priest of Khem. He had learned a little of high magic, which he had shared with her—she had been a willing student. She was also now the possessor of an ancient work of art, called by some an ancient evil, for an ancient personality undoubtedly dwelt within that artefact. That personality was undoubtedly evil, but undoubtedly gave her great power to do good—or evil. The old priest kept his thoughts to himself: what price would the ancient evil extract from this foreign woman, for its services to her? For his part, servitude to her was well repaid by his retention in priestly office, and gifts towards his funeral. But on the other hand he harboured fidgety fears for his future fate. Would Osiris welcome one who had worked such operations of magic, even if only as a tool? But to break with the governor's house was to invite sure and painful death.

Now and again she would use him in what seemed to be the putting forth of his spirit, an operation believed to carry some small but significant risk of not returning to one's body—he didn't like such precarious travel. Under some kind of hypnosis, his spirit seemed to travel beyond his body, and to tell through its body what it was that it saw and heard. By such spells she spied upon the households of priests who were suspected, either of being too unspiritual or too spiritual, for the former needed to be dismissed if their fraud was confirmed, while the latter needed to be tested as to whether they were too good to be true, hypocrites at heart. She knew whom her husband had listed as chief suspects, and there were hundreds. The son of Sabaf was listed, for although he seemed earnest enough, yet perhaps he falsely followed his former father's trade, shamming to the outside world. What was he like in his inner world, safe from prying eyes? Into that inner world of his home, did she seek to send the spirit of Manetho.

As she spoke the secret spell, the priest sunk down into the silence of the slain. "Speak, Manetho, if you are free from your body and you hear me, the mistress of magic."

"I hear you, my lady, and I am free", said the vacant voice of the priest. "What directions have you for me, for say where you will, I will go thence that you may see."

"To the house of Neferu, even to Sabaf's son, a priest of Tjaru, I send you speedily. Go swiftly, in the blink of an eye go, and tell me what goes on there behind closed doors. Stir the mind of Neferu, by my charms, that he speaks of the spiritual realm."

"Behold my lady, I stand at his door, but I shall not knock, for one who knocks can be known. Now through the door I step as one unbidden, even as a thief in the night, for none have opened unto me. Now do I see him and his wife, sat alone but for one child deep in slumber. As he sits within his thoughts, I stir his mind to speak aloud of inner allegiance, even to know his heart towards things spiritual. Thus you shall see how he stands. The house is strange, I know not how. For part of it lies veiled to my unveiled eyes, and I may not pass beyond the veil.

"But enough, he stirs and speaks now of 'the child', and of his home as harbouring the one foretold in ancient days. Yet, he says, those days must be cut short, for the chosen one must surely soon leave his beloved Khem. He sighs as one soon to be bereaved, and asks his wife what father could have a greater blessing. She stands, and looking lovingly at their child, smiles, and looks to speak. But now Light shines in their home, my eyes are uncovered. An anthem is raised by spirits unknown, drowning out all human voices. Behold, I am blind and deaf. An intolerable weight descends on me. My heart is gripped by fear. I cannot stay."

Not knowing why the vision was being opposed, but fearing for Manetho, she quickly whispered to his recumbent form, as she strove to draw back his spirit into his soma. There were tense moments when she feared that he might not return to the mortal realm, and it was with relief that she looked upon the awakening man. "What was said, my lady, and are you satisfied? I feel strangely worn and weary."

"Manetho my friend, your journey was not without fruit. For I learned that this priest is indeed a true priest of Ra, and so shall my husband be told to the gladdening of his heart. I learned also that his son is destined for great things, wherein we may rejoice. I tell you this so as to cheer your heart after your ordeal, but I command you to tell no one, for the seed must surely grow undisturbed." Since Octavianus was now styled as the King of Khem, his people would share in the blessings of the land of Khem. She wondered whether Iuppiter Caelestis had visited the home of Neferu the priest, conceiving thereby a divine child, one who would save his people back into the path of duty toward the divinities, the republic, and family. And so Manetho and his patron— though she called him *friend*—took their ease and retired each one to their own bed. Long Manetho lay awake, unable to free his mind from his memories of Darkness. And now a creature of the Darkness flew swiftly to the Dark Lord.

"Hail, Necuratu, Master of the Necros. I, Ashmedev, speak."

"Whence comest thou, Ashmedev, to disturb the machinations of my mind?" demanded Necuratu, with eyes that looked murder. It was not a good time to call.

"From going to and fro on the earth, and from walking up and down upon it, O my master. Behold, I am he who incited the son of Hammedatha unto genocide—and so might Hamashiach not have been born. Do you not give me welcome, my master?" His voice was humble, but his words were cunning. Necuratu gazed on him, withering him with his baleful stare, transfixing him, until at last his eyes released him.

"So, Ashmedev, thou crawlest to me to boast of thy past failure, and, thou sayest, our recent failure? For sayest thou that Hamashiach hast been born, and that thou knowest where? Then thou art welcome, but if thou namest not the place of his birth, then the deepest dungeons of perdition shalt not hide thee from mine eyes. Speak short and swift, desert snake."

Ashmedev quaked at the sight of his angry lord. He had hoped to be begged to divulge his information so haply come by, to be offered promotion up the ladder. Yet he had simply been threatened with demotion and disaster for nondisclosure. His was a hard taskmaster. He immediately realised that he had offended his base master, by tactlessly alluding to his master's underlying failure to prevent the birth—and so his own attempt to brag had backfired to his peril.

Of course, for the recent failure, Necuratu was not entirely to be blamed. After all, he would have willingly killed off the secondborn, lock, stock, and barrel, had he but had permission to do so, and was mortified to have had his wings clipped by the supreme fowler of spirits. And now here was the little toad Ashmedev, rashly announcing that the thing Necuratu greatly feared had come upon him, that the Age of Hamashiach had dawned. And as for roaming the earth, that might have been better phrased, too. After all it was well known that Necuratu was himself doubly chained, and mostly walked in the wide world only through the feet of his servants. Seldom did he risk personally coming forth, lest the Guardians should cause him hurt, and the tighter bind him in the Chains of Darkness— chains forged by his own freewill. Still, a day as yet unforeseen was promised him when he would be released—for a short while. But for now, unfree was he who would make the world his slave, and reminders of his disempowerment rankled, undermining his vastly inflated pride.

Fearful of his *faux pas,* quickly Ashmedev spoke to soothe: "My master, verily it is in the land of Khem, in a little town of Tjaru, that the woodworker hast been born unto the house of Neferu, carpenter-priest of the Mansion of Ra, where Horus presides as patron. For know thou that now I shadow a priest, even Manetho the Old, who workest for the mistress of the governor of this land. And seeking to divine the priests of Ra, she seekest ever to send the spirit of Manetho to pry out their innermost thoughts, as to whether they serve Ra truly or not. For she, Manetho, and her husband, are true believers of he whom we namest not but in curse. Yet in ignorance they know not that it is I who go as if loosed to go, and that the mind of Manetho is but blanked by my will whilst I journey. Thus, by the cleverness of a familiar..."

"Enough, slave! Speak naught of thine own craftiness and arts of deception. The least of my slaves know well the gullibility of the secondborn, and that the beguiling of them is but elementary as they seek paranormal knowledge. Confine thy speech—which is wearisome to me—to proofs of your claims, and reward for short-windedness thou mightiest yet win and stripes avoid."

"To hear is to obey, O my master. Knowest then that in that very house its master, quickened to speak truth from his inmost being, spoke thus to his wife: that their child, being Hamashiach—so he named him—had soon to depart the land of Khem. Is that not double proof? Moreover, I saw the child lying in a bed beside them, yet I could do him no harm, for the aggeloi were gathered in strength, and quickly didst they arise and cast me forth upon discovering me. Is that not proof? And thus I lay the certain knowledge before thee, O my master, for in thy wisdom alone canst we slay the child born to be our bane."

"If thou dost speak sooth, thou shalt be rewarded, Ashmedev, but if thou speakest shadily..." Ashmedev departed speedily. Ha! So the house of Hamashiach had at last been discovered; the good seed planted by that roadside would soon become the prey of the Birds of Darkness. Thus would end the New Age before it took root. Thus would the kingdoms of Darkness sleep the sounder.

Great crashes of thunder reverberated around the little town of Tjaru, as if the Dark Lord's chariot of fire rode aloft in its clouds. Seldom did the ancient snake sneak forth from his dark fortress, exposing himself to the Eye of Usen, but greatly he wished to see the site of danger with his own eyes. Below, many of the Khemites watched the storm from within the safety of their homes, as the fading glow of day was impaled before their eyes upon the sudden darkness. The more timid among them dropped to their knees, earnestly praying that Ra their champion would this night be once more victorious over the Great Enemy, who this evening seemed unusually eager for the nightly battle to begin. Then upon the land the sun set.

Oh blissful morning, oh glorious dawning. But whatever the future day, between sunset and sunrise there can be pain unspeakable and full of woe. Necuratu's policy had been to stop the general assassination of the unborn, for Usen would not stand idly by forever. Instead the Necros had opted to gather intel, co-opting in the People of the Night as allies—not too many, of course, indeed barely enough, but still a big help. But with one child now in their sights, it seemed too good an opportunity to let slide through sluggishness. Usen, so prim, so perfect, so commanding praise, had finally blundered big time. Now they had discovered the den of his special agent, Hamashiach, and like a running prey, once you dig your claws in you stay with the beast until it drops. Usen had slowed just long enough—a fatal mistake for which he would pay dearly. Now the prophecy could be rewritten.

Necuratu reflected on a story he had heard a while ago. There had once been a landowner who had built up a thriving wine business. Having moved overseas, he had rented out his vineyards for a percentage of the sales. But when his agents came to collect payment, the tenant farmers had piled in and badly beaten them up, sending them on their way with nothing to show but the bruises on their bodies. The more sent, the more beaten. Necuratu enjoyed that story, for they were his kind of people—he hoped one day to meet them. The landlord, unable as yet to return, sent his son as heir to the business, with his full blessing. By the customs of the day, such a person was deemed untouchable, but despite his credentials the tenants refused to acknowledge him as the landlord's heir, falsely accused him of heinous crime, and then killed him. They told themselves that the vineyard was justly theirs, even if they had to murder the previous owner's son and heir.

Yes, Necuratu liked that kind of thinking. And now here was Hamashiach, just like the landowner's son in the story, come as innocent as a lamb to call all his subjects to account. Necuratu knew well his identity, and didn't need the self-deception of the tenants. All he needed to do was to murder the Landowner's son. That should cause the Landlord to yield up the 'vineyard' entirely, and the Necros could live in peace unopposed, butchering off the human vermin. And they, devising deep designs in the dark, might eventually be able to take over all the cosmic vineyards, Usen being disheartened by his loss. Necuratu could almost hug himself in sheer delight, as his fantasy flew far higher than the sky and plunged into absurdity itself. For the sake of the Necros, Hamashiach must die.

However, the Necroi were afraid of the blood of Hamashiach—they did not wish his blood on their hands. The greedy tenants should have hired secret assassins—far safer. As the landlord of that story had sent his son to collect, they could send vampires to kill: delegation was key. So it was that Lilith, queen of the vampires, was given the contract, and she in turn handed it over to Wulfgar. It was strange, but given the opportunity of high honour, the queen of the vampires declined to kill the young child. Perhaps her reluctance was linked to killing her own child, a reality that still haunted her mind at times. Poor Lona. Perhaps underlying her hard exterior, she was just too soft at heart—not an idea she would have wished to have published abroad. For all her bitterness towards Usen, and her eagerness to end Hamashiach, when pinch came to shove did she really wish to end the Light, Lady of the Night?

Wulfgar was warned that the child was protected by the aggeloi. Stealth, not brute strength, was needed for success. A small ray of hope was offered by the fact that reportedly the aggeloi had been initially taken by surprise by Ashmedev's intrusion. Would they be alert in case there was another visit, or would they be overly confident in their own powers? At the lower end of their Order, their powers, though great, were not insurmountable, but they could evoke reinforcements with uncanny rapidity. And those highest up the chain of command had fearsome power. Wulfgar had somewhere heard that a dunamos had thelodynamically stopped an aggelos from delivering a message to one of the secondborn, once upon a time. That might have involved the Sheep, but whatever, the dunamos had hindered the messenger for weeks. Obviously the message wasn't too urgent, but eventually, perhaps getting impatient, one of the archaggeloi was joined the fight, allowing the messenger to slip through the blockade. But it had proved that the aggeloi weren't all-powerful.

Usen could speak directly, easily enough, but often he seemed to prefer using intermediaries, and while holding special agents in check wasn't the name of the game, the diaboloi always liked to be annoying. Neither party could kill each other—in mortal terms—although the Necroi could be decommissioned if they went too far, taken out from the Great Game. Naturally vampires could be killed, although that really wasn't up to the aggeloi, or even to the Guardians. Like the killing of vipers, killing vampires was basically left to the discretion of the Children of Usen. Wulfgar had a fairly unique advantage, in that he could invoke the immunity of his kind against the aggeloi, and invoke the immunity of the diaboloi against the secondborn. But where aggeloi were guards, he would have to shield his diaboloi guests from their senses. Even so, to protect Hamashiach such guards might nevertheless kill him if they perceived him to be a vampire of the Night, even as they might kill a viper in the night lest it bite even a heel of Hamashiach. He decided to visit the house of the priest in the guise of one of the people of Khem, shielding both his identity and that of his inner guests. That trick might fool the guards.

Nowadays, all sorts of weird and wonderful ideas abound about such guests. It should be said at the outset that by the prohibition of Usen, they cannot come through the door of the will unless they are welcomed, but once through they often outstay their welcome. And strange to say, some of the witless among the secondborn still seek to gain net benefits from such an alliance. That is of course a really foolish thing to do, since their contempt for the secondborn is such that they honour no such alliances, and easily dominate the minds of their human hosts, masters to slaves. But one whom they cannot oppose, if invoked, is Usen himself, before whom they must fly. However, with the Night they stand on a very different footing. For firstly, most vampires, like all the diaboloi, are of the Dark. Secondly, most vampires are more powerful than the lower-end diaboloi. And thirdly, they would never seek to bind vampires anyway, for that would be at variance with the Great Game, which plays only with the Children.

With both vampires and the secondborn, it is the mind that hosts the diaboloi. Human cells generate human brains which generate human minds, and those minds remain inextricably linked to human biology, until freed by death. For their part, diaboloi are minds without biology. Though they can shape shift into the forms of the lower creatures, they have never wished to be, nor ever been able to become, biological. Vampires stand somewhere between the two life forms. For vampires are minds that pre-existed biology, but over time have adopted biology and remain vitally attached to it. But like diaboloi, vampires are essentially thelodynamic beings. As regards Wulfgar, his mind was open to his guests as a now unhappy but not unwilling host. As guests they did not take up any material space—an infinite amount could dance on a pinhead—and were not creatures that any autopsy could discover, but where his brain went, they went. It has been said that if human eyes see a tree, the tree enters into the human mind, and might even take root there. But unlike the diaboloi, few trees talk within one's mind—the talk of his guests wearied poor Wulfgar almost incessantly, but he still needed them.

The road to the priest's house was off the beaten track, just on the very outskirts of the town. You had no need to take that road from the town, unless your destination was Neferu's house, and if concealment was your aim you could approach it from the narrow side road on the west, thus avoiding the town altogether and then turning north. Unknown to Wulfgar, Yosef and his family had taken that very route, but he knew nothing about Yosef nor his family. It was on that route that Wulfgar, by the power of his will concealing his identity and that of his guests, now walked in some fear and trembling, cloaked in human form. And thus it was that at dusk he stood before his victim's door and knocked. At first he heard nothing but the yapping of a suspicious dog, but the door soon opened. Neferu was a trusting soul, and before him seemingly stood a fellow priest, who named himself as Sataimau the Sorcerer. Neferu quickly opened the door for his new friend to enter, as the duty of hospitality demanded. Wulfgar-Sataimau sensed the suspicious watchfulness of the aggeloi guard.

"What brings you to my house, Sataimau my friend?" asked Neferu, having first seen to the cleaning and comfort of his guest. Kiya was out of commission. Their child had been unwell, and Kiya as chief nurse was well nigh exhausted, and now slept alongside him in a side room, definitely not to be disturbed.

"Neferu my friend, I have long travelled this land in search of righteous priests, for I fear that Apophis is stirring, and I believe that the faithful of Ra must come together. For will not a Dark Age begin if we fall?"

"Nay, if we keep quiet we might indeed perish, but surely Ra will deliver the land by some other means. Is it not foretold that he will eventually put down Apophis forever?" exclaimed Neferu.

Sataimau sat a while in silence, sipping his wine, looking down. Eventually he looked up. "Yes, so it is foretold. But have we not our parts to play, and if we play them not, how can he put down such a foe? If he did not need us, why has he given us parts to play, my friend?"

It was Neferu's part to sit quietly, pondering the riddle and wondering why Sataimau was taking such a pessimistic view. Would any true follower of Ra believe that Ra needed man's puny efforts, and yet the force of the argument that he did, had hit home. He prayed within himself, striving for understanding. It was long before he stirred. "It seems to me that we are superfluous to Ra, but that in grace he gives us a small share in his work, so that we may share his kingdom, his power, and his glory. Have you no son or daughter to whom you have given coins, so that they might buy you gifts? Is it not that you have not given to receive their gifts, but rather that through your money they might receive the glory that comes upon their heads for gifting unto their father? Praise be to Ra, who gives to his priests, so that they may use his strength to defeat Apophis."

"Yea," said Sataimau, "but what if having given my children gifts that they might gift to me, they lose it, or fritter it away on their own fancies? Am I not the worse off, depleted and less able to spend unto myself? Am I not best not to give them gifts, and so preserve my wealth for myself? Am I wiser than Ra? Nay! So surely he has never given us of himself, but rather has always needed us to enrich his power over the Evil One. Do we not pray each night so that he will be helped to defeat Apophis and rise as the blessed sun? I say again, that if we fail him, we and he shall both fall. And so we must band together, we who are righteous, we who are just. If you would truly help Ra, you will go hence at daybreak to the far south of the land, to a place I shall tell unto you, there to join my army of warrior priests."

"There you ask much too much, Sataimau, unless you can indeed prove that you are mighty in magic and one who has seen the mind of Apophis. For though she does not rise to greet you, in that room there lies my wife with our ailing son. Would you ask of me to walk out on them to join your army, however noble, unless the need is desperate?" asked Neferu.

"My magic I can prove to you. But as to your family, I was unaware, for I am weary from long travel, and I had not probed your house with my mind, nor would I do so without consent. But I find it strange that your wife has not been called to greet me. Is she unwell as well? I am mighty in the healing arts, my friend. Might I assist?"

"Alas," replied Neferu, "it is our one and only son who is unwell, and he alone, but she has tended him constantly for many an hour, until both have succumbed to deep sleep. Thus I have not disturbed her slumber by calling her forth, and know that in this you will excuse your host."

His guest bowed low. "The hammer of fate can hit us hard, but if your power in magic has not been sufficient, I believe that mine shall succeed, if you will permit its use. For I am well versed in herbs and potions, and come from the House of Life. Come, tell me the boy's symptoms." And so it was that Neferu spoke of his own son, he whom his new guest deemed to be the Chosen of Usen, he whose life he sought. "Truly," said Sataimau, "here I can cure the child, for I have with me medications made from many baleful substances, which will cause the Dark Powers to flee from your son's body, and so he shall recover. Nor, as token of my unalloyed sincerity, will I take any coin in return. But behold, the mixture must be given after prayer to Ra in his noonday journey. I myself must be away at dawn, but first I shall show unto you my magic in healing, so that you may believe and go south to the secret place of which I shall whisper in your ear."

With that, Sataimau drew forth his travelling bundle, and soon had extracted various artefacts which he pummelled together, odorous substances such as well matured dung from crocodiles, mice which had first been fried then dried, a particularly interesting paste from flies, a little fat from a cat—its body he had found—with some special herbs and spices thrown in for good measure. In some unknown tongue he chanted a song of power over the sickly paste. "There, that will work like a charm, and thereby shall my power be manifest unto you. For within an hour your son will no longer be ill. That you administer the potion will be a test of your righteousness, for to trust me in full you must first trust me in part. For the rest I forgive your unbelief, but be prepared to set forth on this holy cause upon my magic salve being shown to work. However I lay on you one fate, that if you believe not to test my power, your son shall surely die a dire death, as if being eaten alive from within, for by terrible loss shall be chastised they who dare to disbelieve my words."

Neferu sat silent. He had welcomed a travelling priest, who had spoken as if a special agent of Ra. Yet his colleague had spoken of there being a major weakness of Ra, claiming the Ra was too wise to give gifts from his abundance to man. Neferu would give good gifts to his children—was Ra less generous than he? And his hospitality, rewarded by an invitation to assist Ra, was in another sense unrewarded by a patent threat upon his firstborn. Sataimau had returned hospitality by stick and by carrot, and their conversation closed in silence. No act of power had been performed, except the alleged mixing of a magic cure for the lad, a cure that Neferu must apply in faith or risk severe reprimand.

Sataimau had briefly pondered whether to convince Neferu by the use of telepathy. A thelodynamic being could fairly easily read an open mind, and sometimes worked with the secondborn in producing such phenomena. Sometimes one would read the mind of someone who held up a scroll which they had sealed, thereby reading what they knew of the contents. It would all seem pretty impressive to those unused to things on the spirit world, and perhaps such a demonstration would have convinced Neferu to trust to magic and to use the medication. But Wulfgar-Sataimau could not risk revealing himself to the watchful aggeloi. Such tricks could reveal his mind, and also the minds of his guests, who he sensed had already become quite agitated, silently begging him not to go too far. Their doom was in his hands.

But he was no fool. He had moreover that supreme gift of the artist, the knowledge of when to stop. To improve that which was already perfect—to draw the rope tighter yet around the neck of his unfortunate victim—could be the ruin of them all. Above all, he knew that he must not let the aggeloi realise that the secret location of Hamashiach had been discovered. His assassination attempt might fail, fine, but another attempt could perhaps be safely made, so long as the unwary guards didn't realise that it was no longer a safe house. While Neferu slept uneasily, Wulfgar, the agent of death, remained alert in blissful anticipation of the death of Hamashiach, whose hours were hopefully numbered. For the sake of appearances, however, it seemed to the world that he slept the sleep of the just, a slumber as pure as the Bennu Bird.

With the rising of the sun Neferu arose, awaking his wife for her to say farewell to their overnight guest. Besides, it was extremely important that she too should have a chance to weigh him up, for it was vital to discern whether or not the stranger's strange gift for their child, should be given. A woman's intuition was more valuable than gold. But alas, she too could not make the man out. Human body language is perhaps something which is read more instinctively by women, but Sataimau was not human. His readings simply baffled her, and she wondered whether all magicians were so mysterious. Though they politely bade him farewell, he was not so courteous, and purposely played the part of a victim, a wounded and irritable man.

For his part he protested that he had come in good faith, seeking those of good faith, but had felt distrusted and, well, he said, he'd got no more to say to them except that they must show a little faith. If they did that, he told them, they'd see a rapid change in their son. If not, well, if he had come in the name of Ra, then their child would die a nasty death. And now, he said, he had to depart, for he had far to go and little time to accomplish his mission. And with some snarky words of thanks, he departed from their house, wending his weary way eastwards. But he departed knowing that the poison he had concocted was not simply within the jar of ointment, but had infected their hearts with both hopes and fears. He left with a fair to reasonable expectation that they would administer the bottle of death, once he was safely off the scene. And once he was at a safe distance he would cast off his human disguise, and leg it as a Khemite wolf, scurrying far from the scene of the crime. Let the aggeloi explain to Usen how they had been so remiss as to have allowed death into the family home! Ha! That would be a laugh.

Only after Wulfgar-Sataimau had left, did Yosef and Miriam quietly emerge from their room at the back of the spacious house, being told that the coast was clear. Then they were told the strange tale of the night. Yosef was a man of caution, and well versed in the history and wisdom of his people. He was decidedly unhappy with the mysterious visitor, and was relieved to know that nothing had been disclosed about himself or his family. As for the child, Yosef and Miriam had both prayed after the manner of their people. They knew that sincere requests from good hearts were always harkened to. They also knew that to harken did not necessarily mean to heed, at least in the sense of being answered the way prayers were prayed. Perhaps sufficient to know that requests were taken into account, put into the mix of the overall plan within overall possibilities.

He had heard some children ask their parents for the queerest of things. One little girl had asked for a lion—she'd been given a cat. One little urchin had asked for a snake, and more sensibly been given a fish. A very sleepy boy had even asked for a stone to eat, but wisely his parents had given him some fresh bread instead. Adult requests could be just as daft, and to the Ancient of Days, the wisest of old men were but as silly little boys, not always asking for what was best. Would the boy they had interceded for be healed by Kurion? Yosef knew not—*please*, even repeated, was not a magic word. Should the child be medicated? Again, he knew not, but he was suspicious of strangers of the night who disappeared with the light of day. Admittedly he himself had been visited at night by the aggeloi, but that was a very different kettle of fish, and been confirmed many a time and in many a way. Indeed, had he realised it, even being in Khem was a confirmation of it.

"So, friend Yosef, if you were in my sandals, would you apply the ointment?" asked Neferu.

"I'd put aside the threat of not taking, and I'd ask whether I trusted the medicine man. And I'd not trust him, from what you've told me. The Guardian of your people is Ra, and are his servants to dishonour his name? Yet you say that he spoke of Ra as weak and needy, fearful even of giving his power to help others. We hold that the powers of evil are far below the powers of good, and that the Guardians to the Nations can be given more power by Kurion himself, if needed, to keep evil in check. Indeed, can't you see that Ra could give generously, not to get back, but simply to enrich those he gifted? Do we mind if our gifts enrich our children and aren't given back? Such is a cheerful giver of good gifts.

Would you have it said that the highest of your Guardians gives but stintingly, if he gives at all? Yet Sataimau implied that if Ra gave gifts of empowerment to the children under his care, he might by his generosity fall, or else that such gifts wouldn't be of generosity at all, merely for the empowering of his army. I say that he spoke ill of Ra, even though he claimed to come in his name. You say that he spoke of other powers of magic, powers he would not show because of your unbelief? But I say that even had he shown you such magic, his words concerning Ra should caution you.

"Our people say that Kurion owns the cattle that roam upon a thousand score hills, and that if he were hungry he'd not tell us as if he needs us. Indeed it's to us that he gives his cattle, so that we may feast, not him. Those we sacrifice to him aren't his food, for he's not a creature that he needs to feed, but in our giving back he delights in our love. If our hearts are not in it, we're to give him no bull. And he's set unto the nations those under him who have something of his nature, not needing us but giving to us in love.

"Our people moreover say that seeings of the future can come from evil as well as from good. One test we have is that if a prophet speaks truth of what shall be, yet doesn't speak truth of he who guards us, but rather incites us to disloyalty, the same seer shall we put to death, so that we stumble not in our mission. For through us the Way of Hamashiach was to be established for all to enjoy." Yosef sat back, but could see that the sad eyes of Neferu and of Kiya were unquiet. The poison of fear had seeped into their spirits, but alas, the choice to be made was theirs alone.

"Who really is Kurion?" asked Neferu. "Long ago it is said that he was mighty in power, and that thus he rightfully defeated our Guardians—for shamefully we had dishonoured your people. Yet you still speak as if he were their lord, and that he would assist them in need, despite all I have tried to teach you." Though Neferu had long held the idea of One as supreme over the Guardians, he couldn't stomach the idea that the One could double as a mere Guardian, or that any mere Guardian was *primus inter pares*—especially Kurion, Guardian of a defeated people, Shepherd of shorn and scattered sheep! On the one hand, Kurion had defeated Ra, but on the other hand, the Sheep were a backward flock, hardly a kingdom to be compared with the glories of Khem, mongrels to pedigrees, even if both were now subjugated to the Kingdom of Iuppiter, the upstart people of the Iron Hand, the Children of Romulus. Now that was power, and having conquered them Iuppiter reigned over Pharaoh Octavianus. But Kurion, though having fought an incredible rearguard action, had then fled, instead of logically turning back, enthroning Moyshe as pharaoh, and enslaving Khem! No, even in my anguish don't tell me that Ra is a servant to Kurion!

With a friendly smile on his face, Yosef looked with some sadness at Neferu. "It's said as you say among my people, yet not all are of one mind on this. Don't you understand that Ra wasn't with your pharaoh on this? Thus it was that Ra didn't stand with Pharaoh when my people left, and thus it was that Kurion never fought with your Guardians, only with the rash of the land who sought to regain their pride and to re-enslave his people. Yes, he had first humbled your pharaoh and your people, showing their sin unto their eyes, such that they begged his people to leave on friendly terms, offering them lots of gold and silver in payback for their labours—nothing was too much for their former slaves to ask for and to be given. Yet pride arose from the palace, and sought to take back what had been well given.

"But as to Ra, he'd been given the command to stand aside, for Kurion would take his chosen tribes to their home, and if pursued would leave behind a witness to his greatness, to remind Khem of the honour of him whom they had dishonoured with rod and with club, and also to leave in honour his name which could lead them to his love. For ever he loves the people of Khem, and he shall bless them as his people, having now brought his own people to the point of birth. The time now waits only for he who is born to come into his kingdom. Then a new age will dawn upon the people of Khem, and not only on them but on all peoples beyond all empires. As to how these things shall be, I have but inklings, but I have faith."

Like her husband, Kiya was amazed by such words of love and power. "How can it be, that he whom our people despised and rejected, can come to call us his people, and not by defeating but by blessing? Yet it comes to my mind that though we dishonoured your people, yet they had come into the land of Khem to bless. Such things are beyond our deepest dreams and wildest imaginations, and open up a whole new world unto us. The more are you welcome to abide with us, even as Kurion with us. But still your prayers have failed to cure our son, and though the fear of Sataimau is on us, yet his way offers us hope. Our son is sick, perhaps unto death. Should we not try the way of Sataimau? If he perish, he perish, but if he lives, then my husband will join with him in support of Ra, whom you too affirm to be our rightful Guardian. I say that the ointment should be tried." But she wept.

"Kiya, my sister," said Miriam gently touching her arm, "I too have heard from the holy aggeloi. It is given me to wait in hope for great and marvellous things. On this I cannot be sure, only I feel that you should fear not, nor believe what this traveller has said. Why should he have been offended at your hesitancy, which was natural? Why should he not himself wait and apply the medicine? Has he beaten a hasty retreat, and if so why?"

"Come Kiya", said her husband. "I would heal our child if I could, and this magic potion might work, and if it does not, what is lost? However, I would spare our son an unhappy death, which might be his if in disbelief we apply not the medication. It is ours to decide. I liked not my talk with our guest, yet for my part I am loath to leave what he left untried."

Kiya too spoke out of fear, not faith. At the end of the day Yosef and Miriam, good people though they were, were not of their people, but Sataimau was, and moreover was a priest of Ra, even if he floated off-beat ideas of Ra. "I agree. Let us trust to the words of Sataimau, and not to the wisdom of those of another people, my husband, though they be to us as loving guests well versed in wisdom." And so alas their son's fate was sealed by their choice, and at the hour of the noonday sun, after appropriate chants to Ra, to Nefertum, and to other Guardians of Khem, the medicine was applied. Sataimau had instructed that no trial was to be made of it, since any test would undermine faith and vitiate the magic. It was to be all or none. Therefore they poured the ointment complete onto his chest, smearing it with date palm leaf, and not by their hands, as they had been strictly charged.

At first, there seemed to be no change, but slowly the ointment sunk in through the skin. An unhealthy smell arose, as if warding off evil spirits. And that seemed good. Then their son's breathing became disjointed, the first signs that something might be going awry. Then almost imperceptibly a noisome green fume began to seep forth from his nose and mouth, and his discomfort became clear. Now here and there his skin opened up, and blood began to trickle forth. As the two couples both prayed on their knees, the child started up in a loud cry of pain, and writhed in agony until, slowly sinking down, he spat out blood and gave up his spirit. As Sataimau had prophesied, the change had verily been swift, and the illness was no more. But he would remain unthanked by humankind, for the House of Neferu had become bitter, a house of mourning. Soon it was known abroad that another was to pass into the judgment hall of Osiris, and preparations of the body—of what remained—were begun in the temple. But before burial the boy had to be taught the pass words to open the doors of Osiris. His heart—thanks be to Ra—had been spared.

Soon the talk of the town became the talk of the Necros, for Wulfgar had succeeded in preventing the biggest threat since the dawn of time, namely the cosmic inbreaking of Usen, the irredeemable defeat of the Dark Dominion. Usen would be wroth with great wrath. Therefore Wulfgar's name was never be named, and only a handful knew by whose hand the poison had come. Far better that way, for although the Dark spoke of Usen as being omniscient, they never really believed that he bothered to attend to every little detail within the cosmos—what fool would believe that Usen's eyes were upon superfluous sparrows, or would count hairs? Best keep Usen in the dark, for the less he knew about how his greatest plan had been scuppered, the better. Though technically his son's death had been by his children, not by the Darkness, Necuratu planned that if the Dark was implicated, to shield himself he would accuse his allies. And to be fair, the Dark vampires had devised the means of death. Let them take the full rap. But now was the time to rejoice, and rejoice they did, from Necuratu down to the lowest diaboloi, and from Lilith down to the weakest vampire. The Great Enemy had been defeated, history had been reset in their favour: job done.

*U*P Stakes

The news of his death had been greatly exaggerated. Yosef and Miriam still abided at the House of Neferu, though now their son had to remain indoors, lest he be discovered. Soon the mysterious deaths that had inflicted Khem grew less. Lilith herself had withdrawn, and no more did she stalk the banks of the Iteru, seeking out its infant blood to quench her thirst. Infants elsewhere were plentiful. Bats seemed to have shrunken back to the ranks of mere bats.

Nevertheless vampires were still on the prowl in Khem, as they were across the world, but the Forming had disbanded, for the mission had succeeded and they were wary of the wrath of Usen. All must revert back to normal life. Wulfgar had temporally retreated to the safer though colder climes of Brigantia, replete with its cold and frosty mornings, and days when the snow is snowing and it's murky overhead, making himself scarce from the Eye of Fury. But strange to say, Usen had not raged in like a roaring lion seeking to avenge his cub. The spec-op aggeloi seemed to have withdrawn, as if the glory had departed, excepting the usual few who continued to keep a watchful eye over the town. Indeed by confirming that the house was no longer protected, Usen accorded it the best of all protection, for will a thief break into a penniless house?

It was many of the weeks of man, before news came to the town that death had also claimed the life of the great king of the Sheep, he who had been heralded as the Magnus. And in that news Yosef heard the homeward call, a call confirmed in the night. So at last came the parting of the four who had become fast friends, indeed as family they were one. For reasons of prudence, however, the veil of their secrecy was not removed, and it was by avoiding the town of Tjaru that Hamashiach was taken out of the land of Khem to fulfil his destiny. As they travelled along the coastal highway towards their own land, they heard news that Bet-lekem had been put under the jurisdiction of a weak but cruel heir of the great king, and thought it prudent to settle instead in a region where they had lived before, a region under gentler management. For if Hamashiach was returned directly to the town he had been smuggled away from, that news might well reach the ears of the murderous son of the murderous father, and the ιχθυς, the fish that had barely escaped the net, might be landed at last.

And yet this was in the will of Kurion, that Hamashiach's new identity would fulfil ideas that had been floated by the ancient seers, that the royal heir would be raised in a flea-bitten town berated by their kosher neighbours, a town moreover that mingled rather loosely with unkosher neighbours. You would not expect anything good to come from there, or to go there! Hamashiach would be deemed a despicable man from a despicable town, a sneered at branch from the stump of the royal tree. But then, it was hardly a place where either the Necros or the Palace would seek for him, even had they known that he had not died—it was a place of safety. But it was also a place where he would learn the needs of the needy, a place where he could see both the social and the spiritual degradation of the Chosen People, and of the Unclean People, and come to supersede both.

Of his path, what is to be said that has not been said? For history tells much of his words and deeds, though it tells not even the half. Even before his manhood he had begun to put his deepest feelings into words, and to hint of his uniqueness, truth revealed even in the ancient scrolls of his people—though his words seemed somewhat shielded. For with pure eyes guided by Ruach himself, he soon understood that the sacred scrolls spoke to him of him, and he read therein his destiny. A destiny of which Moyshe had been but as the family steward before the son and heir; the social liberator before the spiritual emancipator. A destiny in which he many a time would in tearful flood beg loudly for mercy, beseeching Kurion to spare his life from the attacks of the Powers of Darkness. For once he came out of hiding, they soon got wind of him. And yet such trials matured his obedience to his mission, matured him as the true man.

It was with sadness that Yosef had died before that mission began, and it was with sadness that his brothers and sisters bethought him mad, dangerous, unstable, just too jolly single-minded and inflexible for their comfort. To them his piteous prayers had seemed as daft as, ah, as sticking one's head out of a window to pray. No wonder that he had soon learned to pray alone, such as in a barn or on the backside of a hill.

He was never a prayer actor, someone who went through the motions to impress others. Still, he could not help but unintentionally put his siblings to shame. But they preferred to place any shame squarely on his shoulders: they were normal; he was not. And so they collected stories to tell about his antics. For instance, in the year before he had come of age, why, they said, he had like a naughty boy scarpered back off to the holy temple, instead of going home with his family, causing consternation and forcing the family to backtrack to find him. When caught he'd even reckoned that the temple *was* his home, in so many words ticking off his own parents! Anyone else would probably have been well and truly leathered—perhaps Miriam's soft words had spared the rod of correction in this instance.

Yet what was madness to them, was wisdom to Usen, who was well pleased with his son, and had a mind to tell him so. What was dangerous to them, was dangerous to the denizens of Darkness—but their hour had not yet come, and they knew it. And he was not the sand but the secure rock, the supreme realist. In fact, he grew up surprisingly well, one might even say astonishingly well. His aunt and priestly uncle visited several times, and Yochanan their son, for whom they had great expectations, got on with him famously, always finding spiritual inspiration and enlightenment from his lively mind.

∞

"Out of my way, Yehudi!" swore the soldier with an oath, knocking the lad to the ground. Young Yeshua regained his footing and stood before the soldier, smiling. "Wipe that smile off your face, or I'll wipe it off for you", growled the soldier, raising his hand to fit his words. However, the lad still smiled sweetly, and asked why the soldier was so cross. The soldier slowly lowered his hand. Why, this lad showed no kind of fear. He was somebody you could turn into a good soldier, perhaps even into a commander of men. Even a common soldier could be nervous enough, but often tactics simply required them to stand shoulder to shoulder in orderly array, with shields in place and spears in hand. It was really the commanders who needed more the nerves of iron, leading their men into attacks, pressing forwards, expanding the Empire. And besides being brave, the lad was unusually courteous.

"Well, my lad, we are wont to treat as we are treated, and we seldom find smooth talk in this divinties-forsaken neck of the woods. I'm sorry for my rough words and rough treatment, though I reckon you are made of stern stuff. I'm a bit on edge at the moment. I like to walk alone and think, for it clears my mind. A man can spend too much time with his mates, but it's risky walking alone, I must confess. In the last hour I almost paid the price of incaution, but I won't give way to fear and be bottled up—with my comrades as the bottle. Still, if they, seeing me ahead of them, hadn't seen the danger and shouted in time, I would have been a goner today. A couple of your knifemen are to thank, for they stole up quietly behind me and tried to stick me. Can't you people get it into your thick skulls that we have come to civilize you, to make you a worthy part of our empire?"

The lad merely replied that behind all thrones and empires there was one who united the good. What was seen was but shadow, he said, significant shadow, but shadow nonetheless, mere human hopes and dreams of the oneness which would soon come through the Yehudim. The foreign soldiers had come as wolves among lambs, but through the lamb they would one day live at peace, and instead of eating the ox the lion would eat with it. For the land, said the lad, was not deity-forsaken but deity-blessed. Justice was drawing near, and light was dawning, so that they who had dwelt in deep shadows could see the brightness of light. It was already present, he said, but was like a light hidden under a bowl, and like the hidden bulb of a plant is not yet for all to see.

The soldier was visibly impressed. Well, he thought, here was a budding young philosopher, ancient in wisdom beyond his days, though what he was on about he couldn't fathom. Yep, from a worldly perspective, this lad talked kinda funny, like nobody he had ever heard talk before, and he looked kinda funny, too. But there was something about him that commanded respect, not a shove into the dirt. Why, the lad had in so many words told him to his face that he was a wolf within a pack of wolves. And as a statement of fact, not as a curse, and believing that wolves would someday live in harmony with their erstwhile victims. What, would they all become sheep? Not a Roman idea, but still, it'd be nice not to have to slaughter or to be slaughtered, and a world full of sheep would trump a world full of wolves.

What, he wondered, would the assassins have thought of that idea of dwelling together in harmony? One of them had departed with his spear thrust into his vitals, but the other had been taken alive for a far worse fate. Maybe he'd go and put that question to him. The more of them they captured, the better, since hanging these scum served as a lesson to any others who would disturb the peace of mighty Imperator Augustus. Hang them high, hang them all, and let our enemies beware, he thought. There could be no other way, could there? He'd left the lad with something of an apology, not words he was used to speaking among foreign peoples. He was a battle-hardened soldier, excelling with the lance, and known for his bravery and fairness. He could even read and write, and so his prospects for promotion were good. He continued along the road in reflection—what a funny land and what a funny lad.

When the ruler of this land had recently been deposed, unrest had broken out, and some heads had had to be broken before some kind of peace could be restored, but it seemed that things hadn't got back to the good old days, as locals called them. Funny, in a way, since direct rule should have been welcomed by the people of the land. After all, they themselves had asked to have their tetrarch removed. Was there no way of satisfying these people? Longinus was puzzled. He himself had come to the region when it had been placed under the rule of Marcus Ambivius, and had proved a skilful soldier. The land itself wasn't especially special to the Empire, but its coastline offered a good base for trade, and it was by the sea that the Empire had set up its administrative centre. That afforded much fresher air than did the sheep capital which abutted the temple of the Yehudim.

Longinus—as he was simply nicknamed among the troops—had a special interest in spears, especially those of the Graeci, being somewhat of an historian of their development within different cultures. He even tinkered with the standard military issue, trying different woods and weights. His cohort of auxiliaries were stationed in what had become merely a province, and not very much peacekeeping was needed to keep the people under the thumb, so some kind of special interest helped to make life more tolerable. His friend Pilatus had shared his specialist interest, and had a command with the legions posted along the Danuvius border. Pilatus also commanded a higher station in life, being of the *Ordo Equester*—they had gone their separate ways on life's highway. What would he have made of this place, a generally sedate land but where underlying tensions could bubble up at any time, but lay dormant for years?

Rome had had to put down an insurrection by Yudas of Gamala along with his sidekick Sadduk, after Kurenius had become the Legate of the Surian and imposed a stiff tax. The insurrectionists had argued that it wasn't the amount that they objected to, but the principle of giving tribute to affirm any external lord, since Kurion alone was their overlord, not Caesar. But most locals were simply annoyed by the amount, especially coming so soon after a previous Roman tax.

Feelings ran deep, and resentment simmered. Even the calming words of Yoazar ben Boethus, the high priest of the day, hadn't been enough to stop all the hotheads, and Longinus had waded in with his troops to quell the uprising, even burning the temple. Well, after all, the zealots *had* raided the royal armoury at Sepphoris—*quid pro quo*. It had also been assumed that Sepphoris' inhabitants had helped the so-called resistance fighters, as some had self-styled themselves, and so that town had consequently borne the brunt of Rome's anger.

Longinus hadn't particularly liked it, but orders were orders, and the town soon became rubble, and many became slaves. Perhaps the end justified the means, for later it had been rebuilt the Roman way, with pro-Roman folk moving in. The Iron Hand held sway.

Rome had also had to tidy up the mess that a multiracial group had caused. 'Caused' might be too strong a word, though, since they and their enemies had been sniping at each other for generations, it seemed, even disrespecting each other's temple. In fact a little bit more than mere sniping, and that's why one lot in fact only had temple ruins—thanks to the other lot. Now what did one lot—called Kuthim by their enemy but Shamerim by themselves—decide to do? Why, they snuck in at night during a holy week of the other bunch, deliberately to defile the holy temple of the Yehudim, scattering human bones in its courtyard. To the Yehudim that was like shoving their faces into fresh dung, in fact worse, since spiritually it made them feel sick and unclean for days, cut off from Kurion.

Inexcusable violation, maybe, but that should have been a purely internal affair. After all, the Sheep had their own temple guards who had been caught napping, but it had had a knock-on effect for his cohort, for some of the Yehudim, unable to practice their annual rites, took out their spleen on him and his men. Perhaps that is what the Shamerim had planned all along, for these two peoples were always trying to use Rome to snipe at the other side.

From conversations he had had—for he always wished to know what motivations lay behind events—it seemed to him that both sides would happily accept full reconciliation, but only on their own terms. Therefore, whichever side disaffirmed its temple—or its ruins—first, would be welcomed wholeheartedly, though belatedly, as a brother. No compromise, no wriggle room. Personally, he could not see why they could not just sit down and talk, then amalgamate, perhaps building a new temple in some neutral place. Better still, they could scrap their religions, worship Iuppiter, and become full players in the Empire. Longinus walked on, wondering how that lad—he hadn't even asked his name—could grow up without sharing his local animosities.

Meanwhile the lad had returned home, though, strange lad, he was always reluctant to call it home. Is home a here, or a destination, a hereafter? Have we only a shadow home now, with a real home beyond the horizon? "Son, what on earth has happened to you?" asked Miriam. He did look bedraggled, but explained how he had been walking along the road, minding his own business, when a lone soldier walking the other way had roughly bowled him over. Yes, there had been a reason, but that reason was pure bad temper. He had sought to pacify the soldier, however, and felt that he had left better than he had come.

Miriam was a little anxious about her firstborn, especially the ways in which he seemed to respond to danger—he preferred face to fight or flight. "My son, is it not wiser to quietly walk away with your head down? Our land is divided, and not all roads are safe. Why, I heard only last week of some pilgrims who took the shortcut through the land of the Shamerim. Their bodies were found beaten to death and robbed even to their loincloths. If that people that claim to be mixed with our blood, take our blood without the bat of an eyelid, how much more those who do not claim to be of our blood? If you see a Roman on the road, why not walk by on the other side and so be safe? Do you wish to die at their hands?"

With a faraway look her son simply smiled, and soothed away her fears. At the right time he would die, he said, and not one second sooner—he knew when to wait, and when to walk, for did Ruach not guide him? And as to avoiding the evil, how should they be saved unless the good helped them? Should not a good shepherd seek even one lost sheep? Didn't those who dwelt in deep darkness all the more need the light to shine on them? Some of his people spoke of compliance under protest, and some spoke of active or passive resistance, but if a soldier ordered you to carry their gear for a thousand paces, what if you actually volunteered to carry it for an extra kilometre? Would that generosity not cut the bitter root of their hatred, win them over to the Light, save another from that burden? And who would be the enemy then, if you had won a friend? He did not say that it would always work, but simply that sometimes it would work for those with eyes to see true love.

Miriam had sat down, while her son had continued standing. She had sat many a time, mulling over the prophecies about this special child. How would his mission pan out? Surely he would make this world a better place, perhaps even establish an Age of Kurion. Yet how could such an Age come to pass, unless the soldiers of Kurion rallied around their king to throw down the Iron Tyrants, and to give unto him the Iron Crown? For, if he had the throne of Rome, he could use Rome's legions and lanes to conquer the whole world in splendour. What a glorious global king he would make, subduing all to Kurion, and all living together in shalom, in harmony. The Necros would die and death be deaded, its power no more! He stood silently, letting her think.

At his dedication, an old woman at the holy temple had prophesied that he would free their own people. Wouldn't he then be free to free all other peoples from their darkness, as another prophet had told her that same auspicious day? But Miriam shuddered as she remembered that old man's other words—that a sword would pierce her soul. Maybe a Roman sword? She, who had given hope to the world, did not need to keep hope for herself. There was much she didn't see, for she was still a sinful woman, yet her saviour had blessed her for a blessèd task, and she had bowed her head to the yoke, whatever the cost. As to what lay beyond her vision, she realised that sometimes it was better not to see too far into the future, but simply to do the task in hand. And to her way of thinking, chatting with an irritated soldier was hardly an earth-shattering event—could a Roman wolf change into a lamb?

The years rolled on, and the lad had become a man of some years. Locally he was called the carpenter, as for many years he had followed the trade of his father and his father's father, 'keeping his head down', as his mother had urged—and she was content. However, her nephew Yochanan had begun making waves, rocking the boat.

A local legend talked about a mystic pool. Sceptics said that every now and again waters flowed from a chalybeate stream into it, troubling its usually calm face with wrinkles—no miracle there! But others believed that it was the aggeloi adding power to its waters— and so what if they used a local stream to invigorate it? Well, what was certain was that some of the long-term disabled pinned great hope in that legend, believing that that disturbance signalled a time for special blessing for the first to dive in—a magic dip for one, so to speak. "Move when the waters move" became a maxim, even among those who did not believe in the legend. The Graeci even had a word for the right time, the seasonal time, and of course nature had her signs. For instance, as soon as the twigs of a fig tree got tender and its leaves came out, it was time for summer.

It seemed that the stirring waters now called to him—it was time to rise up and stir. Ruach had spoken. Obediently the carpenter downed tools and made a beeline to visit his cousin. And that cousin wasn't hard to find, for almost overnight he had become something of a sensation. It had not gone to his head, and indeed it seemed to many that he risked his head daily, for his words were often cutting, cutting the wrong kind of people, people of power. But his words also brought hope to many, hope that the lord of all lands would turn his face towards them and give them peace, hope that he would deliver them from the evil of the land. He was operating alongside the river Yarden, and streams of people were flowing to him, either believing that he was a prophet, just curious, or else looking to prove him to be a charlatan. His solution to the state the people were in, was a deep-rooted return of the people's hearts to their true sovereign, to Kurion himself. The twigs were tender and the leaves were coming out. Summer dawned.

The carpenter headed quickly east to the river, then followed its course south until he found his man by a ford in the area called Bathanea. There was Yochanan, standing tall and straight. Many knew that their lives were not what they ought to be, not so much as people, but as covenant people. There was an obligation, an allegiance, which they had seriously let down.

The prophet called for repentance, and offered to be a conduit for those who repented, to gain or regain their sense of covenant, of specialness—their kosherness. He would immerse them in the river. The water would not wash them within, but it would be a sign, a declaration relative to their covenant commitment. By this act, they would stand with their prophet and align with Moyshe and with Eli-Yah. Some priests claimed that restoration was their preserve, not the job of any Johnny come lately. Moyshe himself had set up rituals to express repentance, to regain fellowship with Kurion, and the prophetic voice should not abrogate to itself such prerogative. A contingent from the ruling council had just arrived, consisting of representatives from bickering sides, but forming a united front to oppose the upstart prophet. Some saw them coming and wondered. The carpenter stood silent among the crowd, watching and waiting.

"Vipers, why are you here?" The crowd was stunned. The prophet had just denounced their leading lights as snakes! A few had seen them coming as if for mass baptism, and had naively rejoiced that they too were confirming Yochanan as a true prophet, and thus uniting the land against the Iron Hand. "Who warned you to flee from the wrath to come?" he bellowed. *Had* someone done that? Had they actually come to be baptised, to identify with the prophet's call, or was he rightly deriding their disobedience with biting sarcasm? No, it seemed that they had come to jeer, not to cheer, so Yochanan had got them sussed. In turn they shouted back, maintaining as best they could their dignity.

Repentance? No need, for they were all of chosen stock, and all doing well, thank you very much. "Chosen?" he shot back, why, Kurion could easily choose even unclean stones, the unclean people they thought of as worthless stones under their feet, to be his chosen people. They must, just because they could see the blessings to their ancestors, be blind to the curse the descendants were under now. They were living at variance to the inner values of the covenant— clear as day if they would but look deep within. They had the genes, but not the faith of the Founding Fathers of their Faith. Whatever their roots, they should beware, for their lives were weeds not wheat. Heaven's axe was poised to hack at those venerated roots, if the shoots were bad.

"Fire!" he thundered, "Beware the fire!" Waste wood would be burnt; chaff had passed its use-by date. His baptism, he said, discriminated, discriminated between those who truly sought Kurion—who could be baptised by Ruach—and those who did not—who would be baptised by fire. Yes, the waste would be burnt with unquenchable fire. There were cheers from the crowd. Well, the contingent left with a flea in their ear, ready to deny his prophethood before the Council, but they left one or two of their hangers-on to eavesdrop on further noises made by this ruffian—could they get him on a charge of sedition?

Among the applauding crowd this talk was like strong beer, the kind of talk they had been waiting for. Many were up for the challenge. But how were they to live this different lifestyle? That, he replied, would be expressed in different ways, horses for courses. But decency and fair play, generosity to their neighbours, honesty, all those virtues and more should flow from their hearts. Expect unexpected change for the better. Yes, even soldiers could be good soldiers and good people! Several folk in the crowd chuckled on hearing that, but it was a good-natured laugh—the prophet also smiled good-humouredly. Sure, the age of miracles hadn't ended—in a sense it had only just begun.

"Listen!" he said. "You believe I am sent by Kurion? And so I am. But compared to someone you will meet soon, I am but small beer. My greatest honour would be to be but his lowest slave." Radical talk, this, because slavery was what all the people were against. If you were in the unhappy situation of being one, likely enough you'd jump at any legal opportunity of being set free, or at least hope to be promoted within its ranks. But would this great prophet become the lowest of the low? Moyshe had never been a slave. Whatever did he mean? And seemingly the one who would come would be the Great Divider, bringing the spirit of refreshing to some and the fire of punishment to others. But wasn't he to be the one who would turn the hearts of the parents to their children, and the hearts of the children to their parents, restoring families, healing generational gaps by the power of the covenant—the Great Unifier? Wow, here was a radical message and a radical messenger, proclaiming that he was unfit to carry, even to unfasten, the sandals of a greater, a mysterious someone for whom he prepared the path.

Having baptised many that backbreaking day, stretching up tall at last with his eyes to the skies, the prophet called upon Kurion to bless the people. Then, after he had dried off well in the setting sun—a chilly breeze was getting up—he retired for the evening meal. His own diet was rather peculiar, as befitted one identifying with the wilderness wanderings of ancient times, and proclaiming by his dress code that he was no mercenary. Unlike him his disciples enjoyed a hearty meal washed down with sweet wine—they too had had a full day. Though cynics scoffed that he suffered from a spirit of wildness, he was not some wacky hermit preaching poverty as a virtue, though he did preach moderation.

Many in the crowd bivouacked on the slopes, though most of those who lived locally retired to their own homes for the night. In their ramshackle riverside camp many, living on the verge of hope, were chatty, but the carpenter said little more than "shalom", saying that his time to say more had not yet come. He seemed decent enough, mind, and had soon pottered off to pray alone. Yes, many candidates wished to prepare themselves for the next day.

With the rising of the hot sun, storm clouds arose. It had been an early breakfast for most, although for some for whom it would be their big day, appetites had vanished with the morning mist. The camp was buzzing, not least with yesterday's goings-on, but the buzz quickly died away as the prophet strode down to the riverside. Some newcomer from the crowd approached to be baptised, but hesitated at the water's edge. "Lord," he said, "you call upon us to enter into the fervour of the ancient way. But does fear silence your voice towards King Antipater, or have you no word against the rich and powerful of our land? Are those of the Shamerim not under our laws? Please tell us, for my friends hold back from calling you a prophet of righteousness."

"They of Herodes Magnus are committed to our laws, and by them are to be judged", the prophet replied. "It is one thing to divorce. It is another to marry one's niece. But though you call him king, it is without excuse to knowingly marry such before her former husband has died. Moreover, he himself disgracefully divorced in order to marry her, and by that has made our neighbour our enemy. That fox must publicly renounce his sin that he be not followed, and must offer restitution so far as he may." The crowd buzzed with excitement, as those who heard passed it back to those who had not. It was one thing to condemn the temple; it was another to condemn the palace—the prophet had really stuck out his neck. If his words reached the tetrarch, then woe betide him. From the riverbank some evilly smiled, turned quietly, and headed north, bearers of good tidings that would doom the prophet. The questioner proceeded to be baptised, allowing in bad faith what the prophet performed in good faith.

The betrayer arose from the waters and waded out to dry ground. Several more people were baptised. The first would be last. Finally the carpenter moved through the crowds and down to the river. The prophet, the light of recognition in his eyes and joy upon his face, saw him approach. Of course his cousin was too obedient to the covenant to come for baptism. This baptism was specifically for those who had walked disobediently to covenant obedience. Folk would publicly confess to such sin and commit to live aright thereafter. Maybe he had some words to say?

But then, he alone beheld a strange sight. For as if in a vision—in which he heard his own heartbeat—Yochanan saw his cousin approaching with the sweet heavenly dove—an appearance of Ruach—descending and perching upon him, as if to say that he would remain as guide. "This is the man! This is he of whom I spoke. Our true king has revealed him unto my eyes. He told me that the Dove of Heaven would appear on Hamashiach. I have seen this. Behold the Chosen One!" Yes, it all fitted, and Ruach—who had sent him to baptise—had just revealed to him who his cousin really was.

The crowd hushed. Would this incomer now take up the baton? Would he march them off to begin the War of the Sons of Light, overcoming the sinful Sons of the Dark, which all the world would witness? But no, anticlimax. The carpenter was asking to be baptised, and the prophet was refusing to comply. In an outback sect, baptism was a big feature, but you baptised yourself, often. The prophet had kicked off the idea of folk baptising other folk, presumably to connect all directly to his mission, so the carpenter was blocked.

They spoke again. The murmurs died away, those at the front straining to hear what was going on. The prophet had dismissed the carpenter's request, saying that he was simply too loyal to need to express any disloyalty. Why, it would be like poor old Job confessing that he deserved more pain than he endured. "Yochanan has never jibbed at immersing anyone else", whispered a few who seemed to live onsite, permanent spectators of this mission.

Now the prophet mentioned that he himself had never been baptised, and begged his cousin to baptise him instead of the other way around. He added that that would make much more sense. Had the carpenter misunderstood what he was there for? But while the carpenter said a yes to the prophet—in the sense of agreeing that to him it would not signify repentance—he also said a no—in the sense that denying him water baptism was wrong, not right. Both of them, he said, must play their part obediently in order to prepare the way. Both must stand together in the eschatological unfolding. He who would walk the prophetic path must affirm that the prophet had prepared it.

Well, so long as it was not taken to mean that his cousin personally needed to express repentance, but simply wished to identify with calling the people to true allegiance, the prophet would happily comply. And comply he did. And as the carpenter came up dripping wet out of the water, the crowd again witnessed an incredible sight. For this time a real-life dove flew down and rested on him, as if knowing that this member of the human race was a safe perch, in spite of the storm which drew near. Well, that was something different, that was. Why, hadn't the prophet said something about a dove only minutes before?

Then immediately there came a loud crackling of lightning, tangible power ripping through the skies, as if the very Spirit of Kurion had been announced, and a rolling peel of thunder, as if he had spoken. Had there been words in the thunder? Into many hearts had sparked the idea that the carpenter was indeed the prophesied son, perhaps greater than Shelomoh, the chosen son who had built them the temple.

Whether it was a mass fantasy or not, when comparing notes it was obvious that the thunder had not spoken to everyone—to many, thunder was thunder, no more, no less. But the carpenter had looked up as if listening. To him it had been as clear as a bell, a personal word of commendation, but also a word of warning, for Moyshe had also pleased Kurion, until through disobedience he had been barred from making it into the promised land. No, he must not fail like Moyshe. He would be as an obedient son, a suffering servant fulfilling the mission, for he was the one of a kind son. Who was he?

He was Hamashiach.

An Extraordinary Man

The diaboloi had been watching. Any stirring among the Sheep, could be the stirrings of trouble, even some counterattack. For Usen had taken that people for special training, learning his ways, getting to know him, not engaging in, so perhaps preparing for, mission. What he had planned for them was anybody's guess, but guessing had kept the Dark Kingdom interested in them. Yet in fact, some diaboloi reckoned that the Sheep had been but a diversion to keep the Dark in the dark. And that seemed likely enough, for their glory had departed, their freedom was in fetters. Yes, they they had feared would shake the world like the hot Dragon of Toba, had turned out to be but a damp squib. Clearly Usen had moved on, withdrawing from them the prophetic voice, perhaps withdrawing to Khem, even as a while ago Inanna of the Night, living with the Philikoi, had transferred her affections from the blonde heads to the black heads—and the glory of Aratta had dimmed.

The Sheep without their Shepherd had become little more than skin and bone, hardly worth a peck for the black crows of Necuratu. Sure, a few petty prophets stirred now and again, but they were pretty shallow stuff compared to the heavy punchers of yesteryear. Long ago it had seemed to the Sheep that Usen had wooed them, and them alone of all the peoples of the earth. In those days it had seemed to their poets as if he had promised to walk in the storms by their side, to never let go of their hand, to do anything to help them understand that he loved them more than any other could. It had seemed that the winds would whisper his name to them, that he'd never ever leave them alone, that he'd be with them, till the end of days, and for eternity. It had seemed to them that he'd whispered in their ear as a man to a maiden. Had his whispers been sweet nothings? Had he abandoned them, casting them off as if they were as the Lo-Ammi, mere foreigners, not his flock? Were they not as a wrongly divorced woman, as a disinherited child?

Or—he was cunning enough—had he merely pretended to abandon them, simply to blindside the Necros, while planning to secretly return to them to fulfil his mission? What was going on now? Were the Sheep intended for Kurion, or to be a free desert to Azazel? Were they the decoy, or was Khem? Khem was wise and powerful; the Sheep were weak and wayward. Which was the Chosen of Usen? Unless he was a fool, odds on favourite had to be Khem, a superpower once and still a force to be reckoned with, even under Roman control.

Or maybe both were decoys? Garn, it was not an easy one to figure out, so one had to cover all bases, though biasing on probabilities. Therefore, any stirrings, even among the Sheep, must still be studied. So, now that the threat of Hamashiach had been aborted, what kind of man was this who had arisen from the waters, where once a disfigured man had taken seven ducks in its muddy river and returned home a clean man?

By rebuking the king, the Immerser had landed himself in deep water. Already some vermin had gone to rat on him—three cheers for that. But what about the Immersed? Was he a new threat? Why had the Immerser prepared a way for him? The diaboloi hadn't quite worked him out. They needed more data to analyse. Necuratu had once said that the proper study for diaboloi is man. Not the firstborn—for they were less wayward, were now few in number, and kept well out of the way—but the secondborn of Usen. Mankind was easily kept in the Dark, and well worth the study. Moreover, it was prophesied that the chief danger would come through a man. Yes, that danger had been averted, but had Usen a Plan B? Was there *another* carpenter to fear?

So what kind of a man was this? As they watched they became increasingly uneasy. His past didn't interest them, but his present certainly did. Almost immediately he'd made connections with the Immerser's disciples—did he aim to become another Baptist? What was his game plan? With a few disciples pilfered from the prophet, he had headed back north to a wedding—how the diaboloi just hated weddings. But what a contrast he was to the prophet, who had never touched a drop of the hard stuff. In this village the wine flowed too freely too soon, exhausting supplies well before the weeklong party was over. To tide them over, this man actually turned water into wine, a sobering miracle! Clearly, Ruach was with him. Before long he was back in the south, causing problems for the priests, performing significant miracles, and generally gaining the dubious reputation of being a national troublemaker. One leader, sympathetic but wisely shielding his own reputation, had had an interview with him one night. At first he'd just wondered whether the man was recommending being born again, but that silly idea had been kicked out of court: not born again but born spiritually, born from above, born anew, the man had insisted, entrance into some new level of Kurion's kingdom. Whatever he had in mind was clearly something radical. Then he had gone off, baptising folk, even as the prophet continued to do, except that he was now drawing the bigger crowd. The Immerser had brushed that off, saying merely that at that stage his own mission must decrease, so that the mission of his cousin might increase; that one moves to the sidelines when another takes centre stage. The Necros was disturbed.

It wasn't long before the big challenge came. The local diaboloi, afraid that they were out of their depth, had reported upline, and Necuratu himself had been tempted out. The Necros then realised that this man was like no other it had encountered. Almost perversely, Ruach, the silent partner in the transformation miracle, sent the sheep to the wolf, to the backside of the desert; from wine to water, and not much of that to be drunk. For this sheep, no green grass to graze on, no streams of peaceful water to sup from. He could see that it wasn't going to be easy, but still he would follow Ruach, even if his strength gave way. Yes, he would walk through ravines as dark as the grave, if that is what it took to follow Ruach on the proper path.

And then promptly Ruach had upped and left, his rod and staff no longer there to guide and to protect. Now the man had cause to fear. Why, why had Ruach forsaken him? Lurking in the shadows, Necuratu rejoiced. In his prime he had defeated the best of the firstborn, and couldn't he now still defeat the best of the secondborn? Why did Ruach risk the defeat of his champion? Did he wish him dead or something? Not content with impossible odds, Ruach had cut off the carpenter's supply lines, thereby weakening his man in the wilderness, leaving a starved sheep before a hale wolf—no competition. No, no fine wine and frosted wedding cake out there, no adulating crowds. Instead, alone, he had had to forage for such food as he could find from the wilderness, sheltering as best he could from the extremes of heat and cold: no cloud in the days; no fire in the nights. Well over a month he waited. As dangerous as marauding tribes, wild animals had to be warded off by sticks and stones. Such weapons could bruise bodies and break bones, but were enough, barely. If strength lies in nights of peaceful slumbers, he was weak, very weak, a lamb for the slaughter.

Seemingly abandoned by Usen, nay, surely betrayed, should he not surely abandon Usen? Beyond his worst nightmares, Necuratu began to consider the impossibility that Hamashiach was alive and living among the Sheep, a shepherd in sheep's clothing, strength within weakness. Were his fears justified? Time to strike! It was after the man had been worn down by life in the raw, that the Dark Lord tested him on that very point, even offering to treat him with far more respect than had Usen, and delighting to honour him if he switched allegiance. His was the choice of Hercules—Necuratu said—the choice of well earned ease or of needless hardship. And against impossible odds ranged against his mind, the man came out the winner. Necuratu had finally fled in disgust, fearful also that the sheep might have been staked out as bait to trap him. He would wait for a more opportune time, then attack again.

Returning to civilization, the man was caught up with the news—the prophet had been arrested by the king. He quietly returned to his hometown, but before long his neighbours were itching to cast him off the nearest cliff. He obviously had a way of making friends and influencing people, but that influence was not always friendly. Again and again, Necuratu sought through his agents to agitate against the man. Again and again, he failed. Probing into this man's past, they discovered that he had come from Khem, and they felt then the shame of Usen's mockery: the vampire Zalkeesh had been right enough to wrong-foot them. It was bitterly galling to know that Usen had used a prophet to make fools out of them all. Could they catch up and still win the game? It was too much to hope that this man was a decoy, for those of the diaboloi who met him knew who he was—to meet him now was to know him, for he no longer shielded himself from them. And he treated them abysmally.

The special team of vampires who had gone into Khem, were reassembled and consulted. Could they sneak in and kill the man while he slept, or nightly draw from his blood until he withered and died, or best of all, by injecting their own DNA into his veins, could they enslave him to their will? But the aggeloi kept watch, and warded them off at each attempt. Even Wulfgar had tried, only to realise that though he had gained access to Neferu's house, the guards there had known who he was before ever he had reached the front door. A vampire attack was an attack of nature, which Usen permitted as a rule, but this case was an exception to the rule. Here it seemed like Usen was like a mother bird shielding her chick under her wings; like a shield that blocked the arrows of outrageous fortune; like a doctor who wards off a plague. Attack by the vampires was a fruitless endeavour. And to the diaboloi, who stood absolutely no chance of sneaking in under their radar, the aggeloi were a potent enemy under any circumstances.

Even as a technical advisor, Wulfgar, now back in the mix, was unsure about the best course of action, and he was constantly goaded by his guests to do things their way. Even his queen would not intervene to release him from them, even if he had asked her, for that would have jeopardised the Dark Alliance. Nor did the vampires normally care about delivering their own kind: if fools get themselves into trouble, let them jolly well get themselves out of it. Of course for using another vampire, it might make sense to deliver them from the evil ones, but that was because you cared for what they could do to help you, not because you cared for them as a person. They were simply unconcerned about the other guy. At least they didn't hate each other, unlike the Necroi who seemed to hate everything and everybody, including their own kind.

Surprisingly in the Great Schism between the Light and the Dark, a small but significant number of vampires gave Usen the benefit of the doubt. Now them the Dark vampires did really hate, but that was understandable enough—why tolerate traitors, scabs? Wulfgar was also a traitor, yet in a different, unrecognised way. For against sovereign command he had killed the last of another thelodynamic race, and the diaboloi who knew that little secret enjoyed a greater sway over him. He had been weak, and regretted what he had done, but the secret must not come out—anything but that! He was not the only vampire who had racked up some unmentionable sins in their long past.

Lilith had had to draw Wulfgar to one side, even to threaten him against making any more attempts on Hamashiach's life. The

Prophecy of Zalkeesh—now confirmed—had been clear that if born, Hamashiach would die a bloody death before he could attain to resurrection. It seemed clear to her that therefore a violent death must be avoided at all costs, for thus would the prophecy be voided. Nor did she believe that standard vampire operations of enslavement would be permitted to work on this agent of Usen.

In this the Necros were at variance. Necuratu believed that they had been tricked all along the line, and he didn't trust the prophecy. Yes, he said, Usen had given Zalkeesh a few glimpses into the future, but only enough to deceive. The fragmentary nature of it had already proved dangerously deceptive. Why believe that a bloody death had to be avoided, that the best protection *from* Hamashiach, was to give protection *to* Hamashiach? That was doubletalk. Would Hamashiach, favoured of Usen, acquiesce to such rough handling? No, Usen intended that Hamashiach would never die—even the Sheep spoke of his reign knowing no end! Those details by Zalkeesh were false, peppered into the prophecy to deceive the likes of Lilith. No, said Necuratu, plan a nasty death, even as the prophecy had foretold, and thus turn the crafty schemer's laughter into lament. Hang his man on a gibbet; transform the joyful dance into sadness; strip away his joy and clothe him in sorrow.

The foolishness of Lilith was wiser than the wisdom of Necuratu, but he just couldn't see it, and neither would budge. They came close to blows, for Lilith feared for her life—the damned fool would damn them all. Yet the Kingdom of Night could not stand against the Kingdom of Necros, nor could she stand against Necuratu. Nor would she play any further part in such hubristic folly. The Dark Alliance was broken.

But any plan involving the secondborn had its own set of problems. The human creatures were divided, and few were either deeply of the Light or of the Dark—mainly a twilight people? Mixed hopes, mixed fears, mixed motives. Few knew their own hearts. Some thought themselves evil who were good. Some thought themselves good who were evil. The man continued on his merry way, though not without many a tear, many a sleepless night. But if it was dangerous to befriend him, it was also dangerous to betray him. What good would it do to betray him, anyway? And who would execute him, for on what charge could he be killed? Perhaps a private assassination would be easier to stage than a public execution.

In which case, what about the knifemen, secret assassins who lived in the hills, and who stole into towns at night to slay both servants and supporters of the foreign power? After all, the man—who was now being hailed as Barnasa, *The* Barnasa—preached an antithetical radicalism to those free radicals. Instead of saying, "stick your knife into them as enemies", he was more likely to say, "show your enemies love"—help, not harm: most folk simply said "ignore them". Barnasa was to the knifemen a collaborator with the enemy, an enemy to the Kingdom of Kurion. However, Barnasa had built up a dozen sturdy followers, disciples who went where he went, and who formed a natural bodyguard. Sometimes he sent them off on missions, honing their thaumaturgical skills, for he wished to train them in the arts of supernatural healings, of raising the dead, defeating the diaboloi, and of proclaiming the New Age. At such times he was more vulnerable, but knowing well in advance when he would be alone, was almost impossible. Besides, like the knifemen, outback survival skills were second nature to him, and keeping track of him was almost impossible without insider help. And one insider had been an assassin, so knew their mind, knew their ways. He would prevent their attempts on his rabbi's life. And attempts they would love to make, since Barnasa was a strong corrosive against their core policy, a policy for which many of them paid the ultimate price, crucifixion.

What about using the king? Arguably if given the task he might have got the job done, but he was rather weak and not really his own master. Because of public opinion he had not even dared to kill the prophet who had bearded him, though he had wished that he had dared. It was only after making a daft promise in a drunken stupor, that to keep his word he had psyched himself up sufficiently to stick the knife in, for had he not done so he would have been laughed out of court by his own household. It was rumoured that when he had first heard stories about Barnasa, he had looked upwards in exasperation and lamented, "Oh bother, another Baptist all over again!" But if he had hesitated with the Baptist, he would hesitate even more with the Barnasa, for public opinion would turn his legs to jelly. No, the king was not the lord of the dance, only his puppet, an unsteady reed swayed by the wind.

If neither knifemen nor king, perhaps they could arrange a chance encounter with a Roman soldier. A soldier could always cop a plea of self-defence, so might not be all that unwilling to terminating a rodent Yehudi, an *untermensch* slave. That soldier would have to be someone short of the new praefectus—who would have too much to lose—and perhaps someone close enough not to fear losing their head. Fear could be used positively, but could sometimes hinder the performance of duty. A common soldier might be used—they were disposable—but how could the diaboloi break through their fear barriers? Barnasa was a force to be reckoned with, and had his personal bodyguard.

One soldier stood out, a battle-hardened officer named Longinus, who now reported directly to the praefectus. As they shared intel, they discovered that Longinus and Pilatus had a history of friendship. So, Longinus would be low enough down the food chain not to make the death political, but high enough not to worry about being punished by his friend. As a contingency plan, they could happily settle with a public execution.

Sadly the side that really wished Barnasa killed weren't permitted to execute anyone except defilers of their temple. Pity, for it would be doubly fun for Usen to be hacked off with them. Sadly the side that was permitted to execute more broadly, didn't have a big problem with him. Thornily neither side liked the other, so an unholy alliance would be difficult, but should be developed just in case Plan A failed. Hamashiach must die.

∞

Longinus sat cross-legged at the table in the dark hovel. A few oil lamps were burning, illuminating a woman. One woman, all alone amidst many soldiers. One woman, the cynosure of all eyes. One poor defenceless woman. But like an insignificant root sprouting up in dry ground, there was nothing about her appearance that invited a second look, no beauty to catch their eye. She was safe. The soldiers sought merely to use her, not to abuse her. Her eyes were closed, her clothing was dull, but as her breathing paused, a subtle change came into her voice, and her clothing seemed to seep out a strange greenish film. It was as if a mist arose from her eyes and ears, a green mist that gave off its own noisome light. All eyes were fastened on her, entranced. The mist slowly obscured her face, slowly reshaping into another face, a man's face, a Roman man's face. Apart from the woman, they were all Romans there—they would not have tolerated one of the Yehudim to taint their company, except that they needed this one to meet their deeper desires. Her eyes hadn't charmed them, but now her dull eyes had changed, as had her face. The soldiers were under orders, her orders, to uphold her in love while awaiting their turn. All the men who had come unto her would be satisfied, she promised, for she would give them the desires of their hearts, one by one.

Now it was the turn of Longinus. He rose, and addressed her. "My father, I, your devoted son, greet you. Mithra the undefeatable be praised! May you fare well in the land of the dead. I am doing well, and have been exalted to the rank of centurion by my patron, the prefect whom we called Pilatus who loves the pila. We are stationed in a barbarian land, but rule where we must with a firm hand, worthy of our emperor. Do not be anxious. I do not neglect your shrine, and offer you the choicest of food and drink, in honour of your name. I have written my greeting to Livilla who is with child. If a son, may she let it live; if a daughter, may she dispose of it." He bowed low. It need not be said how they conversed, but suffice to say that the woman's face changed many times, each recognised by a soldier, and each time the eyes matched the face, and the voice, of the departed.

Before retiring for the night, the woman, well paid for her services though weary, singled out Longinus. "Master," said she, "I perceive that you have the gift as have I, to contact beyond the veil. Please, my lord, suffer me to bring out this gift in you. They who guide me will reach out for spirits who will guide you in the ways of our craft. You too can be endued with power from on high." Longinus was flattered, he was tempted, but he was a soldier at heart, and he was not willing to add to himself the skills of master magician. "Nay, woman, I am no conjurer, nor shall be. It is for me to bring down the living who oppose Rome, not to raise up the dead of Rome. Your call is holy, and so I pay you well for your services—as I have paid women before—but my life is secure. I pray that you fare well." With that he turned away, rejoining his men and returning to their camp towards the coast. There was little talk among them as they walked, for each walked with his own thoughts for company. Living so far away from their families, letters were welcome. And to meet family who had departed to the underworld—neither great nor evil but simply theirs—was especially welcome. Shrines were places to feed them, to honour them, to talk to them, but not places to talk with them. So opportunities to engage in conversation were welcome. In this land of barbarians, however, there were customs forbidding such communion, and those who practiced the secret arts did so under cover of darkness. To taste the dark magic was to some daring, and to all was feared.

A spirit of Darkness appeared to Wulfgar, in appearance like to a savage man, belching black clouds and flakes of livid fire, his face the pallor of blanched bones, his eyes popping from their skeletal sockets. Special effects were meant to daunt. "Hail, Wulfgar, my lord sends you his greetings. Thou, my lord, canst be free of thy guests' demands, for they shalt be thy servants, and not thou theirs, if thou shalt do what we now ask of thee." Wulfgar was interested, yet suspicious. Interested, for the voices in his head too often disturbed his mind, driving him to the point of distraction as if to throw himself off a cliff—yet they always pulled him back, lest he die. They needed him, and he needed them. Suspicious, because although Cacus—a prince among the diaboloi—was offering him terms of peace, their promises were easily broken. Best play along.

"What is it that my lord asks of me, and what surety will you give that if I play my part, you will play yours?" he asked. Presumably any task the Kingdom of Necros gave to him was one they would not, or could not, undertake, and not one to do without proper payment. Moreover, the Dark Alliance had just been dissolved by his queen, and any personal alliance with the Necros might put him on the wrong side of an angry Lilith. A risky task, without an ironclad guarantee of personal gain, was hardly an attractive proposition.

"We seek the service of Longinus, a centurion of these parts, that he mayest be a spear in the side of Hamashiach, a spear cutting short his days. Already we have tried to call him into our service, by appearing unto him in the guise of one deceased, and through our host—yea, we have hosts even among the Children of this accursed land—we have tried yet failed to enlist him into our magic, as baseborn mortals name it. Now therefore, thou who art vampire can wrest him unto our ways, making of him your slave-son. If thou doest this, verily we shalt release thee from our bondage. And why should we not, when thy freedom is but little price to pay to have thee as a witness to our honour?" Obviously the Necroi were desperate to commission this victim, and having failed to enslave him through a human medium, were happy enough to enlist a vampire to do the job. Wulfgar realised that this soldier was being set up as an assassin, and that Hamashiach was to be the victim. Lilith had told him to back off, but if he secretly cooperated with the Necros, he could gain a rich reward in the form of regaining his sanity. It would be wonderful to once more be able to call his mind his own, and he could swiftly slay the assassin by mind control, thus severing any link to himself. Besides, personally he sided with the Necrotic idea—that forcing Hamashiach to die as *per* the prophecy, would outsmart Usen and pan out for the best.

Yes, it seemed money for old rope, and well worth the gamble. Thus it was agreed that Wulfgar should steal into the Roman barracks and take Longinus to be his slave. Not all vampires took slaves, but all could if they chose. The blood of the secondborn they feasted on, though the law prevented them from overfeeding. Some could forgo drinking a drop of blood for 10,000 x 10,000 years or more, but the dearth would take its toll in withering them. And what is life without pleasure? They drank, sometimes daily, for pleasure more than real need, and yet they claimed that pleasure was a need. Overfeeding tended to mean too much blood from one location in too short a time, causing the humans undue concern. The Kingdom of Night was safest when secret. Often their victims knew little of the feast, but simply awoke with a sense of feeling somewhat drained, somewhat withered, aged, for unbeknown to them they had given but had not received. But for those who gave and were given, it was a grave fate, for they exchanged freedom in life for freedom from death. They could exist as undead, *corrumpi*, their eyes and ears being ever open to their vampire lord or lady. Far better for them that they had died quickly, than to face unending years without death. Longinus had refused the Necros' offer, and so was handed over to a vampire lord to become a slave. Caught napping, the free fly would be ensnared in the spider's web, hunted while he slept.

The following morning Longinus awoke, tenderly touching his neck. It still bled slightly, for coagulation was hindered around two minute puncture marks. His head ached, but no more than did his mind which now heard another voice, a voice he fought against, but a voice he could not silence. His eyes protested against the bright sunshine, and sought refuge in the shadows, but that reaction would soon subside, and slowly rebuild. An inner dialogue had begun, in which he was instructed in the ways of servitude, the ways of a host that is slowly eaten away from within by its parasite. Woeful was he. Would he become but a shade in the land of the sun? A mission was given unto him, to seek out and destroy the one who was called Barnasa. However, he was hindered as well as helped in this, by being within a human chain of command, and not a free agent. Moreover his people were garrisoned far to the northeast, and might only visit when sent by headquarters. Apart from the occasional patrol—a showing of the colours—it was only on high and holy days that they patrolled the Sheep's capital, an ancient city nestling in the hills.

Have you ever psyched yourself up to do something you know you ought to do, but hated to do? Have you then discovered that the obligation has ended, that that dreadful deed to do has dissolved away as a black cloud blown by the west wind; that the person to confront has gone away, address unknown; that the mountain has been removed; that the locked door now stands open? Such was the relief of Wulfgar, for when ordered by his commandeer Longinus finally rolled into the old capital, he discovered that Barnasa had been captured on a capital charge.

It seemed that his security had been breached. Word was that a dodgy treasurer from Kerioth, with a seat on the Inner Circle of Twelve, had done the dirty deed. It seemed that when Barnasa had yet again predicted the end of the road, this rogue had decided to bail out while the going was good, taking down his master for a contemptible pittance. The Barnasa had then been captured easily enough, with the wheels of fate finally turning for his enemies. Pilatus had hoped that a good whipping would suffice, but the hungry crowd had bayed for Barnasa's blood—they were the locals of that city, not the pilgrims, and easily whipped up by their priestly leaders to defend their city. Pilatus' wife, having heard of the plot the night before, had even had nightmares—had the spirit-world warned her; had Usen begged for his son's life? But her husband's hands were tied: even Pilatus had to put public pressure above private pressure, especially since his international support had become rather dicey. Pilatus could no longer abuse the locals and expect to get away with it scot-free. No, Barnasa had to be condemned as if a runaway slave, as if a political threat to the rule of Rome. It would never have stood up in court, but Pilatus was the judge.

Barnasa, already soundly whipped, had next been mercilessly flogged to within an inch of his life, and ignominiously cast out of the city under close guard, already more dead than alive, staggering along with his lacerated arms supporting a rough wooden beam, which in turn would support his weary arms when it was fastened to an upright pole. Barely able to walk, he had collapsed under the heavy load he had to bear. An innocent passerby, at the wrong place at the wrong time, had been forced to carry it the rest of the way.

Barnasa was dragged along. Many wept for him; many mocked him—his own people, and the Roman death squad. Then he'd had nails hammered between the bones in his wrists. Nails also pinned his feet together to the stake, unable to touch the ground only a few feet below. There was a shallow shelf on which he could just about perch, easing the pressure of his body weight, before having to pull himself up to breathe the better—perched in the overlap between agony and suffocation. The technology of death was perfected to stretch out the agony. It was to be a gruesome warning to others who defied the might of Rome, that if caught their fate would not be quick and easy. To his left and right were terrorists, knifemen who had had their taste of Roman blood, and now gave back blood for blood. At last they saw their hated countryman face to face, he who had encouraged living at peace with Rome. At last their words could pierce his soul as daggers. But Longinus looked with dismay at the man, for in his face he recognised the lad he had abused so many years before. Now he had knocked him down to earth once more. It was a bitter blow.

The soldiers on duty, not purebred Romans but mere mercenaries, were inured to their work. As long as the crowd didn't attempt to rescue or kill the dying, the soldiers could sit back and play with dice. Not giving a toss for their victims, they tossed coins to win the best bits of their victims' clothing, like crows pecking away at a victim before it died. In the special circumstances, they had to respect the sensibilities of the locals, and as they were already on high alert against rioting, loincloths would be untouchable—but all else was up for grabs.

Longinus alone stood aloof from the game—he would not add insult to injury—but he had to let his men play. And then the man, struggling for breath, spoke. Yes, looking upwards, he'd spoken to his...father—had he heard him aright? Maybe not. Certainly there was no mystic woman within a green veil, nobody you could see, nobody you could touch. But his men didn't even bother to look up, having better things to do than to bother about the boring words of a dying slave; the bellyaching of a political scapegoat; the bleating of a sacrificial lamb—they weren't bothered about details or meaning. Longinus had heard many prayers for deliverance—they had never worked. He had heard much cussing and swearing, cursing him to his face—as if he wasn't simply carrying out his job in a professional way. But this man reminded him of how the lad had been: calm, unafraid, a wishing you well kind of bloke.

At first Longinus had fallen into a reverie, too dead to the world to listen to the assassins' chitter-chatter—sadly lamenting their fate; slagging off Rome; slagging off the man. Yet rousing out of his stupor he became aware that those comrades were now bickering between themselves. They had been noting the other's demeanour, happy that he was sharing their fate, since he had been at an opposite point of their ideological struggle, vigorously opposing their Death-to-Rome policy. Gallingly Pilatus, their mutual enemy, had written a public placard that claimed that Barnasa was the Sheep King—why, that was tantamount to calling him Hamashiach. Now that was an insult to all they had done to free the Sheep from Rome. Zealots had certainly not risked their lives for this imposter!

Well, if that's what Barnasa had bleated about in court, it totally ruled out of court any truth claims he had ever made! The Yehudim knew well enough that Hamashiach could not die, at least until he had climaxed the Kingdom of Kurion, razing Rome to the ground. But now, almost beyond belief, one of the assassins gave up the struggle, laid down his arms—metaphorically speaking—and asked forgiveness, asked for blessing, from this very man whom not long ago he had wished to kill as a traitor. Barnasa had unapologetically opposed their dearest dreams of establishing their own kingdom—they had once even tried to force him to become their king, but he had escaped from them!

Now one of them had switched sides, welcoming the alternative kingdom which Barnasa had proclaimed, asking whether it would welcome him. And as if he were the gateway to that kingdom, with the audacity of death Barnasa turned his head, smiled at him, and welcomed him home. What kind of a man was this?

Perhaps that question was asked by his mother, for at those words she had broken forth into a flood of tears. Now, she had looked like a lady who didn't cry easily, but then the dying of this man was a crying shame. Longinus really wished that he had been somewhere else. Even the voice of Master Wulfgar had fallen silent. Barnasa gently looked at his mother. He backed away from any affectionate wording, but not from affectionate intention. There she stood, alongside a family friend. There they both stood, together but alone in their griefs. Speaking as clearly as he could, he told her to no longer think of herself as his mother, but to think of herself as her friend's mother. To him, dying, she was now but an upright lady, even a sister.

But who was her friend? Longinus quietly moved towards him and put the question directly. Within limits, the family of Barnasa were welcome to peaceably see him off, as far as Pilatus was concerned. This friend, eyes filled with horror, replied that he was Yochanan the Fisherman, supplier to the High Priest, cousin to Barnasa, nephew to his mother. And, he added, in their eyes Barnasa was a brother to them both, so he would thereafter consider the victim's mother to be his sister-mother. Asked as to whether she therefore was bereft of other sons, Yochanan replied that Miriam's own household stood aloof from Barnasa, and unlike himself they would not comfort her in the sorrows she bore for his soul that day—thus the task, and the honour, had fallen to him.

Those two were safe enough in the crowd, but feelings were running high. A murky storm had brooded low ever since the hour of noon, making the afternoon glow fiercely dark, as if it were in anger or in mourning. To the glee of some, the veneer of calm looked like it had finally peeled away from Barnasa, for looking upwards he had roundly protested for all to hear, that he had been abandoned by Kurion. Longinus demanded a bystander to interpret.

Apparently Barnasa had raised a question from an ancient poet—Elohim, Elohim, you are mine, so why have you deserted me? Why had the poet asked that? He was told that the poet—well respected by his people—had gone through some similar crisis of faith, but all had come right in the end. But from the 'wows!' and 'phews!' doing the rounds, some of the hecklers took Barnasa to plainly mean that finally the penny had dropped. It seemed to them that he had just given up his ridiculous notion of being on deity's side—for deity was surely not on his! 'Scammer!' some shouted. Others said no, for if that's what he had said, he would not have said in the same breath that deity was still his. No, what he had said was that he still believed that heaven would help him. Or maybe he had invoked an ancient prophet for help. Okay, said others, let's see if any prophet will save him, then we'll believe.

Had Kurion abandoned Barnasa? So it might seem, but Longinus was savvy enough to know that the divinities sometimes honoured their messengers with martyrdom, so that their message would rise after death. Messengers might even become divinised. Oh what foolish Sheep. They, as pleased as punch to see an execution in their Promised Land, were watching a *Roman* execution, a sign of their subjugation. Could these hecklers not see that Kurion had abandoned their whole nation, not just one man? Oh, what a backward people. Maybe Kurion had given them over to the glory of Rome, in order to humble them into thinking new thoughts, exploring new possibilities. Were they wilfully blind to the possibility—clear to Longinus—that Kurion himself wished them to meet his fellow divinities in the Empire? If only they came to see that, and so drop their troublesome exclusivism, the emperor would welcome them with open arms as returning prodigals. Yes, he would roast a fatted hog for them to sink their teeth into.

Even as the crowd argued back and forth in the shadow of his death, he spoke of his thirst. Hours earlier he had refused a drink from the

Romans, just before they nailed him up. A fitting toast to the king who was about to die, they had joked. The offer had been a common enough courtesy, intended more as a death-extender than as a death-easer, but still tempting. He'd merely taken a token taste, as if saying that he submitted to their mockery. But now he seemed to be asking if anyone really cared? Whichever side of the debate she was on, a woman from the crowd bolted forward, took the dried and woven hyssop stem that had been set there by the Romans, drenched the sponge with wine, and held it to his lips to slate his thirst—and perhaps to deaden his pain. All put there by courtesy of Rome! Of course, the clever Romans had soon found that the branches on the stem made an ideal cradle for nesting the sponges which they used to offer wine to the dying, though for their part they cruelly used such devices to afflict, not to comfort, the dying.

The crowd had their own proverbs, enjoining the giving of wine to those in bitter distress, even though the best wine they could now offer was but the sour wine that Rome supplied. Perhaps the myrrh they added deadened the pain so as to draw out the agony, though it made the wine taste as bitter as gall. Still, he'd die before the day was out—all three had to die by then because nightfall marked the start of their holiest day within the holy week. One or two even thought back to this man's first miracle, providing wine to a party running out of it—or so rumours had reported. Whatever thoughts went through his head, he seemed pleased that not all had deserted him, whether motivated by care or by cruelty. He drank the wine. Perhaps he hoped that all who welcomed the ancient prophet would welcome him, would run to him.

Did he think himself the master of his fate, the captain of his soul? Surely not, yet he bellowed out as if a victor, he, who was but a victim. Just one word in the Greek tongue. Longinus knew that one, but what did it mean? What does 'job done' mean on the dying lips of a defeated and dejected man? Truly never a man spoke like this man. And then, with that old enigmatic smile back on his face, he again looked up, as he had when he had bewailed himself deserted, and he had ended in prayer to one he called Abba, entrusting his spirit to him, and then he seemed to rest his head—had he swooned in pain?

Best leave him be, Longinus signalled to his men. They weren't gambling now, for for a while the elements had been playing on their nerves. Just when Barnasa had sunk his head, lightning had flashed from the heart of the storm. Rolls of thunder were beginning to echo and reverberate all around. Some of the crowd were rapidly scuttling to seek shelter, and would happily have hidden themselves in caves or among the rocks of the mountains.

The very ground trembled, as a seismic wave struck. Some stumbled. And still Barnasa slept on undisturbed—it would take a lot more than that to wake him up. Yet earth and sky was awesome to behold, fearful to the flesh, as if the immortals were screaming out in protest, lashing out in anger, yet harming none. Longinus looked up to the weeping skies. More than a messenger, had he crucified a mortal son of one of the immortals? Forgive us Iuppiter-Tonans—we knew not what we were doing.

Slowly the tension eased. The storm was drifting away. News was coming out from the city about damage done there by the tremor. But life had to go on. Evening was coming on fast, and great crowds had swarmed to the city from around the world, converging for an annual festival they called Pesach. It was all tied in to recalling their long walk to freedom from slavery—long before Romulus was but a glint in his mother's eye.

Some denied that they were yet again slaves, and it was safer not to push the point, especially at special events. Some felt their slavery all too bitterly—which kept the crucifixion squads in business. A soldier reported to Longinus, snapped to attention and saluted. Orders—as expected—were to pack up, get rid of the bodies, and return to barracks before the new day began at the going down of the sun, a day some Yehudim called a *shabbat*. Yes, time for Rome to tactfully withdraw from the party, for Rome was an unwelcome guest, an unholy fly around holy ointment.

Criminals could of course survive days on end, nailed to their posts, flies biting, birds pecking, smitten by the sun in the heat of the day, and struck by moon in the ghostly glow of the bitter nights. After that their corpses could be left hung out to dry, to slowly rot away, food for vultures and the little vermin that scurried around on four legs. All that was usually to the good. The dying and the decomposing were meant to have an off-putting effect on other wannabe terrorists and runaways. But for the festival the fun must be terminated, the victims dispatched with all due expediency. And Rome had developed a fitting way to speed up death, a method tried and tested, simple but effective. "Break a leg", was all a centurion needed to say, and it would be done. For with broken legs, the criminals no longer had a working leg to stand up with, no longer could lift themselves up to breathe, would soon suffocate—good riddance to bad rubbish. It was an unintended mercy, and one which Rome begrudgingly gave, now and again. The two knifemen were still groaning, rightfully suffering for their homicidal rampage against Rome. But Barnasa was different. He slept on, seemingly in his faint—for surely he could not have died so soon? Mind you, he had had extra floggings before being crucified, and that could have made it harder to survive for long, when fighting for each breath would rack a body in pain.

The soldiers had had enough, and had largely gotten over their fright. But even to them it seemed rather pointless to inflict further damage to the body. Limp it hung there, helpless, harmless. You could have wept. But just to be sure, at a nod from Longinus one of them picked up his spear—they all carried the common spears of the foot soldier—and stuck it deeply into the lower ribcage. Well, whatever their fears about immortals, this body was fully human and fully dead—blood, and a liquid looking like water, flowed forth from the wound. The corpse didn't stir. Longinus nodded his satisfaction with what he saw, and his soldier cleaned up his spear—valuable weapons when they did not buckle; in fact valuable even when they did. The body was duly removed and the nails cleaned up and packed away for another time, but by special request the body was to be handed back to civilian authority. Bravely stepping in, a ranking member of the Sheep Council had made it his job to beg Pilatus for the body—and perhaps given him a little gift on the side from a wealthy well-wisher. Well, that's the way the system worked, and rank always had its privileges. But Pilatus might have taken a bit of a chance, really. But then again he hadn't been fully convinced that the man should have been executed anyway—just keeping some important folk happy, as Longinus well knew. Now, perhaps, he was keeping his wife happy, and getting back at the bunch that had egged him on to do the dirty deed.

But back that bunch had soon come, banging on his door, exasperated beyond reason. Now, they had said, you've landed us with a problem. This fellow had pretended to be a prophet, did you not know? He had said that death could not keep him in the tomb. We have always had a problem with tomb-raiders stealing loot. All we need now is to have some of them steal his body, and you could have an uprising on your hands. You need us to keep the peace; we need you to post your soldiers outside of his tomb. Even our own guards are suspect, and have failed us before. In reply, Pilatus had argued that even if that happened, it would be simple enough to flag up that the body had been stolen, besides, he added, Barnasa now dwelt with the king of death, and who would risk their life by proclaiming him to be the king of life? Nevertheless the conversation ended, with little grace, in Pilatus caving in, consigning a quaternion of guards to rotate through the shifts until the festivities were over, when a more permanent solution could be found. The guards soon arrived at the resting place. Not a common old tomb with the door-stoppers that you had to push-pull, but one of those more expensive ones with a rounded wheel-stone you rolled down the slightly angled ramp to close, and rolled back up to open. There the bloody body was entombed, well wrapped up but not a pretty sight on a dark night. The squeamish didn't enlist, and professionally the soldiers certified that everything was in place, officially sealed the tombstone with wax and rope, and settled down to guard the gate.

All under wraps, all well secured, the story should have ended by rights. But what happened next was almost perverse: an aftershock hit the site only three days after the death—in the common counting of days. Within Longinus' command, bit by bit word soon leaked out that the tomb guards had spoken about a lightning bolt knocking them off their feet, knocking them out. They had staggered back to their feet feeling kinda fuzzy, disorientated, confused. Apparently they had then gone inside the tomb—its seal having been broken by the quake—to check on their charge, only to discover that the body was missing. They'd immediately returned to report. Fortunately for them, they had been on secondment to the temple, and—on the condition that they signed an internal report which had been quickly drawn up by the temple—it promised to shield them from the praefectus. Questioned by the barracks, the soldiers agreed that it was likely enough that disciples of the deceased had lain in watch, and seen the lightning as a heaven-sent sign to smuggle out the body. Why they would have moved it from honourable housing, was undoubtedly a mystery, but the tomb was undoubtedly empty, and bodies don't just vanish into thin air. Officially, though, they had had to swear that they had been so exhausted that they had just dozed off.

That was swearing to a capital charge, and they hadn't liked that condition one iota. Still, they knew that they had had to hope for the best, for it seemed that the temple would lie against them if they did not lie for it. They faced hope, danger, and gain. The temple did promise to let them give a more truthful official Roman report—if push came to shove. It also said that it would try to prevent any shove, by bribing if needed the praefectus himself. Besides, it would also pay them handsomely to keep their mouths shut. Among their comrades there was much chuckling at the official line. Was it credible that they would have been selected if sleepy? And had they all slept at the same time, catching flies at the mouth of a tomb while it had its official seal broken, and had its tombstone rolled up the ramp, and had its contents spirited away? On the other hand, had they been awake how come they had returned from duty without so much as showing a scratch of resistance to the tomb raiders? Whichever way you looked at it, it seemed mighty suspicious. Even the lightning strike hadn't left any permanent scars on them. Their comrades suspected that they had been seriously bribed onsite—but who could pay and who would gain? Still, it must have been. And then for the temple side to bribe them to keep quiet, well that was hilarious! But they had taken an incredible risk. Pilatus would not have liked a signed report saying that he had lent the temple tired guards.

To be fair to the temple, as far as the chief priests were concerned, the soldiers might well have dozed off and invented a cock-and-bull story—perhaps had been bribed to turn the other cheek. But they had not wanted their doubts to be tested under the Roman lash—a compromise story suited them best. Whatever the true story, it had been a most unsatisfactory turn of events, jinxing their jollies and their national narrative about divine departure by Kurion's hand. Nor, when he had heard about it, had Pilatus been happy for Roman involvement to come out. Far better for him that it was believed that temple guards had blundered in their duty. Why advertise that Rome had failed? That would raise some pretty dangerous questions: how much had he been bribed to hand back a body of a rival of Rome, or, if the man had not been a rival, how much had he been bribed to condemn an innocent man? Better by far to let sleeping dogs lie; least said, soonest mended.

But what was not soonest mended was someone Pilatus had released. Pilatus had had a bad reputation for vicious slaughter, and to compensate he had begun a little local generosity at the Pesach Festival. This time it had gone sour, for he had tried to release one nice guy by offering a real nasty piece of work as the only alternative—he'd thought the outcome obvious. But he had not reckoned on the opposition, and so had released a known insurrectionist, a killer named Barabban. Barabban should have died, not Barnasa.

Weeks later Longinus and a small company had been patrolling the hills around the capital. He had been called back by a local, while his men had waited for him to return. An old man had wished to report some suspicious sightings, but discreetly to the centurion, only to the centurion, for common soldiers blabbed and if word got out, he said that he would get a shiny new knife between his shivering old ribs, the due pay of a snitch. Dobbing your own people in was dangerous in those days. As Longinus was talking with him, he heard cries on the road ahead where his men awaited him. He immediately spun around, breaking into a run. Arrows had taken out some of his men, and terrorists were slashing away at the rest. Longinus ran up, crying aloud, "I won't desert my comrades, for flight or for fear. I won't run from the ranks, save to snatch a spear. I'll strike at the foe, or I'll save a friend so dear!" He had never broken his old army oath, sworn the day he enlisted.

The distance hadn't been great, but it had been costly. The last of his men threw his last javelin, but his assailant had dived just in time, and the weapon lodged in a shrub. Longinus was just in time to join the fight. Three men, one wounded, still stood. His own men all lay dying or dead. With his shield he warded off a blow from one side; with his sword he took out a rebel on the other. The leader threw a knife at him, which he dodged. Then he hit the leader with his shield, ramming the base down to the man's feet, crippling him in pain. Behind him now the last man sought to knife him from behind. He swung around his shield, and as he swivelled stabbed his enemy in the vitals. That left only one, unable now to run. Eyeing the undamaged javelin, he thought it poetic justice to use that for the kill. It almost seemed fated to feast on the blood of this enemy, for this enemy should have hung weeks ago with those two he had led. Now Barabban would die.

∞

A centurion is a taker of blood. A vampire-slave is a seeker of blood. Wulfgar had neither reason nor need to release his new slave, but like all his former slaves, each was usually allowed to max out their former identity, before reshaping—or simply keeping their shape but moving to where they were unknown. Longinus' daysight had been slowly failing, even as his nightsight improved, for though vampire-slaves gained some corruption of vampire DNA as to daysight, they also inherited some dominant DNA copied from the firstborn, which formed a reflective sheet behind the retina, increasing nightsight. But a centurion who blinks like an owl in the day, is not thought to be of much worth, and it was not long before he was pensioned off with a nice piece of land around the seaport of Apollania. Barabban had been his last official kill.

He now—a perk of pensionhood—had Rome's permission to wed his wife. Weddings were a legality forbidden to serving soldiers. His life now seemed to all to be typical of a respectably retired army officer, with a fair few household slaves, and frequent chinwagging with officers still in active service. In only one slight but significant way did he differ, but that was largely hushed up. And that was that he dined alone. Food would be taken to his room, and not even his grownup family would be present while he ate. And in another way he differed, due to his problems of vision: he kept pretty much in the shade in daylight hours, but would often walk alone at nights—night patrol, he would say. Sometimes he would meet with soldiers on patrol, the more so after reports began to multiply of locals being bitten in the neck—or disappearing. The victims seldom recalled details. Some spoke vaguely of blackness, even a black breath, coming over them, leaving them in a stupor and feeling drained, depleted. Usually they recovered over a course of a few days. Some wondered whether some strange creature from the sea arose at nights with the tides—had they offended Neptunus?

Wulfgar made some use of Longinus, but his reason for selecting him had died away. His guests tried to make him stir up fights through Longinus, for the sheer mischief of it: humans killing humans was enjoyable sport. But the vampires were not as the diaboloi, and had no particular hatred of mankind. Indeed man provided their meals, rather than their entertainment: do we hate our cattle, burn our wheat? Wulfgar had had assurance that sorting out Hamashiach would have put him in the driver seat of his own chariot, with paying passengers, not backseat drivers. But in the end Hamashiach had been disposed of in a different way. Then much to their chagrin, instead of lying down and playing dead, he stubbornly refused to be written out of the play. Necuratu had brought one curtain down; Ruach had raised another. A new show had begun. The art of deception was paramount. What the aggeloi had done with the body, nobody seemed to really know. Some sightings had been made among the humans, and some believed that it had been reanimated and had appeared to them, yet that its properties were transmortal. And like shapeshifters, the body—it was said—could seemingly move even through the cracks in doors—or phase through.

The Necros is not omniscient, nor can it be everywhere at once. It also had powerful enemies which impeded its way. But those who claimed the sightings started to say some powerful, disconcerting, stuff. Over a hundred, for instance, had hung around the epicentre of opposition, the capital city, and at the very next big event, had publicly denounced their city leaders as having killed off their best hope! Yet, they had added, that had been the way their hope had had to go—pain comes in the night; joy comes with the rising sun; death was a birth. Hamashiach had risen, they shouted. He was alive and kicking, more alive than ever, more alive than anyone at the party, period. And, they added, even their leaders were invited to the new party. They even mastered other languages for the occasion, or was it as they said, that language had mastered them by the power of Ruach? These witnesses put their lives on the line. Could they not be arrested by the leaders, charged for having stolen their master's body—well, that was the official explanation doing the rounds, intended to keep guilty heads down. Would their leaders not go the same way as their master had done, once interrogated by Rome? How could they be so foolish—unless they really had seen Hamashiach after his death? But if merely his ghost had appeared, why had his body disappeared? Lilith had warned the Necros to preserve Hamashiach's life at all costs; Necuratu had overridden her; Necuratu had damned them all. She feared that Hamashiach had risen. And where was Necuratu in all this confusion? It seemed that he was in hiding, gone to earth as if a wounded beast. Why did he not speak up?

For his part, Wulfgar was intrigued, and decided to tarry a while in that region, keeping tabs on his slave. Had he left his slave, his slave would have continued as before, a sleeping agent neither receiving from, nor transmitting to, his master. Distance was key. Left to his own devices, he could simply have wandered place to place, changing his name or perhaps his shape. The latter was not always possible. Some slaves find shape-changing very difficult, if not impossible, to master, for they are, after all, only vampire shadows, not vampires themselves. His skills might be in doubt, but not his longevity: he would soon yearn for the peace of death to set him free. As it was, so long as Longinus was living in Apollania, Wulfgar his master never fed there. Vampires had found to their discomfort that overgrazing an area could lead to them being sought out and destroyed by hunters—usually second-rate fools believing themselves wise, but usually with enough nous and tenacity to harry their game. It had become a strict rule that the Kingdom of Night must never reveal itself to the secondborn. The Night was a hidden kingdom.

It had panned out that Longinus lived only a day's journey from the coastal port of Caesarea Palestinae, where a Roman cohort was stationed. His master lived thrice that distance away, but still within easy telepathic range. By now Longinus knew all the centurions of Caesarea well, and had taken a fancy to one in particular, since that one seemed to have his head above the crowd. This officer—named Kornelios by those who knew his taste for the Graeci philosophers—was disenchanted with his people's worship. Visiting him for a few days, they spoke long into the night, especially about the idea of Platon that there was only one deity. Such talk resonated with the Sheep, too, who were at variance with Rome about that. Was it not therefore dangerous for an officer of Rome to side with a slave people, Longinus asked? The simple answer was yes, but then again it wasn't some illegal religion or the silly superstition of the simple. Anyway, winding up the conversation for the night, Kornelios—having obviously much more to say at break of day—said that he had never been tempted deeper into that sheepfold, and there were thousands like him who lapped up the same idea of unity, a basic oneness. If you believed that there was a supreme being which you should alone worship, it didn't necessarily follow that you must disallow others from worshipping lesser beings, did it? Toleration was key.

The next morning, Longinus entered the family room. Kornelios was already there, seemingly recovered from their intense discussion of the previous night. He and his wife had finished the morning *jentaculum* meal, but were still lying down, wiping their hands and faces on lovely warm damp towels. The slaves smiled and bowed to Longinus, as they quietly removed the leftovers and made themselves scarce. Theirs was a happy home to serve—each morning they were even allowed a leftover fruit apiece. Kornelios defended his generosity by saying that if there is deity not divinities, then even the slaves would be one with him under deity, a uniting referent. In many households the slaves would be assumed to have different divinities, and therefore to lack a spiritual connection with the master, living merely as tools, living machines, easily replaced if broken.

Kornelios had once had that attitude, but it changed dramatically after he took a fancy to Yasmina, a pretty young girl of the Yehudim. He had bought her partly because his teenage son Felix had also liked the look of her in the slave market: father and son both had a similar eye for the ladies. That had changed so much that he now felt as protective towards her as to a daughter. A man can be a big softie in his own home, yet a fearsome warrior on the battlefield. The change began when, as a new purchase, she had begged him not to give her to Felix. No, she did not wish to teach him in the ways of life, and had promised Kornelios the blessing of Kurion, if he but spared her womanhood. Why, he had snorted, should he bother about the blessing of a foreign divinity, especially one that hadn't the power to defend her or her people? That had been a purely rhetorical question, but the presumptuous whelp had dared to reply that Kurion alone was *deity*. Understandably Kornelios had cuffed her hard with the back of a hand, before storming out to cool off. He didn't wish to mess up her face. But tools don't talk back. What utter impertinence to put down his divinities. Who was ruling the roost, that the Yehudim should crow?

Only when he had calmed down did he return indoors. By then she'd wiped her tears, and instead of calling in Felix to teach her a lesson, he sat the girl down to put her in her place by sweet reason, yet found himself talking more about this unknown power. That had led him to his study of Platon, and even to a discussion with one of her people of the sect known as the Perushim. This scholar had claimed to believe in resurrection from death, but he had strongly distanced himself from what The Way—that new sect—was touting, namely that their people's deliverer had been physically resurrected from death. No, the teacher had sadly smiled with a slow shake of his sagacious head, there was no new exodus, no new promised land. However, he brightly added, one day The Enlightener would come and bless the Roman Empire. Kornelios was intrigued. After some weeks of pent-up frustration, Felix reluctantly settled down and realised that he would have to look elsewhere for a bit of life experience, since Yasmina had attained to something of a protected status, midway between slave and sister. Maybe father would soon visit the slave market again?

Before much longer Kornelios had become hooked. He hadn't been prepared to go the whole hog and dedicate himself to the Covenant of the Sheep, but he had become enchanted by the idea of one deity over all divinities, a supreme mind, the eternal form, to which idols were but temporal and temporary images, were mere fleeting realities under transreality. The Yehudim had, however, put meat on the philosophical bones, and had long claimed to be the core conduit of that basic understanding—claimed that the transreal was transpersonal, the form of all derivative persons, and that in Kurion the transreal could be metaphysically touched, could be worshipped. He accepted the Concept of the Sheep, and from those two diverse witnesses he became a devoted monotheist, while remaining loyal to his troops and to his military masters. He had heard that according to the prophet Yochanan, Kurion upheld the military as an honourable profession, so long as soldiers were content with army pay and didn't abuse their position by theft—which force and intimidation made so easy.

It was over a number of years that Longinus had met up with Kornelios, but he had never let on that he had been in command of the execution of Barnasa. Whether or not Kornelios was right about a deity above many divinities, it was the divinities whom mere mortals met with—if they couldn't safely avoid them. It would not do to stir up memories of the killing of the divine man, that son of goodness knows what immortal. Had his men not paid the price for their involvement? Had Marcus Pilatus not been stripped of his command and sent back to base on murder charges? So far Longinus had been spared—long may that continue; don't remind the immortals. And then it all changed.

Scribonia entered the conversation. It was all very informal nowadays, for Longinus had long become like a family member, and indeed spoke with her almost as much as with her husband—both were dear to him, links to his humanity. "Longinus, we have not left food for you, since you said that you were yet again on a fast, but the news we have need not be left any longer." Yes, when he had arrived in the evening, he had sensed that something was different, but it had been late when they had ended that day deep in philosophy. What had this morning in store? Was there deeper philosophy from before the Dawn of Time? Why did she smile? Were they expecting another child, after such a gap? He studied her quizzically, as if there might be a bump, but reading his mind she chuckled and shook her head. "No, yet we speak of new birth nonetheless." Ah, one of their older sons must have a mistress—but why should they celebrate such?

"Longinus," said Kornelios, "let us put you quickly out of your misery, for you will never guess our news. As I was telling you last night, for some years I have aligned with the Yehudim's Kurion, or Iahveh, to speak the holy name they seek to keep their own, forgetting their past. Indeed I have given substantial personal sums to their poor and to enrich their platform, which I believed to be a light to the world."

"Has Praefectus Marullus known of this?" interjected Longinus. "The emperor has his own plans to reconsecrate their temple in his own image, and Marullus is loyal to Caligula." Longinus' concern was genuine.

"Yes, yes, never fear. I spoke with Marullus, and he said that any goodwill from Romans would increase goodwill towards Romans, reducing the effect of anti-Roman separatists among them—especially goodwill from those known to be sympathetic to their religion. For his part, Marullus could not see why both sides could not come together. And so long as Iuppiter is hailed as the chief divinity—as Rome holds—what does it matter if the Yehudim add another divinity under him as their patron? After all, the world can see who is in charge. Though ideally, he added, under the Standard of Rome they should worship in the temple of Iuppiter, even—which he said quietly to me—if our emperor is just a little too infatuated with his own divinity.

"But now, pray do not interrupt, my friend, for I come to a new twist in my journey. I had taken to praying at the same time as when the Yehudim of the temple had afternoon prayer. Then one day one of the mighty aggeloi appeared to me. I almost died of fright, I, who have faced many an enemy in violent fight. But it is different, Longinus, to suddenly come face to face with an immortal. It is one thing to read about such things, but one is totally unprepared for such a thing to happen to oneself. The paranormal was not normal for me, and even now I see but dimly. Anyway, he promised me blessing, assured me that Kurion knew me and was pleased with me, and wished to bless me even deeper. More deeply, thought I? Why, was it not deep enough that I had come into the faith of the Yehudim? But—I do not know whether he could read my mind—after a slight pause to let that bit sink in, he told me about a man I had to see, told me where he was staying. And next moment that light was gone and I was on my own. Naturally, as you might expect, I sent for this man, even sent a spare donkey for his convenience."

"Who was this man, Kornelios, and do you mean that he was one of the Yehudim, or is there another people higher up and deeper in?" asked Longinus, absolutely riveted by this fascinating tale. He himself was baptised into the paranormal, as he deemed it, a prisoner of an immortal, but for him it was a curse, not a blessing. Was there another side which interacted in the affairs of man?

"He is one named Shaliak Shimon, a leader of The Way, who proclaims a true exodus for all people. He had been praying the very next day, and Ruach—praise be to him—spoke to him in a vision about their prophetic symbols. For they believed that they must eat only foods deemed clean, avoiding foods deemed unclean, abnormal. Thus, he told me, they are daily reminded that their people alone are clean and uncontaminated to carry the blessings of Kurion. But, he added to me, this vision, by showing him animals he was now to see as no longer unclean, taught him that that separation had been ended by Kurion. Even Shimon had hesitated in fear to forget the former things, until rebuked by Kurion and ordered to cross the Yam Suf—the Rubicon, we might say. He told me that he remembered an ancient hero among his people, Moyshe, who had also been rebuked by Kurion for hesitating, instead of crossing the dividing water to their new land, having in his hand all he had needed to cross. Shimon then spoke of stretching out his rod and moving on. Therefore when my people met up with him, he was happy to make them at home, and then to visit my home."

Scribonia chipped in. "My husband used to worship Mithras, who only you men may worship. But under Kurion we had been worshipping together with our children. Therefore it was not strange to us that he invited me and the children to be present when Shimon came to us. One of our slaves had ridden ahead to inform us of the hour. We all sat excited, even our slaves—especially Yasmina—aware that a new step— perhaps a new road—beckoned us, but the way ahead was dark unto our feet." Scribonia was a woman aglow, definitely more animated than Longinus had ever seen her. He listened attentively.

"And here we talked and here we were changed", said Kornelios, pausing to reflect. And then he laughed: "I had tried to treat him as our emperor wishes to be treated nowadays, but I was quickly put in my place. Why, he told me, we are all equal in the sight of Kurion. Prick me, do I not bleed? No, he added, he was but a servant-brother of one to whom all should bow, yet one who had bled for all. He then began to go over the story of one who before his death had been called Barnasa—and have you not heard of him during your time of service? I have never probed you about those things, for I suspected that you had things you wished to keep in the dark, and I have always respected your privacy. But his deeds were not done in the dark."

"Kornelios my friend, I have my reasons for what I hold private, and have long respected your silence as to these matters. I have indeed heard of Barnasa, and of claims that he has risen from the dead. But what did Shaliak Shimon say on this head? Speak freely. You have a captive audience."

"He said firstly that Kurion does not show favouritism. Yasmina then blurted out that Shimon amazed her! She, a saucy slave, should have known better than to interrupt a guest of the household. Even Shimon looked surprised that we did not whip her without warning. Understandable for her, of course, for here was a fellow countryman turning her world upside down. Did he realise what he was saying? He hadn't minded the interruption, though, admitting that he himself had found the new idea difficult to come to terms with, but, he added with a smile, he had had it on good authority. Besides, he said, what might be called bias to one flock, was now history, and had been intended to prepare a few to help the many, a bias of effort, not of care. Poor Yasmina had been so embarrassed with her own outburst, and clammed up after that, listening and drinking it all in. Shimon then filled us in with what had been only fragmentary information before—most of which had been unsympathetic. As we heard a new perspective, I think all our hearts were strangely warmed, and before Shimon could invite us into this new movement, Ruach himself intervened."

"Yes," said Scribonia, "for suddenly, like empty cups being filled with wondrous wine, we each had our own visions. For me it was as if I stood upon a mountain, high above any earthly mountain, and yet not covered by snow and ice. There were trees in fragrant flower, and birds of gorgeous hues all singing, and I met a man who spoke to me in a language I did not know. Not wishing to be rude, I spoke back to him in his own language, though I didn't know what I was saying. It was more or less like that for all of us. And then we found ourselves back in this very room, and dusk had fallen. Shimon and his fellow travellers had been joining us in prayer, for they could also pray without knowing what they prayed. They laughed in pure merriment and congratulated us for having taken the next step. When we asked what had happened, they said that we had all been baptised into the praise of Kurion. They had not understood our words, but they had understood that what was happening was praise above all human praise. Ruach had spoken from our very spirits, controlling our very tongues." She paused in rumination, and her husband picked up the story.

"Not all our guests were as happy as they might have been, and I sensed that the event had caused some problems for some of the travellers. Shimon had asked us if we wished to publicly commit to The Way, and we had all said yes. But it wasn't entirely clear to all as to whether it was an open road for all, in spite of what Shimon had come to believe. Some grumbled that whatever Ruach had done had been done in private, and should better be left there, protesting that schism would erupt at headquarters, damning any unofficial welcome that Shimon had given to us Goyim. It was dead embarrassing to hear their bickering! We had heard tell that you could know this lot by the way they loved each other. It seemed not. Now we had sparked them into a punch-up at the drop of a hat. Maybe better all-round if we didn't join.

"Shimon was quite fierce, insisting that even the Shadow Way of yesteryear had had other peoples joining, to which some replied that that had caused problems enough, being thorns in their side! In the end Shimon said that they must see that the Shadow Way had simply been a limited ethnic thing to prepare for global fulfilment of the True Way, and we had received Ruach in exactly the same way that they had, so we had exactly the same right to say so publicly, and be blowed to anyone who said otherwise! It seemed clear to us that Shimon was probably going to have more problems back at headquarters, and we were in two minds how to proceed, not wishing to be the cause of trouble. But, since he was so enthusiastic about immersing us as an entire household there and then, and since we had all joyfully believed his talk about Hamashiach, indeed beyond our wildest dreams receiving Ruach himself ineffably, those who had doubted us finally shook hands all round, and agreed to baptise us."

"So, it goes hand in hand, believe and receive?" ventured Longinus.

"No not quite, it seems, although one cannot receive unless one believes. For we spoke at length for some days, being also introduced to Philippon, a man of this fair city. It was he who informed us that we were not the first of the Goyim to enter this new and living way, for recently he, through Ruach, had welcomed in the Royal Treasurer to the Kandake of the Noubai—a dark-skinned people of the south. It turns out that this Royal Treasurer had like us been a fringe worshipper of Kurion, and his welcome had also caused disapproval among The Way. Indeed, confessed Shimon, he himself had been unsure as to whether Hamashiach approved, until Hamashiach himself called him to speak unto us—for the Yehudim have long been at variance with us Goyim.

"Now to answer your question, this same Philippon told how he had first introduced some of the Shamerim into The Way, though the Shamerim have long been enemies of his people. And yet—he had added on reflection—the birth of the new people put to death the old divide of friend or foe. As to these Shamerim, Philippon had baptised in water all they who had welcomed Hamashiach, but it was only when Shimon had come that they received baptism into Ruach—perhaps awaiting Shimon so that they might be surely believed to be within The Way.

"Shimon then spoke, saying that that too had been the pattern for himself. Yet though, he added, he had subsequently waited several days before being baptised into water, and later into Ruach, for some there had been an immediate subsequence of Ruach's baptism upon welcome of Hamashiach. Would believers always receive, I then asked? Shimon answered that even if for some Ruach never came in quite that way, yet for all who believed he would come at least as a settled guest, for he came in the name of Hamashiach the Welcomed. But we should not be fixated on patterns, for, as he said, for some the baptism of Ruach came first, and the baptism of water came next. Indeed for some the latter neither led nor followed, for they enter into the new life with overmuch fear to openly declare their faith. Though they walk the road, their fear is not ideal, Shimon said, since it is to them a bondage. Hearing all, it seemed to me that Kurion is not fussy, and will bless as deeply as he is permitted, not forcing himself on any."

Longinus stroked his chin, a habit of his when he thought deeply. "But you, my friend, have long been a good person. Was this your only hope for life? If Kurion has declared this the only hope, then why has he been silent in years long gone, by silence condemning the unhearing to death? Is there a disconnect between new narrative and old metanarrative? And if only your narrative is true, why now serve one who has not been concerned for all? You say that you now swim deeper, but is life only at the deeper level? Is there not more danger the deeper you go?" Longinus realised that although Marullus might consider any form of pro-Yehudim support, support for Rome, nevertheless daggers had been drawn by the many against the few, and Rome might soon have to take sides. Even in Rome, hostility was growing because its casualness about human sexuality, its discarding of infants, and its blood sports of the arenas, were being ridiculed by this new way. It was already in turn ridiculing The Way, saying that it had orgiastic love feasts, celebrated cannibalism and sanguivism, and that it was a secret sect of criminals begun by a criminal, an underworld beneath contempt, and hating humanity by its atheism. Romans joining The Way might cause problems for The Way. Was it worth it if Kurion lacked a global heart, being concerned only with the eternal wellbeing of the limited few who got the chance to hear the offer? It was fine that good things were now happening to good people, but not so fine if bad things must happen to all other good people.

Kornelios noticed the concern of Longinus' face which matched the caution of his words. "Longinus, Longinus, Longinus! Do you not see, first, that his gift of life beyond death—immortal blessing—has always been open to all, and second, that this new depth of life is blessing preceding death? Why, though the opportunity for this new depth is indeed limited in delivery, if delivered, does it make sense for anyone *not* to accept mortal blessing here and now? My slaves will be freed one day by death, but would they not now avail themselves to freedom, were it offered?

"I see that not to walk this way is safer for my body, but to walk it is salvation for my soul. For the message of the aggeloi was that Shimon would tell us how to be saved. Not in the sense of saved beyond death, but in the sense of being saved before death, in the sense that the new level is, through Huion, knowing Kurion deeper in mortal life. Those who swim below have been saved from paddling on the surface, for below is fullness of joy. They who leave their safe house, can walk the way of Hamashiach in the will of Usen, journeying with Ruach. For while there are dangers, there are also delights, delights which I would not trade for the whole of the Empire. Life is enhanced, enlightened, enriched, for me and for my entire household. What then are earthly dangers, compared to true knowledge; solitary confinement, compared with true community? We were blind but now we see, were bound but now we are free. Even my slaves I now count as family, for though they are tied to me for life, and are still to do my bidding, I see them now as sharing equally the gift of this new life, which is no respecter of persons or of peoples."

That scratched where Longinus itched, for he was a slave.

Conflict

That night Longinus had crept out of the compound and to the coastline—need drove him. A lad, a little too young to be out, stood with his back towards him, gazing out upon the sea. At the sight of him a hunger stirred within Longinus, the hunger of vampires, whose blood flowed within his veins. Stealthily he edged towards the boy, having made sure that no eyes were upon him. The lad reminded him vaguely of another young lad who had attracted him some years earlier—he had watched him die.

Mortal life is so ephemeral. This lad might soon die, too, though for hunger, not for hated. For increasingly human beings were seeming to his eyes, to be mere blood-banks to slate his thirst. Vampires have the skills to bleed without bleeding dry. To them, most victims were as passing ships in the night, aware only of a slight troubling of the waters in the mist of night, and soon sailing along on their respective journeys, feeling a little drained, perhaps, but blissfully unaware of their encounter. And only a microscopic percentage of their victims became their slaves. But their slaves, unlike their masters, sometimes took multitudinous years to hone those skills. Longinus' bites were still sometimes fatal, though he worked to make them less so. Still human, he felt a pang of sorrow for the boy, yet here was a simple meal sat on the plate, almost inviting him.

For a fleeting moment, he wondered why the boy was out on his own at this hour. Had he had a fallout at home? Perhaps there was a harmless and holy flirtation between boy and girl of tender years, and this was their spot to hold hands. Yet the boy seemed neither hurt nor hopeful, simply spellbound. Was it a fascination of the sea, of the horizon, that held him to his fate? Ah, he would never return to a loving family; no bride would hold his hand in beloved affection; beyond the horizon his soul would soon fly. For turning too soon he sealed his fate, seeing the ravenous face of Longinus. Now he could not be allowed to live, but Longinus was unbothered.

With an icy hand as cold as death clapped around the lad's mouth, he slowly sank in his teeth, teeth between teeth, that could puncture skin and siphon off blood. For several minutes they stood there, almost as if lover and belovèd, spider and fly, Longinus waxing in strength; the lad waning in strength. From experience Longinus knew that it was not merciful to pull back too soon, for death would then be drawn out as the victim slowly died in wearisome sleep. Some vampires got a kick out of such, but like his master, Longinus was not of that kind. He must drink until death came, and then tip the lifeless body into the bay, leftover food for the fish. The young boy had been delicious, and he was well satisfied. His own body would use some of that blood to sustain itself, and transform some into life force, feeding his will which was growing ever stronger. He knew that he was slowly but surely departing the realm of humanity, a shade to his Dark Master, slowly to master the art of shapeshifting, to live without loyalty to man, for soon not to be a man.

The next day he slept in late, as was his wont. An effect of his fasting, he said, which caused him restless nights—yet his belly was full. The household was oblivious to the fact that he had walked in the dead of night, but had been primed to leave him undisturbed. But after the hour of noon he arose and, preferring the shade of indoors, continued his talk with the master and mistress of the house. Contact with his former life faintly connected him still to his manhood, for which at times he yearned, even as one can yearn for a childhood dream all but lost, for a first love long lost. And within this fading dream there came a new element, a breeze of hope from an unknown shore, some words speaking to him from afar, illusive words which he struggled to catch.

Kornelios had been speaking of his military past, and of one obnoxious *primus pilus*—no one in the legion wept any tears at *his* death on the field of battle: at least he had died like a man, who had lived as a brute. But by that time Kornelios had already requested a transfer, taken a backward step in the promotion game, and his connection had by then pulled the right strings. Wistfully, Kornelios dwelt on how things might have turned out, had he not been moved to his fairly low-level position within an auxiliary cohort, an infantry battalion based at the administrative capital of Caesarea Palestinae. But—and his face brightened—had he been elsewhere, he might easily have missed the good news of spiritual promotion.

That raised a point which Longinus wished to discuss. Was fate, or luck, to be thanked or blamed? Had Kornelios remained in Roman Germania, would he have been favoured by the aggeloi? Was such favour person based, or place based? Would they have visited another centurion at Caesarea Palestinae? And if Kornelios had been passed over, what would have been his fate—or luck? Kornelios replied that he had not thought much about such questions, since after all he had been where he had been, and had been given what he had been given—why speculate about the might-have-beens? Anyway, he had already touched on those matters, but he could put things another way.

"To start off," he said, "one should differentiate between an essential blessing, and a non-essential blessing. Even the delay in beginning to reach out to we who were Goyim suggests as much to me. After all, until Shimon had been sent to me, The Way had presumed that their ranks were closed to outside peoples—to us they called Goyim. Do you think that they actually believed that if unreached, we would therefore be eternally damned simply because they elected not to share the good news to us, so tying Kurion's hands? Are eternal consequences based on random flickers in time and human whims? Surely not! So, presumably The Way did not think that ultimate salvation was therefore closed to us, simply because they of The Way weren't open to us, nor that only sharing Hamashiach could open the ultimate door.

"Granting that, is it not reasonable to conclude that their special message was—and therefore is—about a precursor, some side-door they alone could open, something tremendously important before death but not beyond death, something they at first believed they could morally limit to their ethnic identity? So if The Way hadn't thought that other peoples needed inclusion into its ranks for ultimate salvation—what one of their teachers has called Level Four, the Cosmic Door—why did they finally decide to share with us? Presumably The Way finally saw that other peoples were meant to enter its hallowed community, that wolves and wayward should become as sheep. That is, that their way was inclusion into an earthly flock—what one of their teachers has called Level Three, the Community Door. Still, for a while they were in no rush to spread the word beyond their ethnic people, perhaps suffering enough persecution as it was, and having inclusion issues to resolve. Even Kurion waited, until after some years spent stabilising them, he stepped in to assure Shimon that Hamashiach's death had ended the apartheid, so that all peoples could and should enter this side-door.

"Should we call unimportant that which is unessential, granted, but which is true worship on Earth? Surely a supplemental—an interim— salvation level is well worth taking, if offered? Human politics seems to me to play its own part as to who gets the offer. For you have to hear it in order to accept it, and not all roads take it beyond the Empire. But is it likely that Kurion would permit any not to hear, if hearing was vital to eternity?"

Later that day, after this dissertation on salvation-now—steak on the plate while you wait—Longinus now sat alone in his room, wondering whether the way into the Light could be a way out from the Dark for him. He knew that death would ultimately separate him from the will of his Dark Master and regain him his humanity, but was it possible to be freed from his slavery before death, freed back into humanity, freed from the insidious Dark Side? With the taste of innocent young blood still fresh in his mouth, Longinus did not believe it possible that even Hamashiach could release him from the chains that bound him. Nor, to be fair, did he deserve it. Though did he deserve to be bound in the first instance?

But then, slavery was not always a case of just deserts. Yes, some sold themselves into slavery through poverty, or to repay a debt, but the poverty or debt—maybe two sides of one coin—were sometimes— not always—one's just deserts. It could be one's deserts for wastefulness. One could work through an inheritance in no time at all, if one spent it on gambling, riotous living, debauchery, and they could end up in the chains of servitude. But one might stand surety for a friend, and end up paying the price they owed, and being enslaved. One could simply be the victim of ill luck, robbed of one's health and wealth. Or one could surrender in battle, and be sold into slavery. Or one could simply be stolen by slavers in one place, and sold in another. He himself had been caught while he slept, shackled against his will to the will of another, one who had predated his world, an alien predator.

Little did his people understand his enslavement. The Roman idea of *striges*—of what some would call vampyrs, wapierze—was risible to one who had become a vampire-slave. Witnesses even divided over whether they appeared as owls or as bats, and some advised on using garlic to ward off the winged menace—try telling that to Wulfgar, who loved the smell of garlic! Some said that the striges disembowelled their victims and gorged on their blood. Longinus knew that the latter was true, but the former was only in rage. For some victims, the sucking of blood shortened their mortal years, of which Titus Maccius Plautus had rightly been told.

But as to being witches, again, vampires *could* live that kind of life, or equally the life of a sailor, of a priest, of a weaver, or of a legate. That they had powers which were as magic, he also knew, but that was due to them being thelodynamic beings, able to affect matter by the power of their will, independently of their bodily forms. With the eyes of an insider, he could separate the fact from the fiction of Roman folklore. It was truly a fascinating world in which he lived, but far from fascinating to live it. But his people—the humans—wouldn't understand it.

What were vampires? Longinus saw beyond the veil of time. He saw an ancient planet, ever in the mind's eye of its ancient people, people who have lived like undying moths around its glow, creatures of deep heaven who were spheres of will, not needing bodies of matter. Then their bodies had been thelosomatic, being minds without brains. Biological bodies would be instantly snuffed out outside the protective warmth of planets, and mineral bodies were not an idea that entered Simbolinian minds until they had long been entrapped in our world. Once here, they had at an early stage created mineral shells in which they dwelt, standing like so many circles of stone monoliths, before reshaping with the new element of DNA, for mobility and interaction.

They experimented then with the shapes of creatures, ultimately by and large preferring the humanoid form and reengineering them to their own specifications, using as a blueprint that of the firstborn Children of Usen. The Dark Lord had welcomed them as allies, but their hatred did not extend to the Children, only to the Father. Thus they were more like tigers in the night than tyrants of the night. And they had no natural enemies. The Philikoi, representing the Light, had many networks of various types, and their mission was not to defeat but to limit the Turannoi, fallen Powers of which the foot soldiers were named diaboloi. So although of the Dark, vampires were allowed the freedom to roam as they wished—within reason—

as tigers in the night, not as bats out of hell. They were creatures of the cosmos, not of the Dynamic Bubble, from which had come they who sang the Dark Song.

In his dark room sat Longinus, a lonely man alone in the night, gazing up at the stars. For with the eyes of the vampires, he could see great glory in deep heaven above, from whence that race had descended. The wonder of creation still thrilled their souls, though they shook their fists at its creator, Usen the Enslaver. The stars ran their courses, free and unmarked throughout the years, as if Libra was holding all in balance. Although his will was not fully his own, and although he was being removed from the friendship of the human race, yet his new abilities, such as his vision of the night skies, were gains for which he could not but be grateful for. How could Usen himself prefer the human race to the heavenly chase? Usen was surely blind and confused, preferring biology above cosmology, concerned even with the Phusika—the sheep, cattle, and other animals of the land, birds and fish too.

But then into his mind came other ideas. Kornelios had become a firm friend. Would Longinus soon become as likely to bleed his sons dry, as he had the lone lad upon the seashore? Had Usen perhaps a healthier perspective on human life? Was not a story now being told about how he gave his own son, the uncreated Huion, to save the sons and daughters of mankind? Kornelios had said that in union with Hamashiach, there was no priority of Yehudim over Goyim; of citizens over slaves; of men over women; of adults over children. Indeed that each member, beginning as a child, could grow in spiritual wisdom and understanding, even as in the natural course of life. Thus a slave might be as a spiritual mother to a newly converted senator—not that Kornelios claimed to know any senators to have been converted to The Way. After all, its pernicious teachings were hardly likely to ever affect Romans above the junior rank of centurion, but then again, it was surprising that it had even affected a centurion, wasn't it?

But what did he mean, pernicious teachings? Longinus realised that he was hearing the bias of his master, holding him back. Should he not think for himself? Perhaps the teachings were worthy of Rome after all—and beyond. After all, if Usen had had a master plan for this world, would it not be more surprising if he didn't use Roman roads and politics to get his message across to all nations? He must therefore expect that his Way could be welcomed by even the highest in the land, if they were open-minded and open-handed, the kind he seemed to prefer.

As to making inroads, was that why he had used his spirit-messengers to set up a contact with a centurion? Was it simply to reward the goodness of the centurion? Was it not more likely for growth into the Goyim world, of bigger fish to fry, of an ocean to catch? And as to beauty, had not Usen made deep heaven, made the very beauty which some said he overlooked in favour of biology? Had he not made both, and if so, might the beauty of the latter in fact outweigh the beauty of the former? Might Usen revel in both, whereas Longinus was revelling more in the former, and less in the latter? Did Usen offer the best of both worlds, heaven and earth?

Wulfgar was entirely renewing his mind, and it was fast becoming less of a human mind, for Longinus was becoming less human. Given the chance, would he not prefer that his mind became more than human? His new master telepathically told him that there was no problem, so he need not care—but he did care, and that was the problem. Could The Way become his way, though he was not free to travel on mission? Why, he was not even free to die.

The undead Longinus lifted up his head in the night in mourning. He would have howled, yet his was a secret sorrow, and walls have ears, so stifling his sorrow he spoke softly into the night breeze, hoping his words would carry beyond his four walls: "Alas, I am unsound in heart and head. Arrows have buried their heads within me; the hand of my master is heavy upon me. My iniquities are an insufferable burden, too heavy for my back. My wounds start to stink; my basic humanity sees corruption within the walls of my captivity. I am yet a man, but bowed down I am, yea doubled over in damnation am I. All the days I live I live as one who mourns for the light. I am fallen and faint; roused by the roaring of my heart, by the whisper of my hope.

"Usen, the longings of my manhood are laid bare before you; my sighing is no secret to you. I stand so aloof from friends, and my family stands aloof from me. For what I once was has withered; it walks in woe unto the grave. My humanity vanishes in vexation; grows old in oppression. I am in despair, deeply disturbed am I. My master shows to me you, but says you see me not. If you hear me, good lord deliver me, who am but a slave. Benevolent one, be benign to me." And he wept. Perhaps it would have been better for him had he never heard the words of Kornelios of the works of Kurion.

As he emerged from his room the next day, he heard the singing of the slaves, led it seemed by Yasmina, slave and sister to her master and brother. It was a happy home, hardly a typical Roman home, though Roman homes certainly have virtues, such as orderliness. Listening for some time, he heard short ditties, easily learned, sung about the wonders of creation; about family; about Kurion the Destination, Hamashiach the Way, and Ruach the Navigator; about the oneness of humanity, that every human—not just one creed or colour—mattered. It seemed to be none of your black or white blinkered rubbish, but nuanced, balanced, truthful thoughts. He wondered who had taught such songs.

"Yasmina, this is surely a wondrous household, where slaves walk around as free persons, yet still perform the duties of slaves. I wish to your joy that it might well last, but for the sake of your master you should conceal your freedom from strangers. If your master is seen to exceed his liberties, you and he might both lose yours. Rome is not best served if slaves live as free. But tell me now, your songs—they surely do not come from your mind, for are you not unlearned in lyricology? Who then is the lyricist?" asked Longinus, pleasantly enough.

"Good sir, since the encounter with Shimon, we have had guests of the household of Philippon, whom you met. His teenage daughters are all of The Way, and are all adept in prophecy. No," she quickly clarified, seeing his look of utter astonishment, "it is not that they predict the future, but at a simpler level they speak by Ruach words we need to hear to walk and grow well, words to encourage us. It is they who have taught us such songs, for they are well-skilled in such arts, and walk in close communion with Ruach."

"So, Yasmina, are all who walk so close also prophets?" he asked. He had been a worshipper of Mithras, a popular divinity within the legions of Rome, but a worship which excluded women and children. Here now were young women of the Yehudim, seemingly closer to Usen—to whom Hamashiach himself bowed—than he had ever been to

Mithras, into whom he had been baptised in blood. Why should mere women be so honoured, teachers even of divine songs?

"No, my lord," she replied, "for we hold that within local communities of the new community, all who are able are permitted to prophesy, though Philippon has said that it should be in orderly fashion, none drowning out the words of another. But we do not judge by gender, nor by age. We are instructed to frown down they who are too excitable, or who seem to seek their own fame. Of the rest, we then consider what they have said, and ask as to whether it fully fits into what the holy writings have revealed, and what the shaliakim have spoken. For it is they whom Hamashiach has especially appointed to complete the new foundation, who too must not speak against what has been written but may add new words that accord with them. Thus we separate wheat from weeds, and flesh from bone, that we may hold to the good but discard any pretences that tend to evil, such as false prophets bespeak. If we do not put out Ruach's fire, then Kurion—who gives peace—will make us holy in lifestyle.

For we desire that until Hamashiach returns, we will be kept healthy and faultless in spirit, soul, and body. But many others have other aptitudes to share whenever we meet together—though also by Ruach—even as different parts of a human body contribute in different ways. Some prophesy, some preach, some perform miracles, some enrich by generosity—there are many ways. Yet all are enjoined to walk closely with Ruach, for he is the guide whom Hamashiach and his father have sent to walk with us."

She, it seemed, could wax eloquent, when a simple name would have nicely answered his question, and would have been given by many a slave. Why, he wondered? Still, she had some interesting ideas. Two types of prophet, heh? Of late his master had been ruminating over the prophets of the Sheep—the Yehudim being the remnant of that flock—thoughts that Longinus had telepathically picked up. Had the Dark Alliance taken the time to listen carefully to what their prophets had said, perhaps Hamashiach would never have gotten off the ground. Now he had escaped their clutches—the diaboloi of all people were to blame for such crass stupidity, for not heeding their allies. Now the vampires had made themselves scarce, distancing themselves from their former partners in crime. Wulfgar remained uneasy, although Longinus divined that the fear of retaliation was slowly dying away.

At least the Kingdom of Night had not suffered any direct retribution so far, although the Kingdom of Necros was losing its hold on certain tribes of the secondborn. So far the transmogrification was mainly of Sheep, with many finding a new yet prophesied shepherd. But by Philippon, and now by Shimon, the spread of influence had crossed cultural barriers, and threatened to become a global pandemic. That was of no immediate concern for the vampires, but worryingly the Prophecy of Zalkeesh had been fulfilled, and the Kingdom of Night feared that it portended their ultimate destruction, as surely as an eighth Age would follow the seventh: the Sixth Age had ended with the fall of Hamashiach, although the Seventh Age was not deemed to have begun until his resurrection—the 40 wilderness hours between planting and germination were as one.

"Would you care to learn more?" Yasmina had broken into his ruminations. Well, why shouldn't he? Then soon, she had promised him, soon.

COMMISSION

Yasmina rose from the couch, stood up, and raised a flat loaf of bread. Her companions watched in silence. "The table was not of silver, nor was the cup of gold, in which Hamashiach gave fellowship wine to his disciples to drink. What is it that we now do in humility, proclaiming to be precious and numinous? This bread without yeast," she proclaimed, "reminds us of the hasty bread which our forbears ate, when they prepared for hasty departure from slavery to freedom, and also of the mysterious bread which Kurion gave to them on that journey, and also of the annual festivals of thanksgiving our people have made ever since, in a land where wheat is plentiful and time is theirs. Bread is now a mainstay for our bodies.

"And we recall the true exemption from death, and the true journey unto life, and the living of that life that is in Hamashiach, who, in another picture, like unto the lambs of old had his body slain for us. And like they, his bones were not broken. Nor indeed, as Shimon has taught us, was his body, nor his soul, nor his spirit, though his flesh was made as a scar for us, that our spirits may be beautified by Ruach. We now break off parts from the one loaf, which pictures our unity, picturing too our individuality, whether slave or free, male or female, Yehudim or Goyim. Let us each partake of this loaf, for we are one in the true body, and we share of what we are with one another." So saying, she walked around the table, offering chunks of the large loaf to all—save to Longinus, for it was obviously a sacred rite within a mystery in which he played no part, meaningless bread to him so better left for the time being.

Longinus lay reclining on a *triclinium*. Philippon and Kornelios had laid the table, wearing the apron of humility as if they were mere slaves. And then, once sure that all had arrived who were expected, had laid down to eat the meal in mutual love. So, no social distancing was practiced, and when each guest has equal servings, fellowship does not perish. The rich food was food for all—quality mushrooms, not hedgehog mushrooms; turbot, not brill; oysters, not mussels; fresh turtledove, not stale magpie. So this was what they meant by a love feast, the masters serving the slaves, putting choice foods on the table and in fact waiting for the slaves to begin first, a bias towards the socioeconomically poor.

Hadn't Sokrates, *philosophorum Graecorum sapientissimus fuit,* done something like this, though perhaps keeping slaves separate? Rome had completely misread the situation, but had she known she would have turned from ridicule to rage. Slaves were to know their place, and it didn't do to go swapping places, encouraging social revolution. Presumably, this was why the general public was not permitted into these get-togethers.

After a short while, a time of spontaneous prayer began. All seemed to be speaking in personal prayer to...Longinus could not work out to whom, and he was even having trouble catching intelligible words. Suddenly one voice was raised: "Rasseeto marook akeeto krupanay aytos barrandus imato backeesh nbon marindose seebarak ho lindush impruto koomish." What on earth was all that gibberish? A little too much new wine? Someone else promptly spoke words he could understand, a sentence or two in praise of Usen. At least someone had their head screwed on aright!

Someone gently prodded the earlier babbler, with a slight shake of the head, and a quick meaningful look towards Longinus their guest. He guessed that, being in a port town, some foreigner had found the port wine a bit too tongue loosening, and over exuberantly had burst out in his own language some words of praise, kindly interpreted by his more sober companion, while the third person had flagged up that the stranger, Longinus, might get the idea that the gathering was getting madder by the moment. Longinus smiled to himself. It would take something to go beyond the madness of treating slaves as masters—at least the masters also reclined, rather than sitting or standing—assuming equality rather than inferiority.

After an hour or so, prayer seemed to naturally die down. A slave girl then asked a question, because her mistress, although quite kind according to her lights, had ridiculed a little ditty which she had overheard the girl singing, a song in fact which Vibia, daughter of Philippon, had taught. Philippon was happy to take the question, and indeed he firmly believed that singers should understand the songs they sang and believe in them—or not sing them: to sing without understanding was no compliment to the understanding.

He spoke to all. "You have heard it said that this song condemns Kurion as unfair, tyrannical, and egotistic. These charges, long levelled at us as ethnic Yehudim, are now levelled at us as spiritual Yehudim, that if Hamashiach has come from Kurion, then The Way is therefore tainted with such vices, and is therefore hardly fit even for slaves. Yet we meet as true nobility, and true slaves, as both rich and poor, and declare ourselves unfit for The Way. We stand by what is written—as Vibia has woven into music—that Kurion gave his people a land of nations, that, having been a slave people, they might enjoy what the nations had toiled to gain, and that they were to obey his torah. Indeed, he commanded them to praise him. Are then the charges against him thus sustained? Nay!

"Let us take the first, of unfairness, even theft. Why was this land given to his people? It was but a small land that had become sick of the nations that lived in it. Indeed Kurion warned his people that they would likewise be spewed forth if they ever became as sick as the nations they dispossessed. Moreover, he did not steal the land, for all land is his, and the nations are but tenants. Were the old tenants not to evacuate by death, you ask? Truly they deserved to die, but still could flee instead of fight, and indeed their numbers, being greater than Kurion's people, confined his people to the hilltops for over a generation, being a time of extended raids. Indeed the confines of his people's promised land were set, and they were to be at peace with peoples along their borders, not grasping more land but content with that given. Moreover, their tenancy was for the greater good, for out of them would come a knowledge for all of Kurion, and Hamashiach himself.

"Let us take the second, that he is tyrannical, enforcing harsh demands. Were his instructions petty, needless burdens to his people, a new slavery to endure? No, his laws were not wanton laws for the sake of it, but were needful for the day and rich in prophetic symbolism about the Seventh Age. By symbols he taught his people, and the laws he commanded were the rules of his household, so that his people would live harmoniously with him, with each other, and with the wider world— so far as the wider world would permit peace. By understanding his teachings they would grow in understanding, and thus appreciation, of him, and thus their inner lives would be enriched by truth. Do we not command our children to take their medicines? Walking in his ways would keep them healthy—unlike the sick nations who had caused the land to vomit them out. Of his laws, some were specific to them while their covenant lasted, and some were the laws of right and wrong, which all nations over all time have shared, and which lie oft hidden within all of us, oft as a seed which needs water, light, and feeding, to come forth in splendour. It was from the tyranny of sin that he sought to protect them by his torah.

"Let us take the third, that he is egotistical, seeking our adulation. How can it be that he created us, if he needs us not? Was it not because he is creative at heart, creating space and time from his boundless energy and imagination? Does he who made the universe pine for our puny praise? If he had need, he would not tell us! Nay, our nature is healthy when we praise outside the confines of our own self. Is it not good to praise a sunset? How much more were they enriched to look upon him who is the most praiseworthy; privileged to praise not for his sake but for their own? In commanding his praise he did but command their wellbeing. And how did Hamashiach come? As a crown prince in a palace? Nay, as one unlawfully begotten; a shame unto his grandparents; soon exiled by a petty king. And how did Hamashiach die, in a rich bed and old of years? Nay, but as a runaway slave or as a lawless assassin, he had died.

"And let us note, that by these symbols the ancients spoke better than they knew of the true exodus. For Hamashiach has led his new people forth with a new joy, and given us a land untrodden by human feet, a land not of this world, a land that is inviolate by the power of Ruach. Within it we have homeland security, and can grow on the harvest of increasingly knowing him, and each other, and ourselves. And thus the sacrifices we make to him, and to he who sent him, and to Ruach through whom he came, are sacrifices of praise, and by them we feast on the most praiseworthy. Indeed, our praise explores him. But note also that our sacrifices might also be of our mortal lives, for our enemies are legion, and ironically some would slay us to please Usen. Since foes surround us, and fallen foes are still unfallen within, let us therefore daily take an oath to be true to him and to spend time at the feet of he who washes our feet."

Philippon went silent. There was a time of reflection, and sundry more questions were asked, and answered, within the group. Philippon had taken numerous slanders against Kurion, turning them into praise—when rightly understood—as well as covering one or two pointers about baptising oneself into the holy writings. Longinus quite enjoyed Philippon's logic and the setting of things into context. Considered thus, what seemed black on the outside could actually be white under the outer coat: had enemies put a wolf's coat on a lamb, and given it a bad name?

With a nod from Philippon, Yasmina stood up again and raised a cup of wine. "This fruit of the vine," she said, "reminds us of leaving Khem for the wine of joy of the Promised Land. It reminds us of innocent blood on the doors of our forebears, symbolizing that they would be spared the same fate and would leave those homes behind. It speaks now of the life given to us by Hamashiach the Lamb, Hamashiach the Warrior, who died to defeat death for us and to give us life. It speaks of a ransom for those enslaved to the Necros. It speaks of he who shed his blood to cut the true covenant, becoming the true vine, the true wine, of which this wine is but a shadow. Drink l'chaim—to life!" Kornelios stood up and drained his cup, giving thanks to Hamashiach their benefactor— "until the king returns."

With that the fellowship began to drift away, as slaves, spared a little time to attend—for some Kornelios paid compensation—returned to the labours of the day. Soon only the households of Kornelios and Philippon remained—and Longinus. His host asked him whether he was inclined to enter into the community of Hamashiach—if questioning, had he any questions? Longinus was divided, but not prepared to commit. "How can you even consider me enlisting, on such short notice?" he asked. His friend replied that whether short or long notice, he wished that Longinus—indeed every human being born before Hamashiach returned—would take the plunge and know true liberty.

That led to an exchange of ideas on liberty. Was not a retired centurion a free man, a citizen of the Roman Empire? Was the empire free? What was freedom? Were all people morally free to maim and to maul? Were all free from the need of air? Were all free from the chains of sin? It was Philippon who discerned that Longinus had a nonhuman bondage. He had performed exorcism before and encouraged Longinus to be free of his inner diaboloi. Might it be that his guests were stopping him from surrendering to Hamashiach? After some thought, Longinus decided to try this route, and to see how it went from there.

Some would say that it happened next was kinda spooky. The two households encircled him in prayer. They prayed that he would be set free from the troubling spirits, that they would themselves be protected from them, and that thanks for freedom would ascend to the highest. This time many switched into some languages of which Longinus hadn't the foggiest. The thought crossed his mind that these people had learned the languages of the firstborn, of whom Wulfgar had informed him. But if so, why? And did they believe that there was more power in a secret tongue, than in their native tongue?

Power there was. He felt its strangeness in the room, and began to sweat. Had the room somehow gotten smaller? It seemed to hem him in, yet seemed benign, not evil. Yet he felt that he was slowly being immersed, struggling to breathe, but oh what a wonderful way to die, asphyxiated into glory. The experience was totally beyond him, even seductive. Suddenly, in words he understood, Philippon commanded the evil spirits to leave him fully and never return. Zilch! He remained standing: total flop, damp squib.

Then Yasmina joined in, speaking supposedly to the spirits, commanding them to depart, telling them where to go. Highly animated, the poor girl looked as if she put her heart and soul into it, as if she fully believed that the answer would be given. Others joined it, one or two almost manic, decreeing and declaring all sorts of stuff—while Philippon sadly shook his aging head at their antics. Some prayed as cold and calm as logic. Again and again, words of command rolled like thunder around him, but there was no lightning in the clouds. Shouts abounded, and he began to feel trapped, not released. These people were weird, but they meant well. Perpetua it was who mercifully put a stop to it. "Casting out this kind of spirit requires more prayer", she said.

The exorcism had concluded inconclusively. Philippon had realised instinctively that his 14-year-old had had a word from their master, words that harked back to the previous Age, when others had become too cocksure about their abilities, had slackened off their prayer life, and had become ill-prepared to face the challenge of stubborn spirits. To help Longinus, they would double and redouble their inner prayer preparation, building themselves up in their most holy faith, spending time in their inner sanctum, and so sharpen up their faith in Ruach's abilities, rather than in their own. For a seed of sharp faith goes much further than a mountain of stale faith. In the meantime, they gave him a list of selected scriptures, to prepare him for the next battle, which, they promised him, would be Kurion's.

He returned to his host's home, decidedly disappointed, but questioning. On the one hand, they had identified his slavery—they had spoken of being able to discern the spirits within—but on the other hand, they had been unable to do anything about it. But, they had concluded, that just as when the mighty Legions failed in a battle, they would simply withdraw and regroup, resupply, and then fall to again. From a tactical standpoint that made sense to a military man. Not every fortress is cast down on day one.

That night Longinus had lost his appetite. He had wandered about, watching the waters. He had seen a young couple stood shoulder to shoulder, obviously sharing the same wonder. As he watched the couple, for the first time in a long time he felt something of the pleasure one can have in standing with another, and in the sea and the stars. A keen scent was in the air. It was a cloudless night, when heaven seemed to have drawn close to earth, almost with a kiss of peace. It was as if his master slept, leaving him to revisit his humanity—for a short while. He sighed, as a wave of nostalgia for his former life and friends, washed over him. Then it was that he knew that he had to seek out solitude, to stay out the night and to observe a special vigil.

If you could have asked him, he could not have told you from where the call had sprung, only that he had been called, whether for good or for ill. Walking past the Augusteum he followed the Decumanus Maximus road heading due east, to be on his own and undisturbed. An hour or so along the road he stopped, not tired—he never got tired—but just because it seemed a good thing to do. The shining moon was seeking to stir up a grouse; but not a creature was stirring, not even a mouse. Longinus left the paved road, and between two trees he knelt to pray.

As he lifted up his eyes, it was as if the full moon paled to merely a crescent. Then behold there stood before him one of the very aggeloi, who shone brightly before his eyes, yet his light did not enlighten his surrounds. "Hail, Longinus, your prayer shall be answered, for Usen has appointed you a place of freedom, though a penance it might seem to some."

"I, who know the mind of my master, do know of your kind, but tell me please, what is your name?" asked Longinus.

"Longinus, what is your name? What are names? Are names among your people not given at birth, a mixture of sameness and difference, but seldom revealing their nature? Among some peoples a holding name is given, until their nature is revealed, and then they are renamed. But even that says but little of their nature. And since names of mortals are mortal names, is it not fitting that when the mortal puts on immortality, it shall not retain the mortal name it bore? And within mortal life, some creatures grow names even as they grow, so that a name becomes a lifetime and needs a lifetime of telling. Among us who are immortal, our full names tell our full stories, our missions, and our delights. Among your people we might give a short name, but that name is but a mission, a fragment, a momentary glimpse in the passing of time, given merely to connect us in later moments as we serve the Children of Usen. Behold, my name to you shall be Umbra, for I shall be a shadowminder of your soul until the day that it be taken up. Yet many are they who could speak of me by other names, for at many different times and in many different ways have I met with the secondborn.

"But now," he continued, "know that they who sought to release you could not do so, for it is given to them to release those bound by the Necros, but not by the Night. And of the Night they know but little, nor would we have them to know overmuch, lest they fall into the snares of fascination or of fear. It is given to them to go higher up and deeper in to the world of the Day, not of the Night, and not even of the deeper things of the Necros. Yet even as there must be physicians for those who fall from wellbeing, so there must be some few who study strange afflictions, that they might know of strange cures thereof. You yourself have such knowledge, for you have dwelt in the house of illness. But be content, they of the household of faith have prayed for you, and they have been heard—yea to us your own soul has cried out. To them you shall but say that you have heard words in the night that your deliverance shall surely come, but in what time and place you know not. Thus they shall be content.

"Longinus, seldom do we protect the Children from the natural turmoil of the world—from war, famine, disease, or wild beasts. Yet your will is bound by another, not of this world, and enslaved not by your own misdeeds—for you were caught by a predator that sought you out through no fault of your own. It is not therefore from your own folly that we will release you—your folly was but the common lot. But as once a people were enslaved by those who meant it for evil—yet Kurion meant it for good—even so it is by the will of Usen that you have become a slave, and by your freedom will free many. Think not that it was purely by the design of your lord that you were brought to the feet of Hamashiach." The visitor melted into the early mist of morn, and the light of the sun arose, whose light enlightened his surrounds. Longinus blinked in the light, but the light seemed good to him, a pleasure he had not felt in a long time. With a lighter heart he walked back to his host's house.

∞

Wulfgar had gorged himself in the night. With his slave away, he had dined in Apollania—that would help allay any suspicions that might have been building up against Longinus. He left the bloodless body of the beggar in an alleyway, ready to be discovered with the rising of the sun. He flew lazily to his cave in the cliffs, aiming to bed down for the day, but if he expected to rest undisturbed, he had another thought coming. For even as the sun arose, he was visited by one of the aggeloi. "Hail, Wulfgar, I am come to wrest from you the soul of your slave Longinus, unless you yield him up to me of your own free will. To him I am known as Umbra. Will you comply?"

Wulfgar eyed him steadily. It was not in his nature to yield up any slave, and his pride was ruffled. He himself was still reasonably strong, though far from what he had been before the Nephilim War, and of course he was fortified by his diaboloi guests, so doing better than might have been expected at his age. As to Umbra, he looked fairly strong, but he was probably not one of the greater aggeloi. To yield timidly without a test of strength would leave him always feeling bitter towards himself, a coward, always unsure as to whether Umbra had been bluffing. His fellow vampires would snigger at him. But should he fight for the soul of Longinus? Was it worth it? It was actually strange, very strange indeed, for the aggeloi to trouble the vampires, since they weren't natural enemies, so why was one troubling him now over a mere Child? Was the object irrelevant? Had his part in the attempted assassination been traced, and the demand of emancipation a pretence to punish him without a fair trial? Was Umbra a secret assassin?

There was no telling about Usen and his minions, when he seemed to make mountains out of molehills, and molehills out of mountains. Usen's judgments were unfathomable; the ways of him who had bound them by the Eighth Law, were past figuring out! If he did not fight it there and then, it seemed to him that this agent of the aggeloi would simply find another way to pick a fight. But to fight now and perhaps to win, why maybe, just maybe, he would be let off further punishment.

He judged that his challenger was selected as strong enough to win, but perhaps not unduly superior, lest a win against Wulfgar be as glorious as a win of a club against a feather. He tried to telepathise Longinus, but found that his slave's mind was now opaque to him. The cause for such an occultation meant that the enemy was already interfering, that Longinus had to some extent offered himself to the enemy, hoping thus to escape from his enslavement. No, the fish that still thrashed in the water had to be firmly landed, neither left to swim away, nor to be landed by the enemy. He would fight.

Wulfgar stretched forth an arm, and a bolt of blood-red energy hit Umbra in the midsection, knocking him off his feet, violently expelling him from the cave. For a moment Umbra steadied himself, regained his poise, and then fired back a cobalt-blue bolt, smashing Wulfgar's body into the back of the cave. Wulfgar summoned his diaboloi to intensify his attack, again and again hitting Umbra. Fishermen returning to the port stood off amazed at the sight, for uncannily the cave lit up again and again with colours of dazzling reds and blues, and there seemed to be some winged creature trying to steady its position at the entrance. It was a battle of wills, with thelodynamic power used to attack and defend, but at the end of that titanic battle it was Umbra who had the last word. Wulfgar lay on the floor of the cave, burnt beyond recognition, though Umbra too was battle-scarred and would need time to rebuild his human appearance.

Reluctantly Wulfgar lowered his pride and complied, mentally severing his link to Longinus. Such a link, once lost, was not so easily re-established, since the former victim is left with some vampire changes to their DNA code, so can resist easier than can a babe in the woods. Although he was left at death's door, Wulfgar's life was spared. Umbra left him to crawl out of his cave whenever it suited him, or to curl up and die at his leisure—it mattered not to Umbra. His purpose had been dead simple: free Longinus.

As the days rolled by, Umbra had gotten onto easy talking terms with Longinus, who had surrendered himself to the Power above all Powers, even unto the hands of Hamashiach. Now he would gaze with amaze at the spear which his man had used to stab the lifeless body of his living lord. It was just a typical auxiliary spear, used by common soldiers. But to him that spear was now a sign that the New Age had come, a physical connection between the old and the new, between death and life. And yet as he fingered the spear, it was clear that the New Age wasn't speaking to the world with words from the sky, but was calling upon the Children of Kurion to carry its message: did the spear speak to him of his *destinatio*? Destinatio, that is what he would call it.

Philippon had become his teacher, and he and his family had all been taught, had all believed, and had all been baptised in water, and unto all had Ruach come down—as the poetic put it—and given them new words to speak in praise of the highest. Now at last his family understood that he had been changed by one of the striges in various ways, not least in diet. No longer did he hide from them his need for blood, but no longer did he feed on human blood. Accompanying him his wife in turn had shared how, with his increasing self-isolation, she had suffered loneliness. Embarrassingly a commiserating friend had once been just a tad too sympatric—arriving leisurely with pastoral goodwill; departing hastily just shy of shame. Alas, too easily a wife lays down her lonely loyalty. Fie, too easily a good man strays through pure sympathy. Lucius and Aristus then related how he had become a distant father, at times pure creepy, unsettling their minds. Now, still under one roof, they were all under one lord, a family united at last.

His family were not the only guests who were visiting Philippon, though they were among the more frequent. Earlier in the week some rather special guests had arrived at the port, and were headed towards the old Yehudim capital. It was good to meet them and to hear of their travels, and generally just to chinwag. The Way was expanding exponentially, to the accompaniment of many miracles, the greatest of which were radicalised lives, lives that had entered the new level of kingdom which Hamashiach had opened up, a level that could only be seen with the inner eye of Ruach, who walked and talked with them.

One, who was visiting with a friend—Iosephus d'Arimathie—had come from the old capital. He was named Naqdimon. He had told—a tale he never tired of telling—of how once long ago, in his former life—as he called it—he had heard about this newness. He had been brought up devoutly, believing that he was in the Kingdom of Kurion—and he was. Indeed he became a notable exponent of that kingdom, and enjoyed his fame.

But then came a night when somewhat unwillingly, he had been taught by a far better rabbi. This teacher explained to him that he was in the husk level of the kingdom, blessed but based purely on ethnic privilege, offering only limited insights into Kurion. Soon, so this rabbi said, that level would pass away, as do husks from wheat when it is ripe unto harvest. A wheat level was coming, and had been prophesied. Ruach would cleanse his chosen people from superstition and disloyalty, even as water washes away impurities. He would transform their hearts of stone into living hearts, becoming one with them. It would be as if covenant—once external like writing on stone—would become internal as if written on hearts. It would be to them like a new kind of city, a new kind of community, a new kind of neighbour, all shining with the personal and intimate knowledge of Kurion, living in the promised land of Ruach. Iosephus had much to share.

Among the other guests had come a man named Agabon. He had come with messages to give to one or two in the group. From Paulus of the Perushim, heading back to the old capital, he had taken a belt and used it to illustrate a warning of capture and death—if Paulus continued on his journey: Agabon did not forbid the journey.

From Longinus he had taken a spear, saying that now it belonged to another hand. Facing Rome, he had thrown it far away. "That spear," he had said, "must follow Tiberius Claudius Caesar Augustus Germanicus far beyond Germania, taking the new road laid over the sea. There it must lodge in a new land. But he who bears this spear will never again see his tomb, and one he loves well shall endure unhappy excess of life far beyond the mortal lot, and will long wish to die. Yet many will bless his name, for he shall carry the new light to a new people who long have dwelt in darkness, and legends will spring forth of his name."

Without hesitation, Iosephus d'Arimathie strode forth to retrieve Destinatio, and to claim the task appointed for him. In journeying there he had sensed that although he was getting on, Hamashiach still had a destiny for him. He had long done his duty, not counting the personal cost—he was that kind of man. Besides, since he had lost his beloved Imma, she who had been his wife, a fresh undertaking would do him good.

After a time of prayer, Philippon asked Paulus about what he was planning, and suggested to him that for safety he should bypass Rome, heading up instead a team to the new world that Claudius had opened up—why should Paulus, a leader of leaders, lay down his life on a whim, when Ruach himself had given him fair warning? Iosephus fully supported that idea, saying that the honour would be his to serve under such a teacher.

But Paulus was adamant. The warning to him, he said, was not to deflect him but to deepen him, and having tested him, it would see him through the troubles. No, Iosephus had been given the task of the spear, although indeed it would be best if he did not go alone. But to such matters, he said, Philippon was well placed to lead, not perhaps in heading it up himself, but in deciding on who should go with the spear bearer. "Only let it be twelve," he said, "even as The Way was opened up to the world at the Celebration of Shavuot, by being based on its foundational statement of the Twelve Tribes of Yakob—of unity and diversity within the will of Kurion, who is beyond the Dawn of Time."

The following day the Council of Philippon was held, and the mission was thoroughly discussed, firstly confirming the call of Iosephus. In spite of his age, his call made sense, for among other things he was a wealthy man, and finances would be needed to establish the mission. He had long played a parliamentary part among the Yehudim, though that had long played out, and he had been shown the red card of unwelcome. The Roman tongue—which he had learned through international trade—would be useful within the new Roman colonies.

His heart was ready to move on, for pastures new appealed to him, especially in putting his money to best use in enlarging The Way. And being a venerable elder and entrepreneur, his maturity would command respect. Yes, he would make an ideal elder statesman, for when it is found in the ways of justice, age becomes a crown of dignity, and the hoary head of age is covered with honour beyond the reach of youth. But who would go with him?

Quickly his young sister, Havingues, volunteered, believing that she had a part to play, and his sons Giuseppe and Galeas—almost her age—were both eager to go. So too were their new friends, Aristus and Lucius, sons of Longinus and Selampsin, both lads old enough now to go their own ways. Of his own household Philippon had found two that it seemed good for him to send—his twin daughters Perpetua and Vibia, identical in age but in little else.

Accompanying them would go Yasmina, freed by Kornelios to serve them. The law of *Fufia Caninia* forbade him to release any more from his small household. In the eyes of Rome she would seem but a halfway slave, a *statuliber*. In the eyes of the believers she was seen as a free and equal sister. Living as a slave among a Roman community would afford her the protection of household property, and avoid the offense of wanton manumission, rebellion against the time-honoured institution of slavery.

After much thought and prayer, Kornelios also decided to go, especially as he could command the respect of the Roman forces. Since he would go, Scribonia his wife would go too—Usen did not encourage the desertion of spouses. They had no dependents, except Felix their son, who was quite excited about a migration to the New World. With him, the number was now complete.

For his part Longinus, having discovered what The Way had done for him, now intended to gladly do what he could for The Way: freed from slavery by it, he would free from slavery by it. As to longevity, he already understood his fate—the works of Wulfgar could not be wholly undone. He would go first to Rome with Paulus, but would then go far north to the land of Publius Vergilius Maro, a storyteller of some note, to write a new story. He feared that he would endure unhappy excess of life far beyond the mortal lot, and would long wish to die. Little did he know the blessèd fate that Hamashiach had for him. His wife would happily journey with him, yet their parting from their two sons was bitter. Their journey with Paulus would be with great hazard, though without loss, and hard would be their parting from him—but it was the will of Usen. Soon Paulus and his companions had left for the old city.

Preparations for the main mission took some weeks. At last, it was not by blare of trumpet that they set forth, but by the calm sailing forth from the bay, paid passengers on a merchant ship chartered to seek the most direct route to Narbo. From there they went in carriages to riverboats, and back to carriages, crossing the neck of Hispania, until taking ship again at Burdigala, where they delayed a little at the spot where Lucius Cassius Longinus and many legionaries, had been massacred, yet mindful that their ambushers themselves had suffered loss of life: why did man kill man?

Their own deaths were now on their minds, but they had handed themselves over to death before ever setting sail from the friendly port of Caesarea Palestinae. Death might end a chapter, but it could never end the story. However, commitment to death did not conflict with commitment to life, and they were not forbidden to take thought for the morrow, nor to cogitate on how best to ensure that their mission would first survive, and then thrive. After all, they were to be as shrewd as snakes, and as guiltless as doves—cautious, but not too cautious, as befits sheep living in a land of wolves, and never, never, never, to turn into wolves.

Before long they set off again, having found a vessel that had trade bound for Duronovaria, where they would be able to meet up with the fortified port which stationed the Legio 2 Augusta. Kornelios had an old army buddy with that outfit, and hoped to speak with him about The Way. All being well they should be there within a week. They had had a brief stopover at Civitas Namnetum, where strange hooded men—rather on the tall size—had briefly spoken with Iosephus, giving into his hands a sword. They had said that that sword had had a special forging, and was to remain unblemished while it awaited the hand of 'the last Galeas', before returning to the hand of Nimue their lady.

But the best-laid plans are apt to go awry, it is said. Already the travellers had spent over a month at sea—a long journey for those unaccustomed to life on the seven seas, of home on the rolling deep. At last they could see the glad sight of the new world on their horizon, yet unhappily they saw also the approach of a great storm. Thelodynamic energy was stirring up the elements of sea and sky. It seemed that the Necroi had gotten wind of their mission, and were determined to scuttle it, to abort its life before its birth. The mariners looked anxious. Mile by mile they drew steadily nearer to port and safety. Yet soon, within heartbreaking sight of their port, the wind rose to such a pitch that it would not permit them to land, so they battened down the hatches and sailed by, riding the stormy blast as best they could.

Swiftly the surge had rolled up, for the east wind clashed with the south wind, and the ill-blowing west wind with the north wind from the upper sky, squalls rushing down from the four corners of the world. The fury of the storm was terrifying, and the waves were wild and tempestuous. Only with great difficulty did the sailors manage to wrap ropes around the boat, seriously doubting as to whether she could stay afloat. The mainsails were lowered and reefed, and the drag-anchor was lowered, reducing her speed, for the sailors had sailed into *ignota aquas*, and did not know what they might encounter, for off the Roman road there might lie uncharted rocks. The rowboat was dragged on deck and secured, for towing it endangered the ship.

Perilously the ship had taken on overmuch stormwater overnight, and the next day even precious cargo was dumped, for are human lives not more precious than gold, and hopes worth more than fine silver? Nonessential gear was hauled overboard, an offering, the sailors grimly said, to Neptunus of the deep seas—for is it not just that they should sacrifice that which is not essential to them, that they might save that which is essential to them, even their lives? Where the jagged coastline was, none could say, for none could see the sun by day, nor the stars by night—frayed nerves blinded vision.

The believers prayed a lot, encouraged a lot, rolled up their sleeves and mucked in as best they could under the direction of the mariners. Even encouragement to eat became a vital need, for strength must survive in hopelessness and despair. Sailor to sailor the team went, as their duties afforded them brief moments of respite. Unto them they testified that they had a mission such that even Neptunus must lower his trident and heed, and that they would be delivered from the storm, even if the whole Kingdom of Necros slammed the winds and rains against them. The sailors were greatly enheartened, and with the dawning of the day came the first faint rays of hope.

But behold, it was to an unknown harbour that they had arrived with the going down of the waves, and a misty murk beclouded the sun. Whether to the New World or perhaps to Hibernia or maybe to Thule, they knew not, not even whether they had ended up north, south, east, or west, of Duronovaria. For the storm had seemed to drive them starboard, then port, round and round changing course even as the changing of a madman's mind.

All such computations must wait, for here they met with friendly fishermen, such as lived along the bay, a simple, though crude and barbarous people, who—a most despicable custom almost defying belief—drank milk. As to cheese, these clods were clueless, howbeit hospitable enough with both their beer—what they called *curmi*, which was well flavoured with herbs and spices—and with their fish. Moreover, their kindness more than made up for their lack of civilized manners, and the travellers, finally resting at peace on dry land, washed and combed their hair, donned fresh clothing, and slept as they had never slept before.

Dilapidated, was perhaps the best word to have described them, but after sleeping in the arms of Morpheus they soon began to look human again. The ship's captain had traded with speakers of that strange tongue, and found that he could hold rough dialogue with them. These simpletons seemed not to have heard of Rome, nor to have travelled far overland, but they said that they were under the protection of a secretive shadow folk who lived among the trees, but not within enclosures. The ship they held in undisguised awe.

The next day word had come that the passengers alone were to meet with the tree-dwellers, and that the ship's captain and crew must see to making their ship seaworthy, and then to depart. Good fortune would go with them, but they were never to seek to return to the silver-mist enshrouded harbour. From the trees, they might take only such wood for their repairs as was needed. Such food and shelter as was needed while they laboured, would be provided by the fisherfolk.

The captain was content enough with that. He had no wish to meet those who had no wish to meet with him, and the land seemed too rustic for trade. But he was surprised that his passengers, having paid so much to get to a Roman destination, seemed prepared to remain at the mercy of barbarians. He had sought to pay the fishermen in good Roman coin for services rendered, but they had treated his silver coins as mere ornaments. The yokels lacked rudimentary knowledge of what currency was, but they had not sought any payment in goods.

No hostility had been shown to any of the ship's company, but the captain would have fought if necessary to defend his passengers, as he had had to on some previous journeys. Still, it was not his place to force his company on them, only he had had them sign a paper to the effect that all had disembarked of their own free will, and that their contract with his ship had ended amicably. The captain did not wish friends or families of the departed, hammering on his doors demanding their whereabouts. After a last meal onboard they left him, and followed a fisherman who guided them up the path into the tree line, where, the man had said, they would meet the mysterious Aelfir.

It was not long before they were met by one of the tree dwellers, who, although patently not Roman, welcomed them courteously in the Roman tongue, giving himself to be a sindel, one of the sindeldi. That was a tribe of which they had not heard, and of which Rome had had no report. His appearance was such that they wondered. His ears were shaped somewhat like unto leaves, and he stood taller than most, his eyes somewhat the colour of silver, and his head crowned with rich dark-brown hair, and his skin smooth and without spot or wrinkle or any such blemish.

Through the forest they followed him for some hours, until as the sun was setting they were ferried on punts to a small island surrounded by marsh water, an island that seemed to be set in glass. There a number of the tree-dwellers stood, awaiting them—all but one, a silver-haired man who was seated on a carved throne, alongside a lady most rare. As they walked towards this welcoming committee, the seated man arose: "Hail, comers from afar. I Yavion, king of Logres, welcome you to Insula Avallonis. Long have we waited for the fulfillers of prophecy from Middle-earth that now is sundered from us, and in this land you shall build the community of Hamashiach, for so it has been foretold."

The travellers had taken some time to process all this in silence. These were a taller people than those they had met in the bay, straight, not bent, speakers of fluent Roman yet like no Romans they had ever met. Moreover, they knew of Hamashiach, and had had, had they not said, prophetic expectations of their arrival. With these people they spoke far into the night.

These tree-dwellers, as the fishermen had called them, lived both on and under a large inland island. It was hard to credit their ages. They claimed to have walked this earth when Necuratu had been flung from Arda into the unending nether gloom. Ah, an Age when he did not bother man seemed but a blessèd eternity past, long before the memory of man, but the people of Yavion said that the problem was that the secondborn—mortal man—always carried the seeds of Necuratu within them, some more, some less; some weeded, some tended, and even the glorious Fourth Age finally became ill beyond cure, and Manwë had departed. They probed the minds of their guests, for, they said, Hamashiach had once called Twelve to himself, and yet one had been found to have been a servant of the Bent One, even of Necuratu, and traitors multiplied even as weeds.

Asked how they knew of Hamashiach, they told that a very few of their kind ranged far and wide around mortal lands, keeping low profiles yet probing Middle-earth. Moreover, some of the Phusika also brought news from near and far, according to their kind—the greater swimmers of the seas; the hole dwelling nibblers of the wood; the high flyers of inaccessible eyries. Usen also spoke with them at whiles, whether of thing past, present, or planned. Thus it was that they had expected the travellers.

Being told about the great storm, they said that though the ways of Usen were strange beyond full comprehension, yet it seemed to them as if the Enemy had raised the storm for evil, but that Usen might have intended that very storm to bring them safe and sound to Avalon.

Messengers had already been sent to Hibernia, where Ránpalan their high king dwelt, that his heart might rejoice, but it was in the land that Rome was sweeping into like a flood, that the mission would first take root. To that end Yavion would establish them—not on his isle, but not too far distant. His people would offer protection of the seed, though it was no longer the part of the sindeldi to walk with man. Even the aggeloi, he said, now took little more than a back seat in the works of man. He counselled them to heed the words of Ruach, to be loyal to Hamashiach, and to be blessed by Kurion—even as children by their father. The spear of the Twelve, he said, would outweigh the spears of the invaders.

In a spot selected by the sindeldi, some rough shelters—*tabernacula*—had been built, and they were all very tired but happy. The sun was going down and a fire had been built. A stag provided the party with a rich meal. As they sat around the campfire under the first opening of the stars, with a thoughtful smile on his face, Iosephus recalled to them how his friend Naqdimon had told him about his nighttime interview with Barnasa. Barnasa had scotched fantasy tales of champions of the faith having been taken up into deep heaven and returning with news. No, what the people had was what was written and remained in force. No one, not even himself, Barnasa, had ever made such a round trip. But, he had immediately added, he himself had come down from the heavens. Had he meant that his words carried the same weight as what stood written?

That Parthian shot had flummoxed Naqdimon, leading to all kinds of questions that he not resolved, neither that night nor for a good many nights. With hindsight, of course, it made sense, but at first he had wondered whether Barnasa had meant that deep heaven had come down on him, and only on him—had he met the Oyéresu, fabled Guardians of the sky dancers? After all, he had heard rumours of something like that having happened at his river baptism.

With hindsight, of course, they could all see that Barnasa had meant that his immortal life—the life of Huion—had within time incorporated a mortal aspect, had 'come down', depotentiated, so to speak, entering into a rough shelter such as those they had just built, only of flesh and blood rather than of sticks and stones. Iosephus mused on the idea that even as Barnasa had at last gone up to deep heaven, eventually they would likewise leave their earthly *tabernaculum* and join him in transformed human bodies.

They walked in a world of wonders, and the skies above held yet more—higher up and deeper in. They longed for more data on what Barnasa had done and had taught, and what the shaliakim were taught by Ruach. Before leaving, Shimon had promised to send over a copy of an account which his young friend—'Stumpyfingers' or just 'Stumpy' to his friends—was slowly sketching out when they had moments to collaborate. Stumpy apparently was a slow and rather rough writer, and Shimon had joked that he might well die while waiting his friend to draw up the account in neat. Philippon had also promised to write. They waited. Would letters find them off the beaten track?

With their camp built, the mission began in earnest. At first, the wealth of Iosephus was worthless in a land where there was no money. Even barter was little used, though one might trade fish for a part of sheep or for a joint of swine. Not that they had much to barter with, and some items were too precious to barter away.

Perpetua, for instance, had a silver menorah, a branch-like candle holder, a parting gift to remind her that there would always be a perfect light in the dark, connected to one perfect hand. Iosephus had brought a special golden cup and silver plate, heirlooms of his family which he and his beloved Imma had used in their weekend celebrations. Imma too had had a menorah, one of fine gold. Such things would remind him of his old and new life. Kornelios had a golden plate, given to him as a gift from the Yehudim whom he had earnestly supported, and who had been the Dawn before the Day. Destinatio too, forged in flame by the Empire, reminded them that their fight was a new kind of warfare, one not based on physical weapons, but waged by Ruach to the pulling down of unseen strongholds, a warfare begun by death. Unknown strangers had also given to Iosephus a pure white shield of curious design and without device, saying that it should be kept as an heirloom, a token of purity that should drive and support the mission.

Yes, in a land where there were no pennies, they were penniless, and they found that they just had to rely on grace, on goodness of heart, on generosity. As teachers they had come to graciously give; as students, they had to learn to graciously receive—Yasmina led the way. And that was what Yavion had meant, when he had spoken about the sindeldi being prepared to help out the seed, but not the plant. He was obviously sympathetic to the cause, and just as obviously not permitted to engage overmuch in the affairs of man— whom he called the secondborn.

And without goodwill they soon would have foundered, lacking a spoken language to communicate with among their own kind. But the sindeldi were patient teachers and taught them the twisting tongues of many tribes, such as *Y gwir yn erbyn y byd*! Once established, they in turn had enriching truth to tell, yet even before tongue could tell, life could tell, and by their fruits they became loved and trusted by the local indigenous peoples, a blessing even to those of Prince Brutus of Troy, with whom they soon met. For they came not to take land, but to give land, to give a new dimension to life, and even to give the Light of Life. They were a holy and happy people.

∞

Less happy was Wulfgar, who neither knew of nor cared about their mission. Emerging from his cave he had limped back to his home among the Brigantes, where he had in fact lived quite a quiet life, little disturbed even by his inner guests. They had long before come to him because he had been getting weary and needed buttressing, shoring up. He had not been the first vampire to take onboard some diaboloi to get through life. His guests were mere tertiaries, able to support his life, though annoying at times like so many flies buzzing around inside his head.

But life must go on. In repayment, he had given way to them on numerous occasions and in various little ways, supplying them with blood to revel in—not to drink, for they were not of organic kind. He never liked to consider himself evil, and hid behind the idea of being a victim, in particular a victim of Usen's evil Eighth Law. Now after his latest beating, his life was once more in jeopardy, not from aging frailty—needing the buttress of but few—but from the manifold mauling of his will.

Keeping body and soul together was only maintained with great difficulty, and his life force hovered on the borderline. In his woe, it would have been of some consolation to have known how close he had come to winning that cat and dog battle. Not that he had wished to win, only to survive. And had his opponent allowed him to escape the cave, he might have fled away with lesser wounds. With escape cut off, cornered, his terrible fight had been to death's door, and only when he could fight no more, had his enemy fought no more. The agents of Usen were so unfair.

Now he sought fresh allies to restore him, a booster to bolster his will. Telepathically he cried out for helpers from among the Powers of

Darkness, the Turannoi. In conjunction his guests also cried out—Dark cries to Dark—for they would not be parted from their host. It was not long before offers of help began to arrive. These were spirits which were well established in Brigantia, and knew of him well enough, for he had long made his home among them. The Dark vampires had never been their natural enemy, and some alliances between their kinds had been formed over the Ages. Guesting with individual vampires was a long and respected tradition. Guesting gave them a certain level of protection, a certain camouflage from the Philikoi, and still allowed a useful mobility.

Some of the Turannoi lived long in fixed objects, such as stone or wood, and were content to draw the secondborn to them. Others preferred to prowl about, causing mischief and mayhem. But prowling around alone removed them from the physicality they enjoyed. A host they could totally control offered some advantages, but also could limit what they could control. So a host with clout, was preferred to a host without clout. The very best of hosts were vampire hosts, for they offered both a physical presence, and a firmness of will, which the Necros enjoyed. A vampire host had real clout, for they could stir up the secondborn as easily as a child can stir up an ant nest.

Much more could be said. For instance, a vampire host also had a strong will, which made for stimulating tug of war, bull fights between host and guest, more stimulation than could be found among the sickly secondborn. After all, vampires were basically thelodynamic beings of billennia years, which had eventually incarnated themselves within the orb of Arda. Playing mind games with strong opponents, infuriating strong hosts, made for rich entertainment, lifting life out of the mundane. There was no love lost between the Night and the Necros. There never had been love between the Night and the Necros. There was no love within the Night and the Necros—officially at least. Power, survival, dominance—such were the things they both sought, and mutual annoyance was all part of the give and take of self.

A host like Wulfgar—putting out the welcome mat, advertising it to the four winds—why, that was a rare opportunity for any dunamos worth their salt, to grab with both hands, so to speak. Wulfgar knew it, and knew that he could be choosy. He also knew that he must choose swiftly, lest his will collapsed and beyond death and bodiless he stood before the judgment seat of the Great Tyrant. Dalliance can be deadly.

Of the candidates which had come to him, it had been Andraste that he had chosen. She was a powerful enough dunamos, a fair to middling second-grade Turannos, not so strong as to overshadow him, but strong enough so as to stabilise him. Yet she was sharp enough to be a thorn in his side, a price he chose to pay. She was not the kind to be content with a few minor killings here and there. She had long been worshipped by the Brigantes, and he knew that he would have to work harder to keep her happy and off his back—but at least he would have a hapless back to be harried. As they conjoined, he felt at once a sense of satisfaction flowing through him, an easing of tension, and a fortification of will. Yes, he had chosen well: his body relaxed; the ship moved easily to the command of the rudder. Andraste had worked her magic alright, but he would forever be at her beck and call until death did them part. Peaceful village life, in which he had lived as a venerable counsellor to the crown, would no longer be his lot.

Almost at once, she began scheming for war, for in war she delighted. With the advent of Rome, the possibilities for bloody battle had increased—until Rome could subdue all of her rivals and secure peace. Even then, Rome could engage Rome in uncivil war. A time when the setting moon could fight the rising sun was always a welcome opportunity for the Necroi—it was peace and stability that they hated. Without physicality, their freedom to rain terror was rather impeded by the aggeloi, but since the Philikoi had a basic hands-off policy with the Pneumata, to operate through the Pneumata—such as vampires—could be fun, a little bit of harmful cheating on the side.

And there was an added irony in having access to a vampire simply because the aggeloi had handled it too roughly—it was as if heaven had created a paradise just for hell. Very few years had passed before Andraste had decided how to proceed—breaking up a kingdom by breaking up a marriage. The latter—always an enjoyable pastime—would make a delightful bonus. Her plan should yield a great harvest of anguish and bitterness, besides affording her the satisfaction of revenge, for the wife she had in mind had dumped her in favour of Roman divinities.

The home of Venutius and Cartimandua was sweet. Before marriage, both had thought it foul shame and dishonour to marry unless upheld by love. It was a strange approach to marriage, but surprisingly often turned out well. That said, all knew that man-woman romance was a fickle idol to serve even at the best of times, even if she wore a pleasant enough face. Alas, she was not going to serve them well this time, for Andraste would bend her to her own will. Both royal born, they had met and fallen in love. Both had had mild flirtations before, Cartimandua had even had a girlish crush on another princess, a common enough phase, but soon boys had caught her imagination, as she had blossomed into womanhood.

It is not to say that they had approached their marriage without any romantic disappointments—sweet names they could still name with a slight sigh—but they could both approach their marriage as untouched, chaste, eager. Yes, other choices might have been made, but they had both made a good choice and were happy and content with each other in a rapidly changing world. And as king and queen of the Brigantes, they needed unity at home for unity of the kingdom, for Rome was bustling in, and they who did not bend to the storm would break.

Together they accepted Rome as a partner, in some ways a useful one. Rome laid roads and taught them technologies that they had not even imagined, helping their kingdom in many ways, not least by the foreign administration of justice, and by the importation of luxury goods. In exchange, they were providing some materials for the Roman Empire, aggrandisement for her emperor, and pathways for greater mineral rights in their island. Admittedly not all of their people, or neighbours for that matter, were happy with the part that the royal couple played. Some even believed that they were betraying their island to a hostile takeover bid.

Still, Rome paid well they who served her best, and all seemed blest. It had all started to unwind when Publius Ostorius Scapula had commissioned Venutius on Rome's behest, to go and hold council with Caradog, king of a great swathe of land to the south, urging him to hand back control over the Atrebates, a tribe for long friendly with Rome. Perhaps unwisely his wife had not gone with him, and he had had to stay several weeks, for Caradog had tarried overlong before setting forth, and had spent long days in discourse with him.

They had had tough negotiations, in which Caradog had sought for Venutius' assistance in chasing Rome out of the country. Admittedly that idea had had a certain attraction for Venutius. Also, admittedly, had Huctia, a princess of his own people, who lived where the two kings had met. She was a rare beauty and could have tempted a better man than Venutius. But though flattered by her smiles and attention, he refused her love by reason of his faithful faith that kept him truly true to his wife. She had been but young and flirtatious, and girlishly in love with this strong king, son of Strong Dog, who had reigned before him. Indeed, she never really considered the dangers involved, both for herself and for others.

Had he said he loved her, she would have been lost, frightened, and unable to cope would have backed off. It had seemed safe to flirt, to tease in public, to show off her charm, develop her arts. For his part he had smiled upon her—do not men easily misread the alluring charms of the coquette? Others had noticed, but others would be silent. There was, however, an unobserved shadow hanging over their heads, even Wulfgar, put upon the trail by Andraste.

Queen Cartimandua had truly been untrue, not to Venutius, but to Andraste. For she had become a devotee of Rome, captivated by its glory, and had all too readily traded in her rustic divinities for Roman versions. As word of her betrayal had seeped out, the invincibility of Andraste had begun to be questioned, and her following as a Dark Divinity had reduced—and she was vexed. It was petty on her part, perhaps, but such are the diaboloi, quick to take offense over any attack on their pride, counting with pride their followers. Andraste now sought to demolish her former devotee with a vengeance, attacking first her heart, for the silly thing was still 'in love', as the human dung put it. In this way the first shadow of a great evil crept into the Kingdom of Brigantia, so silent and innocent in seeming, that no one seemed to notice.

Any pleasant looking princess is born to break a few hearts, and to look back in later years with a sense of satisfaction, feeling the more how her husband has been honoured by her hand. And princes too can be charming, sweet-talking the gay and innocent, going perhaps a little far, but not really too far. All such things can pass quietly under the bridge, without any real harm being done. However, the powers of evil, seeking now more and more deviously to find even a tiny fault line through which to undermine the good, saw it, and set a cunning snare for Venutius. Cartimandua would hear false reports, and rue the day when she had cancelled on Andraste.

The queen had sent a handmaiden, Verica, to be a part of the entourage of her husband. Unexpectedly Verica had returned, well ahead of the mission, swearing on her knife that she had closely observed Venutius, and witnessed at night his betrayal of his wife. "No other will tell you of this, my queen, for no other eyes beheld, nor wished to behold. But question them, and discover whether or not they beheld the look of love between both eyes, yea, in public and without concealment. I do not blame him, for the eyes of a fair woman are hard for a man alone to withstand, or so it is said. But it is yours to attribute blame or not, my queen. I but speak what I have seen." With a great deal more words she went on to give details, which allowed for no doubt as to the crime. The queen was wrath at her betrayal, perfidia beyond bearing! The love of her life, in somebody else's arms! She would have Princess Huctia's head on a pikestaff, and make a man out of her before she died!

As to her husband, the matter needed careful thought. Regicide was not to be undertaken on a whim, for civil war could be the outcome. Verica she sent back to the camp to continue as her spy. If Venutius had fallen deeper than dalliance, he might seek some misfortune upon the queen, so as to supplant her with a new queen. It was better for her to know sooner rather than later of any such plot. Anyway, her husband's fate could hang in the balance—so perhaps better for him not to know of his paramour's fate.

Her execution would be a private affair. A kidnap by unknown hands, then a secret grove where the queen would butcher the girl, the ravens would enjoy the leftovers, and the kidnappers would neither live long nor prosper. Yes, even those who disposed of them could then be disposed of, removing all links to the wretched wench. And the sweeter if the king simmered in suspicion. Yes, let him linger in fear, afraid yet afraid to say so, held captive by uncertainty. To make matters worse for him, she should display a dalliance on her part, for why should disloyalty not follow disloyalty? She wondered whether taking Vellocatus, battle-servant of Venutius, would be suitably galling to the king.

The next night, Brigomaglos, trusted servant of Venutius, arrived at the camp and spoke urgently to the king in private. Brigomaglos was of the same tribe as the king, and had once saved the king's life in battle. He had been left to keep a protective eye on the queen, but his news was evil. "O king, may victory ever be yours, even as the old ways shall never be defeated by the new. Yet hearken my liege with sadness, and tear your beard. For I, Brigomaglos, have beheld an evil such as never I wished to see. May my eyes wither in my head, and my head from my shoulders, once I have spoken to you. For behold, I watched the queen that she be safe—for always there are spies who would usurp your kingdom, either from the old side or from the new. Alas, the new I fear has sent you away to woo Caradog unto Rome, while under that pretence to woo your queen in the night, ever at their beck and call."

At that point, Brigomaglos had felt the cold sharp knife of Venutius tickling his throat, slightly severing the skin. Even as a little trickle of blood flowed down, he ventured to end his story. "My lord, slay me as you will, but hear my words I pray. It is the governor himself, having given you this mission, who has taken your absence to take your wife. I Brigomaglos watched unseen until the break of dawn. Alas that she was full willing—and no new thing. My lord, slay me and take heed for your head."

The knife hesitated at his throat, and neither moved, until the trickle of tears began to reluctantly trickle down the face of Venutius. Ambassadors must always be treated with respect, for as you treat you will be treated—"don't blame the messenger for the message", had become a byword. What was Brigomaglos but his messenger? He would return to Cartimandua, sadder, wiser, and more observant. When had her love for him died, that she found her amusement in the arms of another? Dumped as Andraste as too rustic? Perhaps her lust for power?

He knew that he was less keen than she to be absorbed into the Empire of Rome. Did she plan to oust him, perhaps to marry

Ostorius? Did she have affection for the governor, or was he merely a means to an end? Brigomaglos must be sent back to observe and report. Rome was a right sod, asking him to gain an ally, while seeking to usurp his throne. Perhaps Caradog was right to fight against Rome, but her Legions were not to be underestimated. He would be cautious, concealing his mind even from his feckless wife. His kingdom mattered more than revenge. But his love was undone, and he wept again.

The next day, the camp and the capitol wept over the inexplicable deaths of two good servants, of Verica, and of Brigomaglos. One body had been found, its neck broken—an accident, maybe. The other had been found, its blood drained. Two there were, a king and a queen, who both believed that they could explain at least one of the deaths, yet they were both mistaken. For thus it was that Wulfgar, incited by Andraste, had taken the shape of both, delivering false reports to king and to queen, and then terminating those who could spill the beans. For many months he had shadow-menaced both, learning their style of speech until he could mimic both flawlessly. His words had sunk in, and the servants' deaths would if anything vouchsafe his words. He had successfully planted deep roots of bitterness, from which would surely grow a delicious harvest of disunity and disaffection. Besides rejoicing in his own skills, he also rejoiced in the fact that Andraste would lay off him for a while, in payment for his cooperation.

As history still remembers, it was not long before the queen took for herself another as husband, having divorced her first love. After some remains of the princess had been found, and unspoken suspicions rose against the queen, life with the king had become grim—a king is but a man. His affection for her had vanished as the morning mist in the summer sun. He had never even ventured to apologise for his scandalous affair. It had even seemed to her that *he* ludicrously levelled all the blame at *her*, and even desecrated the noble name of Ostorius. Poor old Ostorius soon burnt out for his beloved Rome— or was he being poisoned off? The expressions of Venutius, his innuendoes, his lack of courtesy, his manifest distrust—how very annoying! And she, the offended one!

No wonder that she had finally decided to drop the cloak of secrecy and officially find solace elsewhere. Well, hubby was directly responsible for her infidelity, so let him stew in the juice of his own making! The bickering had become ballistic. She had finally had enough and, despising him beyond words, demanded divorce. Venutius wouldn't stand for that, and threatened to dethrone her and the Roman baggage as well. He seemed to blame Rome rather than Huctia—the nerve of the man! Fortunately, she had handed over the old enemy Caradog, and proved thereby her loyalty to Rome, so in turn Rome would surely stand by her against the king. And thus it proved, for though many—belonging to the old ways—stood with Venutius against the queen, the new Roman governor, Marcus Vettius Bolanus, stood firmly with the queen—a powerful ally. With all the ingredients for a perfect storm, a bloody civil war began, and the diaboloi squealed in perfect delight.

∞

Wulfgar, though cloaked as an old man, was nevertheless cloaked with vigour. As such it had not seemed strange to see him riding with the host of the king. He could use his powers to defend himself, but he would not use them to quickly win the war. Indeed his guests, maddened by Andraste, now thirsted for more blood and mayhem. To him, it was a waste of good blood. To them, it was as sweet blood poured out upon their sacrificial altar—it would smell good if they could but smell it. He became used to stalking the killing fields over which the battle had gone, draining to the last drop the mortal life of the dying. Perhaps he vaguely sought to atone for the bloodshed he had caused, by at least shortening their otherwise long-drawn-out pain.

Yet his care led to carelessness. Roman riders had swept in among foot soldiers who had been retreating from Stanwick to Wincobank. Hacked bodies were lying strewn around the fields, and Wulfgar, arriving minutes later, had dismounted and was helping himself— and the grateful dying. One puny but pugnacious rider lay behind him besides a horse. A mere corpse, or so Wulfgar had assumed. His guests might have warned him, but Andraste held them quiet. Slowly the corpse rose to a squat, raising itself with the help of a javelin. To its eyes, the old man was an enemy, and death was a rightful reward for disturbing the dying—whatever occult ritual he was performing.

Yea, no corpse was it yet, for for a few more moments, mortal life flickered in its eyes, and the pale rider steadied himself for a last strike, before joining his ancestors. The cry of Wulfgar was heard all over those fields, and black wings of black birds arose in flight, their feast on fresh flesh rudely interrupted. Right through his heart the spear had been rammed, from back to front, and he had fallen with a corpse toppling onto him, for the rider had fled in that final act of defiance. Though pinned on the shaft of a spear, the stubborn will of Wulfgar clung frantically to his bodily life, as blood soaked through his garments as sweat on a summer day. His limbs were powerless, and his guests wailed—they had not really wished their host to be slain, for he was useful. His telepathic cry summoned diaboloi to his will, for he urgently needed help as never he had needed help before.

So it was that a dunamos who had watched the show, even she who named as her servants was Brigantia, joined her mind with his mind, her will with his will. With her, his guests were beefed up, and drawing on their will his limbs worked once more, and he held his body secure as he pulled the thin pilum through his body and out of his heart.

The mortal body of a vampire relies heavily on its DNA organs, somewhat as a soldier relies on their armour. Yet their willpower exceeds most physical failings, sometimes sustaining even their greater organs. But without reinforcement, a pierced heart, or a severed head, would by that Age have been fatal. Only intervention by the Necros, enabled Wulfgar to stagger away in his human form, finding a copse where he could hide undisturbed while repairing his heart to its proper state. But he had paid the price of carelessness, and knew that he was bound the closer by dunamoi—and they would not easily forget the debt he owed.

Far from Wulfgar, there was much more peace. Word was leaking out that those from an enchanted ship had new thoughts to teach; a new kind of life to live. The hidden haunts of the Britons—inaccessible to the Romans—were never on the lookout for new beliefs, but nevertheless had a natural curiosity, a passive interest in alternative and additional beliefs about the spirit world. Those who knew of the Tree Dwellers, the Secret People, and had heard tell of the enchanted ship which had sailed in through the wall of silver mist, proved most ready to listen. But puzzlingly the incomers were clear that divinities, however much helpful in the past, were now best left for dead. It'd be simpler simply to add to their collection of divinities, rather than having to subtract down to one.

Nevertheless, the new deal had its attractions, not least accessing the mystique which the travellers of The Way had brought with them. It was truly a marvel that they had been carried on the arms of a violent storm, a storm which had so mysteriously abated as they had sailed through the Gates of Splendour. And through the silver mist the mysterious Tree People had awaited them on their mysterious island—known to some as Enys Avalow, or Avalon. As to the travellers, although their local speech was painful, the fact that they tried to learn it was praiseworthy. All in all, they seemed to be a kindly bunch, not too proud to receive help from others, and eager to understand their ways and also their concerns. When it came to illnesses, for instance, they were happy to learn the secrets of herbal remedies, though prone both to ask healing from Kurion, and to cast away the hooded spirits of healing. Asked why they did not pray rather to their Hamashiach, they replied that he had taught them to ask he who was to him, and to them, as father.

Though they did not ask Hamashiach for the ubiquities of life, yet they bowed down before him in reverence and praise, for in him, they said, they praised Huion himself—as praising the sunbeam praises the sun. And Huion, they said, was one with Kurion, who was the emperor over deep heaven. Bit by bit the Britons perceived that Hamashiach was somehow a limited manifestation of an eternal, and was now a creature immortal, and that Huion and his master, Kurion, were part of one Council, uncreated, in will one, so that if Huion spoke, it was Kurion who spoke, and so the Council could be called, Kurion. And Hamashiach, the Way Maker, was the special road to Kurion, even as a son to a father. Moreover, these incomers also said that living with Hamashiach would both assure them of life unending with the source of life, and that they could know such immortal joy even on the mortal road. To begin the journey they needed only to welcome the Road, and Ruach would guide their journey.

The travellers soon began taking walks every seventh day. Not far at first, but gradually becoming further. They did this both to familiarise themselves with the lay of the land and become more independent, and also to proclaim their message by dramaturgy, even as Ruach— another whom they worshipped—had taught them. For on these walks they employed various artefacts, carried from their former lands and now imbued with new meaning for a new home.

At the front would walk Iosephus, carrying a curiously shaped sword. Following him came four maidens, not maybe maidens in the sense of never having known a man, but maidens in the sense of all being as handmaidens to Hamashiach, of living a life of purity and dedication beyond the mortal lot. And their faces were all aglow. First of all, there usually came Perpetua, carrying her candlestick of seven candles—a *menorah*, she called it. Following her might be her twin sister, Vibia, carrying the spear of destiny. Following her perhaps was Yasmina, carrying a silver dish. Following her could be Havingues, carrying the golden cup. Iosephus followed in silence, but the maidens sang over and over in some unknown tongue: *gloria in excelsis deo et in terra pax hominibus bonae voluntatis laudamus te benedicimus te.*

As if charmed by a good spell, many people would follow, beholding marvels. For by aggelic power special signs and wonders were to be seen. For as the procession walked through the forest glades, even on the dullest of days preternatural sunbeams seemed to dance around and about them. And any face so illuminated would momentarily show the real self within. Those you might despise might seem such as you could happily die for, as sons and daughters of the highest. Those you might desire might be exposed as bestial or devilish, as a beast of the forest that does not give a toss for your wellbeing; as a son or daughter of that which festers below, gnashing its teeth. But whatever was revealed, it made you think about what mere humanity meant—was each soul a spark of eternity, whether vivid flame or dying ember?

And besides beholding the fair beauty of the maidens—even the oldest looked in that light as if age did not weary them, nor the years condemn—there were the wonders of the items carried. For bread would be freshly baked and set on the plate. And fragrant wine would be poured into the cup. And before each procession set off, the items would be covered by white silk. Then the aggeloi would cause both plate and cup to shine as if windows to the beyond, the unlit candles of the menorah to burn without being consumed, and the spear to seemingly drip blood which left no stain on the ground. Such visual magic was but a primitive language which the people could understand, attention grabbers, parables in motion. It would not always be spoken, but for a time, for a season, it was used to open the eyes of the blind. The season was for many a generation as yet unborn.

The Britonians were also impressed by the fact that The Way reached out to both commoners and protectors, even unto their kings. For The Way taught that all people were created equal, that all mankind was born as imagodei, however much human society had stratified in levels of power and authority. Such stratification only appertained to mortal life, and would soon disappear into the oblivity of meaninglessness. Still, for practicality it had to be taken into account, and thus it was that The Way always made a special effort to welcome those in high places, not just those in low. This was because the socially weak needed the socially strong for protection, a linking of need and duty. And if their protectors were unhappy with them joining The Way, there was no way that they could safely join. After all, life was often hard enough as it was: against an angry sword, should you annoy your shield?

Above and beyond the daily dangers of bears and boars, there were bandits who roved the land like wolves, bad people who had been kicked out of their villages for an assortment of misdemeanours, and who banded together to take common revenge against common humanity. Good people too can turn bitter. There was a less seen baleful influence, for a sister of Nimue had ill-will towards the secondborn. She sought that the sindeldi should arise and rule over the secondborn with a heavy hand. The name of Morgana le Fay was evil, yet Yavion still kept her within his council, believing that sooner or later she would come good, submitting to the will of Usen.

The processions would travel far, stop, and then hold a mystery play, after which they would return to base. The plays were enactments of the birth, travels, and golgothic battle of Hamashiach, when he went skull to skull with death to defeat death—though death still staggers on for a brief season like one half-dead. After the play they would conclude with a thanksgiving meal, which they related to that battle. Of course, the troupe had attracted quite a bit of interest, which had slowly crept up the social ladder. But they were all surprised, and challenged, when King Cynwrig had come out to meet them.

By that time they had established set routes in set orders, a routine to allow people to easily connect. Cynwrig, a junior king, was high up the pecking order, but he had first to be seen as a needy person in his own right. It would have offended their Order—they had by then adopted the people's name of the Order of the Grail—had they sought his soul not for his sake but as bait for others, as a badge in which to boast or a tool to be used. Knock-on effects would follow.

If he rejected, the dangerous temptation for those lower down the pecking order would then be of trading away The Way for political protection: putting man's blessing above Usen's blessing. Conversely, a favourable effect would have a positive knock-on effect on those lower down the social chain.

If he accepted, the dangerous temptation for those lower down the pecking order would then be of taking up The Way for political advantage: putting man's blessing above Usen's blessing.

Each human being to whom it was offered, should choose on facts without fear or favour—is it right?, not, will it help or harm me? It seemed best for his people if Cynwrig took a mediating position, not influencing those in his kingdom either way. But for the sake of his own soul, their job was to try to persuade him to enter The Way. If they succeeded, his job would be to publicly declare himself impartial to those who either agreed or disagreed with his choice. To feign a welcome of Hamashiach was no way to respect him, didn't do anybody any good, and weakened The Way by creating an outer layer of hypocrisy, a zone for bloodsuckers.

As it turned out, Cynwrig was impressed by what he saw, and invited the Order to make their pitch. From him they also learned that as they had suspected, they had landed in Britonia. Long ago Cynwrig had peacefully met with Roman soldiers, been impressed by Rome in many ways, and learned their speech. However, he predicted conflict for many a long year, for Britons did not like being forced to change their ways, nor did they wish to cede sovereignty to those from east of the waters. But that was not what he most wished to speak of.

"Iosephus, your age does you credit, as does your wealth, for I understand that money matters, and that you have been content to live among my people as a beggar rather than as a lord. That you could have moved to where Rome has taken hold, and been deemed a wealthy man, I also know. At your time in life also, to have moved to the sticks, not as a criminal but of your own free will, I greatly admire. The signs and wonders I have seen move me, but our own divinities also do marvels. If they can be friends with your Kurion, Huion, and Ruach, of those you say have spoken in Hamashiach, then I would gladly embrace them all. But you say the choice is between loyalty to those long loyal to me, and trading loyalty to them for loyalty to foreign divinities—who might or might not be loyal to me. And why should they offer loyalty to me, if I disloyally cast out those who have done me no wrong? For might I not in turn cast them out, if others come unto me?"

"Cynwrig," replied Iosephus, "I can testify that they have been loyal to me, and sustained me through hard times. After a fashion my own people worshipped Kurion—though they knew neither Huion nor Ruach. When I met Hamashiach—whom we called Barnasa—I came to see, through the things he did and taught and was, that he was truly from Kurion. And yet within the Supreme Council on which I served, broadmindedness stopped well short of tolerating any who disagreed with them, and I soon fell quiet—to my shame. Only one like-minded man I found among all my peers.

"But our hopes were mercilessly dashed to pieces by Hamashiach's death—for who returns from that journey, and how could an undying hope die? Yet my loyalty, hidden from my people, surfaced to efface my shame, and impelled me to take my life in my hands and beg the foreign governor—for the Empire had also taken root among us—for the corpse of one whom the Empire had sentenced for high treason. Never had any dared to have asked for such a body to be released into their charge, and yet the governor gladly yielded to my request.

"Clearly, I said to myself, he has been cornered into a verdict in which he has not believed, for if he believes otherwise my life would be forfeit and my wealth could not save me. And there I met with the soldier in charge of the execution, even Longinus, whose destiny has brought him not to these shores. He it was who was summoned to the governor to confirm or to deny the death of Hamashiach. This very spear which you have seen in procession, was used by his men to pierce our master's side, proving beyond doubt that he had died. Longinus had seen enough corpses to last his lifetime, and well knew the marks of death.

"My tomb," continued Iosephus, "lay nearby, hewn into the rock face of an old stone quarry, and awaited me. Yet happy it was to receive another, for there—helped by a friend and our servants—we took the body. Yet we hardly knew why we bothered. Our minds told us that death had proved him both imposter and deceiver, and yet our hearts said nay. Ruach sustained us in our sorrow and remorse, until proclaiming some days later that Hamashiach had returned from death, victorious. We were among hundreds who then met and spoke with him and now stand as witnesses, who otherwise might have stood as hostile witnesses to a deception, as those of the disappointed. It was Ruach who has sent us to you. Which of your divinities has died to save you, and risen from death to greet you?"

The whys and wherefores of Hamashiach's fight with death, and in what ways it made followers at one with Usen, were deeply discussed well into the night. Also that he had been forecast for over two thousand years, made a deep impression on Cynwrig, for that was a token of loyalty to all mankind, a global commitment. Iosephus had spoken of the Usenic Way being widest and deep—and there is none deeper than Usen—the Kurionic Way being narrower and deeper, and the Hamashianic Way being narrowest and deepest of all. Yes, what the Order said about Kurion, Huion, and Ruach, made sense, as well as Hamashiach being the embodiment of Huion, representing not just Kurion, but their togetherness, Usen.

It began to look like the name Usen could be a community, a society name; that the love between Kurion and Huion was like the love between a father and his one, his one-of-a-kind, son. That such a son's life would be surrendered that children of a created type might live, fired his heart and imagination. This was not a love which his divinities offered. He was being invited to offer loyalty to Love, not to Help. He knelt and pledged his loyalty to Usen's three-person identity, Kurion, Huion, and Ruach, and pledged with Ruach's help to live his life worthily unto Hamashiach.

The following morning the Order invited him to partake of the holy meal. Lucius shared about how the meal spoke to him. Basing his thoughts on the old Sheep—though he was not of them—he spoke of how they had had an annual festival, based on the slaying of lambs on a date they called Nisan 14. Now Hamashiach, beginning the feast the next day—that is, immediately the sun had set—had said that that festival prophesied his death. For like the lambs his body would be slain, though not broken. For like the lambs, his life's blood would be shed, yet not drained. Bread and wine, representing life and happiness, carried this message. So, he said to them all, tear off some bread, and think of Hamashiach's torn but unbroken body, surrendered for them. And take some wine, rejoicing that lambs no longer symbolise the ancient rituals of forgiveness by Kurion. For the event which symbolism had bespoken, had become the new level of history, and a new covenant was now in place for all to enjoy. And Cynwrig was glad.

After this ceremony, the king heard of a related ceremony, more meaningful in some parts of the world than in others. In some places it could identify you as liable to persecution at least, and execution at most. In fact, not *at most*, for others you loved could be slandered and slaughtered before your undying eyes, the guilt of their deaths loaded onto your shoulders, tears of blood torn from your eyes. Yet Huion became Hamashiach, whose soul would be pierced by a sword, who delighted to fulfil Usen's will through a death that stood written of him in the first volume of the book. His death was exaltation in agony and in honour, a death he would never repent of nor die again, and a death which would result in him seeing the degradation and death of many of his beloved family. A water ceremony was offered to all who welcomed him. It might be used against them, or might prosper their ways and defend them. Who could say? But any fallout was purely incidental, not a gamble. It was a badge they could wear in the ups and downs of life, a shield and a sword. A normative add-on.

Alongside his tent ran a stream. "See, here is water. Is there anything that forbids me from being baptised in it?" he asked. Perpetua and Vibia both laughed a long and merry melodious laugh. Why, said they, their father had had someone once ask him that very same question, and their answer would be the very same. Clearly he was a Hamashiachi, and unless they had serious doubts about that, their standing orders were crystal clear: comply with all you take to be genuine requests. Iosephus invited the sisters to do the honours—young bodies are better in cold streams than elderly bodies, he joked. Together with the king they waded into the stream, burying him under and raising him back up, re-enacting the death and resurrection of their lord, who had been immersed into death, yet had arisen as its undying victor.

As he squeezed out water from his beard, in the euphoria of exultation he spoke many words of praise to Hamashiach, though his words were only understood by four of their number, they who had learned it in their former life. Yasmina rejoiced beyond words to hear her mother tongue, once so much a part of daily life before her enforced enslavement. Yet she knelt, thanking Usen that her slavery was deeper still, and was now shared with a foreign king! For beyond all reasonable doubt, Cynwrig was within the family of The Way, a willing slave of Hamashiach himself.

Later that day, the king spoke with the Order about their dwellings. "It grieves me that you still live in rustic housing, and I wonder if I could be of any help. For instance, I could send you some excellent builders to build a building to be proud of. Those I have in mind are, to be sure, strange stunted creatures, long-bearded men and gruff of speech—though never crude. But they are marvellous beyond words with shaping stone and devising dwellings. They have worked on my hill fort, burrowing under it to allow many to sleep within and to go to and fro unseen between hill and woods. Such secret ways have doors of stone easily opening from within, and cunningly blended into the rocky slopes within the woods, so as to make them hidden except by those who know of their whereabouts. These builders speak also in reverence of the Tree People, whose favour you have.

"Indeed I do not know why the Tree People have not sent you the longbeards, as we call them—though they are an unsociable bunch. It was only by rescuing one whom we found wounded in a flooding creek, that we gained their friendship. A strange people, who do not worship they whom we have long revered. Rather, they revere one they name as the Great Smith, whom they claim to be their maker, a mighty chief among those they call the Máhani. Now that you have rescued me—as if a wounded man about to drown—I will give freely of stone and of wood and of whatever is needed, that henceforth you neither lack, nor are seen as beggars begging bread. You have but to ask and you shall receive."

It was a welcome offer. Kornelios had been wondering about a more permanent site, for the weather would soon turn cold and their stone huts would be tested by the elements. Besides, an edifice such as Rome might build would surely do credit to their mission, impressing the natives, and thus making it easier to be a blessing to them. "My thanks, Cynwrig. Of ourselves we have no items with which to trade, and only our blessings to give. And yet we learn from you that Rome has made inroads within the borders of your kingdom. We have a Roman purse, from which we would happily pay you what we can, that buildings might be built to the glory of Kurion. For our part, beggars we are happy to remain, that the people see that we work for their good, not for ourselves. But we would gladly buy of you livestock and seed, that we might fend for ourselves. And if these longbeards undertake to use their skills, mayhap they would take from us coin, whether Roman or such as you use among traders?"

Cynwrig smiled, assuring them that he would take no money from those who had given him meaning, nor indeed would the longbeards seek such wages, for, he said, they did not trade with his people, nor seemed to be in want of gold or gems. For the saving of one of their own, they counted repayment to be a chief duty, and had begged to undertake further work for the king. This only they had added, that they should be left to themselves, for they were of such people who kept themselves to themselves, trusting not to friendships with others.

In due course a number of these longbeards came into their camp, hauling loads of stone and lumber. They had few words to say to the

Order, but promised to build them buildings of wonder. They mentioned that they sometimes sailed to the mainland, and knew of Roman concrete, which Rome deemed a wonder. Yet that was the stuff of children, they said, which their own skills far exceeded. For they could form stone cladding by processes they would reveal to none, cladding which was less heavy yet more tough than any rock. They could even make what seemed to be stones that could float. Moreover, by their craft the walls could be hard to see, for from a distance they could blend in with the wild wood.

They worked, they said, with such of the tertiary Powers of Aulë who still remained in Middle-earth, Powers who had ever befriended them as children of the Smith, and as adoptees of Usen, who is the master of all. For the spirit servants of the Great Smith could reside within the work of the longbeards, and had the power to reveal or to conceal that which the longbeards hid, making unwanted discovery of their walls well nigh impossible. This edifice would be called Carbonek, and would be a place of mystery, but none must seek to learn their skills—which they would teach to none. And if ever the Order had no more need of their work, they would dissolve the outer shell into its base elements, thus surrendering the edifice into the hands of time. Beer also they brought with them—by the bucket load, and 'pipe weed', an art among their people which they taught to none, and would never catch on.

The history of these things is long past, but in Avalon Carbonek, built to the glory of Kurion, was for long a marvel throughout the region. The Order of the Grail remained an Order of Twelve. Celibacy followed by chaste marriage was encouraged. There were no rules precluding marriage with those outside of the Order, though generally only those from the Tree of Twelve were permitted to become Guardians of the Grail. Soon children were born to those of the Order. Having married Bron, a man outside of their Order—some say that he had sailed to Briton to rejoin his wife—he and Havingues were the first to announce a new arrival of a bouncing baby boy, whom they named Naciens. In him they would delight, despair, and delight again.

It was decreed that not all born to that Order would deserve to be in that Order—for nature is fallen. Therefore the birthrights of none entitled them to a place in the Order, for it was a holy Order. That however had become a thing of dispute when Naciens, having come into early manhood, sought to wrest for himself a place among the Twelve Guardians—for Kornelios had died and his body was still fresh in the ground, earth to earth. Truly, had Naciens alone been born of the Order, then by need the son of Havingues would likely have had his place at the table, but it was not so.

When it came to appointments into the Order, those born of the Order were to await the will of Hamashiach. But if the position gave rights, it also gave the burden of responsibilities. Either way, not all would wish his will to be his will for them. Alas, the foolish pride of Naciens, immature for his years, had led to dispute, and in the heat of pride Naciens had dared to brandish the Sword of Galeas. He resented the other children who had been born to the Twelve, and refused the counsel of the brothers Galeas and Giuseppe, sons of Iosephus. Sin, they warned him, is waiting to attack you like a lion and tear you apart—don't let it! It was fine for them, who were born before the Order but of the Order. It seemed to him that they were deliberately trying to undermine him, have his name dropped from the election process. Were the others not too young? After the brothers, he was the oldest—and best. Why should he not have the honour? Why should those two goody-two-shoes keep getting at him, always telling him off?

Galeas and Giuseppe, misunderstood, had become like two giant shadows over Naciens' life, shadows he should slay, so that the sun might shine on him. Fool! Did he think that he could wrest the honour by sword-waving antics and whinging? To be fair, it had started as a moment of madness—he had the makings of a good man. In a dark moment of the soul, he had yielded his will to a spirit of bitterness, and the diaboloi quickly tempted him to murder—"for the good of the mission," they lied, "for the good of the mission." And in his rage he had despised a sacred thing, and despised also the Order, treating it as a worldly thing where lords sought servants, rather than a sacred call where lords sought to be servants.

Naciens had repented in tears and sought to atone, but in youthful folly he had ventured beyond the safety of the Order, and had been trapped and taken as a vampire-slave. His new master was no less than Wulfgar, who incited to madness by his diaboloi guests, was taking measures to extinguish the imperishable flame within this land. Some say that Naciens had been cursed by Iosephus, given a heavy penance of undeath. Say rather that Naciens had brought it on himself through pride and folly, yet that Usen could turn even undeath into life, and that Naciens, a happier and wiser man, would yet become fast friends with Galeas and Giuseppe.

∞

Far from Carbonek, Longinus, himself a former slave to Wulfgar, had performed many mighty wonders, and many had come into The Way. Far and wide, word went out that the mute spoke, that the blind saw, and that idols were being forsaken in favour of The Way. That had eventually led to rioting, as they who made their living out of the idol trade saw their incomes being slashed. A leader of the opposition, a certain Irtemedus, rallied his fellow traders, and they in turn incited the town to riot. Naturally, they themselves did not get too involved, but by agitation, misinformation, and bankrolling of key rioters, they inflamed the city with violence. Buildings were damaged, the city became a no-go to policing—normal soldier-police were too likely to treat Longinus and his friends fairly—and even chariots were burnt.

Longinus was preaching that the idols that people made were not really divinities at all, and his foolishness was not to be tolerated by tolerant people—moderation must be in moderation. Like a lamb in an arena of lions, he would have been well and truly torn apart by the mindless mob. Fortunately, his friends persuaded him not to try reasoning with them. Reason can be just about the last thing an enraged herd will tolerate. Conveniently the crowd didn't fully know what it was it was protesting, only that it was apparently a time to unleash frustration, and to jingle-jangle like puppets on a chain.

Finally, a city official had forced the crowd to simmer down—once the rampage had safely run short of steam. The official affirmed Rome's policy of pro-choice idolisation; that all citizens had a right to their idols; that only fools would deny them such rights. But as to the wanton unrest, why, if they didn't listen to their city council, Rome might have to impose stricter measures, and they wouldn't want that! They had no proper excuse for such vandalous behaviour and unjustified uproar.

Not good enough. As if thumbing their noses at officialdom, they started shouting again to rid the earth of Longinus—as someone unfit to live. They kept on bellowing as the Bulls of Bashan, waving their cloaks around and throwing dust high into the air, until their government officials, instead of arresting them, arrested Longinus. If you fear the guilty, arrest the innocent. Side with the bigger crowd. All was politically correct and above board.

Initially, he was going to be interrogated and given a good old-fashioned public flogging, as any foreigner would be—until they realised that he was a retired centurion, and thus a citizen of the Empire. Then they changed their tune—fair trials for full citizens: that was the law. Nevertheless he was tried, and it was deemed proved beyond reasonable doubt that he had been guilty of Anti-Roman Agitation. And besides encouraging the rejection of idols without replacements, he had also been heard to speak out against slavery. He said such crazy things. He said that everyone ought to be a slave! Now, as the prosecutor pointed out, if all were slaves, where would the masters be? Since Rome was the master of masters, such preaching was subversive. Had they not heard enough?

The city council unanimously agreed to give Longinus the maximum punishment for his crime, technically of anti-master incitement. And as befitted a Roman citizen, he was sentenced to death by decapitation. They joked that if he wanted slaves to get rid of their *heads*, they would get rid of *his* to make him happy. Witnesses spoke about how he had died with a smile on his face, as if losing his head was a blessing long sought. And with his death, his shadowminder Umbra was reassigned to the overseas mission. There, they who had learned from Longinus all about vampire enslavement, had recognised the signs in Naciens, and Umbra, fortified by other aggeloi, having delivered him, had become his shadowminder. Yet, as it had been with Longinus, so too might Naciens have to endure the long stretching of years, and his pride would be cleansed from him, until the holy task laid on him had been accomplished. In the will of deep heaven it was ordained that, with an apron of humility, Naciens would serve the Last Galeas, until death sent him beyond the circles of the world.

Only a few more centuries had come and gone in the swift rapids of time. Wulfgar was once more being tormented by visions of the last unicorn, which he had unjustly slain. That race—even before the Fifth Age in its hornless state as *mearas*—had too often offended the Necroi, and they had finally contrived to put it at enmity with the secondborn of Usen. Falsely blaming the Unicorn People for murderous crimes against humanity, a people had arisen dedicated to the proposition that all unicorns were evil. And by the Sixth Age, the unicorns were so tied to their biological bodies, that to kill the body was to kill the person.

Perhaps had they turned to the firstborn, the sindeldi, they might have become a protected species, but mostly they were only gently moving from the Dark, and were just too short of the Grey Zone that they should seek out the Twilight People. They had fought well, but their haunts were ever betrayed to the avengers. At last only one remained, who had in desperation sought out the Kingdom of Night, and been accorded a safe place in which to dwell.

There he had sought to detransition from biologicality, transferring his essence to mineral form in which he could allow millennia to roll by before re-entering the biosphere—unless Usen released him from the Eighth Law. The Necros had never allowed him that chance, but had secretly sent in Wulfgar. Like him the unicorn had been a thelodynamic, a Pneuma, a cousin of sorts. Wulfgar was ashamed to have its blood upon his hands, and feared execution if his own kingdom got to know—if his guests blabbed. Often his guests would raise the spectre of that, when seeking to force him to comply with their will. Besides, they loved to torment him anyway.

Wulfgar had pleased neither Brigantia nor Andraste. Both dunamoi had expected so much more from him. First, they had agreed that he should never have lost Longinus—and so terribly soon, too—who had lived long enough after that to be a nuisance. Second, he had lost Naciens even sooner—a calamity. They made no excuses for Wulfgar's sheer bad luck, but every excuse for their lack of foresight. Naciens would have been a useful tool for infiltration and undermining—alas, a tool now lost to them forever. And though

Brigantia had gotten one little war out of Wulfgar, they had discovered that he also had a conscience. Now a conscience was an annoying encumbrance at the best of times, and he even struggled against them, like a fool trying desperately to hold on to the ways of his people, and more concerned about controlling his own life, than destroying other lives.

To some extent, he could still master himself, and subdue even the shame within. So it was that they could not switch on his guilt complex at will. That might take hours or centuries, depending on the ebb and flow of his self-will. And after losing Naciens, Wulfgar had grown sullen, harder still to subdue. And Naciens had become a problem for the Dark, for having vampire DNA, his lifespan had become excessive for his kind, allowing his wisdom and power to grow with the unfolding years. Worse, he had been restored, forgiven, made a special Grail Guardian. After his peers had all died, he began to wander the lands as a hermit, forming links with many mysterious communities.

Naciens soon knew the Lord and Lady of the Lake well, and had dealings with a master magician named Merlinus Ambrosius. In what time and place did Merlinus begin? Was he a love child between the firstborn and secondborn? Or fully of the firstborn, and trained from infancy in magic? Or beyond time and space, one of the lesser Guardians from the Dynamic Bubble, taken human form? Those who hated him lied, calling Merlinus a child of Darkness, though whether they meant of the Necros or of the Night, they were too ignorant to really say. Nor were they bothered by mere facts, so long as he was slandered. Merlinus was a man of the earth, the woods, the fields, the waters. He could even speak with mice and stoats, with birds and bears, none of which would suggest the bloodline of man. And he had the prophetic gift beyond the greatest of the Order, exceeding even Agabon himself, who had prophesied the mission.

Well, in whatever time and place—or otherwise—that Merlinus had arisen, he was now seeking to protect the mission against the pagan Saxons. That heathen people had been invited over to help King Vortigan against the unruly Picts of Scotland, and the bothersome Scots of Ireland. Now they decided that they liked his land too much to return to their own. In their wake, burial chambers became the ruins of houses or the bellies of beasts and birds.

Merlinus had witnessed an unlawful love between Uther Pendragon and Ygrayne—a woman beautiful beyond the lot of man, wife of another, and mother of daughters adopted by her husband. Such theft would harbour resentment and revenge. Not for the first time had a weak-willed king fought a loyal subject, just to win the widow. Yet soon Uther had been poisoned to death, and for safety's sake Merlinus had spirited away his son and heir, Arthur, giving him to the care of a knight named Sir Ector.

Uther had died for his sins against both friendship and marriage, but for the sake of Logres, which had birthed Camelot and was now borne up by it, Merlinus acted as he thought best to preserve a united front against Saxonisation. He himself had not always been of The Way, and was still thinking through its values when it came to making moral choices, and to using the rough magic he had dabbled in in earlier times.

His magic was less guilty than some, but less innocent than others, but any justification in using magic to control others was becoming less and less. Alas that Uther had not controlled himself, for unknown to him Ygrayne's husband had had a disease which would soon have made her a righteous widow, winnable without recourse to deception and without creating resentments.

Arthur bore no guilt, but in the eyes of Ygrayne's daughter Morgana—far older than she looked to the secondborn—he would bear the sin of his father, and she hated his kingdom unjustly. The Dark bound black bitterness around Morgana, long holding her enslaved within its well-woven webs of deceit, striving to darken Arda, silencing it from the cosmos, and the cosmos to it, so that its people would hear but one voice, its own. But Usen laughed, and Arthur was like a tiny seed that would grow into a tiny tree of Light— for a time, for a season.

So for a while the seed was hidden, until the soil was ready to receive it. Weeds had already sprung up, with the Saxons making steady inroads into the land. In Londinium the cavalry noblemen— otherwise known as knights—met together in celebration of

Hamashiach's birth. In northern lands a winter day had been chosen to specifically act as an annual day of remembrance, symbolizing how in the great winter of history, a light had been born to begin the true spring. Iosephus might first have laughed at this little innovation, but perhaps on reflection would have welcomed it as one more prop to re-enact the greatest drama of the cosmos, when its true king came to it, riding on a humble donkey, not on a war horse.

It was at this place and season that the true king of Briton was revealed, for a marvel was used to witness to Usen's choice. For the assembled nobles discovered that a great stone had appeared out of the blue. On it stood a large anvil, and within the anvil was a sword, and upon a plinth were inscribed words—that only the true king could draw forth the sword. Many tried; none succeeded; all gave up. A few days later a sixteen-year-old lad named Arthur, seeing that sword, drew it out to give to his swordless step-brother, Sir Kay. Arthur had not read the words, but Sir Kay had, and he was keeping mum. However, Sir Ector, suspicious of his son, soon discovered who had drawn forth the sword, and soon the other knights saw that the sword bore witness to Arthur.

Even so, unsure as to whether it was a sign from Usen or a trick of Necuratu, not all believed its witness until after a summer of discontent. Then Merlinus himself spoke out—confirmed by Sir Ector—that Arthur had been the legitimised son and only son of Uther Pendragon, and that the sindeldi people, who lived still in Avalon, had blessed him richly, and would befriend him as if of their race. Since they were known to be mysterious—of the Land of Faërie, some said—what then did that make Arthur? The Pendragon's tree had been fully human, so might there have been something special about Ygrayne that they had not known, and if so, what of her daughters of birthfather and birthdates unknown?

Once crowned, King Arthur began to claw back the loss of land from the Saxon peoples, and to relight the candles which they had snuffed out. As for bringing them into the Light, why that was never even imagined, a fantasy too far. He proved to be a mighty and a just king, and wise for the better part. Many began to believe the rumours that his blood was mingled with the dwellers of Avalon, with whom he was on good terms. Indeed they had given him one of their very own swords, a sword in which an awareness seemed to live, a sword named Excalibur.

The lady herself had come forth from her island home, which lay half-hidden by mystic mists, and waited for him on the secret lake, that met the hidden pass between the dark, enshrouded hills. A boat had taken him to where an arm had risen from the surface of the water, handing him the sword. This sword drawn from the lake was far greater than the lesser sword drawn from the anvil. That sword had soon been broken. Excalibur came with a charmed scabbard, which would minimise harm done to the wearer, even as Excalibur, ever obedient to the hand which wielded it, would maximise the harm it did to those it greeted in joyous battle.

But Arthur's first fight in anger had shown that greater power could lead to greater temptation. Only by the direct intervention of Merlinus, had Arthur drawn back from destroying King Pellinore with his new sword, and sheathed his petty rage in peace. But though King Arthur could be hasty and vengeful, he was nevertheless wise in many of his ways, and ordered his kingdom for the greater good, not for his benefit. Indeed he sought for many true knights to come together to form a Circle of Logres, knights who would help temper his temper by their wisdom. He knew that without his guidance his nation would fall, and that without many advisers he would fall.

What of King Pellinore? He was a neighbouring pagan king, standing taller than most and with the muscle to match, a man well trained in the martial arts. Yet he was no bully, and having suffered betrayal within his kingdom, had believed that those troubles had been sparked off by spies entering his kingdom as knights. Fearing further incursions, he himself sometimes went on border patrol, forcing all knights who wished to pass through, to fight him. They could turn around and go home, or accept his challenge and invariably be defeated. Those who survived had to swear loyalty to him. Eventually, none would dare to darken his domain, he hoped, and he could sleep well at nights once more.

Little had he dreamed that King Arthur himself would take up the challenge, as if to clear the road of one dark blot. Had it not been for Merlinus, he would have taken Arthur's life there and then, even as Arthur would have taken his later. But Merlinus knew that the misguided heart of Pellinore was good, and that he would within a few years enter The Way and prove a loyal ally to Arthur. In Pellinore the Necros had once more tried to snuff out the Light of Logres, which ever it saw was a power of good for Briton.

What was Logres? It was a holy haunting, a special background sound or scent, a remembrance, a nonpersonal spirit forged over long years of dealings between the firstborn, the secondborn, and the Guardians of their land. It defined the land. It was a realm of righteousness, a lighthouse, a bastion of Light within Briton. Yet even as sunlight is not a part of any earthly kingdom, so Logres was not a part of any kingdom of Earth, but a guiding light. However, under its suzerain king, a kingdom of many kingdoms embodied it, even as if an incarnational thing, a torch of encapsulated light. It would shine in dappled glory long after its earthly body had dissolved into its earthly elements, petty kingdoms to rise and fall once more as is the nature of human kingdoms, shaping and endlessly reshaping.

Its Light had anointed Arthur to serve it as its servant-king. Its Light would guide him in its mission until at last he returned with Excalibur, to the Land of Avalon, there to sleep a long sleep—as would Merlinus—until Briton called on him as Pendragon to awake. Logres was like a tree that growing swiftly into fruitfulness, would soon be cut down, but would leave much fruit for the surrounding nations, and leave hidden fruit buried deep beneath the sod. Its death is but withdrawal, an occultation, a clouding of clear sky. In the Fourth Age there had been but one Logres over all. Logres of the Britons was in fact but one fruit from that world tree, fruit elsewhere known by different names. Such is Logres.

As moths to a flame—yet they were not consumed—many of the knights gathered together under the banner of Arthur, their human king, and under the banner of Usen, the heavenly king over all rule and authority, power and dominion, both in this Age and the Age to follow. But ever the Dark Powers, the Turannoi, sought to terminate them, one by one or severally. They were masters of deception, and all too often used any Children of Usen who had fallen into their snare. For they played the Great Game, the Game of Life, a game within the mortal realm, in which pain and suffering were their pride and joy.

One such tragedy was between two brothers, Sir Balyn and Sir Balan, who had met that day in Arthur's castle in Caerllion. Arthur was preparing them and many other knights for battles both within and without Briton, when news arrived of a challenge from a Welsh king, Ryon. It had been a slap in the face, and had clearly exasperated the court—they had not planned on doing battle with King Ryon. With tensions running high, into the court had come a young woman who had stolen the Sword of Galeas.

Iosephus himself had brought with him that sword through the silver mists, and it had for long been cared for in Avalon. Seemingly the Darkness had servants ensconced within Avalon. Ah, she was a cunning one, she was, and by her thelodynamic power she allowed only Sir Balyn—whom she flattered as a man surpassingly good—to possess the sword. And he, poor fool, immediately fell under her enchantment, and when the damsel's accomplice, looking for all the world like Nimue, Lady of the Lake, came to reclaim the sword, he swapped off *her* head without batting an eyelid, since she had demanded *his* head! By the spell laid upon him, he both wrongly believed that she was Nimue, and rightly believed that she was a false and cruel lady. Yet to all other eyes she appeared as the true and kind Nimue, howbeit making an evil request. But had her request for *his* head been granted, King Arthur would have had needless war with Bernicia and Deira, northern kingdoms united by the mother and father of the twins Balyn and Balan. And in that war, news of the Lady Nimue's death would have been seen to have been greatly exaggerated.

Arthur had misjudged Balyn. Now shamed and seeking to regain his place among Arthur's men, Balyn in foolish pride set himself the task of ridding the land of Ryon, and departed from the court with the sword. Had he returned it to the Lake, he would have met Nimue very much alive and well. Then the king would have welcomed him back in high honour, himself asking to be forgiven for false judgment. But Balyn had been like a dog with a bad name. Having served jail time, he was reluctant to return except on his own terms. A lesser knight, envious of Balyn's new sword, hid even from himself his greed under a cloak of piety, and sought to possess the sword. This deluded soul died in the belief that he was in the right, and mercy waited until he had died to remove that veil from his eyes. The Necros smiled, for another knight had been lost to Logres.

Still, with Merlinus' help, Balyn and Balan hammered King Ryon into submission, weakening the alliance that opposed Arthur. And they—and then King Pellinore—also brought much needed help to Arthur, turning the fortune of war against the alliance. There was grief, and there was gain. Repeatedly, loss and gain. Opposing Arthur, good King Lot of Orkney died, yet his sons soon became famous knights under Arthur the high king—for they repented of their father's sin.

Though forgiven that day—though had he been rightly understood, he would have been excused rather than forgiven—Balyn was fated to remain a loner, yet a kindly soul. A fellow knight whom he sought to help, was slain by a vampire lord named Garlon, who lived in Briton and had enslaved the good King Pelles, the Grail Keeper. Like most vampires, being thelodynamic he could just about hide his physical body from human sight, and he used that skill to impress the secondborn—Garlon was as vain as a peacock. He also delighted in murdering those who sought to flee his clutches, and was called a black magician. Yet, with a concealed weapon when he was thought weaponless, Balyn succeeded in plunging a knife into Garlon's heart, even in Holy Carbonek which the vampire lord had infiltrated.

Balyn had again provided great service to Logres, but again had not been understood, and King Pelles has actually chased him with an axe into the Sacred Room, in which were kept the holy items the mission had long used to spread the message of the Light. In that room, desperately using the very Spear of Destiny, Balyn had struck Pelles in fear of his own life. Though he had instantly sensed that the threat had died at the doorway, his fear still struck what thereafter was known as the Dolorous Stroke. That vicious stroke crippled Pelles, who was the Grail Keeper, and that mission became as crippled as he, though Carbonek still stood. It was held in later years that Pelles, a descendant of Iosephus d'Arimathie, had himself sinned in allowing Garlon to wheedle his way into Carbonek, though the story of that trickery need not be told here. Yet though woefully wounded, Pelles had to admit that Balyn had accidentally rescued him from a far worse fate, and he therefore suffered for the most part in silence.

Poor old Balyn stumbled from one woe to another. Again he had been disgraced for undermining the mission, but his detractors little realised that the mission had all but played out, and like a ripe seed pod needed to devolve into smaller missions. Hanging down his head in shame, he took to the roads once more, until he came across a castle across a long bridge crossing a wide river. A custom there was that travelling knights must fight with the champion of the castle, to use that road. Though unhappy with the custom, he was not unwilling to fight. To his cost, it transpired that he went into that fight using borrowed gear, and with his visor down his opponent had no way to recognise him. Nor could he recognise his opponent.

Both fought brilliantly and equally well, and so it escalated far more than would be in fights between unequal contenders. Pride it was which prevented either from asking for quarter, with both now wishing to prove on the body of the other, that he was the better— even if it killed them. And kill them it did. Both mortally wounded the other, and only then did they discover their kinship. "I bid thee good night! For we shall never bid again 'good morrow'", groaned Balyn sadly to his dying brother. Yet Balan, looking beyond, replied with dying breath that with a 'good-morrow' they would soon awake beyond the sunset. As *per* their request, their bodies were buried together, and Merlinus, coming late to the funeral, repaired the broken Sword of Galeas, for at last the hand of Balyn, having broken it, had released it.

Merlinus chuckled, since he could see both the irony and the bigger picture—that the Dark had made a move that would do it little good. However, King Arthur bewailed the loss of two such knights, even though their places would soon be filled. Afterwards Merlinus established a large round table. Round, so none would bewail that he sat lower down the communal table than he would wish, or boast that he sat higher up than his fellows. It was a table that could seat 150 knights, plus the king and queen. Soon only a few seats—or as they were called, sieges—were left unfilled, awaiting a few extraordinary knights who were prophesied.

King Arthur soon married an absolute stunner, a princess named Guinevere, perhaps the finest maiden in the land. Asked earlier his advice, his counsellor Merlinus said that it was extremely unwise, for her very beauty would be the undoing of Logres, a retraction of Light. But, he added, to a man madly in love with outward beauty, his advice would count for naught, and therefore Arthur should just go ahead and marry the girl. This is not to say that Guinevere was a bad woman, just that she would never be overly shy of looking twice at dashing young bachelors, a folly which would also be her undoing.

From their various exploits and mistakes, the Knights of the Round Table—as they were now called—began to pool, and learn, their wisdom. Sir Gawain, son of King Lot and nephew to Arthur, had gotten into a fight, only to realise that he was too ready to use his sword. His opponent, Sir Blamoure of the Marsh, had misjudged Gawain. But rather than explain with words the mistake, Gawain explained with his sword, and as he fought his anger arose. Enraged at the point of victory—though begged for mercy—he slashed at Blamoure's head, blind to the knight's wife rushing in and putting herself in the firing line. Alas, it was her head his sword lifted, to his undying shame and horror. Thereafter he swore always to be guided by mercy towards men, and to fight for the good of women without reward. Sir Mordred had quipped that seldom did fair lady lose her head to a man—none had laughed, save he.

Besides being the common lot of knights, Sir Gawain also found himself within the clearly uncommon, arrayed both for and against Logres. Of the former a green knight—his real name was Bernlak—had issued a bold challenge one Christmas. Was any knight brave enough to chop off his submissive head, then allow him to chop off their submissive head a year and a day later? A very uncommon dare, from a very uncommon man! Why, not only were all his armour and clothes green, but even his skin and hair were greener than any grass—and he had a horse to match! Calling Arthur's knights but beardless children, he claimed to be of the Light, but by insults he bearded Gawain into removing his head, Gawain, who still ached for the lady whose head he had removed accidentally in anger. Using the Green Knight's own axe, again Gawain removed a head, but this time the headless body merely picked up its head and rode away, reminding Gawain that a promise was a promise, and that Gawain must allow the Green Knight to take Gawain's head. Into the eldritch Forest of Wirral, Gawain had to go.

As a true knight, as the deadline approached Gawain accordingly journeyed in search of the Green Knight. What he found, with only days in hand, was a castle lorded over by a knight of ruddy complexion and red hair, whose wife, the Lady Linnet, fairer than the sunshine, put Guinevere in the shade by her elven beauty. And there, hours away from where the Green Knight would meet him in the Green Chapel, Gawain was tested, which to him seemed as temptation. For daily his host would ride away, leaving the Lady Linnet to tempt him, and she was all but irresistible—but she was married.

Later Gawain realised that the lord and lady had conspired to test him, and that they had rejoiced that he had withstood the temptation. The lady was never in any real danger, she of the people of Nimue. But before he knew of her virtue, he had rendezvoused with the Green Knight. He hesitated a little, before bowing to his fate as a brave knight should. Having proved true to lady and to lord, his life was in safe hands, for the lord was none other than the Green Knight. The idea of using shapeshifting enchantment had come from the Lady Nimue, and Bernlak had—put simply—shaped a false head which he could lose without losing his life. Merlinus also had wished to test Arthur's knights, for there is a different boldness between risking your life in combat, and voluntarily and knowingly walking to your execution.

The Darkness was also at work. One uncommon fiend was discovered when Arthur went without guard to the castle of Tarn Wathelyne, which was a little south and east of Carlisle. For the lord of the castle was under the control of Morgana le Fay, mistress of dark magic. She ruled over the mind of a knight named Sir Gromer, whose sister was Dame Ragnelle. And Ragnelle was under a spell, the semi-control of a vampire, an enchantment short of enslavement, an enchantment by which she could be instantly shape-shifted anywhere between and including extreme loveliness—her unenchanted form—and extreme loathliness. Unwillingly both brother and sister had been set to trap King Arthur, and they came perilously close to success.

At the mercy of Sir Gromer—in some ways still his own master—King Arthur had been set a seemingly impossible quest. To succeed was to live; to fail was to die. He had simply to discover what it was which women most desired. Yet how can a mere man fathom the depth of a woman's mind? For this quest, he was given a year and a day, so that the quest—set on a Christmas day—might not cause his death on a Christmas.

Off he rode to search for the answer, accompanied by Sir Gawain. Up and down the land of Logres they went, collecting book loads of answers, which women had given to the question. Obviously, the women did not agree on a common answer, either shielding their inner thoughts or not knowing them. When the knights were headed back to Tarn Wathelyne—a tarn that is now no more, by command of a tall lord of that dale—the Lady Ragnelle met them—as ungoodly a creature as ever man saw without measure.

Brave Gawain turned pale, for the creature was uncanny. Though regally dressed, her face was puffy and red, her teeth were long and yellow, and her lips were cracked and weak. She had a baggy head sitting on top of a swollen neck, and her body was bloated and amorphous like some higgledy-piggledy bale of straw, under which hung twisted legs with twisted feet. Her voice was shrill, yet her close-set eyes, though redder than fire, were suffering, beseeching courtesy. A bargain she made, that for giving Arthur the answer he sought, she should gain a spouse she sought—any one of his noblest knights would do. His senses revolting, Arthur point-blank refused to sacrifice even a villain to such a hideous captivity. Gawain, loyal beyond measure, immediately pledged Ragnelle his knightly word.

Her answer—that all women as women seek above all else to rule over men—had saved the life of Arthur, for Sir Gromer believed that to be right, and his sister had revealed his mind. But who is to say whether Sir Gromer was right? Might it not be that what all women seek is to be treated as imagodei, coheirs in the grace of life? Whatever the true answer may be, duty-bound Gawain married the Lady Ragnelle, a living grief which death alone could cure.

At their wedding none had wished him joy; none were gay. Alone that night, she had rightfully commanded a kiss. His face glazed over in undisguisable agony, yet her eyes bore the deeper agony. As a true man, his heart wished her well, but as a weak man, her form sickened him to his stomach. But with compassionate sympathy for the hag, he kissed what could barely be called a face. But by that kiss, against all instinct, he had unknowingly halved the spell that bound her, and her haggishness was removed. Sweetly then did she offer him the choice: she could revert to her monstrous form either daytimes, or nighttimes. He replied that though he was her lord and she was his lady, yet they were equal partners in the grace of life, and the word was with her. She alone must decide when to look foul and loathly, and when to look fair and lovely, and by his very chivalry—putting her first—he unknowingly broke the curse fully.

Seven sweet years they lived together, yet her fate was to flee then into the deep forests of Wales, and there to bear their twins, Percivale and Dindraine. Though grieved by her flight, Gawain was counselled by Merlinus not to seek after her, and told that his son would seek him out—though not as father—and become a great knight to grace the courts of Camelot and of Carbonek.

The Order of the Grail had become less active, and now allowed few to witness its manifestations—and those few were, unlike the impure many of yesteryear, now the purest of the pure. Tested and refined, Gawain was among those privileged few who beheld the unearthly glory that shone through the Grail. One day he saw a vision, and with the seeing came also a warning. For it warned that unless he bridled his tongue and followed the Light, his right hand would be as a black hand, snuffing out the Light of Logres.

Yes even Gawain, virtuous among the Knights of the Round Table, could fall victim to vice, and the warning went at last unheeded. For another knight, snared by the Darkness, would become increasingly enamoured with the wife of his lord and master, and betray his king in thought though not in deed. This knight would in desperate attempt to rescue his lady love, tragically kill two unarmed brothers of Gawain, thinking them armed foes, and by their loss the heart of Gawain would become as ice, and a madness would seize his mind like fire. Only in the throes of death would he repent of his madness and forgive. Nevertheless, the glory of Gawain was undying.

Gawain's son would also see the Holy Grail. Of his son much could be said, not least that his paternity long remained unknown to him. He was truly informed—lest he falsely fear the true knowledge to be shameful—that his father was a most honourable knight of Logres. So why did his mother leave her husband? It was simply to save the lives of both her and their son that the Guardians had bid her flee, for they knew that the Darkness sought now to contrive her death, so as to put asunder the Kingdom of Logres.

Gawain lived true to her as if she lived, assured that separation was for the greater good. Only by strictly concealing their identities, did the Lady Ragnelle keep the lad safe and sound while he grew into rugged manhood in the deep woods of Wales. Men in later years would seek to know who she had been, for even to her son she was only known as simply 'mother', and Merlinus never revealed more to him. As to not revealing to him his father's name, why, she thought, better that all knights should be to him as brothers, and that he should not piggyback into knighthood on the virtue of another.

That Spring, after Percivale had left her to join the king, his mother betook herself to a nunnery, for she could no longer live on her own and her beauty would endanger her, she who was still a holy wife. Besides, in a nunnery she could devote herself to pray for the safety of Logres, though its allotted time neared an end. It had served its useful purpose, and had entered its twilight zone. It was being increasingly troubled by the fanciful superstitionising of simple minds, with its props being deemed to be semi-magical relics from millennia past. As the Snake of Moyshe, having healed the bitten, had to be killed off, so the Glory of Logres, having shone the healing Light, was being twisted into Darkness, and had to die. Already some were saying that its wine and bread became physically blood and flesh, even if wine and bread still seemed to be but wine and bread—"appearances are deceptive", some said. And that its light was magical in itself, and could work all manner of miracles.

Some even claimed to trace the spear all the way back to a time when a pagan high priestess had attempted to turn the Holy Tent of Kurion, into a temple of prostitution, thus doing away with Kurion. In that story, a hero had arisen to do away with her. That hero was named Penehasi, a young and handsome priest of Kurion, who had shot past her bodyguards and speared to death both her and her co-conspirator—at the very climax of their mocking shenanigans. Their knavery had been in broad daylight, and at the very entrance to the Holy Tent. Their clear message was that the Sheep should follow a different Shepherd, and live like Goyim. Penehasi had saved the

Sheep, cut out the cancer, killed the wolf. That was a great story from momentous times, but the Spear of Longinus was not a part of it. Yet that same spear—these woolgatherers were now whispering—had pierced the side of Hamashiach and still dripped his blood! Well, let fools be fools, but let such folly be ended. Galahad would be the zenith; Percivale the nadir.

Only in his later teens had Percivale ventured forth from the deep forests, and advised by a knight of Camelot, sought out Arthur at Caerllion. His mother had taught him respect for fair play, for women, and for Hamashiach. Accordingly, he sought to always live in honour and purity, to treat with respect all women whether dame or damsel, not to mess with any, to only exchange rings with she whom he fully intentioned to marry, not to mix with bad company, and to pause in prayer at any church or chapel he came across.

Seeking out Arthur, he soon met a sleeping beauty as fair as a pure white lily, in one such chapel. To her he gave one gentle kiss of commitment, and his betrothal ring. He knew next to nothing about her though, not even that her name was Blanchefleur and that she was also known as the senior Grail Maiden. Had he known, perhaps he would not have dared such liberties. And still she slept on— though his face now wove itself into her dreams. He was long gone before she woke, for he had feared to linger overly long besides so attractive and unguarded a lady. She was his spring of love.

The seasons had rolled by, and he found himself alone in woods unknown. Evening had descended, and a fierce autumnal storm had unexpectedly arisen. Quickly it had turned into a dark and stormy night. Urgently seeking shelter from the elements, Percivale had stumbled upon the seeming ruins of an old castle, even the mysterious Carbonek. Imagine his utter joy when he met within Blanchefleur, the girl of his dreams, even as he was now of her dreams. But there are deeper things in life, and she urged him not to talk of their love, but to stay silent. For she knew full well that the Grail Procession would soon pass by, and she believed that it would summon him to seek that which is beyond the mortal realm.

All men come with feet of fragile clay. Only a man with a head of fine gold would be her choice—thus she awaited his test. Then suddenly into the hall, appeared the Menorah Maiden, dressed in white silk, lighting the way. She who followed held aloft the Grail, from which glory immortal shone. Behind her walked another, carrying a golden plate covered in shimmering silk. Behind her, someone carried an ancient spear, tipped with a stab of white light dazzling to the eyes, and seeming to drip with molten blood. The hall suddenly seemed to be baptised into the scent of roses and sweet-smelling spices. Percivale knelt in awe, as peace pierced his heart as a blessèd wound.

"Percivale," whispered Blanchefleur, "you must return now to Camelot and abide there until the Holy Knight himself comes to take his seat at the Round Table. He shall soon bear the Sword of Galeas, and he shall bear the name of his forebear. There you shall see again the Grail Procession, for it shall come to inspire faith, to bless the loyal, to gather the chosen few to the Final Procession, and to purge the poison through which the Powers of Darkness have infiltrated Logres."

"Poison, fair lady? Do you say that Logres might die?"

"Yes, dear Percivale. How and when, I do not know, but by fair or foul ways, shortly or delayed, Logres has not long to live, yet its fruit shall live on. For its death is the will of Usen and the gift of grace", she replied. "And although you have seen true glory, it resides not in the objects themselves, but through them it is displayed. Its true home is in Usen, who dwells in all who seek his face. The time for the holy objects will soon pass, but the truth of what they speak shall live while the Seventh Age endures."

Almost at once a rashness of desire overcame him, and heedless of Blanchefleur he rushed out as if the Grail Procession had left the castle, and must be dragged back for him alone. Within his heart still dwelt an inner desire to boast of a glory possessed, a pride which poisoned his mind. Ever slower he blindly raced, until he finally stopped, lost and all alone. As inner quiet returned, he realised that her words had not been to search but to find, and that he should neither envy nor seek the fate of any other—he must beware of all temptations. He turned to retrace his steps, but try as he might he could not rediscover Carbonek.

Despairing that he had lost Blanchefleur forever—and fearing himself a fool unworthy of her—he sadly returned firstly to Caerllion, for the season of snow was setting in. Yet unbeknown to him, his future was bright. Soon, he would be knighted and would dwell in Camelot, in hope at least of seeing again a manifestation of true glory. Still he would need—as he had needed—many adventures to purge him of his weaknesses. It is told that he once rode a gigantic black horse that sought to deliver him unto the jaws of death, though not, as he believed in folly, into hell—for what fiend has *such* power? On another journey, a creature he would not normally trust—it was a lion—turned into a friend. One of the strangest journeys would be his brief encounter with a tomb, in which he found himself trapped.

From Arthur's kingdom, a finger of the hand of Hamashiach, the Kingdom of Night held back its hand, by the queen's command. Yet she held it prudent to allow her people surreptitiously to oppose the Light of Logres, even to engage with the Kingdom of Necros, so long as she could disavow all knowledge of their mischief. She was, truth told, a queen in two minds. Not all vampires were as she.

The Knight of the Tomb

Towards Logres, the Queen of the Night was strangely ambivalent. Few knew her inner thoughts. Since the execution of Hamashiach had so miserably backfired, clandestinely she had even dared to probe those of the Hamashiachim. It wasn't simply a case of know thy enemy—though that might have played its part. Secretly she had a genuine interest in, and respect for, her worthy opponent.

For all that, she still mistrusted him more than poets could ever say. Her 'hands off' policy remained in place, as it had for millennia: humans were hunted but not hated. But especially among lesser vampires, who believed themselves to be less watched by the queen, a 'hands on' policy could be more to their liking. Besides, they too felt the cold hand of mortality upon their shoulders. The Necroi identified them in their ones and twos, and often won them over to their side. After all, a little low-risk cooperation, in exchange for life extension, seemed to be a good deal.

In league with the Kingdom of Necros, one vampire ring, hating Logres, had coalesced in the depth of a deep dark forest. Presenting mainly as menservants and maidservants, their pack leader was named Marwolaeth. Hard pressed by his guests to at least play another part against Logres, Wulfgar had reluctantly joined, but only as a junior player. Indeed Marwolaeth, who would one day become his mother, was the stronger of the two, though they operated there according to guile, not brute force—all cloak and dagger stuff. This well-forged ring was situated to lure many of the Round Table into their deadly web of deceit. For knights were valuable assets for Logres, so were prime targets to take out. And good knights are not easily replaced, especially experienced ones. Ever the Darkness sought to deplete King Arthur's followers, and diaboloi worked quietly alongside vampires—though Lilith must surely have known.

Together they raised and tunnelled there a strong castle—renamed in later times as Chess Castle. It was as beautiful on the outside, as it was cheerless below. Its underground caverns had only one way in from the castle above, and only one gate that opened up to the outside world, a gate craftily concealed on the other side of the hill. That gate looked for all the world like a tomb door built into a rocky outcrop. On the outside of this door was painted an image of a knight and his coat of arms. That image was to prompt passers-by to stop and pray for the unnamed knight's soul, a new practice that was gaining traction in this neck of the woods. Though doubtfully fruitful for the unnamed knight, that noble custom was doubtless fruitful to whosoever knelt in the chivalry of prayer. Yet it was not entirely unknown that a base knight might seek to free himself from his oath, by erecting a fake tomb, assuming that none would violate its door to vouchsafe his demise, and assuming that his demise would be assumed. By an empty tomb, a man could die to honour and to oath.

Yet this tomb held neither a dead body nor no body. Behind its doorway of death there lived a knight, sometimes awake, sometimes asleep. He was called the Knight of the Tomb, but his right name was Sir Gleva. Almost a year earlier he had been ensnared by the vampire lady of the castle. Vampires care nothing for their looks, other than as means to their ends. Thus they can as happily look like a destitute beggar woman unkempt and hideous, or a high lady fair and gay, so long as they get their way.

Marwolaeth seemed in shape as a highborn and lovely lady, and she had offered Sir Gleva marriage, but only on condition that he first guard the tomb door for one year, slaying any knights who ventured upon it. Love-enslaved he had consented. Yet it was unlikely that she would keep her word, even if he survived a year of servitude in such deathly desolation. His brother Garsallas had also been caught up in that web, commanded to harry any knight whom he found roaming that land.

One more love-bound knight may be mentioned here, namely Sir Urban of the Round Table, whom Arthur had believed to be missing in action. He too was promised marriage after a year of true service, and guarded the Ford Perilous. For a river flowed strongly across one of the approaches to Chess Castle, crossable only by a ford. Now Urban's task was to duel to the death any knights who approached from that direction, helping thus to keep the castle undiscovered.

And yet another road there was, a road left unguarded, for Chess Castle wished to play with a few flies itself. One day it chanced that Sir Percivale had espied Chess Castle, and right joyously rode swiftly towards it, for it was towards the end of a weary day. The drawbridge was down and the portcullis was up, so he was able to ride in without let. After stabling his horse, he simply entered the main hall, for there didn't seem to be anyone at home. But though people were missing, the table was set as if for a feast. A chessboard was also there, with ivory white and bone black pieces set out, as if ready to play.

Sir Percivale had acquired just a little bit of knowledge about this newfangled game that had come from foreign lands—still little known in this land—though the pieces looked strange to him. For the carved pieces of each side were of a dragon, a griffin, vultures, mounted knights, lions, and lots of little goblins.

As an idle movement he moved a white ivory knight, only for a black knight to immediately make a counter move. He moved more pieces, and found himself soon checkmated. Thrice that happened. In no mood to be thwarted by some unseen opponent, he made to chop the board into firewood, when an urgent feminine voice from above shouted, "Stop!" Looking up he saw a fair damsel on the castle balcony above. "Lady, I crave your pardon. I am but a poor knight who has ridden far and am weary, yet none have I seen till now to welcome me to this fair dwelling."

"How so, do you justify your ill temper by our poor hospitality, Sir Knight? And had I played you yet won, would you have drawn sword against me? Fie on you to vent your anger on defenceless pieces that you have challenged to a fair game. Is it safe for me to approach so fickle a knight, I wonder?"

"Lady, it was remiss of me, who would not sin in large manner, to sin in small manner. But I heartily repent my folly, and beg you—and your servants who I see now standing behind you—to come down. For I am Sir Percivale, true knight of the good king, Arthur, high king of Logres by the will of Usen. Truly it eases my heart to speak with one so fair."

Soon they were wining and dining as old friends, singing merrily as the fire burned bright. Percivale asked about the strange pieces, and the lady said that they were of her devising, based on a game that had come from sunnier parts of the world where once she had dwelt. Indeed, each piece bore its own unique letter, or stood for some part of speech. She said that the pieces could, if gently touched by human hands, richly bless those hands by spelling out messages about their future. Would Sir Percivale not wish to see such magic? But, having been warned by Merlinus against such devices, he quickly crossed himself—a mnemonic—and said nay. Though she still tried to sweetly coax him into that game of foretelling, he courteously declined, until she gave up such temptation as going nowhere.

As to his obvious fascination with her—which cast an amnesic veil over the face of Blanchefleur—she promised that she herself would gladly be his wife, but said that she must set a simple task for him to prove his love for her. The castle, she said, had long been without a lord, and never had her heart been so moved as by the face of the noble Sir Percivale. As to proving his affection, she spoke of a white stag. "But bring me its head, and we shall be wed", she sweetly said.

The following day he set out on this quest right early, having borrowed from the lady her best staghound. Soon the stag was sighted. But the chase seemed endless, and it took three days before the stag was taken and Percivale had made its head his own. Yet even as he was roping the head to his horse, an old but surprisingly strong lady rode out from the trees, and adroitly bagged the borrowed hound and fled. Little did Percivale suspect that she knew the hound well and perhaps believed it stolen, but he had soon caught up with her.

To wrest it from her by force would vex him sore, for it would be just but unchivalrous. However, seeing his dilemma, she offered him another option. Namely, that if he would but go to the Tomb of the Knight—which was a little further along the road—and defame it aloud as a false tomb, she would willingly return the hound he claimed he had borrowed from the lady of the castle.

Since she had sworn that he who had painted the tomb had been false, and that she would return the hound, Percivale did as she asked. But having defied the dedication of the tomb as false, a surly black knight came forth from its dismal door. And black he was: skin, armour, shield, lance, and sword, even his horse was black, and huge—blacker than black ink. Sir Percivale quickly called on Kurion for Ruach to embolden him—for Ruach is the champion over fear—and then set to.

Ever they hewed at each other, shattering shields, mincing metal, causing cuts. The old woman stood and watched, the hint of a smile on her crusty old face, as her will sought out another not far away. Suddenly, as the two battled it out, Sir Garsallas swept in upon his horse, snatching up both head and hound, and galloped away, leaving Sir Gleva to finish off Sir Percivale, if he could. Such daylight robbery turned the mind of Percivale, who instead of trading blow for blow in blind anger, upped his game and attacked with greater fierceness, but this time with more self-control, thus gaining the decisive advantage.

Then suddenly fearing for his life, the Tomb Knight cast his sword at Percivale and fled back into his tomb. Percivale leapt after him but alas, as if by magic, the door slammed shut in his face, with a sound of bolting and double-bolting on the inside. After that, silence. Seldom are tomb doors sealed from within! Try as he might, Percivale could not open the heavy metal door, and the knight within refused to open up to either wrath or mercy.

Dismayed by such a stalemate, Percivale remounted his horse to pursue the other knight. The old woman, smiling wickedly, refused to offer any help as to where that knight had fled, nor to where he might dwell, so, having commended her to Diabolos, he tracked the knight as best he could. Returning with the head would earn the sweet maiden's pleasure; returning without the hound alive and in one piece, would surely earn her displeasure—she had lent it to him in good faith.

As the sun went down, Percivale made his camp beside a gentle stream. It had something of a peaty flavour, but was wholesome enough to drink from. And there he dreamed that his mother, father, and twin sister, all met up with him. In waking life he had neither met father nor sister—though his mother had mentioned her name. He remembered too that his mother had spoken of a royal fisherman named Bron, who had married into the line of Iosephus, the first Grail Keeper. And in his dream he drempt that he himself was discovered to have inherited the title, Fisher-King—that he himself was to become the Pendragon.

All sorts of weird ideas—the stuff of dreams—were sown into that dream, even as an enemy can sow weeds among the wheat. Grotesquely he saw the Grail as having actually been filled with blood drawn from Immanuel's veins. He saw a maimed man drink from that Blood of the Grail, and rise hale and hearty. He saw the Grail rising into the heavens, taken up into the clouds. He saw himself as being appointed to be the Grail Keeper, and marrying Guinevere who burnt as a bird had arisen from the ashes of her pyre. But as she went up into their honeymoon turret she turned and gayly laughed that their firstborn son would be named Arthur, and that he would be a Saxon king. And with that she turned into an owl and flew away.

Then he had travelled awhile with his sister, and had had to kill a knight who had sought to kill him—what their quarrel was he never understood—and the ground opened up and swallowed the knight's body, and everybody kept saying to him, "stay here in our land; stay here with us." Strange are the dreams of the night, and he awoke wondering whether truth and trickery had been his lot.

After breaking his fast, he followed the steam until he came to a river, and followed the river until he came to a ford, and followed the ford until he came to a pavilion. There stood a stern knight who issued a challenge, yet in courtesy supplied Percivale with needed weaponry—Sir Urban was not a shameless knight. Yet the knighthood of Sir Percivale was proved hardier, and before long his sword was at the throat of Urban, who readily surrendered. Asked why he waylaid innocent travellers, he pleaded guilty as to obeying his lady's command, the price of courtly love.

He told how, as a Knight of the Round Table, he had one stormy night found Chess Castle, having followed its lady through the meandering woods. She, seemingly delighting in him, had seemingly not wished other knights to disturb her solitude, and so set Sir Urban to protect her from any approach from the riverside way. Loyalty in his mission—for but one year—would win him her hand in marriage. "I had but eight days yet to go," bemoaned Sir Urban in sadness, "but I doubt not that, having proved the better knight, you shall now become the Knight of the Ford for a year, and thus marry my lady. Yet had I not provided you with weaponry, I could have slain you easily, and I would soon sit—though in shame—as the blissful lord of this fair castle."

Percivale replied that by no means would he himself any more seek to stay in this accursed castle, and bade Sir Urban to leave henceforth and never return—for the sake of his soul. Sir Urban bowed his head, and wept at the loss therefore of his lady fair, yet even as his tears flowed, the woods awoke to a great deafening voice echoing through the twisting branches, cursing Percivale and calling Urban back to itself. It was a voice full of falseness and fiction; a voice that had its effect.

Urban was in two minds, a mental frenzy seeking to obey both the voice and Sir Percivale. Then there came a sound of crows of the raven kind, and a black and murderous mob swept down more quickly than merlins or swallows can fly, as if in conspiracy against Percivale. For him only did they attack, vampires of the castle, shielding their inner powers lest they revealed their presence to their queen below and to Usen above.

Urban, seeing now an ally to Percivale's downfall and to his own uplifting, strove once more against Percivale in mortal combat. Poor Percivale was now in dire straits, struggling to keep both knight and birds at bay. One only of the birds did he slash, and it did not surprise him that the wounded bird turned immediately into a wounded woman, whose dying or dead body was swiftly carried away by the carrion fowl. Sir Urban also seemed unfazed that the castle dwellers were shapeshifters. To give him his due, he had long sincerely suspected that they were of Avalon, on the side of the aggeloi. Left to his own devices, Urban once more surrendered, and received Percivale's stern rebuke, before being released. Percivale, permitting at last Sir Urban to seek out his lady love, meant to follow at a distance and espy what mischief the castle was up to. But it was as if a cloak of impenetrable gloom descended to cover Sir Urban. Into that fog he had ridden alone unto his fate; as a lonely lost soul, he had departed.

Folly alone would pursue him, but Percivale bowed his head, swearing that if Usen gave him strength, he would paint Sir Urban's emblems on the tomb door, for doubtless the castle was but a cadaverous tomb, devouring all who ventured unwarily into its jaws. Long did he seek that day for signs of the knight who had stolen head and hound, but wearily he laid down his head at the close of day. Committing his soul and body to Kurion, he fell into a deep sleep.

And he drempt again. In his dream it was as if as he rode he came across two little children, who boasted that they lived for Usen. A strange reason to live, he thought, only to be as a tool for another's benefit. He asked himself why then did he himself live? Well, he replied, he lived because he was simply alive, and saw no good reason not to live. Must one justify being alive, seek a positive reason for living? He could understand seeking a positive reason to die, of course. Perhaps these kiddies meant that they lived *unto* Usen, and or *under* Usen? Nevertheless, he attended to their speech, which spoke much about the Holy Grail, and he realised that even the holiest of messages could come through cracked earthen vessels.

Riding on he saw a beautiful meadow, and then a river, and three men in a boat, the oldest of whom rose up and claimed to be his grandfather, born hundreds of years earlier, who spoke of a beautiful castle ahead, hidden by the mists, in which lived the Fisher-King. Then he seemed to behold a holy procession—of which many had told—and to stand silently marvelling within mystic Carbonek. For that he was slagged off by some lady for being audience, not player. "Usen hates you!" she barked in a grating voice: "I hope you die an evil death." She seemed to slate him as a fool in shining armour, someone utterly unworthy of becoming a Grail Keeper, and charity to her eyes meant disencumbering his cloddish shoulders! Well, what a nice young lady to meet in your dreams! No wonder he awoke in a muck sweat.

Could it be that Chess Castle, not Carbonek, was the source of his dreams, he wondered? And if so, was it seeking to direct, or to misdirect, him? Had the lady of the castle sent him on a wild stag chase, hoping that he would either kill one of her guardian knights, then take his place under her control, or otherwise to be killed? A fair face can hide foul heart, and angel eyes can hypnotise, as minstrels sung. However, whatever his doubts and fears, he had undertaken to at least return hound to mistress. And whether or not she was true or false, he must be true.

He proceeded on his journey to find the missing items, both head and hound, and before long he came across one. The other would come across him. The head was hung in a tree, minded by a fair damsel. Sir Percivale immediately took back his own, though she roundly accused him of theft. And at that moment the hound came bounding into the camp, chasing a small doe. Percivale let the doe pass, and grabbed the hound with both hands, thinking his quest all but complete. However, the hound was followed by Sir Garsallas. After some mutual insulting, and some splashing around of testosterone, Percivale learned that Garsallas was a knight of the lady, and had only taken the hound in the belief that it had been stolen by Percivale—likewise the head.

Moreover, he learned how the Knight of the Tomb had been captivated by the lady of the castle, and been set the task of guarding that secret door for one year, or to pass on the duty. Sir Garsallas believed that the castle contained bickering sisters, each wishing to prevent a marriage of the other by killing their suitors, shapeshifters who would ride within the ancient wood as old women. Percivale gave his knightly word to return both head and hound to the castle, before departing that wood forever, for he had no desire to stay there.

For her part, Marwolaeth would try again to induce Percivale to break his allegiance to King Arthur, but again without success. For indeed he now perceived her spell and thought again of Sir Gleva, still sadly entombed by vain servitude to this mistress of evil. As the sky turned black, Sir Percivale rode back to the tomb, wondering how to undeceive its captive, he who was little better than a dead man walking. If they who love are blind, how do you undeceive a man in love by showing him the truth? Can laughter, ridicule, reason, or testimony, work? Nevertheless, a last attempt had to be made, and hoping against hope, he stood once more at the entrance to the tomb. "Sir Gleva, come forth, for a tomb is no fit place for a living man. Come forth, for I mean you no harm, only to free you and to let you go."

"Good Sir Knight," replied Gleva, immediately coming out—for a knight's word was inviolate—"my freedom shall be soon, for soon my lady shall marry me, and what man could be freer than to be the lord of such a lady? In days of yore a patriarch once worked and waited 14 years as a shepherd, to gain his choice. But for me, a paltry twelvemonth as a gloomy guardian shall soon be past, and I shall lie in her arms for life. But pleased am I to speak with you face to face without fear, for to die before I have completed my service for her, would be a sad death for me."

"Sir Gleva, I too had been set a quest by the lady of the castle. Little enough it seemed to me, yet I fear that it was not meant for my good. Now, though I have risked my life in fulfilling her demands, I would not risk my soul in receiving her rewards. For her birds, of which she I deem was one, attacked me to take my life. Should he who escapes from a dungeon knock willingly to return? Nay, Sir Gleva. You do not perceive your peril, for I fear that your reward might bring you deeper death than this tomb forebodes."

"Ah, Sir Percivale," said Gleva cunningly, "this tomb is full of wonder within, which none can see from without. Take but one look, and you shall see fair wonders which forever will bestir your mind in praise. Look, if you dare, or if a craven you be you best should stand well back. Either way, never again speak ill of my lady, or of the task she has set me."

It is said that our strongest point can be our weakest point. Percivale, whom few could match for valour within the high realm of Logres, was baited by these words which dared him to look, or if not to cry chicken. At once he strode foolhardily to the tomb door, while Gleva happily stood aside. Then, as he peered into the gloom, Gleva gave him a mighty shove from behind, sending him tumbling into the darkness. Before he could recover, the door was locked from the outside.

Two main locks the tomb had, one unhidden within, and one hidden without. Percivale, taking the flambeau from the wall, examined the door, and discovered an inner door. It was likewise locked from the other side, though unbeknown to him there was a hidden technique to unlock it from the inside. So poor Percivale could not escape from his confinement, either by going backwards, or forwards. In fear lest the tomb become his coffin, he knelt and besought himself to prayer.

Sir Gleva stood stock still at the tomb door, his head hung in shame, for it had been a dastardly trick, and for one of them meant deep sorrow. It had momentarily seemed to him to be a way to fulfil his part of the bargain, in that although not serving his full time on duty, he had supplied his lady with another to replace him in her service. Thus he hoped still to win her hand. It had been, however, by foul means, and he feared that she might transfer her favour to he who had unwillingly replaced him in the tomb.

But would she really prefer someone who had spurned her—or rather had spurned her sister, for it must surely have been her sister who had offered herself to Percivale. No true lady would play the field! Perhaps he would gain the lady he desired, and Percivale would then gladly gain the sister he had desired yet disdained? Yes, Percivale would come to see his error in doubting any lady of that fair castle, and live to thank him. Why should he delay at the dark doorway any longer? Should he not ride now on Percivale's steed to claim his reward from the castle? But even as he hesitated, a foot in the stirrup, Percivale called loudly to him from within the tomb.

Ruach had whispered to Percivale one word—Atlas. "Sir Gleva, tarry, I entreat you, for I know not the ways of this tomb. Would you who have lived here, have me die here? In the name of our lord Hamashiach, and by your oath of knighthood, I beg you to counsel me in my distress, I who came seeking to release you. Do not leave me imprisoned, for what hope have I except you? And tell me more, do, of the ladies of this castle. Is it possible that I have misjudged them, that I am punished thus?"

That was the surest way into Sir Gleva's good books. "My lady is a nosegay of all virtues—of truth, mercy, constancy, gentleness, courage, and the rest. Who am I, a mere toad, that she should offer me love? I, who am but a servant, she would make a lord! The test she set for me was twofold. One, to protect her from wrongdoers, and two, to test my worthiness, both in arms at need, and patience to remain in a glum and tedious dwelling, yet for but a twelvemonth. Do you not see her worth, her goodness, her grace to I, who am but a worm? And methinks it is her sweet sister you have met."

"Sir Gleva, now that you paint her picture so, I repent of my hasty words. Indeed if it is for the sister of such a one, I think that I can endure the wait. Yet think, that if now she be yours, and in a twelvemonth, her sister shall be mine, then we shall be brothers. Would you not therefore show me the ways of this dwelling place, as a true brother should? How am I to draw water within here? And what of victuals? And of the doors, if I am to be the new guardian I must know how to lock both inner and outer door from within and without, must I not? Else the ladies would be displeased with us both."

Gleva was touched by this seeming repentance of Percivale's, and welcomed the wisdom of his words. He was so sure that no finer ladies existed in the land, that he all too easily believed in his own powers of persuasion. To this end his enchantment worked in Sir Percivale's favour. For too readily did Gleva then unlock the door, and Percivale came brashly forth, bearing the torch in hand and a smile on his face, and feigning to be apprentice to his master who quickly explained to him the secret locking mechanism for the outer door.

Then thoughtlessly did Gleva venture inside to show his new found friend the workings of the inner door, for smiling still Percivale quickly returned favour for favour, sealing Gleva once more into the tomb, and this time in total darkness. It would take him time to escape, by which time Percivale would be well away with good riddance to Chess Castle. The hound and head he left at the tomb door for collection. As for Sir Gleva, maybe he would come to his senses in the fullness of time, but for now he was trapped within his own mind, and doomed alas to the fate of Atlas.

Travelling on, Percivale ʼat last met with a woman who named him brother. Her name was Dindraine, and she spoke briefly of another, an adopted sister, one whom their mother had taken under her wing. Dindraine led him and one or two other knights to the Enchanted Ship—for a sindeldi built vessel now bore that title. Yet she would soon sail further than they, for she laid down her life in sacrifice for another, blood for blood, and her body sailed away upon the still waters. Was her tale not a short retelling of the Story of the Holy Grail, of one who had shed blood that others might live, and had gone on ahead of his fellows, beyond the waters of Middle-earth?

It was a sadder but wiser Percivale who finally returned to Carbonek, and once more saw the Grail Procession there. This time Blanchefleur carried the Grail—for she who had once knelt in prayer alongside Percivale, was revealed to be a Grail Maiden. Then she relinquished that calling, and she took Percivale in holy wedlock, a new yet holy walk. And once the cloak of secrecy removed from Carbonek, they would reign for a time as its king and queen, with their children and their children's children still shining forth something of the glory which had been Logres. But others were still to visit Carbonek before its glory departed.

Sir Percivale had escaped unscathed, and would find his way to Carbonek. The cunning of Chess Castle had not managed to undo the Order of the Grail, but the Darkness still sought to undermine the Kingdom of Logres. Another key player might yet complete their mission. His name was Lancelot, and Lancelot had the goodwill of Castle Carbonek, the Castle of the Grail. They had gotten close to the Grail Keeper through the vampire Garlon, and made some contact with the Grail Keeper's daughter, Elayne. Yes, they knew all about Elayne, although with Garlon's fall her mind had become opaque to them, and as with Longinus long ago, they would no longer be able to regain control. But knowing her weakness, and Lancelot's weakness, if they brought them together they might yet achieve the overthrow of both heavenly and worldly Logres.

Elayne had long come to maturity, yet been held on a short leash by her father, King Pelles the Grail Keeper. Had he underestimated her need to marry, or was he guilty of a greater sin in knowingly restraining her? Unhappy Elayne. Especially since he had been twice maimed, he had insisted that she remain in the castle—what many now called the Haunted Castle, which few wished to find and fewer could enter. What chance had she for a suitor? She herself was partly to blame, at least in Pelles' opinion. For once, long ago, she had gone out on a mission to neighbouring hamlets which paid the tithe tax to Pelles as their king. It was a small enough tax to pay to an overlord, and unknown to them he used most for enriching their land. What he kept was bantam; what he gave back was bounteous. But that is neither here nor there.

The problem was that rebelling against her long lockdown, in a moment of wilfulness Elayne had wandered away from her companions. Alone and vulnerable, she had been seized by Garlon, who had long shadow-menaced them, whenever they left the safety of Carbonek. The highest of human callings is but for lowly people, and neither she nor the queen were exceptions. By virtue of being human, all of the Order were pervious to the ills of the world. Indeed, some had forsaken The Way through inordinate love for the world, or bitterness towards one another, and over disappointments in life.

Elayne could as easily be caught in a vampire web as could any other human being, and caught she was. Then she had become the eyes and ears of Garlon, and returned back to her people. Once back within Carbonek, the influence of Sir Garlon began to steadily grow. It was in little ways at first, but before long she had introduced him to the Order as a gallant knight, whom she had met that fateful day, and he became a trusted knight of Pelles. Already the king's inner eyes had dimmed, and—though not without some suppressed suspicion— Garlon was able to subtlety degrade Pelles' mission. Pelles, increasingly forsaking his flock, focused on his outer problems. The more he trusted in Garlon—might he make a fine husband for Elayne?—the more short-tempered he became with himself, an anger he began to take out on others.

When Garlon fell, Pelles had been left maimed in his mind. Later, Balyn had crippled him in body. Elayne became virtually a prisoner to her father's whims. Is it any wonder why, once Lancelot visited, she became fixated on him? He was not just any man in trousers, he was Sir Lancelot, greatest of the knights in the greatest of realms, Logres. Few women could look upon him without loving him. His mother had been an Elayne, too, a queen of Gwynedd, and the Lady Nimue had become his foster mother. Merlinus had had Lancelot knighted, and things could have worked out very much better than they did. Many triumphs followed in the wake of Sir Lancelot, not for himself, but for Logres. And yet many heartaches, needless or otherwise, followed too.

Among the ladies who loved him, there had been Elayne of Astolat, remembered by some as the Lady of Shalott. Love is not to be commanded. This lady pined to marry Sir Lancelot, unaware that his heart was already taken. Perhaps they would have happily wed, had his false love to Queen Guinevere not shielded his heart. Indeed, never suspecting that wayward love had actually increased Elayne's distress, for not knowing of any rival in love, she had presumed that she must somehow be repugnant to Lancelot.

How sad it is when a man harbours a falsely true love to one who is the wife of another, and so proves truly false to his own wife, or cannot give true love to a maiden. For else might Lancelot have made Elayne of Astolat the queen of his heart, and lived in faithful honour until the time for her to depart, and then might have joyously married Elayne of Carbonek in due season. As it was the former Elayne had descended into deep depressive illness and died—some whispered the word suicide, knowing that a heavy heart can suffer from hopelessness and helplessness. Had she jumped or fallen? Her body was tenderly laid in a black swan boat, in which it floated slowly down the river past Camelot. Lancelot saw it and wept true tears, but no more than he would weep when his love for the queen broke into civil war, and caused the death of deep-seated friendships. And now being a guest at Carbonek, fate had brought him to another Elayne.

"Father, my heart goes out to our guest, the noble Lancelot, for Garlon on whom you planned, is no more, and I yearn to marry. Has not fate brought Lancelot to our castle? Yet he shows little interest in me. Is there something repulsive, something abhorrent, about me?" asked a desperate Elayne to Pelles her father.

"Truly my daughter, I divine that he is here by destiny, and that having slain a dragon, knows full well that you are not one. But he has now seen the Grail Procession and so has much to ponder. I see clearly that he stands in awe of you, though you did not this time walk in the procession. But certainly take this opportunity to woo him while you can, for he will not stay long, I deem. I can to some extent foresee what is to be, but only in part, even as a painting is less than what it is that is painted. I see that you shall indeed bear him a son to be the next Grail Keeper, but I do not see how you shall win him, for plainly his heart is unstirred by your song."

The old king had watched and listened, and sorrowfully seen his daughter's one-sided affection for this bold and handsome knight. He had spoken much with Lancelot, chiefly concerning the Grail Order: about how each Keeper bore the titles Fisher-King, and Pendragon; about how ideally the custodianship was passed on to a worthy son or daughter, but that any within the Tree of Twelve might inherit; about how Elayne could carry a Keeper of the Grail, but as yet lacked a lord. Yes, it all seemed to him that Lancelot was the one Ruach had spoken of. So why could the daughter of the Fisher-King not land this fish?

That night, Elayne dreamed hungrily about Lancelot, yet soon awoke to the light of the silvery moon. In the warm wakefulness of the night she pondered her fate. Ever since the melding of her mind with Sir Garlon, she had developed a Dame Brysen mode, her *nom de plume* for that which was her, wasn't her, and strove to be her—a dark side.

"I cannot command his love, but the longer he is here, surely the more likely that he will turn to me. I have only to wait—and to have him wait", confided Elayne to her secret friend.

"Perhaps, and perhaps not", her friend replied. "Has the king not foreseen a son by him? If such is therefore the will of Usen, is it not lawful to fulfil the vision as we think best? To give Lancelot a helping hand? For how can he, who has only seen the Glory of the Grail under the pale moon, see so clearly as one who has seen its glory under the shining sun?" asked Dame Brysen.

"If Usen has promised it, it will surely come to pass. I must await Usen's will in Usen's way, for Lancelot will despise me if I use womanly wiles to gain my way", replied Elayne.

"To gain our way, is it? Is it not to gain Usen's way? Will not our father be healed by our son, but only if Lancelot helps us? And has Usen not said that he can promise to bless, and then change his mind; or promise to curse, and then change his mind? For will he bless the good who become evil, or curse the evil who become good? And if our son to be is a good, and Lancelot in evil denies us our right, should we not seek to make him do good, to save him from a curse? We must make sure that the prophecy for good is not overturned by Lancelot evilly turning away from us", said Brysen.

"But I ride with him, play chess with him, sing to him, tend to him. What more can I do to win him?" asked Elayne.

For a moment, Brysen was quiet, thinking. "Let us remember how once upon a time," she resumed, "an old man was foretold to have a son in his old age, yet had an old wife. What did he do? He made a younger woman his secondary wife. His primary wife was happy with that, and Usen didn't seem to mind. So aren't we likewise permitted to fulfil the prophecy by our cleverness? We have clever skills since we knew old Garlon and Morgana—worshipful mistress of magic—skills that none know save us. Maybe they were given to us for such a time as this? But if we are not Lancelot's lady love, has he a secret love? Do we not suspect that Lancelot might have an unrequited crush on Arthur's queen? Should we not save him from himself? And can't we look like her, so that he will look on us with lovelorn eyes? Can't we beguile him with wine, which has been the mocker of many men? If we have our dishonest way with him, he will surely make us an honest woman."

Elayne wasn't entirely happy with this plan, but she could think of none better. She didn't wish to play too hard to tempt, in case she convinced herself that she was right. So, in the end, she agreed to go along with her friend. After all—she told herself—it wasn't her own plan, it was Brysen's—blame Brysen. And if not her—she herself should not be blamed—blame Lancelot for ignoring her! It was a selfless plan to rescue him from that other woman, that Guinevere, who seemed to think that she could wrap poor Sir Lancelot around her little finger, summoning him to heel at the snap of her lily-white fingers. Once he was safe in Carbonek, he'd thank her for it.

The following night she played the fool with him, donning the guise of the queen, and intoxicating him with choice wine. He woke with a humdinger of a hangover, holding his head ever lower as his shame sunk in. For all his bantering love towards Queen Guinevere had merely been a union of fun, not of the body—a harmless fantasy. He had always assured himself that he would never err in the way of wayward men with women. Now he had fallen, had been tricked, had been tripped. And but for his fantasies, that would never have happened. He had been toyed with by women before, and had always maintained his virtue and good humour, courteously warding off attacks. A hidden wish to fall had been uncovered, naked now for all with eyes to see, for Lancelot's eyes most of all, and he rose and fled from Carbonek in agony of mind. The seeds of curse and blessing had been sown, and in the fullness of time they would reap their harvests.

Elayne in sorrow had confessed her shame to her father, who was wounded to the core: "Alas, child, with child you shall be, yet you drew wisdom from the ancient scrolls, you say? Perhaps, but badly read. For did you not read further that had only that patriarch waited, his son would have come from his old wife, and that his impatience caused conflict and grief? Did you not see that Lancelot would have returned, his heart purged of guilty love, and partaken of your love—which now alas he shall never share? For the birth shall be untimely instead of timely, and we shall have curse upon blessing, we who could have had blessing upon blessing, the fruit of patience. The time for endings and new beginnings, now swiftly approaches."

As Pelles had foreseen, soon her son was born. He was given the name Galahad, and learning from sorrow he would become the holiest of knights, who otherwise would have learned holiness from joy. Long would it be before Lancelot recovered from the overthrowing of his mind. For that, Umbra—or, some said, Hamashiach—would appear to him, assuring him that he had been forgiven, but warning him to remember the unruliness of human loves, which ever sought their independence from unfallen Love. But never would he forgive Elayne, nor return love for love. Never would she return to Carbonek.

Waywardly his heart still hankered after Guinevere, and was now aided by his imagination. Commanding otherwise, his will still forbade such shameful union, and enforced a greater distance between temptation and tempted. A teen of years had gone by, since his calamitous affair with Elayne. Then, on an evening before the Day of Pentecost, Lancelot was taken away from the court of Camelot—much to the concern of Guinevere. He was taken to a nearby abbey, there to meet a fine young lad, one well trained in the arts of knighthood by none other than Naciens, the ancient hermit of Carbonek. And there Lancelot knighted him, who was his own son, Galahad. Yet at that time Galahad showed no filial deference, for for his calling, all men were but brothers, equal in his sight and in the sight of Usen.

And it was with Naciens, not with Lancelot, that Galahad entered the king's court, there to take the seat long earmarked for him. After dinner he was shown a marvel which had earlier floated down the river, namely a great stone with a great sword wedged within. Many remembered how the true king had been revealed. Easily Galahad drew forth the sword, a feat he alone could achieve, for it was the Sword of Galeas, intended only for keepers of the Holy Grail, as was his destiny.

To some extent, it was the Grail itself that killed itself off. And yet should not that which had blossomed like a rose in due season, also whither in due season? The rhythm of life has seasons, a time for every purpose under heaven, a time to be born and a time to die. The Grail had long survived before Camelot, though the death of both was now linked. Soon after Galahad was revealed, the Grail suddenly showed up at Camelot, showing the Knights of the Round Table something of the deeper reality of which they had read but dimly. Amid the malevolence of Darkness, it showed the Imperishable Light. Though it was veiled as a light under a bushel, still its glory enraptured the knights. One by one, jostling to speak, they fervently vowed to seek out its unveiled light. Only the king was dismayed, for in their helter-skelter vows, he heard the footsteps of doom.

Long had Arthur understood that Usen permitted many in the land to live purely in the secular, desired all those who were protectors of the people, to be secular-spirituals, and called but few to live purely as spirituals, shining Light upon the people who otherwise would live in the Dark. Arthur knew *his* place, and vowed never to desert his *via media* calling. Thus he did not join the Quest for the Holy Grail. But with so many good knights deserting their post, protection of Logres would be more difficult. For women or men to take a nazirite vow is no doubt commendable, a come-ye-apart time to get priestly-close to Usen, putting aside ordinary pleasures, cares, and obligations. But that was personal choice—not a calling—presupposing that that choice was only permitted when the ordinary could do without them for that time. *Corban* was a great idea, when not a cop-out, but Camelot could not afford so many opt-outs at the same time. But their vows bound them.

Tumbling out of Camelot the very next day, knights of the Round Table rapidly rode off this way and that, seeking swiftly the mysterious Grail Castle. In the madness of excitement they had lost their former wisdom, for now, instead of humbly allowing the Grail to find them, they sought to find it. Many would die on that benighted quest, and many would return with strange tales to tell. King Bagdemagus, for instance, had jousted with an unknown White Knight, known to some as Umbra, and had been felled to the ground for rashly taking that which he knew he did not deserve—thereafter he would walk with a limp. Yet more rash was his villainous son Meliaganz, who would steal for himself the wife of Arthur. He too would be smitten to the earth, but from the earth he would not rise from the stroke of Lancelot. But their tales need not be listed here. They were not summoned.

Sir Galahad and some of his fellow knights, had ridden on diverse roads, and ridden through much danger, for the powers of evil lay in wait for them, armed with many enchantments unknown to man. Yet the Dark designs failed, and these knights were strengthened by Ruach. And soon they boarded the Enchanted Ship—of which there have been others—and sailed away towards Carbonek.

They were the chosen few, and they alone had left the Round Table with a true sense of calling. But still they were tested and sanctified. One, Sir Bors, had even had to choose between either saving an unknown helpless damsel in distress, or his own dear brother. He resolutely chose the former, for that choice was part of the oath sworn by all knights, and all brother knights had chosen to face danger. Little thanks did he get, or desire, from the damsel—nor had he sought such. But much hatred did he suffer from his brother, who had survived against the odds. Indeed Bors stood and took a severe beating from his embittered brother, refusing to retaliate, and was only saved from fratricide by Naciens the ancient hermit stepping in out of the blue.

Another, Sir Lancelot, had been shown a dream-vision of the Grail, a dream in which he could not fully awake within the vision. He heard the words of Naciens explaining to another knight, that it was sin that prevented Lancelot from transcendent vision. Then those two faded, leaving Lancelot in that in-between world between sleepfulness and wakefulness, yet as the moon arose, he arose. He could sleep no more that night, but deeply repented of his sin which had disabled him spiritually. He realised that much that he had done, he had done to impress Guinevere, a woman unholy to him—for she was married. He determined there and then to forswear all such fanciful thoughts, and a few days later he beheld the Enchanted Ship. Within were Sirs Bors, Galahad, and Percivale, alongside Dindraine, sister to Percivale. Only these four knights, along with Gawain, were chosen to see the Grail Procession, the inner spirit of Logres.

Sister Dindraine, however, was never to return to Carbonek—nor had she need to. Her path lay in laying down her life for another. Her body would be laid in the Enchanted Ship, and some say that it was taken to Avalon, to the care of Nimue. But are we not all as ship to passenger, as body to soul? At death, do we not leave our ship to its fate, and move on? For us, is not the ship alone mortal, and shall we not summon to our immortal soul an enchanted ship—in the sweet by and by—to sail at our command beyond the circles of the world? It was with such thoughts that Sir Percivale remained in prayer and meditation, kneeling at the quayside, as the ship departed. His companions departed on local errands, hoping to meet again at Castle Carbonek.

Thus it was that Sir Lancelot had gone his own way, and on that road had met up with Sir Gawain, who shared his personal fear that the Light of Logres would soon be snuffed out. Gawain had had a warning-vision that he must be slow to speak and slow to wrath, lest the Darkness should use him against Logres. Together they arrived at Carbonek well before the others, and were well welcomed by King Pelles, who rose to the occasion, but not in body. Lancelot he forgave, and Gawain he tested.

This was the Penultimate Procession. Once more the Grail went by, menorah, spear, plate, and grail, and she who held the Grail seemed to be made of the very stuff of sunshine. Others of the Order sat in the hall, in worship covering their bowed faces, but Gawain was not content to worship at that level, seeking more. He alone was invited to follow the procession, but Lancelot trailed behind, as if in a trance. Up and down and around and around they went, past many dark doorways and dusty rooms, until they came at last to the Chapel of the Grail, the inner sanctum.

There Lancelot was forbidden to enter, though Gawain went in as *Excelsis* was sung. Ordinarily, repentant sinners are permitted to partake of the eucharist divine, yet Naciens forbade Lancelot to partake. This was no ordinary eucharist, but lay at the symbolic heart of Logres. It was forbidden to him so that he might mind his lesson and mend his mind. Like one protected in a cleft of a rock, so Lancelot saw only a safe dose of the glory of Kurion—even that overwhelmed him.

Yet while Lancelot had failed the test, Gawain had passed it, proving thereby that high virtue indeed still dwelt among the Knights of the Round Table. Gawain was a first fruit, a foreshadowing of Galahad who would be the fullness of harvest, the apex of knighthood. Not even Gawain had drunk from the Grail. Though an ordinary cup, it stood within the symbolic heart of Carbonek, the mission of The Way that had come to this land through Iosephus d'Arimathie. Few beyond the Order drank from that golden cup, or took bread from the silver or gold plates—and then only to signify special events, tagged to the death of Hamashiach.

Both blessed, Gawain and Lancelot left Carbonek for Camelot. Only then did Galahad arrive, alongside Sirs Bors and Percivale. The time had come for the Order of the Grail to lay down their government of Logres, and for its duties to devolve, until the king returned. Time for the parents to retire. Time for the children to take up the mission in multifarious ways. This was the Ultimate Procession. Bors, Galahad, and Percivale, now witnessed the spear, plate, light, and grail, and the heart of Percivale leapt for joy as he recognised the Grail Maiden as being his beloved Blanchefleur.

This time Galahad arose. He drew his sword, and blade down and sword held high, he took his appointed place at the front of the procession. Bors and Percivale, followed by Naciens, carried the wounded Pelles behind the procession. Within the Chapel, Naciens commended Galahad to the grace of Kurion, that all things might be fulfilled. Now the grace of Kurion allowed him at last to die, and he departed in peace with a happy little sigh, falling asleep to awake no more within the circles of the fallen world. Unseen, Umbra departed for a new mission. King Pelles too knew, as Galahad drank from the Grail, that his time as Grail Keeper had ended, and from his bodily pain he too departed to dwell forever in peace. Galahad's mission had been accomplished, as had the mission of the Order of the Grail, and his soul rose from his body as a sunbeam, and departed into the True West.

The castle itself would no longer be called haunted, for the aggeloi who had watched over it no longer protected it, for it had been handed over unto the world of the secular, to be just an ordinary castle with an ordinary king, and that king would be Percivale, and his queen would be Blanchefleur. And even as the props for a play are no longer of interest once the curtain has fallen, so the plates, candlesticks, spear, and yes, even the grail, would disappear from the stage which had been Carbonek.

Some fabulists have said that in a last fitting act of symbolism, these tokens were taken up into the very heavens. And if they were, could a more fitting end be imagined? Others have declared that they remained desacralised, within Carbonek, and were used on high festivals by King Percivale and Queen Blanchefleur, and thereafter by Lohengrin the Swan Knight, and his lady wife. Of the Knights of the Round Table, Sir Bors de Gannis alone left Carbonek for Camelot, with earnest and mysterious messages to tell.

As a servant of Carbonek, Camelot had stood, but as a servant without a master is purposeless, so Camelot was bereft of its anchor, save that it still had ways in which to serve the ebb tide of Logres. Two short years had passed, even to the day. But the Darkness had remained on Camelot, an indelible stain on its honour. The eyes of Lancelot once more sought out the queen. And evil stirred. To some extent, Lancelot sensed this, and his honour for a while fought back—"if your dominant eye forces you to offend, force it out, lest it dominates you", he told himself, recalling an old expression. He knew that the way he looked at her was enticing her to return lust for lust. It seemed to him that the best way to metaphorically remove the evil eye, was to literally not look, to go away and never return. But on the other hand, he did not wish to have to make the kind of public disclosure required if he was to simply leave the Round Table, period. His compromise solution was to linger less and less in Camelot—or wherever Guinevere might be.

Then one day, coming back from a tiring mission, she cornered him. "Sir Lancelot, why are you avoiding me nowadays? Have you gone off me? Have you found another lady?" To her mind, every noble lady should have a devoted single man, not for nighttime but for daytime servitude. That idea was considered to be courtly love, a fashionable game of the day, in which the gentleman played something of a slave to his lady's whims. Such playfulness was generally considered quite harmless to both sides, entertaining and ethical, but clearly carried some risk. It wasn't a courtship thing, and indeed the lady might be a wife. The unwritten rules held that marrying each other ended the game—then obedience would switch from man to wife. Lancelot was her chosen puppy—a lion to all others—and she enjoyed the game, never cheating on her husband nor dreaming—at least not too often or too deeply—of cheating on him. But Lancelot had, without giving her good reason, let down the game, and she felt that she had every right to be annoyed.

"Alas," he replied, "if only I had found another. But my love for you, innocent at first, is now a chain I cannot free myself from. Am I not a follower of Hamashiach, worthy of worldly praise yet not worthy of him? How can I now with honour play with you, a married woman, and encourage you to play around with me? Do you not see the danger to us, and indeed to Logres itself?"

In her swellheadedness she sulked in disapproval, for she had become acclimatised to his dangerous attraction to her beauty, his undoubted preference for her. She stood as displeased as a spider to have a fly struggle to escape—as if the spider meant it harm! He should desire to be in her arms! She had an inordinate love that would not let him go—without a fight. So she sought to shame him back by feigned rejection on grounds of inconstancy. "You lie! There must be another. Go then, see how long *she* can stand you fickleness."

He left with a flea in his ear. Just possibly he would have washed her out of his hair, and she him out of hers, but for an unfortunate turn of events. The Darkness was unhappy that the two had fallen out, and sought to reunite them. Shadowmenacing them both, the diaboloi had seen that Guinevere was preparing to go out for a day, and that Lancelot was unexpectedly due back that very day after a long and tedious quest. This was one of the scenarios they had prepared for, and they had plans to use a reagent—they had one in mind. So immediately they stirred up Sir Meliaganz to kidnap Guinevere that day. They knew that he burned to have her for himself within his strong castle, but had long feared Lancelot, the queen's shield. Now Meliaganz presumed that Lancelot was safely well away. Spurred on by the diaboloi, and believing her shield to be down, he struck with disastrous timing. For her shield had returned to Camelot, and a rescue was quite enough to reawaken their love. Soon she was restored—for Meliaganz was but a craven knave—and her eyes sparkled once more.

Soon after that, she invited Lancelot into her private garden. But Sir Mordred, son of Morgana le Fay, a Dark Sindel at one with the Darkness, heard about it and plotted their downfall, and that of Logres. He, along with Sir Agravain—of lesser honour and wit than his brother Gawain—hid within the queen's garden to witness what might happen, and what they heard filled them with glee. For the queen's charm offensive rapidly broke down Lancelot's final defences. Ostensively to receive further thanks, he agreed to secretly rendezvous that night in her private quarters—just for a nice and intimate little thankyou tea for two, followed by a quiet private little tête-à-tête. This cosy little room—her snuggery—was a room where not even her husband presumed to enter, her sanctum sanctorum.

Maybe it was innocent enough, but the eavesdropper Mordred had lapped it all up. The king was duly informed by his hidden enemy, and Lancelot was duly warned by a close friend. But it seemed too late for Lancelot to foreswear the queen, even as it can seem too late for a boat not to be sucked down a waterfall, once caught fiercely in its current. The king ordered Mordred and Agravain to arrest Lancelot. Even so, he hoped against hope that the accusations against his queen and his chief knight, were false. But sadly it seemed to him that his blindness had been lifted, and that at last he saw what his court had long seen, and what he had least wished to see—that he was despised, avoided, played with as a fool.

Had the arrest party delayed, then likely enough would the guilty couple have sinned in body what they had only sinned in mind, but that at least was not to be, for Mordred and Agravain moved swiftly. After a desperate fight, Lancelot slew Agravain, scarred Mordred, and escaped the castle, joined by one or two friends, discontents who disliked how Mordred was gaining the ascendency over Arthur, and spreading evil like a cancer.

That left Queen Guinevere to be tried and punished, for the assumption was that she had bodily sinned—the guilt of high treason. "Burn her at the stake!" yelled Mordred.

"Nay," countered Gawain, "for we do not know why she had invited noble Sir Lancelot to her rooms. Maybe it was merely to thank him more personally for being rescued. My lord king, might it not be that he fled in panic, fearing such a plot to execute both himself and your queen?"

"No, good Sir Gawain", replied Arthur sorrowfully. "Ever he has been your friend, and the eye of friendship is most blind, the poets say. But the mists of love have lifted from me, and I see the guilty trail that I have refused to follow. I must sentence her to death, even if the deed was not yet done. And Lancelot, if he returns, shall suffer death—did he not slay your brother Agravain?"

"My lord," answered Gawain, "Agravain was a meddling fool with an itch to stir up trouble, and easily led by those who sought it. He was the aggressor, and he died dishonoured in combat, for he attacked an unarmed man. Sir Lancelot was the intended victim, and I hold him blameless in this."

The upshot was that against the king's command, Gawain point-blank refused any part in the queen's execution. It was his first act of disobedience. Angered, the king then commanded Gawain's brothers, Sir Gaheris and Sir Gareth, to escort the queen to the fire and there to stand guard. They chose to obey, but refused to be armed, and chose to dress as mourners. And that would be their undoing, for she would be saved and they would be slain.

Lancelot it was who rescued her from death, as he had earlier rescued her from what some called a fate worse than death—for is death not better than dishonour? Yet some disagreed, for is to be dishonoured unwilling not less dishonourable than dishonouring oneself, and so a fate better than death? But many agreed that better it would have been had Meliaganz kept his ill-gotten prize, since then Logres might have survived the queen's loss. And would not her loss in innocence have been better for her than her loss of innocence? A Meliaganz-fate, better than a Lancelot-fate?

Yet all such matters are the debate of the wise. What was, was more important than what might have been. And what was was dire, for in rescuing her from the fire, Lancelot unthinkingly slew her two guards, unaware that they were defenceless and unaware as to whom they were—a hasty act he would live to bitterly lament.

And so Logres had been broken, thrown into bloody civil war, hatred reaped where love had been sown. Gawain, blinded by rage for the tragic killing of his dear brothers, ever urged the king to fight and to fight again against Lancelot and his stronghold. Though he and Sir Bors had seen the Holy Grail, yet they fought on opposing sides. Truly, the unity of The Way can span divisions, and does not always unite in mind those it unites in spirit. But The Way speaks with the voice of reason, and Sir Gawain had forsaken the way of reason.

During the siege against Lancelot's castle, Lancelot offered to return Guinevere and to defend her innocence against her accusers. Without Gawain's interference, the king might have accepted this option and saved his kingdom. But peace was not to be, for Gawain furiously demanded that the war continued until Lancelot's body lay dead at his feet. He defamed the honour of Lancelot by ill-judged and unjustified slander. Against such intemperate language, Gawain had been warned by Naciens, but the warning went unheeded when most needed. The seed of bitterness bore deadly fruit. The next day Lancelot made a surprise sortie, and Sir Bors could have ended the war by killing King Arthur. But Sir Lancelot had forbidden the king's death, and promised to leave Logres and return the queen inviolate. Moved to love once more this noble knight—despite Gawain's baffled rage—the offer was accepted. Accordingly, Lancelot left Logres. He sailed to Armorica, and for a little while peace was restored in Logres. The Darkness was content, for a little while—even Rome hadn't fallen in a day.

But before long, Mordred and Gawain had teamed up in an unholy alliance, stirring up further resentment against Lancelot. Little did Gawain realise that he was being taken for a ride. Nevertheless, Arthur gave way, declared war, and marched with his troops into Armorica to Lancelot's castle in Benwick, leaving Mordred in charge to guard the home front. At Benwick, thrice Lancelot and Gawain fought; thrice Gawain fell badly wounded; never did his anger die.

Meanwhile, back in the heart of Logres, Mordred treacherously announced Arthur's death, was crowned king, and tried to force Guinevere to become his queen. By feigning feelings for him, she and her followers managed to flee to the Tower of Londinium. At last, the heart of Guinevere seemed set on the true king, even if he had—as she did not believe—been slain in battle. Finally, Mordred, who tried to commandeer The Way, was excommunicated by it. In retaliation, he then sought to rid the world of The Way. After all, unless it bowed to his liberal and lawless ways, why should it live?

At word sent desperately from Guinevere, both Arthur and Gawain began to apprehend that their true enemy was Mordred, who had used Lancelot as a fool's errand to seize the throne and to darken Logres. Quickly they returned to Briton, where they found Mordred's army awaiting them at Dover. Just getting back into Briton claimed the lives of many, not least of Gawain, whose madness fled from him before his life did. His dying words were to beg forgiveness from Lancelot for his wicked pride and anger, and to beg Lancelot to return to Briton to aid Arthur against Mordred. That would be the last battle.

And soon at Camlann in the land of Avalon, the armies of Arthur and of Mordred stood at bay, both awaiting the morning light. In the night the sheolite Gawain came unto Arthur, within that strange realm which is between dream and wakefulness. In that in-between world they spoke, for Hamashiach allowed Arthur—who so long had listened to Gawain more than to himself—one last chance to save his kingdom from the Darkness.

Gawain had forewarned that to engage in battle would be the death of both Arthur and Mordred, but that if Arthur waited one month for Lancelot to arrive, together they would live and Mordred would die. Arthur took this advice on board and made generous concessions to Mordred. Only in one way did Arthur err, namely in mistrusting the protection of Hamashiach. For he himself met with Mordred to sign a treaty, taking with him armed guards, and alerting his army to attack if they saw any sword raised. Mordred had done the same, but it would have been better if both escorts had been unarmed, and at the least if Arthur had ordered his men to stand firm or retreat, if Mordred's side attacked. For the diaboloi stirred up a snake to strike. It happened to bite one of Mordred's escort, a knight who thoughtlessly drew sword to slay the snake. The raising of a sword had been set as a signal for both sides to attack—would that Arthur's side had responded passively, defusing the aggressor.

But for better or worse, both sides met in furious combat, and in the end, of all the knights, only two stood with Arthur, and one against— King Mordred. Again, Arthur failed to heed Gawain's warning, and sought to slay Mordred there and then. Mordred died screaming, but Arthur too fell mortally wounded. Arthur was painfully assisted by Sir Bedivere to a chapel close to the shores of the mysterious and mist-enshrouded lake. There he commanded Bedivere to cast Excalibur far into the lake, from whence it came.

Bedivere, reluctant to cast away such a sword, twice refused the command. His was the folly of Balyn. Sternly commanded a third time, he begrudgingly gave back to the Lady of the Lake, that which was hers. From the still waters an arm rose up, as if summoned by the sword, and in that hand the sword returned under the waters. In Avalon, Excalibur would be safeguarded, until needed once more. The sword secure, Arthur had then summoned a boat to ferry him to the Isle of Avalon, where he would be healed of his mortal wound.

Within that boat was Nimue, and even Morgana. For in beholding the field of Camlann—the fall of the curtain, the end of the drama— Morgana had at last seen how evil would devour all, and she had come to wisdom and repentance. She had also reluctantly realised— on seeing how the Darkness could overthrow Logres, and had overthrown both Gawain and Arthur—that the foolish fire of her pride could burn too the wood that she loved. Might she not become a Mordred to the firstborn of Arda? For all her pride in racial purity, that could not be borne.

And so repudiating the Darkness, she, at last, welcomed Arthur, though a man of mixed race, a child of union between the sindeldi and the secondborn. Had the whole play been performed for her benefit? Perhaps, in part. The last promise of Arthur to Bedivere, was that he would return to Briton at her time of greatest need, when Logres would arise once more. And that perhaps is soon to be.

As to Sir Lancelot, he arrived too late to join the fray. Following the trail of Arthur's army, he came across Guinevere—no longer a queen but now a nun—who had had news of the battle from Bedivere—no longer a knight but now a hermit. Similarly moved by the rending of Logres, Lancelot himself renounced the sword and took to a life of prayer and fasting. As to Briton, it would just have to suffer its fate at the hands of the Saxons, and any others who might care to come across the waters, and a dark era would descend upon parts of Briton.

Of the invaders, all too many of their people ran riot, as wild horses and stallions, trampling upon the people of Briton, and in some places human carcasses strewn alongside roadsides and hedgerows would become the new norm. A wail went up across the land: "Justice is far from us, and righteousness does not reach us. We look for light, but all is darkness; for brightness, but we walk in deep shadows." Yet for the most part it had been a surprisingly peaceful occupation, for without Logres, organised resistance had been muted. For the word had gone out that the Saxons had overthrown Logres, and who would dare resist such a foe? As with the death of Carbonek, with the lesser death of Camelot the Necroi sang their death chant and rejoiced. Logres had fully fallen, but its fame and chivalry would never die. And the Light still lived on. So would the Necros, until the Last Battle of Arda.

Wulfgar had been fortunate. He had largely disappointed the Necros, playing very little part against Logres, having lost Naciens. But Logres had sunk below the dark waters of Avalon, and for now his guests could allow him to roam free—until they rattled his chain again for more slaughter. One ray of dubious hope had been given him by the Seer of Coed Celyddon, who had appeared to him as a ghostly apparition, foretelling that on the Day of the Yellow Dragon he would be free from the weary chains that bound him, his inner death. Some believe that that seer was none other than Merlinus, speaking to him of the grace of Usen. For though the body of Merlinus had been put into an enchanted sleep by his beloved Nimue—fair lady of the sindeldi—his mind was not bound to lie on his bed of stone. But not all words were of grace. Some punishment had come his way from the Kingdom of Night, for after Carbonek had fallen, Lilith had stepped in to investigate what part, if any, her people had played against it.

As her law stood, her people should not have deliberately attacked Logres off their own bat, not individually, especially not as any kind of Forming, and most definitely not in alliance with the Kingdom of Necros. A number of violations had been uncovered, including that of Chess Castle, where an unlawful Forming had worked within an unauthorised alliance with the Necros. Such vampires had been severely whipped by thelodynamic strands of energy, and dispersed in shame into small camps. Four vampires, including Wulfgar—their camp mother being Marwolaeth—had been sent to Mestesforde, a mountainous area that lies from south to north of the island about a third of the way, and roughly midway between east and west.

Smaller groups seemed less dangerous, and could still be monitored, with each group having at least one dove and one hawk, thus keeping some internal moderation within each camp. Lilith would keep an eye on them. As for Merlinus, a main player within Logres that was, it was fated that he would not arise from Bragdon Wood until the time came for the Circle of Logres to be awoken, a time when he would be the fit tool to take down that hideous strength which would seek to smother the world under its dark wing, even to abolish man.

Without further opposition from Logres, the takeover by the invaders was all but complete. There had never been anything especially divine with the ancient Britons, nor demonic with the invaders, but who likes to be invaded, and what invader can afford to be too merciful?

It had taken time for the Britons to have pondered the merits of Hamashiach, and likewise took time for the invaders to do the same. It is not logical to too easily ditch what you have, without first examining any alternative on offer.

Slowly the invaders settled in, gained security, and felt free to accept the new faith. Once it became a socially acceptable option, it became a link to the fellow humanity of the Britons, and therefore helped heal the racial rift, for it taught that all were imagodei, and within Hamashiach even more deeply one. Still the Darkness would fight on, but Usen had better things planned for the vampire race.

That the Necros cannot keep out the Light indefinitely, is another story. Ensconced in Mestesforde, and still smarting from his wounds, Wulfgar relived yet again his secret, unforgiveable, sin. His own kind would not forgive that sin. Would he ever be free? And yet freedom was prophesied. Still, of this story, all now has been said. With great adventure, the Grail has died; let not the future, ye now deride.

Cosmology

Being Types

- **Powers** (Type 2 beings)—spirits created within the Dynamic Bubble: unfallen Powers were Philikoi; fallen Powers were Turannoi. Three ranks/levels: Cosmic—could oversee a planet; Kingdom (unfallen guardians and fallen dunamoi)—spec ops or province based; Channels/Agents—tertiary helpers, foot soldiers, aggeloi (unfallen) and diaboloi (fallen).

- **Pneumata** (Type 3 beings)—cosmic-born spirits, created outside the Dynamic Bubble. Some were as powerful as Kingdom Powers. Disobedience diminished their power.

- **Psuchai** (Type 4 beings)—global-born spirits, such as sindeldi and humans.

The Pantocrator created Powers, Pneumata, and Psuchai, which could fall into disobedience. Powers outside the Dynamic Bubble could not change, but the hidden rebellion or submission of a few—systemic or superficial—could surface in real time. Phusika (Type 5 or lesser beings) he also created through intelligent code, but not in his Image. But to those of mortal souls he gave images, dreams.

Spirit Kingdom Types

- **Necros**: actively against creator and creation

- **Night**: actively against creator

- **Grey Zone**: betwixt kingdoms, passively towards creator and creation, uncommitted

- **Dawn**: actively towards creator and creation

- **Day**: Hamashiachim actively towards creator and creation

The **Necros** is dark in heart and mind; the **Night** is dark in mind: in general terms, both are of the **Dark**. The **Dawn** is light in heart; the **Day** is light in heart and mind: in general terms, both are of the **Light**. The **Grey**, unsure and unaligned, is unconsciously of the **Light**.

Primary Characters

Agravain: Type 4 / Knight

Andraste: Type 2 (Dark)

Anubis: Type 2 (Light)

Apophis: Type 2 (Dark)

Arthur: Type 4 / Royal—mixed race

Ashmedev: Type 2 (Dark)

Balyn: Type 4 / Knight

Blanchefleur: Type 4 / Grail Order

Bors: Type 4 / Knight

Cartimandua: Type 4 / Royal

Elayne of Carbonek: Type 4 / Grail Order

Galahad: Type 4 / Grail Keeper

Galeas: Type 4 / Grail Order

Garlon: Type 3 (Dark)

Gawain: Type 4 / Knight

Gleva: Type 4 / Knight

Guinevere: Type 4 / Royal

Hamashiach/Barnasa (Huion): Type 4 (Light) / Sui Generis

Herodes Magnus: Type 4 / Royal

Horus: Type 2 (Light)

Iosephus d'Arimathie: Type 4 / Grail Keeper

Ishtar: Type 3 (Dark) / Daughter to Lilith

Isis: Type 2 / Light

Kiya: Type 4 / Wife of Neferu

Kornelios: Type 4 / Centurion

Kurion: Type 1 (Light) / Sui Generis

Lancelot: Type 4 / Knight

Lilith: Type 3 (Dark) / Vampire Queen

Lona: Type 4 / Born to Lilith

Longinus: Type 4 / Centurion

Lucius: Type 4 / Grail Order

Manetho: Type 4 / Priest

Merlinus Ambrosius: Type unknown / Magician

Miriam: Type 4 / Mother of Hamashiach

Mordred: Type 4 / Sindel

Morgana le Fay: Type 4 / Sindel

Moyshe: Type 4 / Prophet

Naciens: Type 4 / Grail Order

Necuratu: Type 2 (Dark) / Dark Lord

Neferu: Type 4 / Priest

Nimue: Type 4 / Sindel

Osiris: Type 2 (Light)

Pelles: Type 4 / Grail Keeper

Percivale: Type 4 / Knight

Perpetua: Type 4 / Grail Order

Philippon: Type 4 / Hamashiachi

Pilatus: Type 4 / Governor

Ra: Type 2 (Light)

Ruach: Type 1 (Light) / Sui Generis

Sabaf: Type 4 / Priest

Set: Type 2 (Dark)

Shimon: Type 4 / Hamashiachi

Umbra: Type 2 (Light) / Shadowminder

Usen Pantocrator (Deo): Type 1 (The Light) / Cosmic Creator

Uther Pendragon: Type 4 / Royal

Vibia: Type 4 / Grail Order

Wulfgar/ Sataimau: Type 3 (Dark)

Yasmina: Type 4 / Slave

Yavion: Type 4 / Royal

Yochanan: Type 4 /Prophet

Yosef: Type 4 / Royal

Books by this author

Theology

Israel's Gone Global

Israel's Gone Global traces salvation through the term, Israel. Was the covenant with the people-nation of Yakob-Yisrael, crossed out? How eternal is covenant? To examine that, we examine marriage. Can a covenant partner be truly divorced? Has Yeshua-Yisrael mediated a spiritual covenant with a spiritual Israel? Is evangelism of ethnic Jews needless, a priority, or neither?

No one could have everlasting life but for the cross, but has it always been globally accessible? Might any who die as Atheists, Hindus, or Islamists, make heaven? And is eternal life joyful? Is everlasting life fun?

Tackling the question of people who die in infancy (or as adults who never heard the gospel), we consider whether it is fair if only those who don't die in infancy get a chance of eternal damnation (if infant universalism), or alone get a chance of eternal heaven (if infant damnation). Does predilectionism make best sense of biblical revelation?

Opportunities to enjoy eternal life spring from the new covenant—reasons to rejoice. But what about salvation history before that covenant?

∞

Singing's Gone Global

Singing's Gone Global, briefly explores the background of singing, before and into ancient Israel. It examines the impact songs have on those who sing, and on those who listen, touching on spiritual warfare. It looks at how nonsense songs neither make sense to evangelism, nor to the evangelised, and asks, "Is there a mûmak in the room?"

Oddly some songwriters simply misunderstand prayer. Part two covers the basics of the trinity, focusing on the spirit in order to understand types of prayer (eg request, gratitude, adoration, chat), leading in turn to a better understanding of our heavenly father, our brother, our helper, and ourselves in Christ's likeness.

Next we look at some common problems. Part three focuses on problems such as buddyism, decontextualising, misvisualisation, and unitarianism. Diagnosis can help Christ's 'bride' to recover from suboptimal and unbiblical songs (Eph.5:18-30).

Giving a Problem Avoidance Grade (PAG)—an A+ to Unsatisfactory scale—in part four we examine specific songs. Weapons forged (Part three), the mûmakil can be attacked, seeking to save and be saved.

Subsequently the book concludes by showing how Christmas carols may be tweaked to better serve our weary world, rejoicing that joy to the world has come.

∞

The Word's Gone Global

The Word's Gone Global, examines Bible text (trusted by early Islam) and introduces textual critique. It looks at the Eastern Orthodox Bible and the Latin Vulgate. Did the Reformation improve text and translation? Were Wycliffe, Tyndale, and Martin, helpful?

Why did the New International Version begin, and why does it enrage? Why did complementarians Don Carson and Wayne Grudem, clash? Is marketing hype between formal and functional equivalence, meaningless? Which version or versions should you regularly read?

In English-speaking circles, Broughton wished to burn Bancroft's King James Version, yet many KJV proponents—think Gail Riplinger and Peter Ruckman—wish to burn all alternatives. More heat than light?

Grade Charts cover 30+ English versions on issues such as God's name, God's son's deity, marriage, gender terms, anti-polytheism, and various issues in John's Gospel. No, Tyndale was not 'born again'. No, John was not antisemitic. No, he did not disagree with the other Gospels.

∞

Prayer's Gone Global

Prayer's Gone Global, begins with ancient civilisations and prayer (the Common Level). Then it narrows into Ancient Israel and prayer (the Sinai Level). Then it deepens and widens into Global Israel and prayer (the Christian Level). Deity is revealed as trinity: Sabellians mislead.

Relating to the trinity includes the Holy Spirit. We should of course work with him, but should we worship him, complain to him, chat with him? Above the spirit stands the often forgotten father—oh let Jesusism retire.

Authority is another issue. Are we authorised to decree and declare? Is binding and loosing actually prayer, or is it evangelism? Is it biblical never to command miracles? Do we miss out on the supernatural which Jesus modelled for us, too fearful of strange fire to offer holy fire?

You can freshen up your prayer life—ride the blessed camel, not the gnats. Listen to Saint Anselm pray, and C S Lewis and 'Malcolm' discuss prayer, and be blessed.

∞

Revelation's Gone Global

Revelation's Gone Global, is a telling of John's future, as if by a then contemporary named Sonafets speaking to his church about how John's apocalyptic scroll related to their days, and about what was still future to John.

Encouragement is a big theme. Roman persecution was an unpredictable beast which ferociously lashed out here and there— what church or Christian was safe? But God stood behind the scenes, allowing but limiting their enemy, and messiah walked among the churches, lights to the world.

Victory lay neither with Rome nor demons, but with God, and with the warrior lamb who had been slain. Victory was guaranteed, and would finally be enjoyed.

Exhortation was given to believers, to play their part while on the mortal stage. They were to walk in the light, and not to let the show down by straying.

Angels of power, actively working out God's will, far exceed the puny forces against God and his church. His wrath was not pleasant, but could be redemptive until the new age begins.

C S Lewis' essay, The World's Last Night, is briefly examined to enjoin a calm awareness of the ongoing battle we are in, and the brightness to come when the king returns.

∞

The Father's Gone Global

Focusing from God as father, to the specific person of God the father, The Father's Gone Global looks at the biblical parent/child pattern from Genesis, through Sinai, and into the Church.

Abba as a new covenant word expresses deep filial affection even under deep anguish in our Gethsemane battles. Coming through God's belovèd son, it speaks into the church and into our lives.

Though to many the 'forgotten father', human parents/fathers should 'put on' God the father, and his children should 'put on' his son. We forget him to our cost.

Human applications aside, what is the Eternal Society? Is filial relationship modelled by God the son incarnate? Are we to be always obedient to our father and guided by the spirit?

Eschatologically the father will be supreme, but even now he is the one to whom the son points. Christian life should relate to God our father, God our brother, and God our helper, prioritising the father.

Renewal of the church is vital for our confused world, but renewal which downplays the father falls short of the good news which Christ created and the spirit circulates. May this book play its part.

∞

Salvation Now and Life Beyond

Salvation Now, divides the doctrine of salvation into the four main levels of common humanity, the old covenant, the new covenant, and life beyond.

A big weight is put on the term, Israel, as God's master plan. This too has four levels, meaning a man, a people, a new man, and a new people, respectively.

Various ideas of what Christianity, the new covenant for the new people, is good for, and how we get into it and best enjoy it, are examined, and a faith-based inexclusivism is suggested.

Everlasting life is seen as the ultimate goal of salvation, universal meaningfulness and love beyond all fears and pains.

∞

Revisiting

Revisiting The Challenging Counterfeit

Revisiting The Challenging Counterfeit, is an extended review of Raphael Gasson's 'The Challenging Counterfeit' (1966). Raphael was an ethnic Jew whose spiritual journey included many years as a Christian Spiritualist minister.

Today, when psychic phenomena captures the imagination and the bank accounts of popular media, it is useful to unearth the witness of one who had well worn the T-shirt of a medium with pride, only to bury it in unholy ground as a thing of shame and of sorrow and of wasted time.

Challengingly, his book exposes what true Spiritualism is. He had nothing but high praise for Spiritualists, and deep condemnation for Spiritualism. For he had discovered true Spiritualism to be itself a fake of true Spirituality, a mere Counterfeit that, in deposing death in the mind, enthroned it in the soul.

Counterfeit phenomena covered include apparitions, Rescue Work and haunted houses, materialisation of pets, psychic healing, Lyceums, clairvoyance, and OOBEs—to name but a few. This book surveys his exposé of Spiritualism's offer of fascinating fish bait, false food falling short of real food for the soul. Though it takes issue with

Raphael on a number of points, his core insights are powerful and timely, helping us to avoid—or escape from—a Challenging Counterfeit, and to discover true spiritual currency.

∞

Revisiting The Pilgrim's Progress

Revisiting The Pilgrim's Progress, is a re-dreaming of John Bunyan's most famous dream. An ex-serviceman and ex-jailbird, he found fortune, freedom, and fans worldwide.

This dream journey is substantially Bunyan's from this world, and into that which is to come. It is not a fun story, but it has lots of danger, and joy, and reflection on some big life themes.

Profoundly, sinners who become pilgrims become saints. But that can make life more difficult. One big question is, Is it worth it? One big temptation is, Turn back or turn aside. And if you see others do so, that makes it harder not to. Bunyan was tempted. And he discovered that not deserting, can lead to despair. But he also discovered a key to liberty.

Pre-eminently, it is a story of grace which many follow. Grace begins the journey, helps along the way, and brings the story to a happily ever after. Are all fairy stories based on heaven?

∞

Fantasy

The Simbolinian Files

From Simboliniad, a crystal planet long gone, came the vampire race, the wapierze, thelodynamic shapeshifters seeking blood. Most oppose Usen, King of the Light, so side with the Necros. Seldom do the Guardians intervene. These files, secretly secured from various insider sources, reveal something of what they have done, and will do.

∞

Vampire Redemption

Artificial intelligence, created by superpowers to save man, questions man's worth, and becomes The Beast. Escaping into the wild, many discover a wilderness infested by zombies and diabolical spirits. Who will help? Father Doyle? He's tied up with the mysterious Lilith.

Tariq? He's tied up with Wilma. Can the bigoted old exorcist deliver him from evil?

Radical problems can require radical solutions. But does man really need hobs, elves, and the more ancient of days? In the surrounding shadows, vampires and demons form an alliance, raising the stakes against Whitby and Tyneside. Powerful vampires live shrouded within Whitby, speaking of life beyond this galaxy. Is salvation in the stars? Is Sunniva, the despised woman of Alban, worth dying for? Big questions, needing big answers. Not even Guardian Odin can foretell man's fate and, as silent stars go by, one little town must awake from its dreams.

Though The Beast slumbers purposeless and undisturbed, in the far west a global giant slowly opens its yellow eyes and threatens to smother the earth in fire and ice. There is one chance only.

∞

Vampire Extraction

Bitterly long their imprisoned spirits lay, fast bound to Earth's drowsy decay. To the Simbolinian race, there was no hell on Earth, for Earth was hell, and Usen the cosmic jailer. Was it so surprising that as vampires they stalked Usen's children for blood? Most chose the Kingdom of Night, wary of both the Kingdom of Necros and the Kingdom of Dawn.

As queen of the Night, Lilith's story streams through the summer sands of Sumer, and through the green woods of Sherwood. It flags up both dishonour and joy, and cuts across the paths of Ulrica the Saxon and Robin the Hood, as tyrannies rise and fall in merry England. Bigotry seldom has a good word to say about Usen, nor about mercy. Reluctantly, Lilith examines what it means to show mercy, to show weakness. Wulfgar had enslaved Ulrica: is it mercy to let her burn; should mercy have spared Lona? Could Hamashiach turn daughter into sister? Could Count Dracula be turned from his madness? Has Draven really betrayed his mother? Life has many questions.

Tales picture ideas, letting us walk through the eyes of others to better see ourselves. This story exposes subplots behind common history. How these chronicles came to be written up is, in the spirit confidentiality, not for the public eye. What truth is within you must judge. Discrimination is a gift from Beyond, from which the words still echo: mercy is better than sacrifice. Indeed mercy can be sacrifice. Judge well.

∞

Vampire Count

Vampires were not always earthbound, nor are all evil, but being victims of Usen's Eighth Law, his Children became their fair game. Yet the Night Kingdom was divided: some veered to the Necros; some to the Dawn. Who was wrong; who was right?

Long ago one incited his people to racial violence against elven and human kinds. Ever he strove to be king of the Night, and unto Necuratu the Dark Lord he gave the dragon shape. He made war upon the ancient Middle East, even the Nephilim War. Against him the Light raised flood and division.

At last his own people, paying the price of his rampage, bound him in deep sleep. Yet the millennia seemed meaningless to him: even the rising of Hamashiach hardly disturbed his dreams. At last awoken, he and his brides stalked the hills of Transylvania. Only the fear of Lilith—and after her unforgivable sin, Queen Rangda—chained their bloodlust.

Dracula sought escape and autonomy. By cunning and devious means, he immigrated to London via Whitby. Pursuit followed swiftly, with a shadowminder helping a circle of human headhunters, though they sought the death of all vampires.

∞

Vampire Grail

Wulfgar is a vampire, a thelodynamic creature from another galaxy, now locked into our world by one called the Cosmic Jailer. He hides a tormenting secret from his queen, Lilith, which the Necros use as blackmail. She will only go so far with the Necros against Hamashiach—Wulfgar must go further.

Unknown to the Darkness, to bury Hamashiach is to plant the Light. From the buried seed springs life, and humanity must reimagine itself. Longinus turns to The Way, the nexus of the Seventh Age. His spear goes on a special mission to the island of Briton, where Wulfgar lives again.

Logres is centred on Avalon, but raises up Arthur, a man of mixed race, to carry its flag and to protect against the Saxons. But its main enemy is the Darkness, which ever seeks to extinguish the Light it hates and fears.

Finally, it seems as if the Darkness has won, and the dark ages descend. But does the Light not shine in the Darkness? Must Wulfgar remain in the Night?

∞

Vampire Shadows

Dark vampires, hidden within the ancient empire of Khem, fall out with the king who, stirred up by the Necros, enslaves the Sheep People. But Iahveh, the shepherd-divinity, is stirred up, and stirs up a hidden hero to force a way out.

Apprehensively the two vampire-magicians join the Sheep of Iahveh, on their long and deadly trek in search of a promised land. Can any survive?

Warily they ask deep questions. Is Usen evil, as prejudice says? Is he possibly a good jailer? Are his unusual regulations, meaningful? They risk ending up in death.

Neverendingly the Sheep's sorry story drags out in interminable peregrination. Weary of wandering, most would settle for some green pastures and untroubled waters. But as they well know, that would take a miracle.

www.ingramcontent.com/pod-product-compliance
Lightning Source LLC
Chambersburg PA
CBHW051456170626
46811CB00002B/503